FIVE PORTRAITS

FIVE PORTRAITS

A NOVEL OF XANTH

PIERS ANTHONY

OPEN ROAD

INTEGRATED MEDIA

NEW YORK

Copyright © 2014 by Piers Anthony

978-1-62467-272-9

Published in 2014 by Open Road Integrated Media, Inc.
345 Hudson Street
New York, NY 10014
www.openroadmedia.com

FIVE PORTRAITS

CHAPTER 1:
BASILISK

~~~

Astrid woke early, as she often did. She left her husband sleeping in the tent and went out to look for pun virus remnants, which sometimes showed up better in the predawn light. She carried a closed vial of elixir, as all the members of her party did, at all times; it was vital to their mission. It was a tedious chore, but somebody had to do it, and they were elected.

She spied an interesting nest and went to investigate. Bees buzzed up warningly as she approached. Astrid merely pursed her lips and blew a breath of air at them, and they quickly spun out of control. After that they recognized her nature and let her be, knowing that she was not a threat to them unless they molested her.

Then she recognized the type: they were quilting bees, whose nest consisted of tiny quilts. It was surely very warm. There was obviously no virus here, for the bees were a pun that had not been eliminated.

She heard a faint panting. Sure enough, there was a pants bush, with several ripe pairs of smart-looking pants. Too smart: those were smarty pants, that when harvested would make the wearer run around madly, or could even run around on their own.

Then there was a spectacles bush with several very nice-looking spectacles ready. Astrid had an interest, as she always wore dark glasses. She folded her own glasses and pocketed them, then took a set from the bush and tried them on. Immediately she became dubious, mistrustful, and extremely cynical. Oh—these were skepticals. She put them back and tried a nice red-tinted pair. Her mood went from sulky to positive; everything looked wonderful. So these were rose-colored glasses. They would do, for now; she was happy for the temper uplift.

There were plenty of puns here, confirmation that the virus had not ravaged this section. But there could still be lurking pockets of it. She had to make sure.

She crossed a barren section where nothing much grew. This was vaguely familiar; she had once lived in country like this. In fact this could be that region, rendered less recognizable by her human perspective. There was a figure kneeling on the ground, facing away from her. Astrid approached. "Hello."

The figure looked up. It was a woman, a large elf with pointed ears and odd four-fingered hands. "Hello."

Then Astrid saw that before the elf woman was a marked gravesite with a plaque: JONE. "Oh, I'm sorry! I did not realize you were grieving."

"No, that's all right. I can't bring Jone back." The elf stood. "I am Jenny."

"I am Astrid. I was just looking for pockets of pun virus to eliminate."

Jenny stepped toward her. "I am pleased to meet you, Astrid."

Astrid stepped back. "Please, I do not mean to seem unfriendly, but it is not safe to touch me. I am poisonous."

Jenny stopped. "I apologize for presuming. You look lovely."

"It—it's a kind of curse. My appearance gives men a particular idea, but I can't be touched." Then, to change the awkward subject: "If I may ask, who was Jone?"

"My last baby daughter. There was a prophecy that she would one day help someone save Xanth from destruction. But then there was a horrible accident and she died. It has been some time, but I still come out to visit her grave. That is surely foolish of me, and I do not generally speak of it to others."

"I'm sorry. I regret intruding. I grew up in this region, but did not know of this grave."

"It is visible only when I come here," Jenny said.

"I will let you be." Astrid turned to go.

"That's all right. There's something familiar about you. Have we by chance met before?"

"I don't think so. I think I would have remembered your—" Astrid broke off, embarrassed.

"My pointed ears? My four-fingered hands?"

"Yes. I apologize for—"

2

"No need. I am unique to Xanth, as perhaps you are."

"Perhaps so," Astrid agreed.

There was a sound in the distance. A figure loomed, running swiftly toward them. It was a giant wolf!

"Stand behind me," Astrid said. "I will deter it."

Jenny laughed. "No need. That is my husband."

"Your—?"

The wolf slid to a halt, changing to a large handsome man. "Ready to go, dear?"

"Ready, dear," Jenny agreed. "Farewell, Astrid. I'm sure I know you from somewhere."

The man became the wolf again. Jenny leaped and landed on his back, riding him like a horse. Then they were off.

Astrid stood bemused. She turned to look at the grave, but it was gone, or at least hidden again. She shook her head, marveling at the odd encounter.

She moved on, discovering a trail in the shape of the letter N. It had an odor of guts. She smiled; that would be an N-Trail. Most folk would avoid it because of the unsavory smell, but such things didn't bother her. Interesting things could sometimes be found along such trails, for those who had the stomach to follow them to their ends. Anyway, this was a very pretty trail, thanks to the rosy glasses.

It led to a lovely little glade that seemed to be a campsite. To whom did it belong?

"Hello, lovely maiden," a somewhat gravelly voice said. "No, don't try to retreat; the trail has been closed off behind you."

Astrid glanced back and saw that it was true; the trail appeared to have become constricted, and there was no clear passage back. "So it seems," she agreed, unconcerned. She removed the glasses and put her regular ones back on, because she suspected that mischief was afoot and she wanted to see things accurately. Now the clogged trail did not look nearly so nice.

"Shall we exchange introductions? I am Truculent." He stepped out of the shadow and stood revealed as a supremely ugly troll.

"I am Astrid," she said.

"And what brings a succulent creature like you to this ill neck of the woods, fair Astrid?"

"I am on a mission to extirpate the last remnants of the anti-pun virus that recently ravaged Xanth," she explained. "I carry a vial of elixir that will eliminate any vestige of the foul virus." She held it up. "We all do; we never want to discover the virus and be unable to destroy it before it spreads."

"You all do? How many are there in your party?"

"Five lovely maidens and four males. One of us has not yet found her ideal companion."

"That's too bad," Truculent said. "She is doomed to find only the worst companion."

"I don't think I understand," Astrid said. Actually she was beginning to get a notion. Trolls had a mixed reputation and a certain crude taste for human maidens. She had encountered one once, and was familiar with the type. "Are you by any ill chance speaking of yourself? I think it is fair to say she would not be interested."

"I am, and she would not. Trolls come in assorted types. Some are noble, some build highways, and some are simply bad news. I happen to be of the latter persuasion."

"Then why do you believe she would associate with you?"

"Because she would have no choice."

He was a brute, all right. But she needed to be quite certain before she acted. "Maybe I am being a bit dull this morning. Surely she would have a choice."

"She would not. Any more than you do, pretty creature."

There it was: her appearance had turned him on, and he had mainly one thing on his brutish mind. But she argued her case, in the off-chance that she was misunderstanding his implication. "Certainly I have a choice! I can associate with whomever I please, and as it happens I have a good man who loves me. I will not be taking up with the likes of you."

"I see I need to spell it out," Truculent said. "I have a five stage process with respect to a tender morsel like you. First I will chase you down and catch you. That will be a slight but pleasant challenge, since you will be confined to my glade. Second I will rape you. That will be another pleasant challenge, as you will surely struggle and scream, enhancing the conquest. Third, I will kill you. That too should be fun, with blood spattering as I bite off pieces of you until you expire. Fourth I shall roast you on a spit until you are thoroughly cooked, as roasted meat is far tastier than raw flesh. Fifth, I shall eat you, swallowing your juicy tidbits and gnawing on your bones. Then I will start the process over with the four remaining girls of your party. This should make an excellent and nutritious week."

Astrid considered briefly. "I don't believe I favor your five-stage process. Neither will my companions."

"I beg your pardon," Truculent said apologetically. "Did I give you the misimpression that you had any choice in the matter?"

"I do labor under that impression. For example, what of the men of my party? They will not readily cooperate with your process."

"I was forgetting the men," the troll agreed. "For them I will skip the rape and still have four-fifths the fun. That will extend my pleasure beyond a week."

"You seem remarkably confident, considering that you don't know what talents the members of my party may possess."

"That merely adds the pleasure of the unknown. On rare occasion a victim does manage to escape my trap. But I believe I have closed the weaknesses, and this little arena is secure."

"I doubt it."

"Then shall we put it to the proof now? See if you can escape me." The troll advanced menacingly on her.

Astrid did not retreat. "Are you sure you won't reconsider? I do not want to harm you if you are reasonable."

"Enough of the humor, delicious delicacy! Try to make at least a token chase of it." He stepped closer.

"Sorry. I decline to play any part of your fell game."

Truculent stood before her, looming over her. "I am losing my patience with you, sweet taste. Must I knock some sense into your innocent skull?"

"You can try."

"Then take this, cute fool!" He swing his open hand and slapped her face. Her glasses flew off. He grabbed her shoulders and stared into her face. "*Now* will you—"

At which point he dropped dead.

Astrid shook her head. "I gave you every chance to relent," she said sadly. "I really don't like killing folk if there is any alternative."

She went to pick up her fallen glasses; fortunately they were unbroken. Their heavy tint was, of course, not to protect her eyes from the sunlight, but to protect other folk from her direct stare. She didn't want to kill anyone by accident. Not even a troll.

Well, it was time to leave this dread glade. But she discovered that the N trail remained clogged; it had not reverted at the death of the troll. The path was impenetrable.

She walked around the edge of the glade. Now she saw why the troll had thought she was trapped: the trees grew tightly around it, forming a virtual wall, and thorny vines bound them together. There was no room to walk between them. This barrier extended high up so that only a flying creature could readily escape it. Truculent Troll had wrought his arena carefully. But in his arrogance he had picked on the wrong victim.

So how was she to depart? She didn't want to mess up anything she didn't have to. She was just checking for signs of the pun virus, and there were none here.

Well, there was a way. In the last month she and her friends had discovered that they had been granted certain additional talents to facilitate their mission. Mainly, they could change between their most familiar forms. Astrid had not had much use for this, as her man Art preferred her in her human form. But now it seemed appropriate.

She carefully removed her sequined dress, slippers, and underwear. She formed it all into a compact bundle together with her glasses. Quite compact; she was able to tuck it under her tongue, thanks to its magic. Then she changed to her original form: a large female basilisk. She was actually an extremely pretty basilisk, but few folk cared to appreciate that, because her very ambiance was slowly lethal.

Now she circled the glade again, this time sniffing the ground. Sure enough, there was the smell of troll footprints leading to a particular spot. It looked just as tangled as the rest, but her nose said there was access. She touched it with a paw, and her digits passed through without touching. One of the trees was an illusion!

She nosed on into what turned out to be a tunnel through the twisted foliage. It wasn't visible, but it was there. The troll must have known it well enough to use it even without seeing it. Where did it go?

Straight to a nickelpede nest. The vicious insects swarmed over it, ready to gouge out nickel-sized chunks of flesh from whatever blundered into their domain. There was no way around it; the vine walls were tight on either side.

Well, she could handle nickelpedes. The taste of her flesh would kill any who bit into it, and of course her stare would wipe out any she saw. So she braced herself and marched into the nest. And through it, untouched. It was illusion too!

The path led to the mouth of a cave. It was closely barred, and locked, like a prison cell. It probably *was* a cell, where the troll kept his future meals. Such as maidens he had caught and raped, but not yet gotten around to killing, cooking, and eating. He would keep them alive so their meat wouldn't spoil. They ought to be rescued.

Astrid changed back into human form. "Hello!" she called. "Is anybody in there?"

"Go away!" a faint voice replied from deep within the cave.

This was curious. "Why?" Astrid called back.

"This is the lair of a troll. Go away before he catches you and adds you to our number. It is not safe here, especially for maidens, which you sound like. We are doomed, but you can still save yourself if you flee quickly."

"I will not flee," Astrid called. "I have come to rescue you. But these bars balk me. How may I open the gate?"

"We'll try to tell you," the voice called. Now there was a scurrying as the captives emerged from the depth of the cave. They were goblin maidens, small and lovely. They paused as they saw her. "You're a nymph!"

Astrid realized that she had not thought to put her human clothing back on. Nymphs were lovely and largely empty-headed; all most of them did was run nude, scream cutely, and kick their feet high, showing off their pretty legs. Few remembered their yesterdays or were aware of their tomorrows; they lived strictly in the present. No ordinary nymph would attempt to rescue captives, because a nymph's attention span was too short to focus on such a task for more than a few seconds.

"Not exactly," Astrid said. "I merely forgot my clothes." She spat out her compact ball, opened it up, and donned her clothing and dark glasses.

"Oh!" a gobliness with lovely reddish brown hair exclaimed. "You're human!"

Wrong again, but Astrid decided not to clarify that aspect at the moment; it was usually more trouble than it was worth. "Close enough. I am Astrid, traveler."

"I am Ginger Goblin, captive."

"Hello, Ginger. I am glad to meet you. Now how can I open this gate?"

"The lock is magic. Only the dread troll can open it." Ginger hesitated. "Who may come upon us at any moment."

"No danger of that," Astrid said.

"How can you be sure? He's one mean brute."

"Because he is dead."

There was a brief silence. "Are you sure?" Ginger asked uncertainly. "He might be playing possum, to better trap you, because you're very much his type."

"His type?" Astrid asked sharply.

"Luscious. He would want to ravish and eat you."

"No, he is definitely dead."

"How can you be sure? Because if he catches you—"

Astrid became impatient. "Because I killed him. I'm a basilisk."

The goblins eeked faintly and fell back, terrified.

"Oh come on," Astrid said. "I'm not here to hurt you. That's why I put on the glasses. Truculent Troll mistook me for a morsel, and attacked me, knocked off my glasses, and I looked him in the face and killed him. It was self defense. Now I just want to undo some of the damage he did, such as by freeing you to return to your homes. I'm a basilisk, but also a woman. I care about the welfare of maidens."

The goblins inched cautiously back to the gate. "We're sorry," Ginger said. "It's a bad time for us. Each day he takes one of us to—to—"

"To rape and eat. I know. But that's over. We just need to get this gate unlocked."

"We can't help you there," Ginger said. "If we knew how to unlock it, we would have done so ourselves and escaped."

That made sense. Astrid signed. "Then I'll have to summon help. This may get complicated."

"Complicated?"

"You'll see." The Astrid braced herself. "Metria," she murmured.

A small back cloud appeared. "Did I hear my nomenclature?"

"Your what?" Astrid asked. The demoness insisted on going through the ritual, and since Astrid needed her help, she had to comply.

"Terminology, language, word, figure, identifier, handle—"

"Name?"

"Whatever," the cloud agreed crossly.

"Yes, you heard your name," Astrid said. "I killed a troll, and now want to rescue his captives, but they are magically locked in. Can you arrange to get Pewter here? He should be able to handle this."

"Why not just pick the lock?"

"I don't know how. Do you?"

The cloud expanded and formed into a sultry female figure with barely enough clothing to avoid freaking out any males in the vicinity. Fortunately there were none at the moment. "Oh, sure. I pick my nose; a lock should be cleaner."

"Then do it, please."

Metria's finger went to her nose.

"The lock!" Astrid snapped.

"Oh. Why didn't you say so?"

Ginger nodded slowly. She was catching on why this was likely to be complicated.

The demoness examined the lock. She put her finger to it. There was a crackle as a spark jumped, and she jerked back. "This is a troll lock!"

"Yes. Can you pick it?"

"Not without being electrocuted. Only trolls can handle troll locks."

"Could Pewter handle it?"

Metria nodded. "He might. Too bad he's not here."

"I have a phenomenal idea," Astrid said patiently. "Why don't you pop back to the camp and tell him about this, and ask him to come here to deal with it?"

"What kind of idea?"

"Fantastic, extraordinary, remarkable, superlative, spectacular—"

"Grate?"

Astrid was taken aback. "Grate?"

"Maybe I misspelled it."

"Great!" Astrid said. "Yes, that's it. You're a genius."

Metria looked slightly suspicious that she was being mocked. "Technically I'm closer to a genie than a genius, but it will do. I'll go fetch Pewter." She popped off.

"Thank you, screwball," Astrid said to the dissipating smoke.

"I heard that!" the last wisp said.

"Oh, bleep!" Astrid swore.

"We have heard of Metria," Ginger said. "She's always mischief."

"She's a member of our party," Astrid said. "She does mean well, in her fashion. It just can be a trial at times working with her."

"We appreciate that."

Soon the cloud reappeared. "Tiara is on her way."

"Tiara? But it's Pewter we need here at the moment."

"But he can't fly. Tiara can."

Astrid counted mentally to ten. It hardly helped. "I wonder whether she will be willing to go back to fetch Pewter."

"No need."

"No need?"

"Superfluous, pointless, redundant—"

"Why is there no need to go back to fetch Pewter?"

"Because she's already bringing him."

Astrid counted from eleven to twenty. That didn't help much either. "Thank you."

"Always glad to help," the demoness said sunnily.

In due course Tiara appeared. Her wild fair hair was gathered and wound around her midsection, its flotation supporting her like an inner tube. She had fins on her hands and feet, and was efficiently swimming through the air, as she had learned how to do in the past month. But she seemed to be alone. Astrid kept her mouth shut, afraid to inquire.

Tiara circled over the forest, spied them, and spiraled gently down, her skirt flapping in the breeze. She landed fairly neatly. She had bright blue eyes, a red cherry mouth, nice features, and a firm slender body. "Hello, Astrid," she said brightly as her hair shortened and formed back into her namesake tiara. "We wondered what you were up to."

"I had a run-in with a hungry troll. Now we need to unlock the troll's gate to let out his captives."

"Ah. That must be why you need Com Pewter."

"Yes. He has a way with locks."

Tiara removed her hand-fins, reached into her small backpack and fished out what looked like a potato chip with the letter C printed on one side, and the letter P on the other side. She brought it to her mouth and kissed it. "Wake, CP."

The chip expanded, forming into an android with a face painted on the front of the head. It was of course a computer chip. "Thank you, maiden."

"For the ride?" Tiara asked.

"That, too."

Astrid smiled. Theoretically the machine was immune to the charms of pretty girls, but that was evidently changing. Com Pewter was no prince, but the kiss had revived him regardless.

"Here is the lock," Astrid told Pewter, indicating the barred gate. "Can you open it?"

Pewter considered the gate without touching it. "This is a sophisticated setup. The lock is protected by an invisible magnetic shell that will short-circuit me if I touch it. The troll surely had it keyed to his identity alone. We need to eliminate the shell first."

"How do we do that?"

"One good bash by a nonmetallic object should do it."

"Then I think we need Ease and Kandy."

"We do," Pewter agreed.

"I will fetch them," Tiara agreed. Her hair grew long again. She wrapped it around her middle, donned the hand-fins, and took off. There was almost but not quite a flash of panties before she leveled out and swam forward. She was still learning to manage such details. Trousers would have solved that problem, but Tiara considered them unfeminine. Soon she was gone.

"How come a common garden-variety troll has such a fancy security system?" Metria asked.

"I can answer that," Ginger responded from inside the cave. "My friends and I were out foraging for flowers, and there were some pretty ones in the glade. We didn't realize that it was the troll's trap. He pounced on us and we were helpless to resist. He told us that he had made a deal with his trollway-building cousins to provide one or more pretty girls to serve their needs. When they come to collect, any of us who survive will be given to them to serve as slaves. We hoped they would come soon, because they can't be worse than Truculent."

Astrid did not like the smell of this. "What kind of slaves?"

"We don't know, but we can guess. The difference is that they probably won't cook and eat us, after. They're more civilized."

Ideas of civilization evidently differed. Still, the trollway trolls were a higher class, and surely better to deal with. "Well, that deal is terminated," Astrid said. "We'll free you so you can go home."

"We appreciate that."

But now there was a heavy tramping along the hidden trail. Trolls!

"Let's hope for their sake that they are reasonable," Pewter said to Astrid. "If not, you know what to do."

"I do," she agreed grimly, touching her dark glasses.

The trolls came to stand before the cave. There were three of them, each uglier than the others. "What have we here?" their evident leader demanded.

Astrid stepped forward. "Let's exchange introductions. I am Astrid. Truculent Troll attacked me and I had to defend myself, as you may have seen in the glade."

"We did," the troll said. "I am Truman Troll and these are my henchmen. How did you manage to overcome Truculent?"

"I am a basilisk in human form."

"He knows better than to mess with a basilisk!"

"He did not give me much of a chance to clarify my nature. He was too busy clarifying his own five-stage process."

Truman nodded. "That does sound like him. Why have you not long-since departed this vicinity?"

"We mean to free Truculent's captives so they can go home. They have suffered more than enough already."

"Those captives devolve to us, now that Truculent is dead. We have uses for them."

"You shall not have them."

"This is troll business. There are precedents."

"It became my business when Truculent attacked me. Any deals he may have made ended with his death."

"We do not agree. The terms of the deal extend to the heirs and assigns."

"We do not agree with your interpretation."

"Do we agree that an altercation between our kind and your kind could become mutually difficult?"

"Our kinds have normally left each other alone," Astrid agreed.

Truman exchanged a glance or three with his companions, then stared down at her. "Then it seems we have a problem." He closed his massive fists as the two henchmen donned hoods that would prevent her from staring directly at their faces. That would provide them only partial protection, and inhibit their vision. Still, it increased their chances of dispatching her before she dispatched them. It seemed they had clashed with basilisks before.

Astrid touched her glasses. She could handle trolls, even experienced ones. But it was chancy; she could not be sure of taking out all three before one got to her with a club. They were of course aware that they would take losses. "I hope it can be amicably resolved."

Truman smiled without humor. "So do I. Do you have a proposal?"

"I do," Pewter said.

Truman glanced at him. "And you are?"

"Com Pewter, a smart machine allied with Astrid. You do not know my capabilities."

"Oh, we do, Pewter," Truman said. "Your iconoclasm is well known. But your power is limited to your immediate vicinity."

"You are standing on the verge of that vicinity. You will enter it if you clash with Astrid."

Truman nodded. "Excellent point. What is your proposal?"

"Surely the goblins have some troll captives, saved for similar purposes as you save goblins. How about a captive exchange?"

"We prefer a good old-fashioned raid and heads-bashing."

"Which would cost you the lives of the captives, making the raid in that respect pointless."

"So it would, unfortunately. But goblin males, in contrast with their females, are surly brutes not much known for negotiation. We would be at war before we came to terms."

"Unless a basilisk served as intermediary."

This time the troll's smile had humor. "Well now! That notion appeals to me. Let's see what offers. This will require a dialogue with the captives. Shall we make a truce for this hour?"

"Granted," Pewter said.

"Granted," Astrid agreed. Trolls were dark and dangerous, but they did honor truces.

Truman's fists unclenched, and the henchmen's hoods came off. They knew that machines and basilisks also honored truces.

"May I say, Astrid, that you are one extremely fetching creature in this form," Truman said. "It is a pleasure to be near—but not too near—you."

"Thank you." At least he was polite about the idea the sight of her gave him.

Truman squatted down to peer into the barred cave. "Goblins, we are in negotiation phase. Are there any troll captives in your home mound?"

"Three," Ginger said. "But we can't say how long they will survive."

"They were alive when you left?"

"Yes. But the female was stripped and tied down for the benefit of—you know."

"Yes. We treat captives similarly. It is to mutual advantage for us to arrange an exchange."

"Yes," Ginger agreed faintly.

The troll inspected the lock. "That's one of ours, yes, keyed to Truculent. No one else can touch it without getting electrocuted. You have a way to deal with it?"

"We believe so," Pewter said. "Assistance is on the way."

Truman turned to Astrid. "Now let's go see the goblins. May I offer you a lift?"

"That is surely faster," Astrid agreed.

"Climb into my knapsack."

She got behind him and did so. Then he stood. "Remain here," he told the henchmen. And to Astrid: "Trust, but verify."

"Agreed."

Then the troll forged into the brush, bashing out his own trail. In a remarkably brief time they reached the goblin mound.

The goblins surged out, brandishing weapons. "Ho! Fresh meat!" their leader cried.

"Not so," Truman said. "I come to negotiate."

"Negotiate, negatiate," the goblin said. "You were a fool to come into our power, poop for brains."

"I bring with me a basilisk."

"Nice bluff, moron! We don't see any—" He paused.

Astrid had changed to her natural form, gazing out and around from the knapsack, not looking at anyone directly. The goblins shrank away, well knowing that form.

"As I was saying," Truman said. "We have three goblin girls from your mound as captives. We will exchange them for your three troll captives. Do we have a deal?"

"The bleep!" the goblin chief swore.

Astrid lowered her gaze. She looked at a tied sheep they were probably saving for the evening meal. It looked her way, and fell dead.

"Do we have a deal?" Truman repeated.

The goblins looked at the sheep. They quailed, realizing that this was no bluff. "Deal," the chief said, disgruntled.

"We shall return in due course with the captives," Truman said. "In the interim, you will bring out your captives and have them ready here. Then we will exchange." He paused meaningfully. "Should anything go wrong, my companion might be annoyed. You wouldn't like her when she's annoyed."

The goblins quailed again. The last thing they wanted was an angry basilisk marauding through their mound.

Truman turned and forged back through the brush. Astrid returned to her human form. "You have an effective way with words, Astrid," he remarked.

"Thank you." She hadn't said anything, but her threat of a glare had been enough. That was his point.

When they reached the cave, Tiara was just arriving, swimming through the air with the man called Ease on her back as if riding a dolphin. Her hair had to be struggling to float them both but was managing. He waved. Then he did a double take. "Trolls!" He drew his trusty wooden board and brandished it threateningly.

"We are in truce, unfortunately," Truman said. "But after our business here is done, if you wish to try your board against my club, I will be glad to accommodate you."

"He's right," Astrid called. "We made a truce. We are friends for this hour. No fighting."

"Oh, bleep," Ease said, lowering the board as Tiara landed. He jumped off her back.

"Here is the situation," Pewter told Ease. "I need to unlock this lock to free the goblin captives, but it is protected by an invisible shell. Kindly bash apart that shell."

"Sure," Ease said. It was his talent to make things easy. He swung the board at the lock. There was a sharp crack, and a small explosion of sparks, and the formerly invisible fragments of the shell dropped to the ground.

"Thank you," Pewter said. "Now let me concentrate. This may take a little time."

"We have made a deal to exchange captives, goblins for trolls," Astrid said. "It's a situation I blundered into, but it is working out."

Ease turned away. He touched the board to the ground, and it became a lovely young woman with dark eyes and luxuriant dark hair. "And hello Kandy," Astrid said.

Both the goblins and the trolls were startled. "What just happened here?" Truman asked.

"I have the ability to change forms between human and board," Kandy explained. "Just as Astrid changes between human and basilisk. When I'm the board, I make sure Ease's aim is good and his strike effective." She rubbed her neck. "Though I must admit that charge on the shell gave me a jolt."

"It occurs to me that you folk are no ordinary group," Truman said.

"We're a special mission to eliminate the last of the anti-pun virus," Kandy explained. "To that end we have been granted certain additional abilities. We are a bit unusual."

"So it seems," the troll agreed, glancing at Astrid, Kandy, and Tiara. "Are all the females of your party as pretty as the three of you?"

Demoness Metria appeared. "Yes."

"And a demoness!" Truman said. "The surprises keep coming."

"Surprises can be fun," Metria said, inhaling so that her decolletage threatened to tear loose and float away.

"I am curious how a basilisk came to associate with a human party, and a demoness, a machine, a girl who floats on her hair, and a board woman," Truman said. "Not that it's any of my business, which makes it even more intriguing."

"We're curious too," Ginger said. "It's not our business either."

"Well, that would be a chapter-length personal narrative," Astrid said. "I wouldn't want to bore you to distraction with a dull literary flashback."

"As it happens, this lock threatens to require a chapter-length effort," Pewter said.

"So we're stuck for the time anyway," Ginger said.

Truman and his henchmen settled down on the ground. "Bore us," he said.

The others settled similarly. What could she do? Astrid began to speak.

CHAPTER 2:
FLASHBACK

〜〜

Astrid Basilisk-Cockatrice was the daughter of anonymous parents who had wiled away a dull minute by generating her on a warm compost pile, then gone their own deadly ways, never to see her or each other again. Why should they? It was their nature to hate all other creatures, including their own kind. They had fought over possession of the resting site, and finally settled it by sharing it for that brief purpose. In minutes they were both days away and not looking back, leaving her to hatch alone. She had to fend for herself from the outset, as all female basilisks and male cockatrices did. She had no particular difficulty, as her very nearness wilted plants and stunned animals, and her direct stare into any creature's eyes was instantly lethal. So she had plenty of spoiling food to sustain her, and was never in any real danger.

Yet she was not completely satisfied with this deadly dull life. It took her some time to figure out what was bothering her. She covertly observed other creatures—she had to hide to do it, because they sensibly fled in horror and/or terror the moment they saw or winded or heard her—and noted that while they too foraged or hunted for food, and generated manure, and fought and slept, they also associated in pairs or even small groups. Sometimes they became very friendly with each other. The mating part was obvious, but why did they continue to be together after it was accomplished?

She realized in time that they associated because they liked each other and enjoyed interacting on a more or less continual basis. This was foreign to her nature, but as she studied it, it began to appeal to her. She wanted to be friends with others, to achieve love, and to have romance. But this was of course impossible. If she encountered a cockatrice he would want to be with her only one minute and never again. That simply was not enough.

She finally concluded that she would never achieve her dreams as a basilisk. Her kind simply were not loving creatures. Yet her impossible desire remained. What could she do?

It occurred to her that the humans might know. They associated with each other all the time, and even made houses so they could live constantly together. She knew better than to approach a human; they were as wary of her kind as any creature was, and somewhat more effective in attacking. She had had a couple of narrow escapes. No creature could overcome her in close combat, but humans used spears, arrows, and thrown stones that were effective from a distance.

However, she managed to spy on one human family by burying herself in compost close behind their house. That not only hid her, it masked her deadly body odor, and she was able to overhear their dialogues in the house. She remained for many hours at a time, mostly listening. In this manner she slowly learned their language. She couldn't speak it, because her mouth and tongue were wrong, but she came to understand it.

One day the man and woman discussed something truly remarkable. It seemed that there was a grumpy old human or gnome called the Good Magician who answered questions for a fee. The fee was a year's service to him at his castle, or the equivalent. Querents, as they were called, constantly sought to bother him with Questions. He didn't like to be bothered, so he had set up his castle to force anyone approaching to navigate three difficult challenges before they could get inside. This significantly cut down the number. Those few who made it in got Answers and paid with their Services, and that was that.

That was what she should do. Maybe the Good Magician would be able to solve her problem. In fact, maybe he would have a spell to enable her to become human so that she could then experience everything she was missing as a basilisk. The more she considered it, the more it appealed to her. She would do it.

Thus it was that she set out for the Good Magician's Castle. She had ascertained where it was. In fact there were enchanted paths leading right to it. Unfortunately she could not use those paths, because they were spelled to exclude dangerous creatures like her. But she followed alongside them, and was duly guided. In due course she reached it, or at least a place in the deep

17

forest that enabled her to gaze at it.

It was beautiful in the human manner, with lofty turrets, a crenelated surrounding wall, and a circular moat that featured a handsome moat monster. There was a drawbridge across the moat, but at the moment it was drawn up. That would be no problem for her; she could swim well enough, and the moat monster would know better than to try to bother her. But she was sure it would not be that easy. She had learned that the Good Magician always seemed to know who was coming—he was after all the Magician of Information—and prepared Challenges tailored to the specific Querent. Also, that the person's magic talent was not effective here. So she would likely face problems that made a basilisk balk, without being able to kill them with a glance. That could be awkward.

Well, she would find out. She emerged from the forest and advanced on the castle.

A man came to intercept her before she even reached the moat. His hand hovered near his hip, where a squat mechanical device was hooked to his belt. "Draw, stranger," he said.

Astrid halted. He wanted her to draw a picture? That was odd. But she could oblige him. She scraped a section of ground clear with her tail, then used a paw to draw a little picture of a nest up in the top of a tall tree.

The gunman paused. "I'll be bleeped," he said. "I can read that. You're saying 'High,' meaning 'Hi.' Well, hi to you too, basilisk. But that isn't the kind of drawing I meant."

It wasn't? Astrid looked at him curiously.

"Look, Bask, I'm a troubleshooter. I shoot at trouble, banishing it. And you're certainly trouble. The worst kind, because you kill folk with your stare. If it weren't for the counter-spell nullifying your deadly gaze and smell, I'd be in deep bleep already. But I'm giving you a fair chance. I mean either draw your gun faster than I can draw mine, so you can plug me first, or get out of here, defeated. Otherwise I'll plug you. It won't actually be lethal, because the magic protects you to that extent, but it will knock you out, and when you recover you'll be far away from here with a geis on you to stay the bleep away from this castle. Now do you understand? This is a Challenge. It's my job to get rid of you so you won't bother the Good Magician with your stupid Question. Got it now?"

Geis? She had not encountered this word before.

"It's a magical obligation," the man explained. "Locks you in so you can't violate it."

He knew what she was thinking? This was scary.

"So are you going to draw or flee, moron?" the Troubleshooter demanded.

She might have been inclined to turn tail and depart, as this Castle business was more complicated than she had anticipated. But there was something about his attitude that annoyed her. So she reversed her mental course and decided to plow on through. Obviously she couldn't draw her gun, as she had no gun and no hand suitable to hold it. This challenge was completely unfair in that respect.

There had to be a way. That was part of the lore she had overhead: there was always a way. She just had to be smart enough to find it.

She looked quickly around. All she saw was a few bright coins scattered on the ground. She knew, again from her eavesdropping, that human folk valued coins, though they really had little or no use for them. Could this be a way?

"You've had enough time, compost beast," the troubleshooter said. "If you don't turn tail this instant, I'll plug you."

Astrid turned tail in that instant, forestalling the gunman's action. But she wasn't fleeing. She was going for the coins.

The nearest was a plugged nickel. She could tell because she smelled the nickel metal, and there was a hole through its center. The gunman must have plugged it earlier, ruining its value. Evidently he liked plugging things, just for the bleep of it.

She began to get a glimmer of the beginning of a notion. Just how much did he like plugging coins? Especially if it became a challenge?

She found a Heaven Cent, a truly beautiful little coin. She swept it up with a paw and hurled it high in the air toward the gunman.

Sure enough, he whirled, drew his gun, and fired. The coin rang as his bullet struck it, knocking it right out of the air. He was certainly a good shot. That might actually be his weakness.

She found a Heaven Nickel and swept it up similarly. She couldn't grasp and hold an object in her paw, but she could throw it by sweeping it out of the dirt. The Nickel arced high in the air.

The Troubleshooter plugged it, again scoring perfectly.

Good enough. Astrid found several more coins, and crammed them into her mouth. They were cold and dirty, and some were truly foul, but she could handle that. When she had them all, she ran rapidly forward, toward the Castle.

"Hey!" the Troubleshooter called, drawing his gun.

Astrid spat out a Heaven Quarter and swiped it into the air behind her. The gunman whirled and shot at it, plugging it right though the center. But meanwhile Astrid was running. When the Troubleshooter reoriented and aimed at her again, she spat out a Heaven Dollar and heaved it up, and he plugged it. She followed with a Hell Cent. That one went up in vile smoke when plugged. Then a Hell Nickel, and Hell Quarter. The gunman got them all.

And she was at the moat.

"Dang," the Troubleshooted cussed. "You diverted me and got through. Nice going, Bask."

It seemed she had navigated the First Challenge. So how was it relevant to her situation, as she had never messed with coins or guns before? Well, it had forced her to use her mind instead of her lethal stare, and practice in that could be an advantage when interacting with humans. She was pleased with herself.

She didn't even need the Hell Dollar, so she made a careful swipe with her paw and skipped it across the moat. The moat monster watched it but knew better than to snap it up.

But her glee was soon doused by a far more negative reflection as she gazed into the water of the moat. So she had made it through one Challenge, really mostly by sheer luck. What made her think she could handle two more? And if by some mischance she did, why did she think the Good Magician could or would actually help her? This whole thing was ridiculous!

As if echoing her thoughts, she heard sonorous music. It seemed to be coming from the blue water of the moat, and it was turning everything else blue: the sandy bank, the motley plants growing on it, even her own body. In fact it was the Blues! She had heard humans speaking of them: music that really depressed people.

She must have activated it by skipping the Hell Dollar, signaling her completion of the first Challenge. So could she change it? *Green!* she thought. And lo, the water turned green, and the music changed. So did the sand bank and plants, all becoming deep green. Now she felt very environmentally friendly, wanting to help the whole natural environment.

She tried again, thinking *Yellow*. Not only did the environment assume a yellow cast, she felt very afraid.

Pink, she thought. The color changed, and so did the music, both becoming very soft and feminine.

So she could change colors, but remained bound to them. This wasn't getting her past what must be the Second Challenge. Playing with it wasn't enough; she needed to counter it. But how?

Well, in the prior Challenge she finally made it work for her. How could she make this music work for her? Music was for listening and dancing, and of course a lizard couldn't dance.

Or could it? She had four legs, but why should dancing be restricted to two legs? She could dance to music, in her fashion. She thumped her legs, forming a cadence, a beat. The music aligned, becoming sprightly. She was doing it!

Except that she needed to get across the moat. Dancing was not helping there. She could swim, but she suspected that this would not be allowed. She tried wading into the water. Sure enough, she did not float; she remained on the lake floor. She would have to hold her breath a long time to cross it—far longer than she was able. She had to find a magical or punnish way. Maybe a music and dance way.

Dance puns. What about Atten-dance? Abun-dance? Depen-dance? Those did not seem promising.

Then it came to her: Ascen-dance! A dance that made a person rise.

The thought brought the music. It became uplifting. She danced, and her feet were light. She moved out onto the water, her whole body almost floating. Her feet touched the water and did not sink in. She was dancing on the water. Ascent-dance-sea!

She danced on across the moat. Halfway across she passed the moat monster, whose green head oriented on her. She paused, smirking—and sank into the water.

She scrambled to resume the cadence, or ca-dance. She fought to recover the music. She managed to get them back and resume her progress. Distractions were deadly! She could have drowned trying to annoy the moat monster. That was an inadvertent lesson, but worth remembering.

She made it to the inner bank and flopped on the sand, panting. Ascendancing was hard work! But she had made it through the Second Challenge.

Soon she perked up and looked around. There was a space between the moat and the outer castle wall. There were a number of gates in the wall, each open and offering access to the interior. So where was the Third Challenge? Astrid did not trust this. Suppose she entered, and the gate slammed shut behind her, and it was the wrong access? The Challenge might be to figure out the correct gate before using any of them.

She walked along the space, eying each gate in turn. They seemed similar, but they did have different names printed on each. She was able to read them because during her spying on the human family, the child had been given exercises in reading. He was saying each word, then writing it with a stick in the dirt. Watching him practice had taught her the written form too. In fact, on occasion he had trouble with his spelling, doing it different ways for the same word. One day the word he spoke was *Feud*, but he spelled it *Food*. He was

21

doubtful, but could not get it right. That bothered her. Finally she had quietly emerged from her hiding place and shown herself to him. He was too young to recognize her deadly nature, so he was not afraid; he took her for a large lizard, which technically she was. She was careful not to look him directly in the eye. Instead she took a deep and obvious breath and held it. So he imitated her, holding his own breath, glad for the distraction from his dull lesson. He took it for a game. That protected him from her odor. She walked to the dirt pad, wiped out his word, and scratched in the correct one. Then she had hastily retreated to a safe range, letting out her breath. He brightened as he let out his own breath, recognizing the correction. Thereafter when he had a word problem, he would signal her by holding his breath, and she would correct it for him. It was a convenient collaboration. She was in effect his make-believe playmate, and that satisfied them both. But all too soon he had grown up and moved on into the things of his own realm, like human girls, and she did not see him anymore. It was sad, but had left her with the ability to read, which now was proving useful.

Not that the printed names were very helpful. They were things like CONJU, ABRO, ARRO, CONGRE, DERO, FRI, FUMI, MITI, and SEGRE. These words had not been in the boy's lexicon, and she was not sure they made any sense. Of course gates could be named anything, sensible or nonsensical, but what was the point of having them in a Challenge if they were meaningless? So she pondered, and cogitated, and considered, and just plain thought. She was not about to try any of them until she understood their nature.

So she walked on, and came to a woman putting together mechanical men from a pile of metal rods, wires, and silly putty. Was she here for a reason?

The woman spied her. "Why, hello, basilisk," she said cheerily. "Have you lost your way?"

Astrid shook her head no, but then changed her mind. Maybe she *was* lost.

"Well, maybe I can help," the woman said. "I am Ann Droid. I assemble and control assorted robots. This one will be RX, a doctor machine. Another will be RNA, a geneticist. Every robot is R-something or other. They can be very useful in specialized situations."

Astrid did not know what a doctor or geneticist was, so stood mute.

"Oh, I forgot!" Ann said. "You're an animal; you can't speak. Let me fix that for the moment." She rummaged in her pile and came up with a small panel. "Hold this and think your words, and it will speak them for you."

Astrid accepted the panel, holding it awkwardly in her mouth. "Like this?" it asked. She was so surprised that she dropped it on the ground.

"Yes, like that, of course," Ann said. "It's a translator. I'm sure you could speak on your own if you had the mouth for it. This merely facilitates communication."

Astrid picked up the device again. "So it seems," it said. "I am Astrid."

Ann eyed her thoroughly. "I must say, you are a remarkably fetching example of your species, Astrid. The cockatrices must be constantly after you."

"They're a nuisance," Astrid agreed via the machine. "I have had to glare several of them off."

Ann laughed. "Human women do much the same thing, though our glares are more figurative than literal. The typical man wants only one thing, whereas we prefer an acquaintance that endures for more than one minute."

Astrid was coming to like this friendly woman. "We do," she agreed.

"So what can I do for you, Astrid?"

This might be awkward. "Are you a Challenge?"

Ann laughed. "By no means! I am merely part of the setting, as it were."

"I am having trouble figuring out what the Challenge is. All I see are mysteriously labeled gates."

Ann shrugged. "Doubtless it will come to you in due course."

So she was not going to help. Possibly she was merely a distraction. "Thank you," Astrid said, and set down the translator.

"You're welcome, Astrid. I hope you figure it out soon."

There were no more gates beyond this section, just the blank wall. Astrid walked back by them, rereading each label. There had to be some clue to their meaning. An array of ten gates with odd names. What was the clue?

She came to the first gate in the row, labeled INVESTI. Investi-gate.

A bright bulb flashed above her head. Investigate! It made a word after all.

She walked back, adding the gate's name to each one. Conjugate, Abrogate, Arrogate, Congregate, Derogate, Frigate, Fumigate, Mitigate, Segregate. They all made sense on their own terms.

Good enough. Now which was the proper one to take? Probably Investigate, as that was what she was doing. She walked to that one and started through.

And it slammed closed, just missing her snout. No access here. So she must have guess wrong.

She tried the next, Congregate. It slammed shut also.

She tried the others. Each shut her unkindly out.

It seemed she had not, after all, solved the Challenge, merely one part of it.

She returned to Ann, who remained busy with her robots. The translator remained where she could take it. She picked it up in her mouth. "I figured out the gates. Each of their names is a prelude to Gate. But they still won't let me pass."

"Perhaps the naming scheme is only part of the Challenge."

"Yes. But I have yet to figure out the rest of it. Are you sure you're not part of it?"

"I am merely part of the setting."

Then a second bulb flashed. The answer would be part of the setting.

"I saw that flash," Ann said.

"You're not the Challenge, you're the solution," Astrid said. "You're here for a reason."

Ann shrugged. "Perhaps."

"Those gates are obviously self-willed. That means they are machines. Robots. And you make robots. You must have made the gates."

"Possibly."

"And you can control them. You can let me through."

"Why should I do that?"

"Because I have figured it out, and you are a nice person, the kind I would like to be, and I am asking."

Ann laughed. "There is something about your phrasing that appeals to me. Select a gate."

"No, please, you select one. I want the one you choose for me."

Ann nodded. "You know, you're smarter than the average basilisk, and a good deal nicer. Take the Mitigate."

"Thank you." Astrid set down the translator and went to the Mitigate. This time it did not slam on her snout. She entered the castle.

A woman met her inside. "Welcome, Astrid. I am Wira, the Good Magician's daughter-in-law. He will see you now."

Just like that, Astrid was in the Magician's cramped study. He was there, poring over a huge tome. "Basilisk, I can change your form but not your nature. I can make your form human, but you will still be a deadly creature whose very nearness is death to most others. Are you sure this is what you want?"

Astrid was not at all sure, but neither did she want to return to her natural haunts. So she nodded. She wanted the change.

"There is another thing. Has it occurred to you to wonder why I am bothering with you, considering that you are a deadly animal most folk seek to exterminate?"

That had not occurred to her, but now that he mentioned it, she did wonder.

"It is because you are no ordinary animal. You have a soul."

That had never even remotely occured to her. How was this possible? Everyone knew that only human beings or those deviously related to them had souls. She was sure she had absolutely no human lineage.

"A night mare was transporting a lost soul to the dream realm when she got distracted by an idea for a truly horrendous bad dream and dropped it. It rolled into a hole and landed on you, where you were sleeping in your burrow. That put it beyond her recovery and she had to move on, chastened. Souls are immeasurably precious, at least to those who have them. Thereafter you were a souled creature, though you did not know it. That is why you became dissatisfied with your normal life. That is why you finally concluded that you would rather be human than lizard. You already had the essence of humanity. Your soul would not let you rest in peace."

Astrid gazed at him with hooded eyes so as not to hurt him. What he said explained so much! She was indeed too gentle to be a good basilisk. "But souls don't accept just anybody," she protested. "That soul should have bounced off me and waited for a better host. I'm a basilisk!"

"You are correct. Souls can be quite choosy. But evidently this one saw in you the potential for it to achieve its full flowering, so it accepted you. It may even have sought you out."

"Sought a basilisk?"

"A dubious business, to be sure. Let's hope it didn't make a mistake."

"I will try to live up to its expectation," she said humbly.

"So I must facilitate your conversion to humanity," the Good Magician concluded. "Now you know why."

She did indeed. What a revelation!

"MareAnn will give you a potion," he said. "You will still owe me a Service."

She nodded again, accepting the terms.

"This way," Wira said, leading her back down the dusky spiral stairway to the ground floor.

They came to a comfortable family room. A woman vaguely reminiscent of a pony met them there. "I am MareAnn, Designated Wife of the Month. Are you sure you want that potion? It will enable you to speak, if you know our language, and Ann Droid says you do, but—"

Astrid nodded without looking directly at her. MareAnn presented her with a sealed vial. Astrid took it between her front paws, nipped off the cap, and gulped it down.

The change was immediate. Her proportions shifted, with her limbs stretching out and her torso condensing, becoming distinctly lumpy. Her tail shrank until it no longer seemed to exist. Her snout shrank into her face. Her scales faded out. What a disaster!

"Now your form is human," MareAnn said. "You should be able to stand on your hind feet if you try. But first put this hood on over your head."

Astrid understood why. She took the hood, which was translucent so she could see out but would distort her gaze so that she would not accidentally kill someone with her stare. Then she slowly and awkwardly climbed to her feet. Her balance was precarious, but she was able to maintain it.

"You are a remarkably pretty semblance of a woman," MareAnn said. "The potion changes forms, but keeps the peripheral aspects. You were a very pretty basilisk."

"Thank you," Astrid said. And she paused, realizing that she had just spoken her first human words aloud.

"You see, you can do it," MareAnn said encouragingly. "However, there will still be a lot more for you to learn before you can safely go out among humans. We'll give you a room to yourself and I will help you all I can."

And so it was. MareAnn had a thing for animals, especially equines, but also for others, and she made sure that Astrid was comfortable and well treated. She spent many hours and days talking with Astrid, acquainting her with human conventions and foibles. One of these was clothing. Basilisks didn't use it, but humans did, so she had to wear a loose robe when she remembered to. It hardly mattered here, because no one entered this castle casually.

Most importantly, MareAnn became Astrid's first human friend. Astrid had never had one before, and found that she liked it very well.

"The Good Magician says that you will need three best friends to fulfill your mission in life," MareAnn said. "I am the first, but I am not enough."

"You seem like enough to me," Astrid said. "I am only newly acquainted with friendship, and don't know what a best friend would be. Also, I have no idea of a mission in life."

"With luck you will learn."

Then one night MareAnn came to her with a mission. "You have an opportunity to perform your Service for the Good Magician in what I hope is a compatible manner. A man has come who will be going out on a perhaps dangerous mission. He will need a bodyguard: someone who can readily dispatch a monster or attacking human when that is necessary."

"I can do that," Astrid agreed. "But a human man—I would not know how to comport myself in his presence."

"True. Fortunately he has a female companion, though he doesn't know it. She will guide you."

"That would help. But why doesn't he know it?"

"Because she is a wooden board by day. It's a curse put on her by a wishing well. Well, not actually a curse; rather it's a devious way of granting her wish. But it seems much like a curse. So she animates mostly at night, when he is asleep."

"I'm not sure I would be adept at handling a situation like this."

"Please, Astrid. This is your chance to go out among the human kind with some appropriate guidance. Kandy is the one who can best help you. She can be your friend. At least come to meet her."

Astrid couldn't refuse, so she went to meet the board woman. Who turned out to be quite nice, once she got over the shock of meeting a basilisk. She agreed to have Astrid join their mission, but insisted on much more formal clothing such as a bra, panties, and a dress. Astrid didn't know about such superfluous things but had to trust the woman's human judgment. She chose a dress with lovely reptilian sequins that reminded her of scales; it was the only one she could really be comfortable in. MareAnn was not easy with it, because the sequins were magic, but let it be.

Thus it was that Astrid joined the Quest to eliminate the anti-pun virus. The dress turned out to be a devious asset, because whenever a sequin fell off it turned translucent, which for some reason made the man, Ease, freak out, and when the sequin was restored, it jumped them to a new location that might or might not be convenient. So it became quite an adventure. Along the way they added others to the Quest, including the machine Com Pewter, the girl in the tower Tiara, the long-haired man Mitch, and Art, an artist who was immune to poison. He promptly became Astrid's boyfriend, because he could kiss her and be with her without suffering, though he was careful not to meet her gaze; there were limits. His ambition was to paint portraits of beautiful women, especially her.

But most important of all, Kandy became Astrid's second and best friend. That truly sustained her. They managed to complete their mission with the help of Merge, a remarkable five-part woman, but still had some mopping up to do.

"And that is how I came to associate with these wonderful people," Astrid concluded. "I am indeed a basilisk, and my direct gaze is instant death, but I am comfortable in this group, and we accept each other as we are."

"That's so romantic," Ginger Goblin said.

"And remarkable," Truman Troll added. "I am glad to have heard it. But who is your third best friend?"

"I have no idea," Astrid confessed. "Nor what my mission in life is. I'm just trying to help these good folk accomplish their mission to exterminate the pun virus and restore Xanth to its natural state."

"I am not quite finished here," Pewter said. "Your narrative has not quite filled out the chapter. You must have left something out."

"Oh!" Astrid exclaimed, surprised, and half a bulb flashed over her head.

"Our appreciation surprises you?" Truman asked.

"Speaking of Art and his Portraits reminded me," Astrid said. "MareAnn said something about portraits that didn't mean anything to me at the time, but now it is beginning to."

"Portraits?" Ginger asked.

"MareAnn said that the Good Magician was in half a dither because though the Book of Lost Answers had been reassembled—I don't know what that means, but I think it's a sort of companion to the Book of Answers that is the huge musty tome he constantly pores over—there was an Answer left over and he didn't know what to do with it."

"Obviously it belongs in the Book of Answers, since it's not lost," Pewter said.

"Apparently not," Astrid said. "The Book of Answers also has the Questions, but this one has no attached question. So it is the Question that is lost. That confuses, befuddles, and perplexes him. So he's grumpy, and that annoys the Wives, who find him difficult enough to deal with already. That's why they swap out every month, getting time to recover from his moods. They need to find the Question so that things can settle down to the normally irritating routine."

"What is the Answer?" Ginger asked.

"Five Portraits."

"Five Portraits?"

"Yes. That's all. I just realized that there are five beautiful women in our party, and Art means to paint them all when there is pausing time. So those could be the Answer."

"And what is the Question?" Truman asked.

"I don't know. But doesn't having the Answer evoke the Question, in human events? It must be hovering close by."

The several assembled folk circled a somewhat haphazard glance. If the Question was near, they did not perceive it.

"We shall keep an eye out for a lost Question," Tiara said. "With luck we'll know it when we see it."

It seemed that would have to do.

"Got it," Pewter said, gratified.

"The Question?" Astrid asked.

"The lock. I have nulled it." And with that he swung the barred gate open.

"Oh, we could kiss you!" Ginger said as the goblin girls stepped out.

"Kindly desist with your threats," Pewter said. But he was too late; the three pretty girls kissed him on both ears and his nose.

"On with the exchange," Truman said. "Then at last we can end the truce, which is becoming burdensome."

"That's right," Ginger said. "You trolls can't do a thing to us as long as the truce holds." Then the three kissed the three trolls, who were helpless to resist, all over their faces, severely denting their ugliness. Ginger even had the temerity to kiss Truman directly on the mouth. A truce was a fearsomely powerful force.

The weird thing was, neither Pewter nor the trolls seemed really to mind.

CHAPTER 3:
FORNAX

~~

The rest of the incident was routine. The trolls carried Astrid and the goblins to the goblin mound, where the troll captives were waiting, bound and chained to stakes. The female troll in particular was disheveled but otherwise seemingly undamaged, except for her wrathful pride. All were glad to be rescued.

"Thank you especially, Astrid," Ginger said as the three goblin girls walked to the mound. "We owe our miraculous rescue to you. I never even dreamed that my freedom or my life would rest on the goodwill of a basilisk."

"You're welcome," Astrid said, moderately embarrassed.

"I doubt we'll ever meet again, but if we do, I will remember."

"So will I," Truman said, not in a threatening manner. "I'm glad we were able to come to terms instead of combat. It gave us both gains instead of losses." He looked at his watch, which surprised Astrid because she hadn't known that trolls had watches. "I would offer you a lift back to your companions, but our purpose has been accomplished and the truce is perilously close to expiration. It would not be safe."

"I understand," Astrid said. "I will make my own way back."

"We will go pick up Truculent's body. There's no point in wasting perfectly good meat."

"No point," Astrid agreed. After all, Truculent had planned to eat *her*. Not that he would have found her edible; he would have died of poisoning. Still, his fate was deserved.

Then the six trolls forged away through the brush and forest. Astrid efficiently stripped, evoking crude wolf whistles from the goblin males, reverted to her natural form, which evoked only dead silence, and scooted sinuously through the other brush and forest toward the cave.

"Good riddance, both!" the goblin chief called after them, honoring the spirit of the occasion.

In due course, Astrid rejoined the others and resumed human form, putting on her clothing so that Ease could stop trying to freak. Then the group of them made their way back to their original campsite. It had been a busy morning.

She settled down in the tent she shared with Art, who was interested in two things, the other being his painting. She was happy to accommodate him, and soon put him to sleep in the normal manner. She had feared that she could never have a normal human relationship with a man, but with him it was possible, and she loved it. Her new life seemed complete.

Then Kandy got a message from the Demoness Fornax. That reminded Astrid how the Demoness had wanted Kandy to be her intermediary in the Land of Xanth, because Fornax associated with antimatter and could not touch any normal matter without both going up in mutual annihilation. Kandy had been doubtful, but made the deal instantly when Astrid was falling to her likely death, to save Astrid. She had been a true friend in the crisis. Now she was serving that role for Fornax.

Then Kandy looked at Astrid. "I wonder."

"Have I made an error in my costume?" Astrid asked.

"No, not at all. Something has come up."

"You heard from Fornax," Astrid agreed. "I understand."

"This time it was different. This is awkward."

"Awkward?"

"The Demoness has observed how you and I became friends, and how we both seem happier for it."

Astrid felt a hot chill. That was the worst kind. "She resents our friendship?"

"No. The opposite."

"I am not following this."

"Fornax asked me to be her friend."

"Well, you are a food friend, and you did agree to represent her in Xanth."

"Yes. That's the problem. My association with her is business. I fear that a friendship with her would be a conflict of interest. I'm supposed to represent her objectively. I can't let any possible distortion prejudice me, because I am dealing with mind-bendingly powerful Demons who insist on absolute clinical neutrality. So I had to tell her no."

Astrid nodded. "That seems right."

"But I felt bad about it. Remember, Fornax enabled me to save you from death in the Gap Chasm. I feel I sort of owe her, even though what I'm doing for her now is payment for that. So I looked for an alternative. For someone else to possibly be her friend."

"That's sensible," Astrid agreed.

"You."

The pause was so significant that it almost knocked Astrid down. "Um—"

"Astrid, I'm your friend, and I would not do anything to hurt you or make you uncomfortable. But it seems to me that you could make her a better friend than I could, because you know about isolation. You could understand her, to a degree I could not."

"But she's a Demoness! They have no interest in mortals except as devices for their nefarious bets."

"That's what I thought. Yet she came to me. You saw what you were missing and decided to join the human society, difficult as that was for you. Fornax believes she is missing something, so she is seeking it, just as you did. There's a similar motive, even if you are quite different beings. Won't you at least consider it?"

Kandy was her closest friend. Kandy had sacrificed her power of decision to save Astrid's life. What could she do? "I will consider it."

"Thank you," Kandy said with evident relief. "You are not obliged to agree, just to give her a fair chance."

"I should talk with her. How do I meet her?"

"Just say her name. She will hear you."

Astrid shrugged. "Fornax," she murmured.

A woman appeared. She was the exact opposite of Astrid, with dark skin, light blond hair, and a dark dress with translucent sequins. This had to be Fornax, assuming a reversed likeness. "Take my hand," she said.

Astrid took her hand.

Then they were flying up off the ground, above the trees, and across the terrain of Xanth, spread out beneath them like a patchwork quilt. Then higher, until the land below assumed the shape of a peninsula embraced by the sea. Then higher yet, until they reached the crescent moon. They landed within the curve of it, where there was a landscape made of honey.

"No newly married couples are using the honeymoon at the moment, so we can borrow it," Fornax said.

Bemused, Astrid could think of only a stupid question. "How can we breathe here?"

"With magic, anything is possible. We can breathe anywhere in the universe, and be comfortable."

"And you—aren't you the Demoness of antimatter? Whose very touch makes everything explode in total conversion of mass to energy? How can we be touching?"

"This is true. I dare not touch any normal matter. My form is a semblance assumed for convenience, crafted of local substance, a simulacrum, governed by my mind. You and I are not actually touching. Usually I just make an illusion, as that's the easiest and safest magic, but I needed to convey you here."

"Kandy said you asked her to be your friend, and she turned you down."

"She has reason. She has to be objective."

"So she asked me to consider it."

"Yes."

"I'm a basilisk! A poisonous lizard. My very nearness can kill."

"Yes. Your situation is not as devastating as mine, but there is a parallel."

Astrid contemplated the semblance of the Demoness. There was indeed a parallel. "You're a Demoness! Your power compared to mine is like a galaxy versus a gnat. Why should you care half an iota about my friendship?"

"Your analogy minimizes the case," Fornax said candidly. "But you have a soul, and I have none. On that basis we can associate as equals. If you are interested."

Astrid remembered what the Good Magician had said about the value of a soul. Now Fornax was confirming it, to a degree. He had said that souls were immeasurably precious, at least to those who had them. That was curious. If no one who lacked a soul wanted one, what was the point? "I am interested, but confused," Astrid said candidly. "I came by my soul by accident, and didn't even know it for some time, and have hardly been aware of it since. Why does it interest you?"

"A soul enables a person to be decent, as you are. To have friends, as you do. To love, as you do. To have larger aspirations, as you do. Demons have none of these things."

"And Demon's don't value souls," Astrid said. "Why would you?"

"That may be complicated to explain. Before you acquired your soul, by whatever means, did you care about such things?"

"No. I realize now that my caring dated from my acquisition of the soul."

"Are you sure?"

Astrid reconsidered. "No. I think I was a bit jealous of the way humans enjoyed each other's company. No cockatrice or basilisk ever wanted company."

"You must have had the potential to handle a soul. That soul may even have sought you out, knowing you would do better by it than some freak in the dream realm."

"Souls have wills of their own?"

"They may. It is a reasonable conjecture."

"And you have the potential to handle a soul!" Astrid said, seeing it. "So you are interested."

"That may be the case."

"Maybe the night mares have another soul you could take."

"They do not. They tightened up their procedures after that mishap."

"You must have something in mind."

"I do. But a soul normally cannot be taken. It must be given, and not entirely."

"I am not following this."

"There was a character named Jumper Spider who was given human form and associated closely with several human women," Fornax said. "In fact two of them seduced him, in friendship. That association eventually provided him with a soul, a composite of portions of his human friends so that he became a souled creature. That in turn enabled him to marry the Demoness Eris, called by some the Goddess of Discord, and when she shared his soul, as happens in marriage, she became like the person she had been emulating. That is, nice. She also became the friend of Jumper's friend Wenda Woodwife. She is much more satisfied with her present existence than she was in the past. Were I to associate closely enough with a souled person, as she did, I might pick up at least a portion of a soul."

"That's why you want a friend!" Astrid said. "So her soul might rub off on you."

"Part of it, at any rate," the Demoness agreed. "Enough, perhaps, to provide me with what I crave."

"What do you crave?"

"The abatement of my loneliness."

"You are lonely? You have unimaginable power! How can you be lonely?"

Fornax laughed. "Were you not lonely at the beginning of your life?"

Astrid thought back again. "I believe I was, though I did not realize it at the time. Basilisks don't have friends."

"Neither do soulless Demons."

"And you, associated with antimatter, can't get close to anyone else anyway. That must be very difficult."

"It is," Fornax agreed. "Touch my hand, and it will allow some of my feeling to show."

Curious, Astrid took her hand again.

Suddenly she felt the utter loneliness not of hours or days or years or centuries, but of billennia: maybe twelve billion years. It was a deep and awful gulf extending beyond her imagination.

"Wake," Fornax said.

Astrid snapped out of her trance. "What happened?"

"You freaked out."

"But only men freak out when they glimpse a woman's panties."

"Men are relatively superficial, compared to women, being really interested in only one thing. There are many ways to freak. Overwhelming feeling is one."

The Demoness was a creature in need of more than Astrid could provide. But at least she could help. She remembered that she was destined to have three friends, each more important than the previous ones. This seemed to be the realization of that. "I fear it is but a grain of sand in a mountain, but I will try to be your friend."

"Thank you." Perhaps there was a tear in Fornax's eye.

"How do we proceed? I am not well experienced in friendship."

"I thought you would know, because you already have a friend in Kandy. I have never had a friend."

"I do have a friend in Kandy," Astrid agreed thoughtfully. "And another in MareAnn. But they led the way. They knew what to do. I am still learning."

"Then we have a problem."

"Maybe we need advice. I can ask Kandy."

"No. Her conflict of interest applies to this. Anyway, she has enough to occupy her at the moment."

"Enough?"

"She is my representative in Xanth. She is now negotiating a Demon Wager."

Astrid was taken aback. "I thought Demons negotiated their own terms."

"Not always. The other Demons don't like dealing with me directly, so they are dealing with my representative. She has authority to speak for me on this particular matter, though she is not pleased."

"Not pleased?"

"She doesn't like the subject."

"Does the subject matter? She just needs to be objective."

"She is finding that difficult."

Astrid hesitated. "She is my friend, and I am concerned. Why should she find it hard to be objective?"

"Because the subject is the Land of Xanth, and she has a certain interest in it."

"I don't want to intrude in what is not my business, but I think it would help my understanding if I knew more about this."

"If we are to be friends, my business becomes your business, and your business mine, as I understand it. So I will tell you. The subject is the destruction of the Land of Xanth."

Astrid was taken even further aback. "As it happens, I too have an interest, being another denizen of Xanth."

"You need not be concerned. It doesn't happen until fifty years hence."

"That helps. But I may live to see it, so it remains my concern. What is to happen to Xanth?"

"It will be invaded by an alternate reality that is slightly more advanced. Rather than suffer themselves to be displaced, the citizens will go for mutual destruction. Thus Xanth will end."

"Is this certain?" Astrid asked with a sinking sensation.

"No. There is an even chance it will survive, if the citizens pursue the appropriate course."

"That's a relief! But then what's the bet about?"

"Whether they will pursue that rather devious course and save Xanth, or allow it to end."

Astrid got a sick feeling. "And you are betting that Xanth will end. That's why Kandy is upset."

"Of course. What is Xanth to me, other than a chance to win a Demon Point?"

"Well, it will complicate our friendship if I die."

"Then I shall have to save you before Xanth ends. And Kandy."

"You don't care if everyone else dies?"

"Should I?"

Astrid signed. "I was forgetting you are a Demon. You lack human emotions."

"True."

"But isn't loneliness an emotion?"

"It must be, but it is not limited to humanity. It existed before humans came on the scene, and will exist after they depart the scene."

That was a good point. Astrid was beginning to see difficulties in this friendship. "At least that is separate from the question of our friendship. Let's focus on the latter. I think we need advice from someone else, but I can't think whom." Then she reconsidered. "You mentioned Jumper Spider. An animal in human form, as I am. Married to a Demon. A mortal/Demon relationship. Maybe they could advise us."

"We'll ask them. Take my hand."

Astrid took her hand, and they sailed up off the moon and into the sky. In half a moment they were cruising past pretty planets, one with icy rings.

"Um, is this the way to Jumper and Eris?" Astrid asked.

"It is the scenic route."

And to Demons there were no limits of ordinary physics. Maybe she would get used it it after a while.

"Um, while we travel, there's something else I would like to know."

"I will clarify it for you. What is it?"

Astrid noted that the Demoness did not question her own ability to answer any question a mortal might have. That confidence was probably justified. "You are a capital *D* Demon. What is the distinction between that and small *d* demons, like demoness Metria?"

"Capital Demons are virtually timeless spirits associated with natural forces who have existed almost since the universe began. Thus I associate with Antimatter, Xanth associates with Magic, Earth with Gravity, and so on. We also tend to have residences, but these are secondary. The fact that Xanth has a tiny bit of odd-shaped land and I have a galaxy means nothing; what counts is the unique associations. The universe would be incomplete without magic, gravity, antimatter, and the others, so we are eternal. Small demons, in contrast, are infinitesimal fragments associated with a particular Demon. Thus Metria is a figment of Demon Xanth's imagination, crafted somewhat in his image but of no actual consequence."

"But Metria is a character, just as I am, and she does things to make an impression on others. That's not inconsequential to me."

"You are a mortal," Fornax reminded her gently. "Your perspective is severely limited. However, if you left the Land of Xanth you would exist as a harmless lizard. If Metria left, she would become a mere gust of wind and dissipate. That is part of the difference mortality makes. Metria has no real substance apart from the magic of the ambiance of Xanth, while you do.

Magic affects you and makes you to a considerable extent what you are, but you would exist without it. She would not."

"Metria can be annoying and frustrating, but she is helping our virus cleanup, and I rather like her. I would not want to see her dissipate in wind."

"You have the capacity to like other folk," Fornax agreed. "This is one of your qualifications to be my friend."

"I suppose I do," Astrid agreed. "Thank you for the clarification about demons. I never had it quite straight before." Actually she knew she would have to mull it over for a while to fully assimilate it, but that would work itself out.

"If my information pleases you, I am glad to have provided it." Fornax grimaced. "I have not before had any interest in pleasing another Demon, let alone a mortal. It is an intriguing exercise."

They came down in a pleasant garden where a handsome nude man and lovely nude women were sunning themselves beside a spider-shaped pool.

"Oh for bleep's sake," the woman swore. "What are you doing here, Fornax? You know you're not supposed to demolish private property."

"Tell them," Fornax murmured to Astrid, letting her hand go.

She should have known it would be up to her. They would not trust Fornax.

"Jumper and Eris, I presume?" Astrid said. "I am Astrid Basilisk-Cockatrice, an animal in human form." She shifted briefly to her natural form, then back. "I have a soul."

"A basilisk with a soul?" Eris asked.

"It came upon me as I slept, but now I am guided by it. I mean no mischief to you. I merely want to talk."

"I feel your soul," Eris said. "But you keep ill company. What brings you here?"

"I am trying to have a friendship with Demoness Fornax, but am in doubt how to proceed. I thought that the two of you might have good advice."

The man became animated. "You're a basilisk? With the deadly stare?"

"Yes. But I wear these dark glasses so that I won't hurt anyone. I don't want trouble, just advice."

"This is interesting," Jumper said, shifting briefly to spider form, and back. "We have not encountered another animal-Demon couple."

"We're not a couple," Astrid said quickly. "Just friends. But we're not sure how to do it. We thought you would know."

Jumper shook his head. "We're not friends. We're lovers."

"And married," Eris said. "Prince Jumper rescued me from confinement by marrying me, six years ago. He is also good company." She bounced a suggestive glance off him, which made him glance back with enhanced appreciation. Obviously she took good care of his one interest.

"Prince Jumper?" Astrid asked, surprised.

"An honorary title," Jumper said. "Princess Dawn arranged it. It's a long story. So we can't really tell you about friendship. The one to ask is my forest friend Wenda. She's very friendly."

"She is also my friend," Eris said. "She married Prince Charming the same year we married. They have half a slew of children. That's another long story."

Half a slew in six years? Surely an exaggeration.

"We will talk to them," Fornax said. She took Astrid's hand and they rose up, up, and away.

"They seem like nice people," Astrid remarked as they sailed past asteroids, comets, and novae.

"She's really changed since she connected with Jumper," Fornax said. "Her power is Discord, but I don't think she has used it once since she met him."

"He really is a spider. He seems happy."

"A Demoness can do a lot for a male, if she chooses."

"Because he is interested in only one thing?"

"Of course. Even small *d* demonesses are very good at that one thing. Men are putty."

Astrid had of course observed that repeatedly in the course of her association with the other folk on the pun virus mission. She had a shapely human body, and when her dress became translucent it tended to freak out any men within range. Metria had also demonstrated her ability to freak out men.

They came down by a palace. There in an ornate playground was a somewhat harried princess keeping tabs on half a slew of children, by actual count. They were all wildly different, but all seemed happy.

"Hey look!" a little boy cried. "A lizard in man form!"

"And a Demoness in girl form," a little girl called.

"Children!" the harried princess cried. "Dew knot approach strangers! They might bee dangerous." Cowed, the children fell back.

Dew knot? That was an unusual accent. Then Astrid remembered: she was a woodland creature who spoke with the forest dialect.

Now Astrid got a better look at her. From the front she was a pretty woman, but from behind she was hollow. She had no innards. A woodwife indeed. How had she borne so many children so quickly?

The princess came to stand before them. "What can I dew for yew, visitors? I did knot see you coming, or I wood have organized better."

"Our fault," Astrid said quickly. "I am Astrid Basilisk, and this is the Demoness Fornax. We—"

"Oh!" Wenda exclaimed, shielding her eyes with a hand.

"...mean you no harm," Astrid continued even more rapidly. "Jumper Spider said—"

"Jumper! Is he all right? I wood bee mortified if anything happened to him."

"Yes, he's fine. He said you might tell us about friendship."

Wenda took visible stock. "Yew want to know about friendship?"

"We two want to be friends," Astrid said. "But we have no experience, because I'm a basilisk and she's a Demoness. So we thought you might be able to give us some advice on how to go about it."

"Maybee I can help. But the children—"

Astrid got a bright idea. "Maybe we can help divert them while we talk. What would do that?"

"It would take a merry-go-round made of eye scream and candy. Since that is impossible—" Wenda broke off, because there it was. The platform was made of flavored ice, the horses of chocolate eye scream, and the poles they were on were edible Popsicle sticks.

The children flocked to it with screams of joy. In half a moment they were all over the horses, riding them while biting off their chocolate ears and tails and plucking out their gumball eyes. Some were even gnawing on their rock candy hooves.

"You really are a Demoness!" Wenda said, amazed.

"Yes," Fornax said. "I'm not supposed to do much magic here, because Xanth is not my base. Don't tell."

"I wood knot ever tell," Wenda agreed gratefully.

They settled down to their dialogue. "Friendship just happens, like love," Wenda said. "When people dew things together and get to know each other. Jumper and I met and helped each other and it grew into friendship. Dew you have anything to dew together?"

"I am looking for remnants of the anti-pun virus that recently ravaged Xanth," Astrid said. "We need to be sure all of it is gone, so that it is safe to reseed puns. But Fornax is not part of that effort. So we really don't have anything to dew, I mean do together."

"Then yew need something that will take yewr attention, so yew can work together. The longer yew share experiences, the more yewr friendship will develop. For example, children. They require constant attention, and can bee very trying, but are marvelously worth it in the end."

"We're not a couple," Astrid said, as she had before. "But that reminds me: how did you manage to get so many children so quickly?"

Wenda laughed. "They are knot mine! I can knot have children." She slapped her empty backside. "They are adopted foundlings who need a home."

"Adopted!" That explained it.

"Foundlings need homes too," Wenda said earnestly. "Otherwise they are lost. I collect any I find." She grimaced. "But we are full up now, and can't take any more until we manage to place some of the ones we have. It's a problem."

"So if we found some foundling children, we wouldn't have to keep them, just find families for them," Astrid said.

"Yes. Yew wood find that remarkably rewarding."

Astrid exchanged a glance with Fornax, who of course was immune to her stare. The Demoness nodded.

"We'll do that," Astrid said. "Thank you, Wenda."

"Yew're welcome. But remember, knot all children are easy to place. It may bee a challenge."

"We'll remember," Astrid said. She took Fornax's hand, and they rose up and away.

Just in time, because the children had demolished the merry-go-round. Only a few sticks remained. The children were thoroughly covered with melted chocolate; Wenda would have an awful cleanup. But she was the type who could handle it.

"Children," Fornax said thoughtfully as they zoomed past comets, novas, and small black holes. "Human children."

"If we can find some," Astrid agreed.

"It occurs to me that there may be some when Xanth ends. Their families will be killed and they will be orphans if they survive. But then they will inevitably die."

"We must save those children," Astrid said with sudden soul-inspired compassion. "Except that we can't, because they don't yet exist. They're in the future."

"Yes. But perhaps we can nevertheless do something. So as to have our project."

"But time travel is impossible!" Astrid protested. "Even if we could go to the future to rescue them, we couldn't bring them back to our own time."

"Why not?"

"Paradox, for one thing. Those children would be in a world where their grandparents lived. They might do something to change their own lineage, and make them never come to exist. So it's impossible."

"Nothing is impossible, with enough magic."

"What, can you travel back and forth in time?"

"Not by myself. But it might be possible to arrange."

Astrid was curious despite her disbelief. "Arrange to violate fundamental laws of the universe?"

"It is not encouraged, but sometimes it happens."

"I don't see how."

"Remember Demoness Eris? She has been around for some time. I know her of old. She had a fling with an anonymous Demon and got a daughter, Dysnomia, whose power is Lawlessness. Other Demons don't associate with her much. She might appreciate becoming useful."

"Lawlessness? How could that help us rescue any children?"

"She would not necessarily honor the laws against time travel or paradox."

"Oh, my," Astrid said. "You don't think small, do you!"

"Size is irrelevant to a Demon. There are only questions of feasibility, and of course Demon Points."

"Why do you strive so hard for Points?"

"Because they give our dreary existences a kind of meaning. We are all-powerful; anything we want to do, we do. That becomes tedious. So we contest with each other for status, and Points are marks of status. Without that we would find existence crushingly dull."

"That never occurred to me."

"Mortals lack time to become jaded. They are too busy just trying to survive. By the time they become surfeit, they are dead. Demons are eternal. They miss the excitement of death, the mercy of oblivion. And of course there is the matter of the soul, another factor that enhances the brief lives of mortals. So they don't need to contest for status."

"I think some do anyway," Astrid said.

"They are foolish. They can't keep status; their early deaths take it from them. So what is the point?"

"Good question," Astrid said. "If we don't do anything useful in our fleeting lives, there is no point."

They came down to land again in Eris's garden. "Did you talk with Wenda?" Jumper asked.

"We did," Astrid said. "She recommended rescuing children. We'd like to rescue some from the future, and bring them back here to live out their full lives in relative comfort. That is the project we have decided on."

"The future," Eris said thoughtfully. "That would be a challenge."

"Yes. So we may need help. We'd like to talk to Dysnomia."

"Oh, my," Eris said. "She is something of a black sheep, pretty wild. I have not been in contact with her for some time."

"Can you reach her?" Astrid asked.

Eris raised a hand and snapped her fingers. Another woman appeared. She was pretty, with good features, long hair, and a nice figure, but she did indeed look wild, following no established conventions of dress or manner. "What do you want, mother dear?" she demanded dismissively.

"These two would like to talk with you, perhaps to enlist your help," Eris said.

"Obese chance! I don't care about any regular people."

"Make an effort," Fornax said.

Dysnomia caught the tone and looked at her. And froze. "Fornax!"

"I am not here to convert you to total energy," Fornax said evenly. "But to enlist your aid, should you be inclined to give it."

It was evident that this wild Demoness had some awe for Fornax, whose destructive power was surely respected even among Demons. "Make your case."

"My mortal friend Astrid will make it."

"Mortal friend!" Dysnomia exclaimed. "Since when did you take to slumming, SeeTee?"

SeeTee?

"The pronunciation of CT, or ContraTerrene matter, a more technical term for antimatter," Fornax explained. "She thinks she is being contemptuous of both of us."

Oh? Astrid removed her dark glasses and looked Dysnomia in the face. "I am a basilisk. I am not accustomed to contempt."

"Why so you are," Dysnomia agreed, evidently taken slightly aback. She was of course immune to the death stare, but she felt it. "You must have an interesting story."

"I do," Astrid agreed, restoring her glasses. "But that is not the point. If you are not going to take us seriously, there is no point in talking with you."

Dysnomia laughed. "Now you have evoked my curiosity. Very well, I will listen."

"We want to travel fifty years into the future, rescue some orphaned children there, and bring them back here. To do that we may need to break some laws of the universe. Such as paradox. Can you help us do that?"

"Paradox," Dysnomia repeated thoughtfully. "That's a tricky one. I never thought to violate that one before."

"So it's a challenge," Astrid said. "Are you up to it?"

"Of course I'm up to it!" The Demoness paused. "I think."

"Then join us for a planning session," Fornax said. "We may set law-breaking history."

"We may indeed," Dysnomia said zestfully.

"Don't crash the universe, dear," Eris called as the three of them took off.

They returned to the crescent moon, biting off pieces of the crescent to chew on as they talked. "Exactly where do you have in mind collecting these children?" Dysnomia asked. "Time is one thing, but geography is another."

"Why not in the troll's glade?" Astrid asked. "He won't be using it any more. It's quite private."

"We can go there physically," Fornax agreed. "Then advance fifty years in time, and collect any foundling children we see, and bring them back."

"What will we do with them once we have them?" Astrid asked. "I mean, yes they are a project, but I have very little experience with children, and can't even be near them for long, because of my, um, perfume."

"I have no experience," Fornax said. "I think we'll have to enlist the help of your friends. They should be able to advise us."

"I will ask them," Astrid said. "Maybe we should allow a little time. I don't know exactly how they will react." She hoped that was not a significant understatement. She herself had not thought of children until Wenda suggested it.

"Take the time you need," Fornax agreed. "Meanwhile Dysnomia and I will work out our strategy for the rescue. When you are ready, just say my name."

Thus agreed, Fornax dropped Astrid off at her camp. The others were there to welcome her back. Maybe it would be all right.

Astrid took a breath and opened her mouth to speak.

CHAPTER 4:
CHILDREN

~~

"Oh, we're so glad you're back!" Kandy exclaimed. "We need you."

"Uh, yes, I—"

"We have found a resurgence of the pun virus! Mitch found it when he was out exploring. We must go extirpate it immediately, before it spreads. Come on!"

And they were on their way, following Mitch. He was Tiara's man, and his hair was as long as hers. In fact he had woven it into a shirt that he wore. Obviously he had been out looking for signs of the virus, as Astrid had. This was, after all, their primary mission. Astrid didn't have a chance to ask them about the children. She hoped the Demon would be patient.

Kandy found herself walking beside Merge, who hadn't made it to the troll's cave. Merge was a pretty girl with multicolored waist-length hair, perfect features, and an outstanding body. She was actually the combination, the mergence, of five sisters who had been separate until their hair was allowed to merge. It hadn't stopped there. She carried her Urn, which contained, or rather served as the portal, for all the pun virus antidote they would ever need to eradicate the menace. All they needed to do was locate the remaining pockets of the virus and douse them before they could spread. And now they had exactly such a pocket.

And there it was. The sign said WELCOME TO PUN VALLEY, but there were no puns in evidence, only awful smelly gunk where they had been melted.

The virus was here, all right.

Merge uncorked her urn and poured out elixir. The gunk immediately shrank into dust as the virus was abolished, but it was of course too late for the puns. They had suffered cruel extinction.

They looked into the valley. It was thickly wooded, with gunk littering the ground and coating the tree trunks. What a disaster area!

"This is too big to cover piecemeal," Merge said. "I'll have to split up." Whereupon she shimmered and split into five young women with different colored hair: Brown, Black, Red, Yellow, and light Blue. They were also nude, as there was only one dress and it had fallen off during the shimmer. Each had a small urn.

"Eyes front!" Tiara snapped as Mitch's eyes wandered.

"Ditto!" Kandy said as Ease's eyes threatened to glaze.

Astrid was relieved that she didn't have to speak to Art. He had learned to keep his eyes in check when not actually painting nudes.

"There's no time to fetch clothing," Brown said. "We have to deal with the virus immediately."

The five girls moved out, efficiently sprinkling elixir on all the sodden puns. So did the others. They were a fair-sized group in all, and made good headway.

Astrid was now working beside Brown. "Your ability to separate may be a problem for a prospective male companion."

"We know," Brown agreed. "Yet at times, like right now, it's useful."

She had a point. It seemed that Kandy's ability to become a board had spread to the others, giving them special shifting talents. She suspected that Demon Xanth had quietly enhanced their abilities, to enable them to better clean out the pun virus, because he didn't like having his land messed up. Her recent association with Fornax impressed on her that Demons could mess in with mortal events when they chose.

Which reminded her of the matter of the children. She needed to grab an opportunity the moment it was offered.

They forged on through Pun Valley, leaving its terrain clean but spare. Xanth without puns was little better than drear Mundania.

"I am ordering a delivery of seed puns," Pewter said. "To restore the valley to its rightful status. The delivery should be soon."

"Our job is done," Kandy said, mopping her grimy face. "The valley is clean, but we're a mess. We'd better clean up. Is there a lake?"

"No lake," Ease said. "But there's a way."

"Why do I suspect this has something to do with bare girls?"

"How else will you get clean?"

He had her there. "So how do we wash?"

"In pun elixir."

They all paused. That actually made sense, to be sure that no vestige of the virus remained on them or their clothing.

"I'm a board," Kandy said, and became the board. It was an easier way to wash.

The five aspects of Merge lifted their little urns over their tousled heads and started pouring. The others stripped and ducked down to rinse off under those streams of liquid. They also soaked and wrung out their clothes and hung them up on bushes to dry. Then the five aspects did the same, pouring for each other, and merged. Merge stood there, gloriously bare, her hair scintillating in all the colors of her aspects.

Astrid noticed as they all dried in the sun how Ease, Mitch, and Art were looking, while Kandy's board quivered resentfully, Metria smirked, Tiara frowned, and Astrid herself felt like doing some deadly staring. That girl needed to find a man soon so she wouldn't be distracting other girls' men. Had she had panties on, all of the men would have freaked out. As it was, they were not far from it.

There was a huge brown shadow. It squawked and a package dropped before them, almost breaking apart. Then the roc bird few rapidly on and away. It was the OOPS delivery. A careless package.

They unpacked it, finding half a myriad of shrink-wrapped puns, which expanded to full size the moment the wrap was off. There were Snow Shoes made of snow; a Yell-O Jacket that would sting anyone who put it on; a bright shining Brilli Ant; a Pine Needle that would sew curses into clothing to cause sadness in anyone who wore it; Sun Dial and Pun Dial Soap they could have used when showering; several Belts: Asteroid, Bible, Rust, Sun; a collection of useful Letters such as D-Tail, D-Fur, Fur-E, Pant-Es, Pant-Ts, Eye-V, Ear-E, Brain-E, Cheek-E, Hair-E, Vein-E, Sas-C, Sis-C; and even a Tea V drink that projected moving pictures.

Astrid had to avert her gaze before she because nauseous. She was almost tempted to jam the puns back into the box and hammer it closed. Xanth without puns was empty, but Xanth with puns could be silly. But she clamped down her gorge and got to work with the others, flinging puns right, left, and away, restoring Pun Valley to its natural state.

At last the box was empty, and the valley was recovering. Art set up his easel and started painting the scene. That was his way to relax, and his paintings were always marvelously realistic and lovely to behold.

"You know, I want to start on those Five Portraits," he said as he worked. "But somehow I can't. The muse won't come. I don't know what's wrong."

"You have Painter's Block?" Kandy asked.

"No, I can paint anything else. Just not one of you. Yet."

"But you're an artist," Merge said. "All you have to do is set up and paint."

"No. It has to be right. The five of you lovely women are somehow incomplete, and I can't paint you."

"Artistic registration," Metria muttered.

He glanced at her. "Artistic what?"

"Enrollment, entrance, ingress, adjustment, disposition—"

"Temperament?"

"Whatever," she agreed crossly.

Art nodded. "Maybe so. It's ironic, because I really want to paint you, you beautiful creatures, and you are all ready to be painted. But something holds me back."

"We'll surely figure it out in due course," Tiara said.

"I hope so." He resumed his nature scene.

Astrid sat on a convenient stool, resting, until she saw others looking at her. She glanced down—and realized it was a massive mound of animal dung. She had been fooled by a freshly spread stinking pun.

She quickly changed the subject. "I have something to say that I hope won't disturb you."

Mitch smiled. "Your direct glance might disturb us, or your deadly perfume, but not your words."

"I talked with the Demoness Fornax."

"The lady dog who tried to mess us up in her galaxy?" Mitch asked.

"Oh, yes," Kandy said, returning to woman form. "How did it go?"

"We have an idea."

Merge was perplexed. "Isn't Fornax mischief?"

"She associates with antimatter," Kandy explained. "She can't touch anything here without it exploding into energy. That's why she needs an intermediary. Apart from that, she's not a bad person. I am negotiating for her with Demon Xanth to arrange the next Demon Wager."

"I don't trust this," Ease said. "She's a seductive wench."

"Aren't we all," Kandy said fondly. "What's your idea, Astrid?"

"Fornax and I have agreed to be friends. But neither of us knows much about how to do it. So we talked with Wenda Woodwife—you know, the 'I wood knot dew that to yew' woman—and she says we should try helping children."

"Wenda does love children," Pewter said.

"So our idea is to rescue some children from the future and place them in good adoptive families. But we'll have to take care of them in the interim. Neither Fornax nor I know anything about handling children, so we'll need your help."

"I don't know a thing about children," Merge said. "But it might be good experience for when I find a man and, well, whatever." She blushed.

"That's a good point," Tiara said. "I feel the same, though I have found my man." She glanced lovingly at Mitch.

"I have a son," Metria said. "He's a nuisance."

"Well, he's half demon," Kandy reminded her.

"True. Ordinary children would not be half the perturbation." "Half the what?"

"Planetary alignment, confusion, devilment, rascality, mischief—"

"Trouble?"

"Whatever," the demoness agreed crossly.

Kandy glanced at the men. "You are oddly silent. Don't you want children?"

"We hadn't thought of it," Mitch said. "But I suppose we could help caretake a few for a while."

"So let's do it," Kandy said, quite ready to support Astrid and her connection with Fornax.

Thus simply it was decided. "I will see about rescuing them," Astrid said gratefully. She had feared that it would be more complicated.

Then she contacted the Demoness. "Fornax," she murmured.

"Good enough," Fornax said.

But something was strange. The others were not moving. They seemed to be frozen in place. "Are they all right?" Astrid asked, concerned.

"They are fine," Fornax reassured her. "I merely froze local time so that we can take as much time as we need to rescue the children, and it will seem like no time to them."

"Oh. Thank you."

"We have had to compromise," Fornax said as they flew to the troll's glade. "Dysnomia concluded that paradox is after all beyond her rule-breaking abilities."

"Oh? Why?"

"If she broke the laws of Time and went back to her origination and persuaded Eris not to generate her, she would no longer exist. Then she would be unable to accomplish anything, such as her own elimination. That's paradox: a self-contradictory argument, like 'This statement is false.' It is essentially nonsense. So travel back in time cancels itself out before it accomplishes anything. Visiting the future has similar peril, because there is the need to return to the present, which is travel to the past, at least from the future. Knowledge of that future would itself change it. Paradox again. She says it makes her head spin, and she does not care to risk it."

"So we can't rescue the children?" Astrid asked, disappointed.

"We'll fetch them. Just without time travel."

"But if they're from the future—"

"This requires some fundamental theory. There is not just a single Xanth. There are an infinite number of Xanths, in parallel universes. Each differs from its neighbors only slightly. Some are exactly similar to ours, except that they are a trace behind or ahead of ours. Only by a second, but if we cross enough parallels, those seconds add up, and we can reach a Xanth fifty years ahead, about to be destroyed. That is where the children will be."

"Just like our Xanth, only fifty years farther along?"

"Yes. So it emulates time travel without invoking paradox. That's an advantage."

"But can we just cross to other Xanths?" Astrid asked, confused.

"We're not supposed to. But sometimes it happens. There was a case when Surprise Golem crossed to another parallel to recover her misplaced baby. Demons can cross, because we are spread across all the parallels; it is merely a matter of which one we focus on. That is what makes us infinitely more potent than mortals. All the parallel Xanths are part of Demon Xanth. But as a general rule we don't do it, because it can complicate things. Duplicated people showing up in a single frame, that sort of thing. It can be hard to keep track. But in this case, Dysnomia will do it. That is the rule she is prepared to break."

"But what is her interest, if she doesn't care about the children?"

"The challenge. She wants to see if it is feasible, or whether it is another kind of paradox. Demons love challenges."

"Such as the challenge of friendship?"

"Indeed."

Something elusive was bothering Astrid, and after a generous moment she pounced and nabbed it. "But if Demons cross over all the Xanths, needing merely to focus on one, what rule is Dysnomia breaking?"

"We are taking you along. That will double you up with the Astrids of the parallels we cross, perhaps making mischief if you encounter one or more alternate selves. That's the violation."

"Maybe I should stay in this one, then, and let you fetch the children."

"No, you will need to touch the children to bring them with us, because you are mortal, with a soul, like them. We soulless immortals can't do that. We have worked it out to bring you, this one time, but that's the limit. The laws of the universe start getting ugly when tweaked, and once is all we can get away with. We won't be able to stay long, either. Demons are close to omnipotent, but this impinges on the impossible. We can't be sure it will succeed."

"So it's risky?"

"That does enhance the challenge."

"What happens if it goes wrong?"

"Nothing to us; we're Demons. But you would fragment across all the Xanths you passed through, and become only a shred of an atom in each."

"I would die?"

"That would be another way to view it, yes."

Astrid felt a chill. Just how much did she want this friendship?

"You are reconsidering?" Fornax asked.

That decided her. "No!"

"That is good, because we can't do this without you."

They came to land in the troll's glade. Dysnomia was there. "Are we ready?"

Astrid knew that meant her. "We are."

"Take my hand."

Astrid took her hand, and Fornax took her other hand. Then the environment started quivering. "What's happening?" Astrid asked nervously.

"We are crossing parallels," Fornax explained. "For us it would be smooth, but your mortality generates some friction. That should diminish as we accelerate."

"Accelerate?"

"Each frame is a second ahead of the prior one. There are many seconds, so we are increasing our rapidity of crossing. To you it will seem like traveling into the future."

"Thank you," Astrid said faintly.

They did speed up. She could tell, because the angle of the sunlight started shifting, as though the sun were moving faster. Then the sun dropped behind the trees, and darkness came. Soon light returned: now they were in tomorrow. It brightened, and faded; now they were in tomorrow night. How many seconds in a day and night? They were crossing many parallels!

The night passed, and another day, faster. Soon the lights and darknesses became a flicker, as they were covering the days so swiftly. In that flicker she saw the trees change, some of them losing their leaves. It was winter. And spring, and summer, and winter again. A year was passing!

The years moved across more swiftly, one two, three, ten, twenty—it became too fast to count. Would they overshoot the fifty?

Then the progression slowed. The years reappeared, and the seasons, and the days. Finally they came to a halt. They had arrived. Somewhen.

The glade had changed. Now it was just a clearing in the forest. A cable stretched across it like a mundane power line. Had electricity come to Xanth?

"No, it is a cable for a car," Fornax said, answering her thought. "It crosses not just from glade to glade, but from Xanth to Xanth. This is one of its stops. Families hoped at least to save their children. But its promise is false; all Xanths in this region will be destroyed."

"What a crime," Astrid said. "Who would tease desperate families like that?"

"They did not realize. The intention was good."

The cable jerked. A hanging car appeared above the forest. It was black, with the words MODEL T printed in its side. It swung down to the clearing, touching the ground as if ready to take on a passenger.

Instead Fornax went to it and opened its door. "All out," she said.

A tousled ten-year-old boy got out. "Is this the end?" he asked.

"Not exactly, but it will do. This lady will take you home with her."

"No. I'm going to the end." The boy turned to reenter the car.

"There is no end," Fornax said. "The cars are traveling more slowly than the termination. It will catch up and destroy the cable and cars."

"I don' care. I'm supposed to go to the end."

"The end is doom."

"And who the sweet violets are you?" the boy demanded insolently. He couldn't cuss because of the Adult Conspiracy, but he had a bad attitude. "You aren't my mother. You can't tell me what to do."

"We are trying to save you from extinction," Fornax said evenly.

"Well go extinct yourself, cousin of a canine. I'm not listening to you." He ducked to re-enter the car.

Fornax looked at Astrid. "Maybe we should let him go. I don't think this one is worth saving."

"No!" Astrid said. It had not occurred to her that the child would be this old or this ornery, but she had to save him if she could. She moved closer to the car.

"And who are you, spectacle face?" the boy asked Astrid. "You aren't my mother either."

"Fortunately," Astrid agreed. "But I'm here to help you even if you don't want it at the moment."

"Help, smelp! I'm tired of all you adults telling me what to do. I'm going on."

But Astrid blocked the car door. "No you are not."

"Get out of my way, stupid!" He sought to push past her, but she stood firm. He could not get back into the car.

"You stay," Astrid said.

Then the cable jerked, and the car lifted and was carried up and away across the forest.

"You made me miss the car!" the boy screamed, outraged. Then something odd happened. Little rockets seemed to fly out of his head. They rose into the air and exploded into dazzling displays. They were literal fireworks!

Astrid removed her glasses and glanced at the fireworks. They turned to ashes and dropped to the ground. Then she closed one eye and glanced fleetingly at the boy. He staggered, stunned. "Now behave yourself," she said.

"What—what are you?" he asked, amazed and frightened.

Astrid put her glasses back on. "My name is Astrid. I am a basilisk in human form. Now tell me who you are and what just happened to you."

The boy had plainly suffered a sudden attack of caution verging on respect. "I—I'm Firenze," he said, accenting the middle syllable, fir-EN-zee. "That's my talent. To go off like fireworks when I get mad."

"Well, hereafter you will better control your temper, Firenze."

A rebellious expression hovered near the boy's mouth. Astrid touched her glasses, and the expression fled in disarray. "Yes ma'am."

"How did you come to be aboard that car?"

"The end of Xanth is coming. My folks couldn't save themselves, but they tried to save me. So they put me in the car and told me to ride to the end of the line, where maybe I'd be safe."

"They miscalculated," Fornax said. "There is no safety when the line ends."

"But—but they did it to save me!"

"They meant well," Astrid said. "And they did save you. We'll take you to our home and arrange to have you adopted by some nice couple."

Now reality was closing in on him. "My folks—they're gone!"

"We're afraid so. Your whole world is gone."

"Gone," he repeated, crumbling into tears.

Astrid put her arms about him. "It's awful, we know."

"Oh, sock mending!" he said, which was as close as he could got to a bad word. "I'm alone!"

"We'll help you all we can," Astrid said as he sobbed into her shoulder. He was after all a child. But she wondered: would any nice couple adopt a ten-year-old boy with a fireworks temper? This mission was already more complicated than she had anticipated.

Then she gently disengaged, because her ambiance would soon overcome him. She simply couldn't stay close to him very long. What irony, if they saved him from the destruction of his world, only to kill him by inhaling poisonous vapor!

Firenze looked at her. "Have I seen you before? There's something about you."

"I'm sure we've never met," Astrid said.

"The other one too. I think I saw you somewhere."

"That's really not possible," Astrid assured him.

The cable jerked. Another car came into sight. This one was low and sleek, bright yellow, with large tires. It swung down to pause in the clearing.

Fornax opened its side door. A tentacular sea creature tumbled out, changing colors as it landed. What was this?

Then the creature put two tentacles together in four sets to form four limbs. The central mass shaped into a body and head. Color flowed, becoming a painted-on dress and a flurry of curls. It looked like a cute six-year-old girl. "Hel-low," she said tentatively.

"We're going to need your help," Astrid murmured to Firenze. "We have another lost child."

Firenze, having cried himself out, revived. "Yes ma'am."

"Hello," Astrid said to the octopus girl. "I am Astrid, a—a friend. Who are you?"

"They call me Squid," the girl said. "'Cause I'm like an oct—oct—"

"Octopus," Astrid said.

"Yes. But I don't live in the sea."

"How did you come here, Squid?"

"My folks—were visiting from another world, when they got caught by the end of this one. So they put me in the car."

So this was an alien visitor, trapped by the end of Xanth. But nevertheless a child. "We will try to help you, Squid. But we don't have any land-living octopi in our land. We will try to find you a family who will take good care of you."

"My family—gone," Squid said, tearing up.

"Can you comfort her, Firenze?" Astrid asked. "You know exactly what she's experiencing."

"I guess. Even if she is a girl." It seemed that her gender made more difference than her species. He went to Squid and sat down on the ground. "Hi. I'm Firenze. I know what it's like. I lost my own family."

"Gone!" Squid cried, falling into his embrace.

So it was working. Firenze was helping. But Squid was a similar problem: who would want to adopt an octopus in the shape of a girl?

The cable car moved on. Soon another car came. This one was a mundane pickup truck. Inside it was an eight-year-old boy who looked quite ordinary. But Astrid feared that this appearance was deceptive, considering the way this was going.

The truck door opened and the boy looked out. "Is this the end of the line?" he called.

"Close," Astrid called back.

"I saw the other children, so I thought maybe it was."

"We are here to take you to a safe place where you can be adopted into new families. I am Astrid, not exactly what I seem, but I'm here to help."

"I'm Santo. My talent is to create holes."

"That's simple but worthy."

"It's not simple. I can make any kind of hole. Such as a hell hole that brings up heat to cook my food. But folk get nervous."

"Don't make any more hell holes," Astrid said.

"And if I want to swim underwater, I can make a hole through the water to air so I can breathe."

"That's a very special hole," Astrid agreed. Indeed, to make one that would not collapse in liquid signaled a far more potent talent.

"Folk don't like it when I make peepholes to bathrooms or dragon nests."

"We will try to find you a family that likes holes," Astrid said. "Yours are really impressive."

Having finally won her admiration, he collapsed. "They're gone."

She went to him and enfolded him, briefly, letting him cry it out. He was after all an orphan.

Then he looked at her, as Firenze had. "I think I've seen you before."

"I'm pretty sure you haven't."

"A—a statue."

"A statue!" Firenze said. "That's where!"

Astrid laughed. "I've never been a statue."

The cable moved on. The next car was a rickety mundane jalopy with a bad paint job. Astrid wondered if the cars were orphans too, trying to be useful in their retirement. This one contained a five-year-old girl with windblown hair. That reminded Astrid of Tiara, whose hair had originally been wild because of its antigravity, before she got it under control. The girl was already crying.

"We'll help," Firenze said. He and Squid went to comfort the new girl.

Astrid was pleased with the way the children were getting along together. They might be destined to be split up among different families, but in the interim it was better if they were compatible with each other. The new one turned out to be Win, whose talent was always to have the wind at her back. That was why her hair was constantly blowing forward. It seemed she could not turn off the wind.

"We can take one more," Dysnomia said. "The rules are fighting back, and we'll have to return before something snaps."

Astrid took the warning to heart. She did not want to be spread across an infinite number of realities.

The fifth car was a giant gemstone, a faceted garnet. How had that gotten in this line? Then she realized that it was a carbuncle. It came to earth, a facet swung out, and a four-year-old girl emerged. She had curly mouse-brown hair and hazel eyes. "Is this—?"

"It is where you belong," Astrid said quickly.

But the girl was doubtful. She had of course been told to ride to the end of the line, and this plainly wasn't. Astrid didn't try to argue. She reached in to catch the girl's arm and convey her out before the car moved on. And missed.

Or rather, mist. The child had become a patch of mist. That was evidently her talent. How could Astrid rescue her if she could not be touched? The car would move on at any moment.

It was little Win who came to her rescue. "Neat talent! Mine's wind. We can play fun games together."

That intrigued the newcomer. She reformed into the girl and jumped down to join Win as the carbuncle moved on. Her name, it turned out, was Myst, after her talent of misting.

Then she, too, looked at Astrid with that faintly odd expression.

"No, we've never met before," Astrid said quickly.

"Still, it helps," Myst said.

"Get them close together," Dysnomia said urgently. "We're about to move."

Astrid and Firenze got the other four children clustered closely in the center of a general glob, and the two Demonesses enclosed them on the outside. "Watch," Astrid told the children. "We have a funny show to show you."

The quivering began, and accelerated, becoming the flickering of day and night, then the backward progress of the seasons. The children watched, fascinated by this show.

"You have the touch," Fornax murmured to Astrid.

"I didn't even know that I liked children," Astrid said. "But I guess I do."

About the time the children began to get bored with the show, they arrived in the present-day glade. "We made it!" Dysnomia said, evidently relieved as she departed. That made Astrid slightly nervous in retrospect. Had this excursion been riskier than it seemed?

"Now we have to get them to our camp," Astrid said. "So they can meet the others. We'll need to feed them and make them a cozy place to stay the night."

"I will transport us," Fornax said.

"Wait," Firenze said.

Astrid looked at him. "There's a problem? Someone needs to poop?"

"It's not that. Huddled together, we felt something. We're not lonely when we're together."

"That's good," Astrid said.

"It's more," Squid said. "We can feel the rightness."

"Well, we are trying to do what's right," Astrid agreed.

"It's that coming here together is right," Santo said.

"And we can tell if it goes wrong," Win said.

"If we're together," Myst said.

This was curious. "Are you saying that you have some kind of magic awareness when you're touching each other?" Astrid asked.

"Yes," Firenze said. "And we don't want to be separated."

"We're all from the future," Santo said. "It's a bond."

That was indeed the single thing they shared: they were all orphans from the virtual future. Astrid didn't know why that should give them any special awareness, but if the idea of it was a bond for them, it was to be encouraged. "I'm glad you are all getting along with each other. You didn't know each other before we collected you, did you?"

"No," Win said. "We were windblown strangers."

"But when we traveled through time, then we felt it," Myst said.

"So are you saying it's wrong to go to our camp?" Astrid asked.

"Not exactly," Squid said.

"But there's something we need to do first," Firenze said.

"And what is that?"

"We don't know," Santo said.

Astrid suppressed her frustration. She wanted to get along well with these children and already knew it would not be easy. Children were more complicated than she had anticipated. "Do you have a hint?"

"We—we need to be sure we can always get together," Win said.

"Even if we're apart," Myst said.

"But when we find good homes for you, you will no longer be together," Astrid said.

"That's why we need a way," Squid said.

This required some finessing. "Why don't you get together and figure out a way?" Astrid suggested.

"Okay," Firenze said. It didn't seem to matter which one spoke; they seemed to have a common thought.

The children clustered together, forming a hand-holding circle.

"There are many," Myst said.

"We'll get the closest one," Squid said.

"That way," Santo said, pointing.

"But that's all tangled thorns," Win protested.

"I'll make a hole." Santo pointed, and a hole appeared. It was a big one, a veritable tunnel through the brush. Astrid was impressed; that was one versatile talent.

The children walked through the tunnel, and Astrid and Fornax followed. "This is not what I thought it would be," the Demoness murmured.

"Nor I," Astrid agreed. "It seems dealing with children is a challenge. Maybe that's what Wenda meant: by the time we learn to take proper care of the children, we'll have a lot of mutual experience and be friends."

"That seems reasonable."

"Is it tying you up when you have other things to do? I can stay with the children."

"Then it would not become a joint experience."

"Oh, that's right," Astrid agreed, chagrined. "I did not mean to be a burden to you."

"Understand this about Demons," Fornax said. "We can be in many places at the same time, and do many things at once. I am currently supervising Kandy's negotiation on the terms of the Demon Wager, and I am reviewing the upkeep of my palace in Galaxy Fornax, and fending off the amorous advances of Demon Nemesis, and doing countless other chores while being here with you. You are incapable of monopolizing my attention. When I seem to leave you, this is to allow you some respite, not because I need any myself."

"I'm sorry. I keep forgetting that you are a Demon. I'm thinking of you as a friend."

"Exactly. That is the point of our association. Already I feel less lonely because of the warmth of your attention."

Astrid was becoming embarrassed, so she changed the subject. "Demon Nemesis?"

"He associates with Dark Matter, that the rest of us can't perceive directly. His local planet is a brown dwarf circling the sun far out, that others have had difficulty locating. He, perhaps alone, has no problem with my antimatter; it does not make him explode into energy, because the interaction is too slight."

"Amorous advances?"

"Demons are not limited the way mortals are, but if he took mortal form he would be entirely typical of mortal males, being interested in only one thing. I have no patience for it."

"My man Art is interested in that, but once his edge is off he has qualities I like, like his artistic ability. He truly does like to paint, and he is good at it."

"It would require a century of amour squeezed into one second to take Nemesis's edge off, as you put it, and then the respite would be brief. More trouble than it is worth."

Astrid had to laugh. "Because he is not limited in that manner either, I suspect. Art falls asleep after once. That is typical of mortal men."

"Demons don't sleep. They merely simulate it as convenient."

"You have my sympathy."

"Oh, I would do it if I had reason. It's not as if I would have to pay more than token attention. But why bother?"

"Well, if you ever needed him for something."

"I am a Demon. I need nothing. Except what I am getting from you: friendship."

The tunnel debouched at what appeared to be a playground, with slides and swings and seesaws, sandboxes, and a little merry-go-round. There was also a raised stage, with benches before it.

"A playground!" Astrid said.

"It is more devious than it looks," Fornax said darkly. "There is a fair amount of magic here."

"This is the way the children can be together?" Astrid asked, perplexed. "Of course they can have fun here, but only when they come here. I don't see how this solves that."

"You will," Fornax assured her.

CHAPTER 5:
PLAYGROUND

~~~

"Can we take a break?" Firenze asked. "Get to know the playground?"

"*May* we take a break," Astrid said.

He looked at her. "You're not my mother, but sometimes you remind me of her."

Astrid nodded. "And?"

"*May* we take a break?"

"Yes. Then tell me what this is all about."

The children pitched into play. The two younger girls, Win and Myst, shared the see-saw, whose central eyeball watched them closely. Squid enjoyed the slide. Santo punched little holes in the sandbox, without touching it physically. Firenze pumped himself up so high on a swing it looked as if he was in danger of flying away into the sky.

"Children have fun," Fornax remarked. "It had not occurred to me before to observe it, but there is a certain pleasure in the viewing."

"Maybe we should join them, to share the spirit."

"And understand them better," Fornax agreed.

The two of them went to the merry-go-round and mounted two of the little wooden horses. Music sounded, and the device started moving. The horses went up and down on their poles. "Wheee!" Astrid exclaimed. "I never saw one of these when I was young."

"I was never young," Fornax said.

After no more than a moment and a half the children came to join them. "I'll race you to the post!" Firenze challenged Santo. Of course the horses were fixed to their poles; they couldn't race each other.

"You're on," Santo said. His horse put down its head and galloped faster, surging ahead.

"Oh, yeah?" Firenze's horse snorted steam and bore down, catching up.

Astrid stared, amazed. The horses remained on their poles, yet somehow they were racing.

"I believe I mentioned magic," Fornax murmured.

"So you did," Astrid agreed weakly.

Soon Astrid began to get dizzy, and had to get off her high horse. Then she jumped to the ground. Fornax joined her by the side of the merry-go-round.

"The children are right: this is fun."

"I'm glad to see them happy. But what is the point of it? They were looking for a way to be together when they were apart."

"We'll see."

Fortunately the children's attention spans were short, and they soon tired of the circling and racing. Then the merry-go-round slowed and stopped, and they got off and rejoined the adults.

"This will do," Firenze said.

"I'm glad you are enjoying it. But how does it enable you to be together when you're apart?"

"Well, it's magic. But there's a catch."

"How is it magic?"

"We can take it with us, so we can use it whenever we want."

Astrid gazed at the playground enclosure, which measured about a mundane acre. "How do you do this?"

"Like this," Santo said.

The children ran to the edges of the park. They pushed against the picket fence surrounding it, and the fence folded down. Then they pushed again, and the edges folded inward. Where they came to a slide, swing, seesaw or whatever, that folded too, as if painted on the surface. They continued, until they met in the center, pushing five edges together to form a box. Then they folded the box, and it became smaller and smaller, until at last it was matchbox-size. Santo tucked it into his shirt pocket.

"Can you reverse it?" Astrid asked.

"Sure," Firenze said. "We can just unfold it."

"But if you are separated, only the one who unfolds it will have the park. That won't bring you together."

"Matches!" Win said.

"I forgot," Santo said. He pulled the matchbox out of his pocket, slid it open, and brought out matches. He passed them out to the others, and took one himself, which he put in another pocket. The others put theirs in their pockets, except Squid, who tucked hers into her painted hair. Astrid decided not to inquire how she could put a real object in fake hair.

"Matches are dangerous in the hands of children," Astrid said. "They can set fires."

"These are different," Squid said. "They don't make fire."

"They match people up with the box," Win said.

"So we can all come to the park, wherever it is," Myst said.

Astrid was unsure about this. "Can you demonstrate?"

"Sure," Santo said. He walked away from them, turned, and struck his match against a rock. There was no flash of fire. Instead he appeared back by the matchbox.

But Astrid was unsatisfied. "I'm sure that playing here is fun, and you can get to the playground when you want to. But you can play anywhere. Why is it so important to have this particular park?"

"We don't know," Firenze said. "Just that it is."

"That's not sufficient. We need a better answer."

The boy's face started to heat. He was about to go into fireworks mode.

Astrid touched her glasses warningly.

Firenze cooled. "Maybe we can find out."

"It'll cost us," Santo said.

"Oh, blip!" Firenze agreed. "It's not free."

"I'm not comfortable with all this mystery," Astrid said. "I think we had better find out what it costs, and why."

"But we have to use it to find out," Squid protested.

"You found the playground without using it," Astrid said. "Now find out what it's for."

The children bounced a glance somewhat haphazardly around. "Maybe we can," Santo said.

They gathered together and linked hands. They concentrated. Then they fell apart, dismayed. "That's scary!" Win said.

Squid lost her composure, reverting to her octopus form. Little Myst started crying.

Astrid picked her up, and she did not fog out. This brief contact should be all right despite Astrid's intoxicating ambiance. "What scared you, dear?"

"Doom!" Santo said, shaken.

Astrid looked at Firenze. "Can you clarify that?"

"I *can. May* I?"

Astrid had to smile. "I'm glad you have that straight, now. *Can* is ability; *may* is permission. You may."

"It's that this Xanth is doomed. Same as our own Xanth. That wipeout is coming toward us, and in fifty years will hit us, and we'll all die anyway."

That probably made sense. War was destined to happen. "How does the playground relate to this?"

"It can show us how to save Xanth, maybe," Firenze said. "If we ask it the right way."

"A playground can save Xanth?"

"No," Santo said. "It can just guide us so we can save Xanth."

That was a technical distinction, but she could appreciate it. "How will it guide you? Does it have a voice?"

Little Myst laughed. "No voice."

Astrid set her down, as she was evidently over her fright. "Then how?"

"If we do our circle in the playground, it will make it stronger, so we can get better guidance," Firenze said.

"But if you can't get a direct answer, how will that help?"

"It's just a feeling," Squid said. "Like hot/cold."

"Like what?"

"A game," Santo said. "Hide something, and when someone looks, say Warmer or Colder, guiding him, until he finds it."

Astrid was missing the human childhood she had never had. "It guides you by making you feel warmer or cooler?"

"Not that, quite, but a feeling of right or wrong," Firenze said. "So if we decide to take the right fork, and ask, and it's wrong, we'll know, and take the left fork."

"Saving Xanth is a matter of taking the correct fork in the road?"

He shrugged. "Something like that. It's hard to explain."

"But it did bring us to the park," Santo reminded her. "Our circle, I mean. In the park, it will work better, and it needs to, because we can't ask which direction will save Xanth. At least we don't think so."

"But there's a catch," Squid said. "We can't just use the Playground."

"Oops, I forgot!" Firenze said, hearing the capitalization. "That's a problem."

"A problem?" Astrid asked.

"It's a Play Ground," Win said.

"For Plays," Myst said.

"But there's no sign of that," Astrid protested. "You were using the swing, slide, seesaw—"

"We can do that," Santo agreed. "But that's not its magic."

"Well, you did fold it up. That's impressive magic."

"Incidental," Firenze said. "It wants to be used."

"You did use it! You played in it."

All of the children shook their heads. "Used for plays," Santo said.

"I hate to seem opaque here," Astrid said, frustrated. "But I am not making much sense of this. Are you saying that it is a play ground, I mean a Playground that insists on having plays?"

"Yes," Squid said.

"And the better the play, the better it will perform for us," Firenze said.

"I believe we need more information than we have at the moment," Astrid said, not wishing to advertise her confusion. "So it's time for you to meet my friends on the pun restoration mission. As we were about to do before we visited the Playground."

The children linked hands, consulting. Then Myst smiled sunnily. Which was interesting considering her misty nature. "Yes, it's time."

"I will move us," Fornax said. "Then leave you to your devices, for the time being."

The scene shifted, and they were at the camp. Fornax was not apparent, though Astrid knew she was close by, observing. There were the other pretty women: Tiara, Kandy, Merge, and Metria.

"Oh, you got the children!" Tiara cried, delighted.

"Three cute girls and two dorky boys," Metria said.

"Oh, yeah?" Firenze demanded, his brow darkening.

"She didn't mean it in a bad way," Astrid said quickly. "She's a demoness."

"Oh, that's why she's the ugly one," Firenze said.

"Oh, yeah?" Metria demanded, her own brow darkening dangerously.

The three little girls laughed. "He's teasing," Win said.

"Oh," Metria said, deflating. "Then that's letter-perfect."

"That's what?" Firenze asked.

"Complete, clear, clean, fresh, satisfactory—"

"All right?"

"Whatever," Metria agreed crossly.

"Firenze, meet Metria, who sometimes has a vocabulary problem," Astrid said.

"I'd never guess," Firenze said as the girls tittered.

"Metria, meet Firenze," Astrid continued. "Whose talent is that he has a fireworks temper."

"I'd like to see that," Metria said, interested.

"Not right now," Astrid said. "We have other introductions to make. Folks, these are five orphan children rescued from fifty years in the future, in effect. We will be finding good homes for them. You've just met Firenze. This one is Santo, with a truly remarkable talent of making holes. This one is Squid, who is of alien persuasion." Squid shifted briefly into octopus mode, and back. "This one is Win, with the wind always at her back, as you can see by her blown hair." Win smiled uncertainly, trying ineffectively to brush her hair back out of her face. "And here is Myst, who can become a patch of mist." Myst obliged with a brief demonstration.

Then Astrid introduced the women to the children, and followed with the men. "I know it's a lot to assimilate all at once, but we'll all get to know each other soon enough. First we need to find places for each of you children to stay while you're with us. Then—"

"No," Santo said.

"We stay together," Squid said.

"Listen brats," Metria said. "We're taking care of you. You should be grateful."

"Listen whats?" Firenze demanded.

"Scamps, monkeys, rascals, jerks, dorks—"

"Children!" Astrid said forcefully.

"Whatever," Metria agreed. "Hey, wait! You're not part of this dialogue."

"I'm trying to keep the peace," Astrid said. "Let's keep the language polite."

"Awww," Firenze and Metria said almost together. Then they looked at each other, getting a faint glimmer of kindred spirits.

"Look, children, you don't have to be physically together all the time," Astrid said. "You have your matches, and can be in touch at any time. Meanwhile, we are on a mission to eliminate the last of the anti-pun virus, so we're staying together, and you are together as long as you're part of our group. It will be easier if each one of you joins each one of us for the nonce, and—"

"Nonce?" Myst asked.

"For the moment, right now," Astrid said. "Not permanently. You need to acclimatize to our world, since—" She saw four-year-old Myst's confusion again, and clarified: "Get used to our world, since you'll be in it for some time. That's easier if you have individual guidance. So why don't you try joining us in this manner and see how it works?"

The children looked at each other, then linked hands. "Okay," Win said.

"Very well. Shall we have women choose children, or children choose women?"

"Why women?" Firenze asked. "Why not men?"

"Because we're the ones who are supposed to be good with children. Men are awkward in such matters."

The children nodded together, appreciating the point.

"Maybe alternate," Santo said.

"Alternate," Astrid agreed. "One of us will choose one of you, then one of you will choose one of us. Who's up first?"

"I'll take it," Tiara said. "I want Win, because of her hair."

"But my hair always blows in my face," Win protested.

Tiara squatted down before her. "Look at my hair." It started floating up from her head. "See? It's got no gravity. It floats. But I learned how to tie it down. I'll tie yours down too. Then you'll be pretty."

"I tie mine down too," Mitch said. "The two of us know about hair."

Win smiled, accepting that. One pair had been made.

"Now I'll pick one," Santo said. "Metria."

"You like fighting?" Metria asked, surprised.

"No. But you're pretty..." The demoness straightened up, smiling. "Wild," the boy concluded. Metria puffed into roiling smoke, but did not argue the case. Another pair.

"Merge?" Astrid asked.

"Myst," Merge said immediately.

"Why me?" the little girl asked.

"Because you can break up into multiple bits of water. I can break up into five girls." Merge fragmented into her five components.

"That's not as good as yours," Brown said.

"But it's the same idea," Black added.

"So we understand you," Blue concluded.

It was a persuasive argument, and Myst smiled, accepting it. Three pairs.

Then it was Squid's turn. "Can you really turn into a board?" she asked Kandy.

Kandy became the board. Squid picked it up and swung it. "Neat." Then Ease picked both up. "I'm never board with her," he said, and the child creature laughed, appreciating the joke.

That left Astrid herself. "I guess that means you, Firenze," she said. "We're the last picks. We're stuck with each other."

"Stuck," he agreed, frowning. But he didn't seem displeased. They had come to understand each other somewhat in the course of their conflicts, and it was possible he respected someone who could make him behave. Some children did. "Actually you don't look bad. For a basilisk."

"For a basilisk," she agreed cheerfully, and kissed him on the cheek. That ruined the moment.

They split up into assorted tasks of temporary family making, arranging sleeping places in the tents and ascertaining food preferences. They even did a bit of scouting for virus pockets, to give the children the feel of the mission. They seemed to settle in well enough.

But there were awkwardnesses with Firenze. He was just old enough to understand the Adult Conspiracy, and to dislike it. When she sat on the ground and crossed her legs, he looked, until a warning touch of her glasses dissuaded him. When Art stepped on a thorn his flying cussword came out BLEEP because of the presence of the child. When she harvested clothing to fit Firenze he didn't want her to try it on him first, because he didn't want her to seem him undressed. And how was she to be intimate with Art, with the boy close by?

The last problem took care of itself. Firenze had had a long hard day, and was tired. When darkness came he lay down on his mat and was almost instantly asleep. She covered him with a light blanket, then quietly joined Art and silently put him to sleep too.

When she woke in the morning, she was surprised to find herself alone. She quickly washed up and dressed, aware that privacy was more difficult now, then went out of the tent. There were Art and Firenze, evidently both early risers, with a painting canvas set up. "A little more purple," Art was saying. "It makes the clouds prettier."

Art was giving Firenze a painting lesson, and the boy was interested! Astrid had never anticipated that.

That reminded her. She had an Answer, "Five Portraits," but no Question. Meanwhile they needed to find a way to save Xanth, fifty years hence. Too bad the two didn't relate.

Or did they? There was an Answer without a Question, and a Question without an Answer. Could they match up? Or if not, could they be made to match up? Then they might have a way to save Xanth.

"Eureka!" she exclaimed.

"We do not reek," Art said, annoyed.

"Maybe she's an art critic," Firenze said.

Astrid had to laugh. "That was an expression of discovery, not a critique of you or your painting. I think maybe I just might have figured out a way to save Xanth. If I can understand it." Then she explained about putting the Question and Answer together.

"Maybe so," Art said doubtfully.

"Maybe we can ask the Playground," Firenze said.

"It can answer that?"

"Maybe. We'll see." He brought out his match and struck it against a stone. And vanished.

Art was startled. "What happened?"

"The matches take them to the matchbox, which is the Playground," Astrid said.

"I believe Santo has the matchbox."

They went to Metria's tent, where Firenze was talking with Santo. "So if we go to the Playground, maybe we'll know," he was saying.

"Maybe," Santo agreed. "Call them in. I'll unfold the Playground." He got to work on it, and soon it was spread out before them.

Firenze put his hands to his mouth, megaphone style. "Alle alle alle infree!"

In three-eighths of a moment the three girls joined them, holding their matches. "We need to decide whether we have the right Question and Answer," Firenze explained. "How can Xanth be saved? Five Portraits."

"Does that make sense?" Squid asked.

"Maybe. The Playground should know."

"But we need to put on a play," Win said.

"We don't have a play," Santo said.

"You need a playwright," Astrid said. "That's a person who writes plays."

The other adults had gathered around. "Anyone here have literary ambition?" Art asked.

No one did.

"Then we have a problem," Astrid said.

"Does it have to be a good play?" Kandy asked.

"No," Firenze said. "But a bad play will lead to a bad answer."

"So it needs to be halfway decent," Astrid said.

"I need imagination to find new types of holes," Santo said. "I could try a play. It wouldn't be great, but maybe I could learn with practice."

"It would be full of holes," Metria said.

"Yeah."

"Firenze, you're the oldest," Astrid said. "Maybe you should try it."

"I guess," the boy agreed reluctantly.

"Idea for the Play," Myst said. "Our rescue from the future."

The other children exchanged a glance or three. "For the first one, why not?" Firenze asked. "It will seem original."

"We'll play while you make a play," Squid said, giggling.

They did. Astrid made written notes based on Firenze's ideas, adapting their rescue to play form. Then they drilled the children on their parts, which were formal presentations of what they had done. Astrid served as Narrator and Prompter. Then they tried putting it on.

The adults went to sit on the benches before that stage. The children went to stand around it. There were no curtains, but maybe they weren't needed.

Astrid took center stage. "We are here to present the Play titled 'Rescue,'" she announced. "Three adults have just arrived at the Cable Station. Lo, a cable car is approaching."

Firenze ran up on the stage, making a chugging sound. "Is this the end of the line?" he asked.

"No, but it will do," Astrid said.

"Then I want to ride on to the end. That's what my folks told me to do."

"The end is doom," Astrid said. "You must come with us."

"I don't want to!"

"I am a basilisk. Do what I tell you, or I will kill you with a stare."

The boy considered it. "Okay, I'll stay." It did not sound very persuasive, but he was after all not a practiced playwright or actor. It would have to do.

"Another car is coming," Astrid said loudly.

Squid scrambled up. She was in her natural form, using her eight tentacles. When she got onstage and saw Astrid and Firenze, she put her tentacles together to form limbs and made herself into a little girl. "I am an alien visitor. An oct—oct—a squid. I need to be rescued."

"We're here to rescue you," Astrid said.

"Thank you." Squid joined their little group.

Santo was the next to arrive, followed by Win and finally Myst. Their group was complete.

"And so the five children were brought here to present-day Xanth," Astrid concluded. "We hope to live happily ever after."

The audience dutifully applauded. The actors onstage bowed, pleased with their performances. Then they left the stage. The Play was done. Would it suffice?

The children linked hands an focused. "Yes!" little Myst exclaimed gladly.

Astrid was cautious. "So the Playground will enhance your ability to choose the correct path. Is this permanent, whenever you are in the Playground, or one-shoot, and you have to perform a play each time you have a serious question?"

"Each time," Santo said.

"Then you will need to phrase your concern carefully, to be sure of getting the guidance you need. If you phrase it carelessly, you will waste your effort."

"We know what it is," Squid said. "Xanth will be saved by five portraits. Yes or no."

"Five portraits of whom?" Astrid asked.

That set them back. "We didn't think about that," Firenze admitted.

"I plan to paint five portraits, to start," Art said. "Of the five beautiful women in our party. When we encounter a suitable setting for each. I just sort of assumed those would be the ones."

"And what connection would those portraits have with saving Xanth?" Astrid asked. "They're just pictures."

"Or with us?" Santo asked. "We're the ones most affected by the end of Xanth."

"Maybe it's not such a good assumption," Art said, troubled.

"There's a connection," Firenze said. "We feel it." The other children nodded together. They were remarkably different in appearance and abilities, but oddly unified in this.

"Maybe we need to know *how* Xanth will be saved by five portraits," Kandy said.

"That's not the sort of question we or the Playground can answer," Santo said. "There needs to be a definite plan. Then we can tell whether it's right or wrong."

The adults and the children pondered, mutually stumped.

Then Firenze brightened. "I remember a picture!"

Astrid focused immediately, not questioning the relevance. "Describe it."

"It was of my great grandparents. With Grandpa, when he was a boy no older than I am, ten. It hung on our wall. Nobody paid any attention to it, but it had been passed down through the generations, a sort of record. I used to look at it, 'cause the boy looked sort of like me, and I wondered if he was like me. Now I wonder—" He broke off, confused.

"Go on," Astrid said gently. "Your memory may be relevant, as it is about a portrait."

"Yes. It's that the woman, Great Grandma, she, well, she—"

"Yes?"

"She maybe looked sort of like you."

Astrid felt a shock of familiarity. "Like me?"

"Well, maybe not, exactly. But she had these big dark glasses on, like the ones you wear. So her face was sort of covered and I guess it could have been anyone. But when I saw you out by the cable car, well, I guess I was more ready to listen to you, 'cause you reminded me of her."

"A fortunate coincidence," Astrid said. "But of course I couldn't be your great grandma. I'm not even human."

"Yeah." He sounded almost disappointed.

"Unless you adopted him," Kandy said. "Or adopted his grandpa."

Both Astrid and Firenze laughed. "Wouldn't that be something!" Astrid said. "A basilisk in your ancestry!"

"I could pretend to have the glare," the boy agreed, making a horrific face.

"But there may be a kernel of relevance here," Kandy said. "He remembers a portrait, and it could be of an adoptive family. Maybe the portraits are of those families."

Astrid nodded. "Five adoptions, painted when they are complete. Art can paint them when the time is right. Then maybe he'll be free to paint the women of our own party, when the fate of Xanth no longer hangs in the balance. And the children, safely embedded in this Xanth, can then work to make sure it doesn't go the way theirs did. That would be completely relevant."

"So what's the program?" Santo asked.

"Whether to work to get the adoptions accomplished, and the portraits painted," Astrid said. "So as to save Xanth."

The children looked at each other, and nodded.

"So how do you invoke the Playground's assistance?"

"We link here onstage," Squid said.

"Then I will get out of your way," Astrid said. She stepped down the small stairs at the edge of the stage. At the foot of it her foot caught on something and she stumbled into an alcove marked DO NOT ENTER. Oops!

She caught her balance. Every so often she did have a problem, because her reflexes were for four legs instead of two. She straightened up and turned to step out of the alcove. And paused.

She was no longer at the foot of the stage. She stood in a flat plain whose landscape extended to the horizon on every side. There was no apparent way back. It seemed that the DO NOT ENTER marking was serious, because it had no visible exit. It had to be associated in some way with the stage, maybe as a place for actors to wait before stepping into their roles, or as storage for stage props. But how was she to rejoin the other members of the audience?

She looked about more carefully. There were scattered trees filled with assorted nests. Was this some sort of bird sanctuary? She walked to the nearest tree to inspect its nest.

A bird flew up out of it. "Auk!" it cried. "A prig!" It circled up over her head and loosed an egg at her. She ducked so that it avoided her head, and it struck the ground where it exploded in a ball of smoke and yolk.

Astrid retreated, but clumsily, almost falling. Why was she suddenly so awkward? Then she realized that it was because of the bird, the auk. It was an Aukward, making her lose dexterity. A groaner of a pun. Fortunately she recovered as she got away from its nest and the fumes of the broken egg.

What had it called her? A prig? She was no prig.

Then she saw a woman at another tree. She was taking an egg from its nest, while the brightly colored bird fluttered helplessly. "Get out of here, prig!" the bird exclaimed.

"This egg is too good for you, Hibiscus," the woman retorted as she walked away with the egg.

Hibis-cus. Like a pretty flower, and the egg was colored too. The prig had stolen it. No wonder the birds didn't like the prigs.

Astrid saw the woman walk to a house made of logs. Now the mad birds were attacking it, bombing it with explosive eggs. The house shook but did not collapse, to their disappointment. Astrid appreciated the birds' position; she would be mad too if prigs stole her babies.

"Maybe I can help," she said to the bird at the next tree. She was feeling unusually serious. "Can you spare an egg?"

The bird indicated its nest, which was marked EARN. An Earn-nest. That was why she was suddenly so dedicated. Astrid lifted out an egg and threw it at the house. It scored on the roof, blowing a hole in it. "Hey, wretch!" the prig inside cried. "You're spoiling the upholstery!"

Astrid took another egg and looped it into the hole. This time the whole house blew apart, sending logs flying. Several watching birds applauded, smacking their wings together as they perched on their nests. The prig was seriously annoyed, but the birds had plainly won this round.

But Astrid knew she couldn't stay among the mad birds, however much she sympathized with their annoyance. Those prigs needed to be eliminated, but that was not her job. She needed to return to the stage, or at least the

Playground. How could she do that?

Well, this was a section of puns. She saw a Cockaphony and heard its discordant cry. There was a Crowker, with a harsh, throaty voice. A Jaywalker, endangering itself by walking across busy paths and trails. And an irrational Loonatic. So could she make up a pun bird of her own whose ability was to get out?

She tried. "I'm a See-fowl," she announced. "Not a Sea-foul. I can see the way out of here."

And she did. There was a plaque marked DO NOT LEAVE that was surely it. She went there and stepped on it.

And was back beside the stage. No one had noticed her stumble. Had any time passed here? Apparently not.

She took a seat and watched the children on the stage link hands and focus. In half a moment they separated. "Yes!" Squid exclaimed happily. "The adoptions will save Xanth!"

The audience applauded again. It was wonderful news.

The children trooped off the stage and rejoined their adult mentors. Firenze came to Astrid. "You were right. We need to get adopted, and get painted. The Playground knows. Now we'll steer that course."

"That's good." She hesitated, then decided to inquire. "You have picked up a working knowledge of the Playground?"

"I guess. It sort of rubs off, when we use it."

"Do you know anything about that DO NOT ENTER nook?"

"Oh, sure. That's the Playground's Storage facility."

"What is stored there that is so secret from regular folk like us?"

"Games, mainly, for children who get tired of active fun. Little hand-held screens with pictures they can move about and score points."

"Are any about birds? Mad birds?"

"Sure. Mad Birds is a big one. These prigs are stealing their eggs and ruining their nests, so the birds are getting back at them by bombing them with explosive eggs. The player is on the side of the birds."

Now it was making more sense, in its fashion. Still, it seemed more like nonsense. "If the birds are trying to save their eggs, why are they using more eggs to get back at the prigs?"

Firenze considered this. "I never thought of that. I guess they are so mad they just have to get rid of the prigs somehow." He smiled. "It makes sense to children. I guess adults don't understand."

"Oh, I think I could get into it, if I tried. Prigs can be pretty annoying."

"Well, you're not human."

"That must be it," Astrid agreed.

The adults got up and returned to their camp, while Santo and the children folded up the Playground. It had been a fair adventure, all things considered.

But Astrid wondered. What were the limits of that Playground? It could be folded up into a matchbox and taken along. Could people hide in it by entering the Storage facility? Would they survive when the Playground was folded up? It was some piece of magic, with its own rules and capacities. There were aspects that made her wary. Too much magic could be mischief as well as help. But she kept her misgivings to herself, for now.

"You know, it might not be too bad," Firenze said as they walked to the camp.

She didn't pick up on his point. "What might not be too bad? Getting adopted?"

"Getting adopted by a basilisk."

Oh. "Well, it's a last resort. You're a smart boy. Folks should appreciate that."

"But I have a temper."

"We'll try to teach you to control it. After all, if I can work with humans without killing them, you should be able to be in a family without blowing your top."

"I guess."

She patted his shoulder. "It's personality that really counts in the end."

"I am learning that," he agreed.

"It's our job to take care of you, the five of you, until we can get you into families and have your portraits painted. The future of Xanth depends on that. The Playground has confirmed it."

"It has. We know what we have to do. But it's hard."

She could not argue with that. "It's hard," she agreed.

"When—when I first got off the cable car, you—"

"I'm sorry if I was abrupt with you."

"That's not it. You—you comforted me."

"I tried to. Of course there are limits, because of my nature."

"Could you do it again?"

She looked at him and saw that he was on the verge of an emotional collapse. He had lost his family and his world, and it was getting to him. He was to a considerable extent the support the other children needed, being the oldest, and he was performing well in that respect. But at times he needed support himself.

"Hold your breath," she told him. Then she hugged him while he cried.

CHAPTER 6:
SACRIFICE

~~~

That afternoon they resumed virus hunting, with the children in tow. They even filled little bottles of the anti-virus elixir for the children to carry so they could participate. Participation, Astrid knew from somewhere, was vital for a child's sense of belonging. The boys were plainly bored, but the girls loved it.

"Look!" Win cried. "A horsie!"

So it was. A nice brown horse was grazing in a field as they approached. Win ran to it, but the horse, startled, neighed and bolted.

And Win's clothes fell off. Astrid, farther away, felt her own dress loosen dangerously. She saw others grabbing their clothing.

Tiara hurried to attend to Win, getting her garbed again. What had happened? Then Pewter figured it out. "That was a young spook horse. A neigh kid. A pun. The sound of it causes folk to lose their clothing."

Oh.

They moved on, and soon came to a lake. There was a ship on the lake, headed for a pier close to them, but then it swerved and went to another pier.

Pewter checked his data file again. "Boon Docks. There's a Magician on that ship who grants boons to supplicants, but nobody knows where the erratic ship will dock, so they seldom get the benefit. Another pun."

Then they came to a house with an old woman seated at a table in front of it. There was a coffeepot and a cup on the table. A sign said MEDIUM COFFEE.

They did not trust this. "What is special about this drink?" Astrid asked.

"You can drink this to obtain temporary psychic abilities," the woman said. "For example, to converse with the dead."

"Thank you, no," Astrid said quickly.

"Or see into the near future. You folk could really use that."

Was the woman determined to lure them into her nonsense? "No."

"You'll be sor-ree," the woman sing-songed as they moved on.

Then they came across several beds set out in the open. The smaller children gleefully bounced on them—and stopped, confused.

Because the beds were not exactly what they seemed. Little Myst was on a Flower Bed, and flowers were sailing up around her. She liked them, but didn't want to squish them. Squid was on a Sea Bed, and was soaked in saltwater. She adored it, but was distracted by the shells. Win was on a River Bed, also wet, concerned about the little fish getting splashed out of it.

Clearly the pun virus had not passed this way.

They cleaned up the girls and went on. Now they found a more normal field of flowers, and all three girls reveled in it. Squid went to the edge of the forest, following a trail of pretty little blue flowers.

"Get back from there, Squid!" Kandy called. "The unknown forest is dangerous."

The girl obeyed, turning her back on the forest. But at that point a small dragon pounced on her. It had been lurking in ambush, hoping for just such a meal.

Squid screamed as the dragon's jaws closed on her. She reverted to her natural form so that the teeth tended to slide around her instead of biting her in half, but already there was blood.

Kandy and Ease charged for the dragon. On the way Kandy became the board, and Ease grabbed it and swung it at the dragon's head. It caught the creature a solid clout on the snout, and it dropped its morsel and retreated. Ease kept after it, clubbing it repeatedly, every strike scoring, until it turned tail and fled, battered. Astrid knew that Kandy was the one guiding the strikes, while Ease provided the muscle. They made an effective team. Still, it was just as well that the dragon had been small, and not a fire breather.

Meanwhile Astrid caught up to Squid. She was in a sad state, with blood on her tentacles, writhing in pain. Astrid picked her up, but she was slippery with blood and slid through her grasp.

"Let me," Merge said as she arrived on the scene. She split into five bare girls, who formed a circle and reached under the child, forming a ten-armed basket. They carried her back to the flower bed and set her down. Tiara quickly harvested fresh sheets from a linens tree and covered and wrapped her.

"I have healing elixir," Pewter said, producing it. He poured a few drops on the writhing child, and the bleeding stopped. Squid relaxed, free of pain, reformed as a girl, and sank into sleep.

"That's not enough," Metria said. "That was a poison dragon, with elixir-resistant venom. I've seen that kind before. It will take her out within hours."

Now Astrid saw that Squid was changing color, becoming sallow. She also smelled the venom, and knew it was true; basilisks were not the only deadly creatures. The child would never wake from her sleep.

"There goes the girl," Kandy said grimly as she reverted to her human form.

"And there goes the Portrait," Art said.

"And so there goes Xanth," Astrid said, horrified.

"Isn't there anything we can do?" Merge asked as she reformed and dressed.

"It would take more magic than we can muster," Metria said. "She's doomed."

Astrid gazed at the child and suffered. The fate of the Land of Xanth might hang in the balance, but the immediate peril of an innocent creature, a nonhuman person in human form the way Astrid herself was, truly got to her. How could she just stand here and watch Squid die? If there was anything she could do—

Then she remembered how Kandy, seeing Astrid about to die, had made a deal with Demoness Fornax to save her friend, heedless of the price of that deal. Was there any deal that she in turn could make to save the child?

"Fornax," she whispered.

The Demoness appeared. She spread the fingers of one hand toward the child. There was a glow. "The venom is gone."

"Oh thank you!" Astrid said, enormously relieved. "But I proffered no deal. What do you want in return?"

"Nothing," Fornax said. "I did it for friendship."

"That's beautiful," Kandy said.

A donkey-headed dragon appeared. "Demon Xanth!" Pewter said.

"Gotcha," the Demon said.

The Demoness Fornax did not move. Astrid realized that she had been frozen in place. Xanth had caught her doing illicit magic in his territory, and captured her. This was disaster!

"She was just trying to save a child," Kandy said, speaking for Fornax, as she had the position to do so. "She wasn't trying to mess with your territory."

Three more Demons appeared. "The Demon Earth, whose association is Gravity," Pewter said, indicating the one with a head like a blue spinning planet. "The Demon Jupiter, whose association is the Strong Force." That was the one with a huge cloudy head with a single red eye. "The Demon Nemesis, whose association is Dark Matter." His head was an intangible blob, extremely difficult to see, though obviously there was something there. "Nemesis is the Chief Judge."

And Nemesis, Astrid remembered, was the Demon who had courted Fornax and been rejected. He had no fear of her antimatter nature, because he interacted only very slightly with either matter or antimatter. He was a suitor balked. This was mischief compounded.

"The case is between Demon Xanth and Demoness Fornax," Nemesis said. "He charges her with magically interfering in his domain. The Primaries do not represent themselves. Who will represent Xanth's and Fornax's cases?"

"I will represent Fornax," Kandy said immediately. "I am her designated intermediary."

"No," the dragon ass said. "You will represent me."

Kandy's mouth opened to protest, but nothing came out. She was frozen also. No mortal had any ability to oppose any Demon directly.

Astrid realized that Demon Xanth had acted strategically to eliminate Fornax's most effective representative and thus ensure his victory. The Demons did not pussyfoot.

"Xanth has choosen his representative first, he being the wronged party," Nemesis said. "Fornax will have a different representative. Whom does she choose?"

Now Fornax was allowed to speak. "My friend Astrid Basilisk-Cockatrice."

Now Astrid froze, for a different reason. "But I have no training, no experience!" she protested. "I don't know anything about a Demon Trial."

"Learn," Nemesis said.

"But—" At which point she was frozen by the Demon.

"You will have a day and night to prepare your cases," Nemesis said. "Court will reconvene in twenty-four hours."

Then the Demons vanished, including Xanth and Fornax. The mortals were on their own. For a day and night.

"Oh, bleep!" Kandy swore, now that she was free to speak. "I have to represent the case I'm against! And do my very best to win it despite wanting to lose it. And argue against my friend."

Astrid was unable to be even that expressive. She dissolved into tears of frustration and hopelessness.

Kandy immediately came to her, joining her in grief. "And most of all I hate having to argue against you, my friend." The others, adults and children, watched helplessly. None of them could change anything.

Squid woke. "Am I better?" she asked, surprised.

Tiara went to her. "Yes, dear. The Demoness Fornax healed you."

"That's nice." Squid got up and resumed looking at flowers, unaware of the scene that had transpired or the disaster that her cure had made. She was truly innocent. She would not remain that way long; other would quickly fill her in.

"I think we had better return to our camp and consider what to do," Merge said. "Eliminating the remaining pun virus is important, but not as important as this. If I understand it correctly, if Demoness Fornax loses her case, someone's healing will be canceled and all will be lost." She did not name Squid, because the child was within earshot.

"That is the case," Pewter said.

"I wonder," Tiara said. "Maybe the children could go play in the Playground?"

"Maybe we should," Firenze said. "At least for a while." As the eldest, he had the best grasp of the problem, and knew why it was better to leave the children out of it, at least for now.

"Yes," Astrid agreed gratefully. "But don't go in the DO NOT ENTER part."

They passed the old woman with the Medium Coffee. "Told you," she said smugly.

Astrid, enraged, grabbed for her glasses. But Kandy and Firenze boxed her in, half carrying her on past. They were right; there was nothing to be gained by killing in anger. It was really their own fault; they should have tried the medium's coffee and gotten a glimpse into the near future, and picked up on the lurking threat. Astrid would try to be smarter hereafter.

At the camp, Santo unfolded the Playground, and the children happily ran into it. Only Firenze looked back, as if he would have liked to participate in the adult discussion but had a greater responsibility. Astrid was coming to appreciate him more.

Then she thought of something else. "Fornax?" she asked.

There was no response. The Demoness did not appear. That confirmed what Astrid had suspected: no Demons would be involved in their deliberation. Demons normally did not interfere in mortal events, particularly those relating to Demon Wagers. They let things play out naturally. That was the point of their bets: they were decided by the vagaries of insignificant whimsy, which is what mortal affairs normally were to Demons.

The group of adults settled in a wide circle. "One thing I'm not clear on,"

Art said. "The Demons have a Bet on whether Xanth will survive. Demon Xanth of course bet Yes, and Demoness Fornax bet No. So how come Xanth is trying to mess up Fornax, when saving the child will help him win?"

"And why did Fornax save Squid," Merge asked, "when she could have won her bet merely by staying out of it?"

"Demons are huge and complicated," Pewter said. "Their reasons for things may be opaque to folk of the mortal realm."

"And Demon Nemesis," Astrid said. "He's been hot for Fornax for, well, maybe a billion years, but she never gave him the time of day, not that he needs it, much less what he really wants. Is he using this to get back at her?"

"What is it he wants of her?" Tiara asked.

"Just one thing," Metria said. "He's male. She's female. You know what that means."

"Oh," Tiara said, blushing. She had learned about men and women, but remained a bit naïve around the edges.

"So is he going to trade his vote for her favor?" Art asked.

"Probably," Pewter agreed. "And without that vote she will surely lose."

"She doesn't want to oblige him," Astrid said. "It's a crime to have a child's life be hostage to his lust."

"Demons don't care about crime," Kandy said. "But you know, I just remembered: in my capacity as intermediary I have picked up some information. Nemesis bet Xanth will survive. It's Jupiter who bet it won't. So Nemesis can't use that particular thing to coerce Fornax. He's already on her side in that respect. That is, what she did helps enable him to win."

"But if she still refuses him personally, what then?" Astrid asked.

"Would he torpedo his own bet to spite her?" Kandy asked. "I don't know the male mind in this respect."

"He might," Art said. "Males can do suicidally stupid things when they get hung up on women."

"So maybe things will cancel out, and it will be up to us to make the case, one way or the other," Kandy said. "Except that we don't want to."

"Actually, I do want to," Astrid said. "I want to save Squid, and not have Fornax punished for doing something decent. But I'm not competent. That's my problem."

"Maybe you can argue it emotionally," Merge said. "As you said, it's a decent thing Fornax did."

"Do Demons decide things emotionally?"

"No they don't," Metria said. "They are soulless; they have no tender feelings. All they care about are the facts, and status. Only if they get souls, or parts of souls, as I did, do they start being at all feeling, and then it's not certain. If Demon Xanth had heeded his half soul, he'd have saved the child himself."

"I was afraid of that," Astrid said sadly.

"Well, let's go about our business, and think about it," Ease said. "We have a day and night to think of something."

What else could they do? They split up and went about their various tasks.

Astrid, left alone, wandered into the Playground to see how the children were doing. To her surprise they were not playing on the swings, slides, see-saws, or merry-go-round. They were gathered by the stage, deep in discussion.

She approached them. "Is there a problem? I thought you would be having fun."

"There is a problem," Firenze said. "Saving Xanth."

"We want to do our part," Santo said.

"That's nice," Astrid said. "But that kind of responsibility is for adults. We don't want to burden you children with it."

"We know how Xanth can end," Firenze said. "We were there, in the future. We're here now because of it. We don't want the same thing to happen here."

"We told Squid about what happened," Santo said.

"Fornax saved me," Squid agreed. "Now they're mad at her."

"That is true," Astrid agreed. "She was supposed to stay out of it. But I asked her to help, and she did."

"Have you come up with something?" Squid asked.

"Only arguments I fear will be rejected," Astrid confessed.

"We want to help you find the right one," Win said.

"But this is too complicated for—"

"So we're making a Play," Myst said.

Astrid considered this. "So the Playground will enhance your group power," she said, working it out. "So you can guide me to the best argument."

All five children nodded.

Astrid realized that it just might work. She needed to formulate the most effective argument to save Fornax, and thus Squid, and Xanth. The Playground might know. Certainly it was a better prospect than her confused pondering.

She was suddenly overwhelmed with gratitude. "Thank you, children," she said, dissolved into tears.

They clustered around her reassuringly. She opened her mouth to warn them not to get too close, then saw they they were all holding their breath.

They knew. She had to smile.

Then they retreated. "But we'll need an audience," Firenze said. "The Playground thinks a play is not complete without an audience."

"The Playground is correct," Astrid said. "I will be your audience."

"Thank you!" the children chorused, then went back to their huddle.

Astrid remained touched by the children's effort. They had given up their playing time to pitch in on the main problem, showing surprising maturity. They were good children. But were they readily adoptable? Firenze's dramatic temper, Santo's formidable and sometimes dangerous talent, Squid's alien nature. Even the two smallest, Win and Myst, might have problems, because the perpetual wind at Win's back tended to blow things away from her, and Myst, sweet as she was, could escape any discipline she wanted to. Ordinary families might not put up with any of that. So this whole effort could still founder.

The children completed their conference. "We're ready!" Squid called.

"What, no rehearsal?" Astrid asked.

"We know our lines," Santo said.

"It's sort of informal," Firenze explained.

Astrid shrugged. They knew what they were doing.

She took her place as the Audience, while the children mounted the stage. It started with a monologue by Santo, in center stage. "I am Cecil," he announced. "My talent is stealing tea cups. I discovered it when my mother sent me to harvest a cup of butter, but instead I stole our neighbor's butter cup. I couldn't help it; I had cuptomania."

Astrid laughed, recognizing the pun.

"I was getting in trouble where I lived," Cecil continued. "Because I couldn't stop, and the neighbors were running out of tea cups. So I decided to try to make my curse of a talent useful. I got a job as the leader of the Curse Fiends."

Now Firenze joined him. "I am the chief Curse Friend." He had evidently picked up on the fact that they called themselves friends, while others called them fiends. They were human beings, but generally not very friendly to outsiders. "My singing Tea Cup was stolen by an invisible Giant, who used a trumpet mute to silence her so that I did not hear her being taken. Now she's in a gilded cage and forced to sing for the giant. I need to get her back."

"I will steal her back," Cecil said.

"See that you do," the chief said gruffly.

Cecil walked around the stage, evidently looking for the lost Tea Cup. He came across Squid, who was singing "La-la-la" prettily.

"Excuse me, have you seen a Singing Tea Cup?" Cecil asked.

"I am the Singing Tea Cup," she said, forming briefly into a large cup.

"But I thought it was a—"

"I am an A-cup," she said. "I wish I were a D-cup. The giant promised I could be a D if I took a deep enough breath. *D* is for Deep. Is it working?" She took a deep breath.

Astrid hesitated to applaud the humor, uncertain whether the children knew the adult implication. They might have heard a woman fussing about her cup size and put it in as incidental dialogue.

"But you're beautiful the way you are," Cecil said.

"I am? Thank you!" She kissed him on the cheek. "My talent is to make all kinds of teas, but it helps to have big enough cups."

"I am here to rescue you from captivity by the big bad giant," Cecil said.

"Oh, he's not so bad. He treats me as well as the Curse Fiend did."

"You don't want to be rescued?"

"Oh, sure. But going from one cage to another isn't rescue. I want to be free to go wherever I want, do anything I want, and have a nice romance. Maybe with you."

"Well—" Cecil began uncertainly.

"Then it's decided! Let's run away to some far-off place where nobody will even find us. Then we can kiss all we want to."

"I don't know—"

She looked at him challengingly. Astrid realized that there was a fine actress in the making, considering that she was only six years old. "Do I have to kiss you again?"

"No!" Cecil said quickly. "I'll do it. We'll flee to a distant land."

The two held hands and ran around the stage.

"Fee fi fo fum!" Win and Myst cried together, using their cupped hands. The wind and mist of their talents amplified it impressively. "I smell the stink of a thieving bum!"

"The giant's after us!" Tea Cup cried in alarm.

"Let's hide behind that Blessing bush," Cecil said. "He won't look there."

"Why not?"

"Because he's making a cursory search."

Astrid stifled a groan. Cursory—curse-ory. Anathema to a blessing bush.

Indeed, the invisible giant was cursing: "Fee fi fo fum!"

They ran to hide behind Win, who was now playing the part of the Blessing. Sure enough, the giant tromped all around the stage, as Myst made the sounds of his footfalls, but never looked there. He tromped away, surely frustrated.

"But what about our deal!" the Curse Friend Chief demanded. "I want my Tea Cup back!"

Cecil sighed. "That was the deal."

"Maybe this will fix it," Tea Cup said. She picked several leaves from the Blessing and swallowed them. Then she walked toward the Chief.

"Ugh!" the Chief exclaimed. "You're Blessed. I'm a Curse Friend. I can't stand you!"

"Then I'll go," Tea Cup agreed. "So as not to cause you further distress."

"And they'll probably live happily ever after," the Chief grumbled as they departed.

The Play was over. The actors gathered at center stage and formally bowed to the audience. Astrid applauded vigorously; she really was impressed.

"Now we can help you," Firenze said, satisfied.

"Well, I'm not sure exactly how," Astrid said. "Some of my arguments are complicated."

"We don't need to understand them," Santo said. "We just need to hear them. Then we'll know."

It did seem worth a try. The children sat on the edge of the stage, dangling their legs, facing her, listening.

"When I come before the Demon Judges tomorrow," Astrid said, "maybe I'll appeal to their self-interest. Demon Xanth has bet that the Land of Xanth will survive, and he'll lose if it doesn't. So will Demon Nemesis. The Demons' main entertainment seems to be watching the oddities that happen in Xanth. What else would they have to be on, if Xanth was gone? So it makes sense for them to decide to spare Fornax."

The children shook their heads. Their consensus was that this was the wrong course. Bleep! It seemed that saving Xanth was one thing, and saving the child was another, and it was the latter that this particular case was about.

"Well, I can argue that though she's technically in violation, she did it for a good reason. To save a child. That should override the appeal of winning the Demon Bet."

They shook their heads again. Bleep once more. The technicality trumped the good reason.

"Well, there's what I learned from Fornax, about the utter boredom and loneliness of being a Demon. They have to vie for Demon Points because that's the only way to ease that boredom. If they want to find some meaning in their bleak immortal existences, they need to do what Fornax is doing, and start doing things for emotional reasons."

But again the children were negative. It seemed that most Demons were not into emotions, regardless of their benefits.

"Or maybe simply because decency is its own reward."

Still no. It wasn't that Demons were indecent; they simply had no concern about the subject.

"But what else is there?" Astrid exploded. "There's got to be some argument that will convince them."

The children shook their heads.

"*No* argument will convince them?" she asked, appalled.

Firenze jumped dawn and came to her. "There's a way," he said. "We feel it. You just haven't found it yet."

"No argument works, but there is a way?"

"Yes."

Astrid considered it, frustrated. "Maybe I am phrasing the question wrong. Suppose I say it how can I best forward my case? Instead of which argument could prevail? Would that make a difference?"

The children nodded yes.

This was odd. Could such a small technical difference change the outcome? The two questions were essentially similar. Well, if it offered hope, she'd take it. "Very well. Let me run through my arguments again, with that in mind."

She did, and the children remained negative. Except for one: that Fornax had acted to save the child.

"But the Demons will reject that!" Astrid protested. "We've already verified that. A mortal human might accept it, especially a woman, especially a mother, but these are inhuman males."

Yet that was the one. Her best course was to put forward an argument that she knew the Demons would reject.

Astrid shook her head, bemused. "Since I have no better alternative, I'll do it. But I fear your guidance has gone haywire."

"We don't understand it either," Firenze said. "But we feel its rightness."

"At any rate, thank you for your help, all of you," Astrid said. "I really appreciate your effort."

"We like you, Astrid," Squid said. "And you're doing it to save me. And Xanth."

"Hold your breath," Astrid said. "I'm about to get all mushy." She picked up the child and hugged her, briefly.

Then they left the Playground, folded it up, and returned to the camp.

"I have an approach," Astrid announced to the others. "I can't say I'm confident, but it has been approved by the Playground, for what that's worth."

"We haven't really tested the Playground," Kandy said. "Let's hope it proves out."

"Exactly what did it say?" Merge asked.

Astrid described the play and the following test of arguments. "So I'm going to remind them that Fornax acted to save a child. Then they will vote against Fornax. But somehow it will work out. If the Playground is correct."

"There's an adage that if you don't have something good to say, say nothing," Art said. "So I will shut up, and go paint a picture."

The others followed his lead, except that they didn't paint any pictures. Meanwhile they went about their business, checking for the pun virus and taking care of children. It all would have been perfectly ordinary, but for the looming Demon decision.

The next day as the hour approached they sat in a circle with the children and waited. What would happen would happen.

The Demon court appeared. Xanth was on one side, in the form of Nimby the Dragon Ass, buttressed by his lovely mortal human wife Chlorine and handsome fifteen-year-old crossbreed son Nimbus. Fornax was on the other side, in lovely human semblance, alone. That seemed horribly symbolic.

"Prosecution, make your case," Nemesis said.

Kandy stood. "There are many arguments that can be made about mitigating circumstances. But we are here to judge a narrow issue: did Demoness Fornax intervene in the Land of Xanth by saving the life of a child who would otherwise have died? Did she thus mess up the natural course of a Demon Wager? The answer is clear: she did. That child." She indicated Squid, who now sat with Ease. "Fornax is guilty. That's all there is to it." Kandy sat down again, beside Squid, who took her hand. Her eyes were dry, but Astrid knew she was weeping inside. She really liked Squid, and hated having to argue the case for her death.

"Defense, make your case," Nemesis said impassively.

Astrid stood. "There is no doubt Fornax is guilty," she said. "The question is why did she do it? That requires a little bit of history. When Kandy agreed to serve as Fornax's intermediary in the Land of Xanth, she did it in order to save my life. It was a business deal for Fornax, but an act of friendship for Kandy, and I am alive today because of that friendship. In the interim I have also become the friend of Fornax. When one of the children we fetched from the future was about to die, I appealed to Fornax to save her, and she did. This was not a business deal, but an act of friendship on Fornax's part. It also safeguards the program we have instituted to save the Land of Xanth from destruction in fifty years, to which the five children are integral. Without them Xanth will perish. So Fornax, for the sake of friendship, acted against her own interest, because she stands to win her Demon Wager if the Land of Xanth is destroyed. Friendship can be like this."

Astrid paused to formulate her continuing case. She saw Chlorine and Nimbus react, glancing at each other, then at Squid, who smiled uncertainly. Apparently they had not known about the peril Xanth was in, or Fornax's part in rescuing it; the Demon Xanth had not felt they needed that information. Not that it mattered; they were not among the judges.

"So if there is such a thing as mitigating circumstances, they apply to what Fornax did. She acted from friendship and with decency, and I think should be applauded rather than condemned. But she did do it. The decision is in your hands."

Astrid sat down, ending her case. Was it sufficient? She doubted it, but it was the best she could do. The three Demon Judges seemed absolutely unmoved.

"The judges will now render their Decision," Nemesis said. "Demon Earth?"

"Guilty."

"Demon Jupiter?"

"Guilty."

"And I also vote—" Demon Nemesis broke off. "Yes, Demon Xanth?"

"My wife and son have required me to drop the case," Xanth said, evidently somewhat nettled. "Accordingly, I withdraw the charge."

"Case is dropped. Court is adjourned," Nemesis said, and the three Judges vanished, leaving only Chlorine, Nimbus, and Fornax.

"We have no brief for you, Demoness Fornax," Chlorine said. "But we do for the innocent child. And for the future of the Land of Xanth, which is our heritage. We are annoyed that my husband did not save the child, though that would have constituted interference in the Wager on his part, so we understand. We thank you for doing what you did on our behalf."

"And we will remember," Nimbus said. Then Chlorine and Nimbus vanished.

Astrid was amazed. The Demons had been in the act of voting against Fornax, as expected. But Chlorine was human, and Nimbus half-human. They cared about children, and the future, which was their future too. And they had made the difference.

The Playground had been correct. This argument had accomplished Astrid's purpose.

Squid got up and walked across to Fornax. "Thank you for saving me," she said.

Fornax smiled, and it seemed genuine. "You're welcome."

But the child did not let it go there. "Why did you do it?"

"I am trying to learn the values of souled creatures. They don't let children die."

"Oh." Squid seemed disappointed.

"And we had to save you to keep our project going."

"Yes." She still did not seem much enthused.

Astrid realized that Fornax needed some help, as she did not understand the feeling of small mortal children. *And she's cute*, she thought.

"And you're cute."

"Oh!" Squid liked that answer better.

And she's like you, in her isolation.

"And you are an alien creature in a human realm, just as I am an alien matter creature in a terrene realm."

Squid was able to pick up enough of that. "You're like me!"

"Yes. I know what it's like."

"It's scary and lonely," Squid said.

"Yes it is," the Demoness agreed.

"But I'm getting new friends. That helps."

"So am I. It does help."

"Can I hug you?"

"That would be dangerous. Will you accept a virtual hug?"

"What is that?"

"I will make an image, like a ghost. You can hug that, carefully."

"Okay."

A ghostly image of Fornax appeared before her. It reached down to the child. Squid put her little arms around it, not quite touching, and hugged. Then she let go and backed away.

"If you ever visit my galaxy," Fornax said, "I have a castle there that is terrene. There I can assume terrene form. Then I would be able to hug you for real, and give you eye scream and chocolate cake."

The Demoness was learning.

"It's a date," Squid said enthusiastically.

Astrid saw tears in Kandy's eyes. That was not surprising; they were in her own eyes too.

CHAPTER 7:
DUNGEONS

~~~

"Now we need to get serious about the adoptions," Kandy said. "Before—"

"Before anything else happens," Astrid agreed.

"How should we go about this? Range out across Xanth looking for promising couples? That does seem a bit—"

"A bit too practical," Astrid agreed. "These aren't bricks to be laid down in a foundation; they're living, feeling children."

"Hey, are you a brick?" Win asked Myst.

"A foggy one," Myst replied, dissolving into a roughly brick-shaped little cloud.

"I'll blow you away!" Win put her face down so that the wind behind her pushed at the mist. Myst quickly returned to human, laughing.

"Maybe we should ask the Playground," Squid said. "It worked before."

A glance circled around, too high for the children but touching most of the adult eyes. "It did indeed," Astrid agreed. "Though not the way we expected. This seems chancy. Maybe we should ponder it another day, then—"

Now the glance descended and circled around the children's eyes. "Let's see," Firenze said.

The children drew together, linked hands, and focused. And fell apart as if shocked. "Maybe not," Squid gasped.

"What happened?" Astrid asked, concerned.

Firenze sighed. "It's, well, it's the best and worst idea. Double or nothing. If we win, we win everything. If we lose, we lose everything. It's scary."

"What, just deciding whether to wait a day before deciding whether to query the Playground?" Kandy asked.

"Not exactly," Firenze said. "There's something big. We don't know what it is."

"We have to ask the Playground to find out," Santo said. "But then we'll be in it, and it'll be happening."

"Then maybe you should stay out," Kandy said. "That Playground's sort of spooky anyway."

"No, that's worse," Win said.

"We can't wait," Myst agreed.

"This makes me nervous," Art said. "How can we be sure that all that magic in the Playground really is on our side?"

"It's neutral," Firenze said. "It doesn't care who uses it."

"It's not the Playground that's scary," Santo said. "Just—"

"Just what?" Astrid asked sharply.

"It's like stepping in a hole," Squid said. "The hole doesn't care; it's just there."

"But it can be dangerous," Santo said.

"Let me see if I have this straight," Astrid said. "Something's afoot, and the Playground relates, but it's not the Playground we need to worry about?"

Again the children fidgeted. "Not exactly," Firenze said.

"We don't have to worry about a hole," Firenze said. "If we're careful of it."

"But whatever it is," Kandy said, "will just get worse if we wait, even for a day? Like a hole that's growing?"

All the children nodded.

"Then we'd better act," Ease said. He generally favored action, whatever the situation.

Again the children nodded.

Astrid glanced at Fornax, who stood in ghostly guise. *I am aware of something, but may not tell you, lest I be guilty of interfering again.*

Certainly that was to be avoided. The last call had been entirely too close. "Let's compromise," Astrid said. "Let me and the children go in, as before, and put on a playlet, as before, and then consider this question again. Get the answer, then get out quickly, before whatever it is strikes. Then we should be better prepared."

"While the rest of us stand guard outside," Kandy agreed. "At least we'll have better information."

"I guess," Santo said uncertainly. He brought out the matchbox.

"Wait!" Astrid said. "We don't have a Play to give yet."

"We'll think of one," Firenze said.

The other children pitched in and soon had the Playground unfolded beside the camp.

"Let's do it," Astrid said. She was not at all comfortable with this, but wanted some resolution soon.

She and the five children walked into the Playground while the others watched. It was clear that nobody was easy about this, but no one had a better course of action to suggest. Fornax walked invisibly beside Astrid, looking uncomfortable. She wanted to speak, but didn't dare. Astrid couldn't blame her, after the close call of the Demon trial; any transgression would be caught and punished.

The Playground was exactly as before, with nothing out of order. They approached the stage. "Now we need a Play," Santo said.

But before they could devise anything, something else happened. The edges of the Playground curled up as if tweaked by unknown hands.

"It's happening!" Win cried.

"Get out of here!" Astrid snapped, urging the children back toward the entrance. "Before it closes up! Run!"

But the entrance was already curling worse than the rest. Their escape was blocked. This was clearly a trap; they were to be folded into the matchbox.

Astrid didn't know whether they would survive that. The normal furnishings, such as the swings, slides, and stage, were obviously made to handle it. But what about living things? Best not to risk it.

Was there any alternative? Maybe.

"This way!" she cried, herding them to the DO NOT ENTER section beside the stage. They all piled in as the folding closed around the stage, crumpling it along marked lines, like cardboard.

And there they were in the Storage chamber, where the Mad Birds battled the Nasty Prigs. Astrid was relieved to see that no folding was occurring here. Maybe that was the design, to protect living creatures when the Playground was not in use. They were safe for the moment.

But how were they to escape, if the Playground beyond was becoming a matchbox?

"Mad Birds," Win said, looking around. "Neat."

"This is where they are stored," Firenze said. "They just go right on fighting the prigs, when off-duty."

"Can we go back now?" Myst asked. "I have to poop." She could say the word when it was literal, just not when invoked as a cussword.

Astrid hastily checked the DO NOT EXIT pavement beside them. She stepped on it, but it did not budge. That suggested that there was no escape there. She controlled her alarm. "Not yet."

"I can't wait," Myst said, beginning to cry.

"Change into mist and do it then," Squid suggested.

"Okay, don't blow me away." Myst changed and hovered as a little cloud. After a generous moment a small blob of mist separated and floated off. Then she changed back, her business accomplished.

Meanwhile Firenze was looking around. "No exit?" he asked Astrid quietly.

She nodded grimly. "It probably won't open until the Playground gets unfolded. That's actually for our safety. We could be stuck here for some time."

"We'd better consult," he said. Then he addressed the other children. "It's happened. Now we know what it's about: we're caught inside the Playground Storage chamber. We can't go back the way we came. It smells like a trap."

"We knew it was coming," Santo said. "But not how to handle it. At least it's not so bad."

"Is there another way out?" Squid asked.

Firenze spread his hands.

"I could make a hole," Santo said.

"Caution," Astrid said quickly. "That could be like punching a hole in a balloon, when we're floating inside the balloon." The other children winced, understanding the analogy. If the Playground blew out or collapsed through a hole...

"It could," he agreed. "I'll stick to small holes, when we need them."

"So then how to we get out?" Squid asked.

"Let's consider a direction," Astrid said. "You can link hands and decide whether it's right."

"You point," Firenze said. "We'll decide. Directions are simple; we don't need to enhance our power with a play or anything."

That was a relief. Astrid pointed randomly. The children grouped and reacted. "Cold," Myst said.

She pointed a quarter to the right. "Warmer."

Another quarter turn. "Hot."

"Then I think we'll go this way, since it seems there is a way out," she said. "But stay together, because we don't know what else we'll encounter, here in Storage. There could be dragons, trolls, or goblins."

"Maybe we'd better figure out how to handle those, just in case," Firenze said.

"I could make holes in them," Santo said.

"Perhaps you should wait on that," Astrid said. "I can handle most creatures with a simple stare. We can warn them, then stare them, and if that doesn't do it, then you can hole them."

"Okay," Santo said. "Just tell me when. I can get in trouble when I do it on my own."

"I'll bet," Firenze said, smiling. "Same way I can get in trouble when I get mad."

"Yeah," Santo said, smiling back. The two boys seemed to like each other. One was a natural leader, the other a potentially deadly antagonist. It was best that they get along well.

Astrid started walking across the plain, and the children followed. The three girls were in the middle, the two boys at the back. The mad birds and prigs ignored them; they weren't part of that game.

They passed a clump of pie plants. "Meal break," Astrid announced. "We're lucky this is here."

"It's part of making the path good," Firenze said.

So it was no coincidence. That made sense. The right route needed not only to get them out, but to safeguard them along the way. The children's ability to sense the right course, even without the enhancement of the Playground, was increasingly impressing her.

They filled up on redberry, blueberry, and yellowberry pies, together with little cups of soda pop that popped vigorously when drunk. Other children found places in the bushes to do their stuff. They rested briefly; then, refreshed, resumed their walk.

"I wish I knew what you are thinking, friend," Astrid murmured to ghostly Fornax.

"I wish I could tell you," Fornax replied.

Astrid got an idea. "But maybe I can guess. There could be a Demon behind this ploy, arranging to get trolls or some such to steal the Playground and keep us prisoner, making it seem like a natural event so you can't act to stop it without disqualifying yourself."

Fornax was studiedly neutral.

"And I'm guessing that that Demon is Nemesis, who will let us go only if you agree to become his plaything."

Fornax made no expression, but her image seemed to be giving off a wisp of steam.

"Because he has seen how you have made yourself vulnerable by forming a friendship with a souled person or two, and learning to value the lives of mortal children. To him that's foolish weakness."

"I must depart for a while," the demoness said, and faded out before the steam further intensified.

Astrid glanced around. "Not that she told us anything."

"Not," the children agreed almost together.

"You know, I don't care much about big or little D Demons one way o the other," Santo said. "But I think if I tried hard enough, I could get to like that one."

"I already like her," Squid said.

"So do I," Astrid agreed.

The path led to a trench slanting downward to a closed door. On the door was printed the word DUNGEON.

Astrid paused, not wholly positive about this. "I'm not sure we want to enter a dungeon."

"But it's the way out," Win protested.

"That's not typical of dungeons," Astrid said. "They are better known for having no way out."

"We don't think there is any other way out," Firenze said. "We know it looks bad, and we may not like it much, but that's the route."

"Our alternative being to remain among the mad birds and prigs indefinitely," Astrid said with a sigh. "Hoping that whoever folded up the park and stole the matchbox will change his mind and let us go."

"Not if it means someone else gets bleeped," Firenze said.

"Ooo!" Win and Myst said together. "You tried to swear!"

He glanced at them. "When I get older I'll swear a blue steak if I want to." A blue streak stabbed from his forehead, exploding into a blue fireball.

"So will we," Win said enthusiastically. "Or at least a pink streak." Then she glanced at Astrid. "Can big girls swear?"

Astrid smiled. "Yes, if they have reason."

"So do we go down?" Squid asked.

Astrid sighed again. "Yes, I think we have to. But stay close to me, in case I have to stare someone. And you be ready with a limited hole, when I tell you, Santo."

"Yes'm," the boy agreed.

Astrid stepped down inside the trench, the children following. They reached the DUNGEON door. It had a big handle. Would there be a similar one inside, that they could work to get out again? Well, Santo could make a hole in the door if he needed to.

Then she thought of something else. "Myst, if you had to go through a solid door like this one, could you mist out and do it?"

"Not through the wood. But I could mist through the keyhole, or under the door."

"That will probably do. I'm just making sure we can't be trapped inside."

"We can't be," Santo agreed.

Astrid worked the handle. It moved, and the door swung inward. Inside was a cave lighted by burning torches. It wasn't clear what fuel they burned; maybe they were magic. At least their party could see where they were going.

Not that it helped much. The cave was huge, with many passages leading away and down. They could readily get lost in it. They were already lost to a degree; there was no sense and making it worse.

"Where do we go from here?" Astrid asked somewhat rhetorically.

The children got together, briefly linking hands. "That way," Firenze said, pointing to a reasonably obscure opening in a wall. "Except—"

There were too many excepts! But Astrid tackled it. "Except what?"

"There's danger. But the other routes are worse."

"The last time we took a course with danger, we got folded up into the Playground," Astrid said severely.

"We're sorry," Squid said.

Astrid was immediately sorry herself. "It's not your fault, dear." She glanced at the other children. "None of your faults. We discussed it, and the adults agreed. We risked it, and paid the price, because we really didn't have much choice. A Demon may be messing us up, indirectly. But it is annoying."

The children stood silently, waiting for her to finish. So she did. "We'll go that route. Do you have any idea what the danger is?"

"Just all around," Squid said.

"Then stay close to me and be alert. If you see me taking off my glasses, do not look at my face. You know why."

"We know," Myst said.

Astrid marched into the opening, the children close behind. Almost immediately there was a problem: it was dark. Astrid could handle darkness, especially in her native form, but she wasn't sure about the children. "Um, maybe we should take a torch."

They backed out and Astrid went to take the nearest burning torch. It wouldn't come. It was fixed in place. "Bleep," she muttered.

"I can help," Santo said.

"Do it," Astrid said, stepping back.

Santo pointed at the base of the torch. It disappeared, and he neatly caught the torch as it dropped. "I made a hole the same size as the base," he explained. "So there was nothing there to hold it anymore." He proffered the torch to her.

"Keep it," Astrid said. "You can be our torchbearer." But privately she wondered what would happen if he made a similar hole in someone's neck. He might be as dangerous to others as Astrid herself was.

He picked up on her expression. "I know. My talent can be dangerous. So I don't use it much."

"The way I don't use mine," she agreed, squeezing his shoulder.

"Yeah. I guess you understand." He grimaced. "I'm not very adoptable."

"We'll find someone," she said, hoping it was true.

They resumed their progress through the cave passage, now with light. It wound deviously around as if trying to lose them, before opening out into a rock garden. All manner of intriguing minerals were displayed: garnets, streaks of copper, silver, gold, and sparkling faceted gemstones.

"It's a mine," Firenze said, impressed.

"For when they need something in a game," Santo agreed.

"Hey—who are you?" a gruff voice demanded behind them.

They turned as a group to discover a squat ugly goblin male, redundant as the description was.

"We are just travelers passing through," Astrid said.

"Well, get out of here. This is restricted territory."

"We would like to," Astrid said. "What is the best route out?"

"Anywhere that isn't here, slut. And give back that torch you stole, brat."

Astrid reined in her ire. This actually was what passed for politeness, goblin style.

Santo frowned. "Stole? We need it for light."

"Too bad, creep. Give it back." The goblin reached for the torch.

Firenze stepped in, knowing that insulting either Santo or Astrid was dangerous. "You are beginning to annoy me, goblin. Don't do that. You wouldn't like me when I'm annoyed."

"Yeah, bleep for brains?"

"Yeah." Firenze's face began to change color. Astrid did not rein him in.

"Well, can it, fizzle face. You're in goblin country. Make any trouble and you'll wind up in the cook pot."

Fireworks began erupting from Firenze's head. "Are you sure you want to annoy me, poop face?"

The goblin gazed at the erupting display and reconsidered. He backed off. "I'll be back," he promised as he retreated.

The other children dissolved into laughter. "You sure fried *him*," Win said gleefully.

"Well played, Firenze," Astrid said. "But we are indeed in goblin country, and had better move on before he returns with a gaggle of goblins."

They moved on, passing the mining outcrops. "What's a slut?" Myst asked.

"A goblin insult for any girl," Astrid said. "Don't use that term yourself."

"Oh, like jerk for a boy."

"Close enough," Astrid agreed.

The route led down to an underground lake. It was surrounded by stone walls; there was no way around it. There did seem to be a continuation of the route beyond it. "Ooo, we can swim!" Squid exclaimed, dipping her toe.

Immediately a fin appeared, slicing through the dark water, and teeth snapped as she yanked her foot back. This was evidently not a people-swimming lake.

Now there was a clamor behind them. The goblin horde had gathered and was in pursuit. "I think we need to get across that lake," Astrid said. "Promptly."

"How?" Firenze asked.

"There's a raft," Santo said. So there was, moored at the water's edge. It had small rails around the edge and a mast in the center with a furled sail.

"But no paddle," Myst said. "And we can't even use our hands."

The clamor behind them was growing rapidly louder. It sounded like not a few, but a few hundred angry goblins. Way too many to stop without considerable carnage, assuming she could Glare them all. Astrid knew she had to think of something in a hurry.

"Win," she said. "Can you increase the wind at your back?"

"Sure, but it really messes up my hair."

"You look cute with your hair forward," Santo said.

"Really?" Win was pleased.

"Get on the raft," Astrid told them urgently. They piled on, sitting in the center except for Win at the edge, facing in. She joined them there, and cast off just as the goblins burst onto the scene. "Unfurl the sail, boys." Firenze and Santo did so, with Astrid taking the torch. "Increase the wind," she told Win. "A lot."

Suddenly a blast of air passed the child and filled the sail. Astrid feared it would blow out the torch, but the torch clung desperately to its fire. Maybe it had come up against high winds before and knew how to balk them. The raft leaped forward, tilting dangerously.

"They're getting away!" a goblin cried angrily. The others milled about, keeping their toes clear of the water.

"Why aren't they throwing their spears?" Squid asked, looking back.

"'Cause they don't want to lose them in the water," Firenze said.

That seemed to be so. The goblins watched helplessly as the raft fairly skidded across the lake. "You'll be soor-ry!" a goblin called.

Myst made a face and waggled her hands at her ears, teasing the goblins. "Nyaa nyaa, blips!"

"Ooo, what you said!" Squid said appreciatively.

"Well, I can't say bleep yet." Then she looked surprised. "Did I say it?"

"You don't need to," Astrid said. "But just so you know, you can't say it as swearing, because of the Adult Conspiracy. But you can say it as a technical term. That's not swearing. Just as you children are able to say Poop as long as it's descriptive and not cussing."

"That's weird," Squid said.

"The whole Adult Conspiracy is weird," Firenze said. "When I grow up I'm going to get rid of it."

"Yea!" The other children applauded.

Astrid did not comment. Somehow, no matter how determined they were to eliminate it, when children grew up they joined the Conspiracy. That was part of its weirdness.

"Why did they think we'd be sorry?" Santo asked.

"Maybe they were just trying to scare us," Firenze said.

Again, Astrid did not comment. She feared the goblins weren't bluffing. What was waiting for them?

"Is there something down below?" Myst asked. "I see a dim glow."

"Some seaweed is phosphorescent," Astrid said. "That is, it glows."

"Neat! I want some."

"But the sharks are in the way," Firenze reminded her. "They think little girls are the tastiest."

"Blip."

They reached the far side. "Douse the wind," Astrid told Win. The gale shut down, leaving the girl with only her normal flutter of hair in her face.

The raft nudged the bank. There was a tying post there. But before they could disembark, there was a scuttling sound. Astrid poked the torch forward, its flickering light showing what was there. Oh, no!

"Nickelpedes!" Firenze said. "They'll gouge out nickel-sized disks of our flesh!"

"Now we know," Santo said.

They sat on the raft, just offshore, as the vicious insects thronged at the brink, clicking their pincers. It was definitely not safe to land.

"I think we need to think of something else," Santo said grimly. "I could make a hole through them, but it would just fill in from the sides."

"I could poke them with the torch," Astrid said. "But there would be the same problem. Same difficulty with Staring them; only those that met my gaze would die, and they really don't use eyesight much."

"Maybe I can help," Squid said. "I can swim pretty well. I could fetch some of that seaweed."

"From the lake?" Astrid asked. "Don't even think of it."

But Firenze was more understanding. "Your ancestors are sea folk."

"Mocktopuses," she agreed. "We can imitate more things than people. I can look like a poisonous snake. The sharks will scare."

This was interesting. "But what use is seaweed? The glow won't bother the nickelpedes."

"Where I come from, glowing things are poisonous. Maybe they are here too."

"But would the nickelpedes be stupid enough to eat it?"

"And some taste good," Squid said. "Creatures eat them, and they die, and then the seaweed eats them. Maybe this is that kind."

"But the sharks aren't dead," Santo said.

"Do sharks eat greens?"

Santo laughed. "I don't think so. I get your point: anything that does eat the seaweed maybe dies."

"Like nickelpedes," she agreed.

"Maybe you have something here," Astrid said. "But since you aren't poisonous, I think it's too risky for you to go down there."

"I wonder," Firenze said. "How poisonous can you look, Squid?"

Squid dissolved into the semblance of a cobra with a bright orange bra. She hissed and struck at him. The other children screamed, and he almost fell into the water. Astrid was amazed; the child did indeed look deadly.

"I don't like to have you take such a risk, but maybe it will do," Astrid said. "You certainly scared us."

"Okay," the cobra said, and slithered into the water, where it became a brightly colored poisonous jellyfish.

Fins converged, hesitated, then retreated. They knew poison when they saw it.

They waited tensely while Squid was below, out of sight. How long could she hold her breath? Or did she need to?

Then a mass of glowing seaweed floated up. It had a sweet, pleasant smell, like fresh candy. Firenze reached for it, but hesitated. "Is it poisonous to touch, or just to eat?"

"Both," Squid's voice answered from the middle of the mass. "I'll do it."

The seaweed moved to the bank. Then Squid jumped to the rack, in her octopus form, hauling seaweed after her. She ran among the nickelpedes, dragging the weed along so that it formed a long double string behind her.

"How can she handle it, then?" Firenze asked.

"I'm immune, silly!" she called.

The nickelpedes seemed briefly taken aback by this spectacle. Then they rallied and pounced on the glowing, tasty-smelling seaweed, gouging out chunks of it to consume. For at least a moment and a half they reveled in this unexpected meal.

Then they started screaming. Astrid was startled; she had never heard a nickelpede scream before. They writhed, waving their claws about. Some rolled over on their backs, dying.

It did not take the rest long to catch on. They retreated. In another half moment the flickering torchlight showed no living nickelpedes. Squid had cleared the field.

The little girl reformed. She walked to the water, jumped in, then out again, rinsing off. "I did it!" she said, pleased.

"You sure did," Santo said. "My talent can be dangerous. So is Aunt Astrid's. Welcome to the club."

Aunt Astrid? Well, why not? "Congratulations, Squid," she said. "You may have saved our lives."

"I was just lucky it was poisonous," Squid said modestly.

They walked on along the seaweed path, careful not to touch any of it with anything but their shoes. Soon it gave out, but the nickelpedes did not reappear; they had been thoroughly traumatized. Then Astrid corrected her thought, for the benefit of the children, in case she had to explain: scared, rather than traumatized.

They came to another subterranean, or rather, underground river. Rivers seemed to serve as the boundaries between sections of the dungeon. This one also had a raft, but it was moored on the other side. It seemed that no one stayed long in the nickelpede domain. Astrid was sure it wasn't safe to swim.

"I can fetch it," Squid said eagerly.

"If you can do it safely," Astrid said.

"I can cover her," Santo said. "I can put a hole in any fin that comes after her."

"You won't need to," Squid said. She jumped into the water, assuming the likeness of a shark. When the fins converged, all they saw was one of their own kind.

"Neat," Santo said.

"I heard that!" the shark called back.

But that alerted the real sharks that there was something different about this one. They converged—and sheared off, because Squid had released a cloud of black. Not only did it conceal her, it looked downright inedible, if not dangerous. It was evidently another trick of her species.

"That's neat too," Santo murmured, keeping his voice low.

The raft bobbed as it was untied. Then it moved toward them. Squid was pushing it from below. Soon it came up against the near bank, and Astrid caught its rope. "We've got it," she called.

Squid popped up. "That was fun. I never was able to do that much before."

"You are a creature of many talents," Astrid said. "Some family will be lucky to have you."

Squid frowned as she flopped out of the water. "I don't want to go to some family. I want to stay with all of you."

"You'll stay with us, via the Playground," Santo said. "Wherever you are."

"I guess," Squid said unenthusiastically.

"We have to save Xanth," Firenze said, almost regretfully.

They boarded the raft, and Win blew them across, as before. There was no wind behind her; it seemed to form at her back and blow forward.

Now they faced a new network of passages. The children linked hands and concentrated on one, and they walked that way. But they were nervous; danger remained.

This tunnel opened into a large cavern with many stalactites and stalagmites. Some connected to each other, but most were separated, looking like huge long teeth. Astrid remembered that the way to tell the names apart was the center letter: if it was a C, that meant Ceiling, hanging from, while G meant Ground, rising from. It was also somewhat like an odd forest that had only tree trunks and parts of tree trunks, no foliage.

There was an ear-wincing scream. "Fresh meat!"

"Oh, bleep!" Astrid swore. "Harpies! They'll attack soon."

"And no seaweed," Firenze said.

Santo glanced at Astrid. "Your talent or mine?"

"I hate to start killing anything, even harpies," Astrid said. "But they can be the most unreasonable fowl."

"Foul fowl," Santo said, and the girls tittered.

Now one of the dirty birds showed, clinging to a stalactite with her talons. She had the head and chest of a woman, and the wings and claws of a vulture, and she was supremely dirty and ugly.

"I can help," Myst said.

"Dear, mist won't stop these nasty creatures," Astrid said.

"Yes it will."

More harpies showed, surrounding the little human party. There was no way to run.

Astrid had learned not to dismiss the children's offerings too quickly. "Can you tell us how?"

"I can do different kinds of mist. Different colors. Different things."

The harpies started to spread their wings, ready to launch downward.

"Such as?" Astrid asked patiently as the flutter of a gathering mob threatened.

"Sleep gas."

"Oho!" Firenze said.

"But that would put us to sleep too," Astrid said.

"Not if I blow it away from us," Win said.

"Charge!" a harpy screeched. This launched an ugly flight.

"Do it!" Astrid cried, putting her arms around the other children. That left Win and Myst in front.

Myst transformed into a purple cloud of mist. Win blew her up and forward. The harpies converged on that cloud.

And collided with each other, dropping to the cave floor, dazed or asleep. Those who had not yet plunged saw that and retreated, cursing with bleeps that fairly scorched the stalactites.

"Enough," Astrid called. "You have vanquished them."

The mist coalesced into the little girl, and the breeze eased. "Neat," Myst said.

Astrid hugged her. "Neat," she agreed.

"I'm hungry," Myst said. "I lost some of my stuff."

"In the mist the harpies breathed," Astrid agreed. "We can all use a good meal, and a good rest."

"But it's a long path back to the surface," Santo said.

Astrid considered this. "The harpies must forage above ground. They should know a faster route. We can ask one of them."

"They won't tell us anything," Firenze said. "Or if they do, they'll lie. You can't trust a harpy."

Astrid smiled. "I didn't say we'd ask politely. I'm tired and frustrated, and my basic nature is beginning to surface."

The children looked at her, not getting it.

Astrid picked up a harpy who was stirring, waking up. She held the creature with one hand clamped around her two bird legs. The harpy was solid, but only about a quarter the weight of a human person, and she stank. "Wake up, fowl-face," she said. "We have to talk."

The harpy blinked awake and looked at her. "Go bleep yourself, girl-face."

"First let's introduce ourselves. I am Astrid BC. Who are you?"

The harpy laughed raucously. "Astrid BullCrap? Forget it."

"I would rather not have to be forceful with you," Astrid said evenly. "But the children and I are tired and want to return to the surface now. Is there a shortcut there?"

"Think I'd tell *you*, child nanny? You don't have the bleeping guts to make me do anything."

"What is your name?" Astrid asked.

"You can call me Bleep!" the harpy said, and the air around her crackled with the force of the expletive.

"I will call you Hagar Harpy," Astrid said. "For the purpose of our dialogue, you will answer to that name."

"*What* dialogue?" the harpy cackled. "I'm not telling you anything, except what a naive creep you are."

"Perhaps I need to be more explicit, Hagar. My full name is Astrid Basilisk-Cockatrice."

The harpy screeched in laughter. "You're a bask, sweetface? And I'm the queen of the fairies!"

Astrid used her free hand to remove her dark glasses. She kept one eye closed and the other with only a slit open. She glanced fleetingly at the harpy.

Who stiffened as if stunned. "Oh, for bleep's sake You *are* a bask!"

"I am," Astrid agreed as she replaced her glasses. "The children and I are hungry, and if you are kind enough to show us a quick way to the surface, I will let you go unharmed. Otherwise, we'll make a fire and roast *you* for our meal. I'm sure you won't taste very good, but as I said, we are hungry."

The children were starting to smile, appreciating Astrid's technique.

"It's that way," Hagar said, pointing with a wing. "Now let me go."

"I will let you go when we stand safely on the surface," Astrid said. "Provided that does not take too long."

The harpy let loose a torrent of bleeps that made smoke curl up. But she knew she was caught, and had to cooperate. She guided them up a winding tunnel to a chamber with a closed door similar to the one they had used to enter the Dungeons. It said EXIT. But it had no handle or knob.

"So how do we open it?" Astrid asked.

"From the other side," Hagar screeched. "You can't open it from inside."

"Are you sure?" Astrid asked.

"Yes, I'm sure. We have to call to someone outside to open it for us. So now you can eat me if you're going to. I think you're bluffing."

Santo looked at the door. "I can hole it."

"Let's wait on that," Astrid said. She glanced at Myst. "Your turn," she said.

Myst dissolved into mist and floated under the door. Soon she disappeared. Then in under two moments the door swung inward. There stood Myst, smiling.

"I'll be bleeped!" Hagar screeched.

They walked through the doorway and up out of the slanting trench beyond. "Thank you for your assistance, Hagar," Astrid said, and released the harpy.

The dirty bird didn't hesitate. "Up yours, moron!" She zoomed back down through the doorway and slammed the door shut. There was of course no expression of appreciation for her release.

"Harpies can be reasonable," Astrid said. "You just need to know how to talk to them."

"Yeah," Firenze agreed. "But would you really have—?"

"If there were no other way," Astrid said. "If we could make a fire without fuel to burn." She glanced at the torch she still held. "Maybe the torch would have been enough."

"But eating a harpy?" Squid asked, revolted.

"We do what we have to, to survive," Astrid said. "I suppose I come from a rougher life than you children do. I mean to take care of you as well as I can. That means protecting you, guiding you, loving you, and feeding you."

"You've been doing that," Santo said. "We would never have gotten this far without you."

"We love you too," Win said.

"You'd make a great mother," Squid said, and the other children agreed. Astrid, suddenly choking up, did not comment.

"But remind us never to make you mad," Firenze said. The other children nodded soberly.

"Now let's go find a pie plant," Astrid said briskly, changing the subject. "And a blanket plant. We're not out of the Storage chamber yet. We'll eat and sleep and see where the path leads tomorrow."

"Yeah," Firenze agreed, speaking for all of them.

CHAPTER 8:
WOLF COUNTRY

~~~

They found a pie plant, and a blanket plant, and a clear streamlet to drink from. This was nice country, with tree-covered mountains and verdant slopes.

"Now we can make tents from the blankets," Astrid said. "But I prefer not to sleep out in the open; there could be predators."

"She means hungry monsters," Firenze translated for the other children.

"Also, there may be rain," Astrid said, glancing at the sky where thick clouds were looming. "So let's find some secluded nook."

And there, not far from the pie plant, was exactly that: a grotto set in the side of a mountain slope. That represented shelter from the rain and some safety from marauding night creatures.

There was a pile of fragrant hay that would be perfect for a bed to lie on. Suddenly that was all Astrid wanted to do. She spread blankets over the children as they lay down and slept almost immediately, then settled down herself. She hadn't realized how tired she was from the dungeon experience.

She woke some time later, to darkness. Then she realized that it wasn't the night; she was in a closed hood over her head, and some faint light squeezed through the cloth. Also, her arms were tied behind her. She struggled, but only her legs were free, and without the use of her arms they could not do much.

"Ah, the sleeper wakes," an insidious voice said.

Uh-oh. This was surely mischief. "What?" she asked.

"No need for confusion. I am Fowler Fiend, the hungry and lascivious proprietor of this grotto. I dosed the local stream with sleep potion when I saw your party coming. Diluted, it was slow to act, but that gave you time to come here and make yourselves available, saving me the effort of dragging you here. Your party makes a fine collection of delectable morsels, and you, my dear, will make a very nice entertainment piece until eventually I tire of you."

So this was another solitary male of the same type as Truculent Troll, bent on assorted savageries. One thing about her human form was that it happened to be very pretty in human terms, and that always made human or other humanoid males get a certain notion. She wasn't sure whether that was an asset or a liability for her. It might be better if she could turn it off as convenient. But she couldn't.

Now she understood how they had fallen into his trap: they had been tired and careless after escaping from the dungeons, and never thought to do a check for local danger. So they had eaten and drunk, then slept as the potion caught up with them. And been caught in the fiend's fiendish trap.

"Thank you for that explanation," she said politely. "But I believe it would be better if you gave up your dark designs and simply released us. I am not exactly what I may seem to be."

"You seem to be a luscious maiden shepherding five tasty children," Fowler said. "It hardly matters, considering the use I will make of you."

"You really don't want to do that." What she didn't say was that if he got too close to her, and remained too long, her poisonous perfume would first make him drunk, then kill him. She had taken out a cave troll that way before.

"Oh, pshaw, tart, of course I do. In fact I'll do it now." Rough hands caught her ankles, forcibly spreading her legs. She tried to kick free, but he simply jammed in close and ripped off her clothing. "Ah, lovely! The pleasure will be all mine."

What to do? She could change to her natural form, but her head would still be hooded, rendering her primary weapon moot, and her arms would still be tied. All it would do would be to reveal her nature, and get her quickly killed; the fiend would not risk her Glare. No, it was better to keep this form, accepting the fiend's assault if need be, so as to render him unconscious in due course. Then she would be able to see about working her hands free. At least the children would be safe until she untied them.

"What's happening?" That was Firenze's voice, as he woke. The sleep potion seemed to have affected the larger people least, or maybe they had not drunk as much as the others had.

Oh, no! What a violation of the Adult Conspiracy it would be for him to be aware of the rape! She had to protect him from that.

"We drank sleeping potion, and have been captured by a fiend," she called. "I am trying to talk him into letting us go."

"That won't happen," Fowler said. "First I will have my fiendish will of you. Then I will see about roasting the brat for my breakfast."

"Your will?" Firenze asked. "What is that?"

"Nothing!" Astrid said.

"Plenty," Fowler said as he settled in close to her body. "I am going to ream her as she has never been reamed. Okay, chick. Time for you to writhe and scream. Sound effects enhance the action."

"Writhe and scream?" Firenze asked. "Is he hurting you, Aunt Astrid?"

"No! Not exactly." What could she tell him? She needed to keep the fiend close enough to be overcome by her ambiance, while not lying to the child.

"What, not hurting yet?" Fowler asked. "I will remedy that. Take that, bleep." His open hand came down to strike the side of her hooded head with a resounding smack. The blow was not as bad as it sounded; she was tough.

"You hit her!" Firenze exclaimed.

"And a real pleasure it was," Fowler agreed.

"You're making me mad."

The fiend laughed. "An angry child. Fancy that."

If only the fiend would breathe enough of her perfume to be affected! But his head was high as he talked. So far. It irritated her that she would have to facilitate his foul design in order to knock him out.

"Really mad," Firenze said.

As if emotional fireworks would accomplish anything.

Fowler continued to bait the boy, while he held Astrid down, enjoying the nastiness. "Go ahead, blow your stupid little top, you arrogant twerp! Meanwhile I'll abuse this slut all I want to."

"Don't call her a slut!"

"What will you do, boy, cry?" The fiend laughed again. "Maybe I can make the slut cry." He struck Astrid again. This time it was in the stomach, and she gasped in pain.

"That does it," Firenze said. "I'm letting loose."

"You do that, scamp. Bawl your fool head off. I don't care if—" He broke off.

Astrid heard crackling as Firenze's temper flared, literally. The fireworks were flying from his head, probably zapping through the hood.

"Now that's interesting," Fowler said. "Radiations of fire are burning off your hood. Your whole head is glowing. That's a tantrum you can call a tantrum."

"Yeah?" Firenze asked. "How do you like this?"

There was a swooshing sound. "Yowch!" the fiend screamed. "You burned me with a rocket!"

That was interesting indeed! Firenze's fireworks had evidently become literal.

"There's more where that came from," Firenze said.

There was another swoosh. "Yowch!" the fiend repeated, burned again. He jumped off Astrid. "I'll pulverize you, imp!"

"I'd like to see you try it, earth bag."

Astrid had to smile. The child couldn't say dirt bag, but was trying.

She heard the pounding of the fiend's feet as he charged at the boy with mayhem in mind. She winced, knowing that Firenze remained tied. He couldn't defend himself.

There was a louder woosh. "Owww!" Fowler cried. "I'm burning up!"

Desperate to see what was happening, Astrid scraped her head across the grotto floor. The hood snagged on something and tore off. She stared, amazed.

Firenze's whole head was a mass of fire. His hood had burned off. Before him Fowler was rolling on the ground, trying to put out the fires in his clothing. Just as the fiend managed to smother the flames, Firenze aimed the top of his head in his direction. A jet of fire like a rocket trail shot out and scored, setting the fiend on fire again. "Owwww!" he screamed. He scrambled back to his feet and ran away, flaming.

Myst appeared. "I'm free. Don't burn me." She ran to Firenze and quickly untied his bonds. Then she came to Astrid and did the same. "How come your dress is up?" she asked innocently.

"The fiend was beating her up," Firenze answered, saving Astrid an awkward explanation. "That made me really mad."

"You're a terror when you're mad," Myst said appreciatively. "You roasted him."

"Thanks," he said, his head cooling to a dull glow. "I never got that angry before. But when the fiend started beating on Aunt Astrid I just couldn't hold it back."

"Well sure," Myst agreed. "He deserved it. Why was he hurting her?"

"He wanted to make me cry," Astrid said quickly. Then, to Firenze: "Those fireworks are more than just temper. You were able to jet fire at the fiend."

"Yeah, I guess," he said, surprised. "I didn't know I could do it. I just did it."

"We'll have to see if you can do it without getting mad," she said as she went to untie and unhood the other children. "This may be a weapon."

"Yeah," he said with more enthusiasm. "I thought it was just my bad temper."

"It might be that you kept your talent under control, to avoid embarrassment, but when you started getting mad, that control slipped. It could be separate from your temper."

"I guess," he agreed uncertainly.

"Try invoking the fireworks without getting mad."

"I don't know."

"Try. This could be important."

He focused. His head started to brighten. "I'm not mad."

"Keep going."

His head heated up. The other children came to look. "I'm not mad," Firenze repeated. "Just heating my head."

"Shoot a bolt of fire."

He concentrated. A firework rocket shot from his head and exploded above them, singeing the ceiling of the grotto.

"Wow!" Santo said.

"I'm doing it!" Firenze said, amazed. "I'm not mad, and I'm shooting off fireworks!"

"Hang on to that ability," Astrid said. "It just saved me from some, um, awkwardness."

"I guess," Firenze agreed.

"Practice it, so that you can do it anytime. We may encounter other monsters. You need to be able to protect yourself."

"What, are you leaving us?" Firenze asked, alarmed.

"No, not at all. But I didn't do a very job of protecting any of you this time. I'm not a good mother figure."

"Now wait, you've always protected us," Firenze said.

"And you always care about us," Santo said.

"And you make a nice mother," Squid said.

"Don't you understand? I let us get into this mess. It *was* my fault. That never should have happened."

The children stared at her. "How could you know?" Win asked.

"Not your fault," Myst said.

"It was my fault. I should have been more alert."

A glance circled around and among the children. Astrid realized that she was being difficult, and they were trying to figure out how to handle her. Then they took hands, briefly.

"You made a mistake," Firenze said.

"We all make mistakes," Santo said.

"It happens," Squid said.

"That doesn't make you bad," Win said.

"We love you," Myst said.

They had come up with one of their group answers. The way they talked in turn was a tip-off. But it wasn't enough. "How can you love me?" Astrid flared. "I'm a basilisk."

"You're a wonderful person," Firenze said.

"We know that," Santo said. "We don't care what kind of creature you are."

"We're pretty wild ourselves," Squid said.

"And you didn't hold that against us," Win said.

"Ever," Myst concluded.

There was moisture on Astrid's glasses. She realized what it was. "Bleep. I'm crying."

"We weren't criticizing you," Firenze said quickly.

"It's not that. These are—these are good tears. It's your support. I messed up, and you're helping me. I don't deserve it. But I'm grateful for it."

Then they were clustering around her. "We need you," Firenze said.

"And you need us," Santo said.

"So it's fair," Squid said.

The two smallest girls just squeezed her hands.

"It's fair," Astrid agreed.

Then the children retreated, knowing better than to stay too close to her too long.

But it was time to get moving. "Let's eat and run," Firenze said. "We know where the path goes."

They went to the pie plants. But they weren't enough. "I'm thirsty," Myst said.

"We need you to be healthy," Astrid said. "And we may need your mist again. You must lose water when you mist."

"Yes."

"But there's sleep potion in that water," Firenze said.

"There could be," Astrid agreed. "We shouldn't risk it. But we do need water." She considered it. "Could you children link and find a way? I know you can't do it directly, but maybe you can tell us cool or warm as we consider ideas."

Firenze shrugged. "Maybe."

"This could be like the game of Nineteen Questions," Astrid said. "If I can think of the right questions."

"Maybe," Firenze agreed again.

The children linked hands. "We want to find potable—I mean, drinkable—water," Astrid said. "Is it this way?" She pointed across the field.

"Cool," Firenze said.

"This way?" She pointed a quarter turn away.

"Cool," Santo said.

"This?" She pointed opposite her original direction.

"Cool," Squid said.

"This?" She pointed the remaining direction.

"Cool," Win said.

Astrid paused. No direction was right? Then she got a notion. She pointed down. "This?"

"Less cool," Myst said.

Astrid realized that made sense: dig deep enough, and you should find water eventually. But they had nothing to dig with.

So she tried once more. She pointed up. "This?"

"Warm," Firenze said.

As in rain? But there was no cloud. She needed a new approach. "Next question: who can best help me get it?"

She pointed to Myst. "Cold," Santo said.

Then to Win. "Cold," Squid said.

Then to Squid. "Cold," Squid said, smiling.

To Santo. "Medium," Win said.

"I could make a hole down to water," Santo said. "A well. But it might be pretty deep, and the water could be muddy."

So Astrid pointed to Firenze. "Hot," Myst said.

"Me?" Firenze asked, surprised. "I don't know how to get fresh water."

"Let's figure this out," Astrid said. "You can be a real hothead. Maybe that relates."

"Yes!" he said, because it was his turn to speak to the question.

"So how would heat relate to fresh water?" Astrid asked.

"No way," Santo said. "It just puffs it into steam." Then he paused, surprised. "And that's hot. I mean, it's close to the answer."

"Steam is hot boiled floating water," Astrid said. "Cool it down, and it's wet water again. And—" It was her turn to be surprised. "And that water's clean, because nothing else steams. Not dirt, not poison. That's the way."

"But it floats away," Firenze said. "We can't drink it."

"We can if we recondense it. We just need to catch it in something cool. That's part of the magic of steam: it doesn't like to be cooled."

"But how—"

Astrid looked around. "Sheets," she said.

The children looked at her blankly.

"I'll show you." She went to a bedding bush and harvested a large white sheet. "Now we will hold this over our heads. Santo, fetch a pot and fill it with water."

Mystified, the boy found a pot and dipped it in the stream.

"Firenze, focus on that pot and heat it until the water boils out."

The boy did as he was told. His head turned color, radiated fireworks, and got red hot. He put it near the pot, and the water started to heat.

"Squid and Win, hold the far corners of the sheet. I'll hold the near corners."

They did, and as the pot on the ground came to boil, the three of them held the sheet above it, to catch the rising steam. The steam condensed as it found the sheet, soaking it through. It sagged in their hands, dripping.

"Now bring a clean pot," Astrid said.

Santo did.

"Now we twist," Astrid said, twisting her side of the sheet while the two girls held the other side. Water dripped into the pot.

"Neat!" Santo said. "But there's not much water."

"We'll do it again." They stretched the sheet out over the still boiling pot, catching more steam.

Progress was slow, but after several sheet wringings the pot was beginning to fill. They were getting potable water. Astrid had taught the children a new magic trick.

Finally they were able to drink it. At last they were ready to travel again.

The children linked hands, consulting.

"That way," Squid said, pointing.

"Good clear route," Win said.

"With clear water," Myst said.

"But there is danger," Firenze said.

Astrid sighed. "What else is new? Is there any feasible way to avoid it?"

"Not really," Santo said.

"But it may be hard to fight without losing some of us," Squid said with a shudder.

"Something that my Stare can't stop?"

"No," Win said.

"Or Santo's holes?"

"No," Myst said.

"But we won't want to use those weapons," Firenze said.

"Not use what we've got?"

Santo spread his hands. "It doesn't seem to make sense."

"So we will be alert," Astrid said briskly. "We make a pretty good team, after all."

"You make a good leader," Santo said.

They moved on. The path was indeed clear, and there were edible fruits and good water along the way. It was pleasant enough. Except for the children's premonition, which Astrid knew better than to ignore.

They crossed a large field with tall weeds that barked when disturbed. "Dog fennel," Astrid said. "It barks but doesn't bite."

Fortunately they didn't need to disturb much of it. There were paths crisscrossing it every which way. They followed their chosen one.

Then she saw something ahead. "A wolf!" she said.

"There's more," Firenze murmured.

Astrid checked. There were wolves at each of the intersecting paths, including the one they had come on, blocking every way out of the field. They had walked into an ambush.

"I'll face forward," Astrid said tensely. "Santo, you face back. Firenze, you face to our left. Girls, face to our right. If they attack, you know what to do. But don't act until they attack. I will try to negotiate."

The children quickly moved into the formation she had described. The wolves would face a deadly Stare, or get holed, or burned, or blown away by a fierce wind. But Astrid hoped to avoid mayhem if at all possible.

The wolves advanced on all sides. They were not charging, just coming closer.

"Halt!" Astrid called. "If you understand me, stop in place. We can defend ourselves, and you will suffer if you come any father."

The wolves halted, to her relief. So they understood at least that much. Many animals did understand human speech, though they could not speak it. But they might think she was bluffing. That would be unfortunate on their part. But neither did Astrid want a pitched battle if it could be avoided.

"I think they're werewolves," Firenze said. "They have that look about them."

That was interesting. They did have that look. Astrid remembered meeting Jenny Elf, and how her husband the werewolf had come to pick her up. She hadn't recognized him as a wolf at first, but now she recognized the type. Maybe she could use her feminine charms on the leader, so they could parlay. "Are you werewolves?" Astrid asked the wolf ahead, whom she took to be the leader. "I'm a shape changer myself. Change, and we'll talk." She stood up straight so that her good human figure showed. Maybe for once that prettiness would get her out of trouble instead of into it.

The wolf just watched her. "I will demonstrate," she said. She shifted to basilisk form, then back to human. But her clothing did not change with her. It dropped off when she changed, and did not return when she changed back. Now she was naked, except for her dark glasses. However, that well might set a male wolf back. She hoped she wouldn't have to fight off his amorous advance in lieu of his physical attack.

The wolf changed, becoming human. Astrid stared, surprised.

It was a woman. As naked as Astrid was.

"So you are a basilisk," the werewolf said. She was lean and muscular, but also a fine figure of a female.

"I did warn you that we could defend ourselves," Astrid said. "But I have not removed my glasses. How about a truce while we talk?"

"Truce," the woman agreed. "I am Wulfha, bitch leader of the Pack."

Bitch? Then she remembered that this was the standard term for a female canine. "I am Astrid Basilisk-Cockatrice, surrogate parent to these children. I will protect them against any threat."

"A basilisk protecting human children," Wulfha said, bemused.

"You have a problem with that?"

"I am merely surprised. Why are you intruding on our territory? This is Wolf Country. We normally hunt here."

"We are merely passing through. We got caught in this place through no fault of our own, and are trying to make our way out. Yesterday we were traversing the Dungeons."

"And what did you find there?"

"Goblins, nickelpedes, and harpies. They were not friendly."

"Yet you survived."

"You doubt?"

"I merely marvel. Few emerge from the Dungeons."

Her skepticism seemed reasonable. "I caught a harpy and reasoned with her." Astrid touched her glasses meaningfully. "She decided to cooperate, and guided us out. Otherwise we would have roasted and eaten her."

Wulfha laughed. "You spoke her language!"

"I did. Am I speaking yours?" That was couched as a question, but it was a threat. The truce could end at any time.

"You are. Let's extend the truce a day and night. We will offer you the hospitality of our den and safe passage to the next territory, in exchange for a service you may be able to render us."

"As long as this service does not imperil the safety of the children, we will agree."

"My word as a bitch: it does not," Wulfha said. Then, to the pack members: "Change."

The wolves shifted into human form, male and female. All were naked, of course. Astrid was sure the children found this interesting. "Werewolves and centaurs don't wear clothing," she reminded them. Then to the leader: "This service?"

"Involves a young inexperienced cockatrice. We have not been able to approach him to establish guidelines."

Oho! "That I can do."

"Then it's a deal. You have nothing to fear from us."

"It's okay, children," Astrid said. "The weres are our friends, until we move on tomorrow."

"Okay," Firenze said, perhaps a bit more heartily than he felt.

"This way," Wulfha said, walking along a path through the fennel.

They followed, and soon came to the den. This was another grotto, with a fire burning before it. Children stood there expectantly. There were introductions all around, then they settled in a comfortable circle. Assorted fruits were served, and there was even boot rear and tsoda popka, which the children enjoyed.

"You must tell us your story," Wulfha said. "It is surely an interesting one."

"That might take some time," Astrid said.

"We have time. What we lack is news of outer Xanth, which we have not seen in our lifetimes. It's not a bad life, here in Storage, but neither is it very exciting. Sometimes we raid the Dungeons, just for diversion."

Some diversion! So Astrid dived into the way they had been mysteriously trapped in the Playground, and their adventures in the Dungeons and with Fowler Fiend.

"Oh, him!" Wulfha said. "He caught me once, foraging near his home in my human guise. I was young then and didn't realize his nature, nor did he know mine. He grabbed me and wanted to—" She hesitated, glancing at the assorted children. "Kiss me. I changed to bitch form and almost bit his head off."

The children burst out laughing. "Aunt Astrid didn't want to kiss him either," Squid said. "We set him on fire."

Wulfha smiled understandingly. "He is more careful of us today."

"Now about this cockatrice," Astrid said.

"He came on the scene a few months ago, completely undisciplined. We don't know how to deal with him."

"Oh, surely you can take down a solo cockatrice, knowing his nature," Astrid said. "You would have had more trouble with me, because you don't know the talents of our group, but you could have made a good fight of it."

"We suspected you were not bluffing," Wulfha said. "There was something about your formation and the way the children focused. If I may inquire—?"

"We will demonstrate, if you wish."

"Thank you. It is true we can handle a cockatrice. But we survive as a Pack by making good use of our resources, whatever they may be, and there are times when we could use the Stare of a cockatrice. Such as if the trolls caught one of us, perhaps a bitch, and held her for hostage, she facing troll type abuse if we did not capitulate."

"I am familiar with troll type abuse," Astrid said.

"Did he survive?"

"No. But I did make a truce with his associates, and we were able to do each other some good."

"Exactly. This cockatrice refuses to treat us with respect, and if he doesn't change, we will have to take him out. That would be a shame."

"A shame," Astride agreed with a smile.

"He will be foraging in our country tomorrow morning."

"I will be there."

Then the children got to show off their talents. Myst fogged out and reformed, delighting the wolf cubs. Win blew a cub harmlessly across the ground without being affected herself. Squid assumed the likeness of a wolf cub, then a patch of nickelpedes, looking so realistic that the cubs skittered back. Santo made a hole through a rock. Astrid could see that the significance of that was not lost on Wulfha; a head was softer than a rock. And Firenze heated his head and emitted a lovely display of fireworks.

"We would have taken losses," Wulfha conceded.

Just so. Astrid was confident that those losses would have been prohibitive. The truce was better, for both sides, as it had been with the trolls.

They had a pleasant afternoon and evening. The girls were already making friends with little bitches. The wolves set aside a comfortable alcove for the guests. "You are most appealing in your human form. Are you personally attached?" Wulfha inquired quietly.

"I am married to a human man."

"Then you will be sleeping with the children."

"Yes."

"One of our males will be regretful."

Astrid knew that in some societies favors were not limited to food and conversation, and marriage was no necessary barrier. "My close ambiance is deadly. Only my husband is immune. Any romantic liaison I might have would have to be quite brief, and I am not looking for one."

"Of course." Wulfha was politely disappointed for the interested male.

There was one other aspect that Astrid did not care to mention. Truces were fine, but were not always perfectly honored. She did not want to sleep apart from the children, just in case. And when she did sleep, she would assume the basilisk form, a tacit reminder to any male who might happen to forget.

"I met a werewolf briefly in Xanth," Astrid said. "He was married to an odd elf."

"That would be an unusual liaison," Wulfha agreed.

"No, I mean she was odd for an elf. She was large, and her ears were pointed, and she had four fingers on each hand. She rode him like a steed."

"There was surely an interesting story there," the bitch said.

"There surely was." Astrid had hoped that Wulfha might know something of the matter, but evidently news of the outside Xanth did not penetrate the realms of Storage.

"With accommodation spells, all things are possible."

"What kind of spell?"

Wulfha smiled. "You're a basilisk, so would not have had much use for them. They enable widely divergent creatures to mate, even apart from a love spring. Thus a huge giant and a tiny imp could make it, if they chose. Certainly an elf and a wolf."

"I am impressed."

"It is one of the useful incidental spells, when different species wish to associate. I understand they are popular with goblins and trolls."

Astrid began to appreciate how the goblins and trolls had been able to ravish their captives without killing them. "I suppose so. Not to my taste, however."

"Tastes vary widely."

The children linked hands briefly in a seeming bedtime ritual. Then Win came to Astrid to kiss her goodnight, the wind blowing her intoxicating perfume away. "Danger," she whispered.

Oops. "From the wolves?" Astrid whispered.

"No. They're okay. A raid. We think trolls."

"Settle down quietly. I will alert the wolves." Then Astrid kissed the girl quickly on the cheek and packed her off, like an affectionate mother.

She approached Wulfha. "The children have a sense," she murmured. "There is danger. A possible troll raid, while you are distracted with guests. Do trolls have a taste for were bitches, with accommodation spells?"

"They wouldn't dare," Wulfha said.

So she did not credit children's fears, understandably. But the threat was real. "Then let me talk to that interested male, though this is not what he seeks."

Wulfha withdrew, and in a moment a muscular male approached. "Let us walk apart a little, and talk," Astrid said. She had not dressed since losing her clothing earlier, and knew he was looking. He couldn't help it; he was male.

He was glad to agree. "I am Wolfram, lead wolf warrior of the Pack."

A female canine was a bitch; a male canine was a wolf. "You are the one I need to discuss this with. It is possible that you and I are being magically watched, so we want to look affectionate, though you need to understand that this is not real. My perfume will first intoxicate you, then kill you if you do not escape it quickly. If you bring your face close to mine, hold your breath."

"I understand, with regret," he said, trying not to make his study of her body too obvious.

"Wulfha doubts it, but I am satisfied that a real threat exists, perhaps a raid by trolls who seek to surprise you while you are distracted by guests. I believe you need to be on guard tonight."

"Because children fear?"

"They are not ordinary children. They have anticipated danger before, and it has come to pass. If you do not prepare for a raid, I will have to move the children to a safer place for the night."

"I will prepare for a raid. We value our children too."

"Thank you. Hold your breath." Then she kissed him on the cheek.

Plainly pleased, Wolfram departed. She knew she had impressed him as much by her body as her words, but that would do. Soon she saw him quietly conferring with other males. Wulfha might be the Pack leader, but the warrior took any threat more seriously.

They settled down for the night. Astrid changed her mind and retained her human form, so as not to give any indication that she thought anything was amiss.

Myst dissolved into mist, floated across, and reformed beside Astrid. "It's close," she said.

"The wolves are ready."

"Maybe not."

This was bad news. But before Astrid could decide what to do, there was a whistle in the air, followed by an explosion. White gas puffed out.

"Get away from it!" Astrid cried. But already several wolves were waking and choking, and wolf cubs were whining, terrified. It was a gas attack!

Then several trolls charged into the camp. "Get the children!" one called. "And get out before the wolves mobilize!"

A troll grabbed for Santo—and fell back, a hole through his body. Another caught up to Myst—and his hands found nothing but fog.

Then there was a concerted growling from behind the trolls. Five large wolves attacked, teeth snapping viciously. Suddenly the troll raiders were the prey.

Astrid herded the children, including several wolf cubs, away from the gas and the battle. But it was brief; the trolls were soon routed, and fled, except for the one with the hole. He was dead.

Santo was crying. "I killed him!"

She hugged him briefly. "It was self-defense."

"I never killed before."

"You did what you had to do. You may have saved the other children."

"Yes," Squid said, hugging him. That did seem to comfort him somewhat. Then Squid hugged two of the bitch children, as they too had been traumatized by the violence of the attack.

The wolves returned with blood on their teeth. They nodded to Astrid before moving on to the nearby stream to clean up.

Wulfha approached. "Now, belatedly, I believe. Our children would have been subjected to brutal ravishment and consumption. We owe you, Astrid."

"No. I fear it was our presence that invoked the raid. The trolls thought you would be distracted, and there were extra children to grab."

"Perhaps." Wulfha looked down at the dead troll. "Holed through the center. Your boy did that."

"It was necessary," Astrid said. "Santo had no choice. He's only eight years old."

Santo was still crying. Wulfha went to him and took him in her arms, as Astrid could not. "You have been bloodied, Santo," the bitch told him. "You may have saved one of our cubs from fates worse than death. You're a hero."

He simply cried into her bosom. Astrid stifled her fleeting jealously. She couldn't comfort any of the children like that, lest she kill them.

The gas dissipated. The males returned, no blood remaining. Wolfram assumed man form. "I admit I doubted, but we prepared, perhaps because of your intoxicating kiss. We owe it to you, Astrid."

"You owe it to the children," Astrid said. "They saw it coming."

"And had we meant to be untrue to our truce, they would have seen that coming too," Wulfha said.

"They knew you were true to the truce."

"They are remarkable children. Can we persuade you to stay with us?"

"I regret, no," Astrid said. "We are seeking an escape from Storage, so we can return to our own group."

"I thought as much. You have earned our respect." Wulfha stroked Santo's head. "You will grow to be a remarkable man."

"Thank you," Santo said, his tears abating. The comfort of the werewolf bitch had evidently been potent.

The rest of the night passed uneventfully, but there was a camaraderie that had not been there before. The truce had become meaningless; the werewolves were now their friends.

In the morning Wulfha led Astrid out to a rocky section of ground. Astrid was not concerned about leaving the children alone; they were quite safe with the wolves. "He should be along soon."

"I am ready."

"Astrid, if you do not find your way out of Storage, please return here. We will welcome all of you, and I would like to be your friend."

Astrid liked the warrior bitch. "I think you are already my friend. If we can't escape, we will return here. It would be a good environment for the children. But we have to escape if we possibly can."

"There," Wulfha murmured.

The cockatrice came into sight. He was not at all furtive; he had no fear of any living thing here. That was of course part of the problem. He had become arrogant in his ignorance. He looked to be about nine years old, in human terms: right between Firenze and Santo.

Astrid walked toward him. "Cockatrice!" she called.

The creature paused, glancing her way. That was mischief already; he had not learned to avoid possible eye contact unless he meant to kill.

"Do not look directly at me," she said as she approached him.

He responded by staring directly into her face. She was sure he understood her; he was being rebellious.

Annoyed, she strode right up to him and kicked him in the tail. "Stop it!"

He hissed and launched at her, jaws gaping. She caught him around the body, whirled him around, and flung him to the side. "Behave, or I'll stomp on your head."

The cockatrice rolled back to his feet, unhurt but amazed. He had Stared her, and she hadn't been affected. He had attacked her, and she had fearlessly dumped him. Had he lost his power?

"Enough games," Astrid said. She shifted to basilisk form and Stared.

He rocked back. As a basilisk he was largely immune to her Stare, but not completely. He was juvenile; she was adult. It made a difference. Her mature Stare was difficult for him to handle; he had surely never experienced the devastating power of an adult before. It was a humbling experience. As with the harpy, she was talking his language.

Now she hissed at him in basilisk talk. *I am here to acquaint you with the rules of interaction,* she said. *Listen and pay attention, or I will run you out of this territory and chomp your foolish tail.*

Who are you? he asked, cowed.

I am Astrid Basilisk. I come on behalf of the werewolves. Here is the thing: if you keep bothering them, behaving irresponsibly, they will come in human form wearing dark glasses and club you to death. But if you treat them with proper courtesy, they will give you the run of their territory and leave you alone. All you have to do is never look at them directly. With one exception: if they should happen to have trouble with trolls or the like, they will call to you, and you will join them and Stare at the trolls. Do you understand?

The cockatrice gazed at her, not responding.

Astrid shifted to human form, picked up a solid fallen branch, and menaced him with it. "Agree, or I'll beat you into submission."

He now respected her ability to do exactly that. Grudgingly, he agreed.

"There are other things," she said, setting down the branch. "Such as the company of folk your own age, even if they are of other species. Even one of our kind can get lonely. I know; I've been there. That's one reason I assumed human form: so I could interact with folk who had minds. If you hood your gaze, the wolf boys your age will hunt with you and share their kills and maybe some of their stories." She smiled. "At present I'm sure you have no use for girls, but you might find it interesting to learn something about them too, so that when you grow up you will know what to do with a young lady basilisk, instead of fighting her. Should a wolf bitch need to negotiate with a troll, you might accompany her, so the troll would know she is protected. She might even reward you with a kiss, like this." She leaned down and kissed him on the snout.

His legs weakened like jelly and he sank to the ground, a small cloud of hearts orbiting raggedly. He had never before been kissed by a pretty female of any type, and her kiss was as potent as her Stare.

It didn't happen instantly, but in due course she did get through to him, and he agreed to cooperate completely. He had a small crush on her, which helped. She gave him a name, Colby, to which he would answer in the future. Then she brought him back to meet Wulfha. He dutifully avoided directly gazing at her.

"This is Colby Cockatrice," Astrid said. "He is sorry he has caused you trouble, and will not do it again."

Colby bowed his head submissively.

"He will avoid looking at you directly, and will not try to use his Stare on any of you. If you call him by name, he will come. And help you when you need it, such as if you have troll trouble. In return you will give him free rein of Wolf Country, to hunt and frolic as he wishes, and you will not cause him any mischief. Your children may associate with him, both wolves and bitches, cautiously. It is a permanent truce. Agreed?"

Colby bowed his head again.

"Agreed," Wulfha said, amazed.

"Good enough," Astrid said.

Colby went on about his business, and Astrid returned to the den with Wulfha. "How did you get through to him so quickly?"

"I spoke his language."

"I saw you kick his tail."

"As I said: his language."

Wulfha laughed. "And he couldn't Stare you to stop you."

"I suspect that did make an impression," Astrid agreed, smiling. "I also kissed him."

"That would have wiped him out. Wolfram's still in a daze."

"Prettiness has its uses."

"So you used the carrot and stick."

"Doesn't everyone?" Astrid asked innocently.

"Not quite so effectively."

At the den they found the children happily playing together, teaching each other new games. But it was time to move on.

The wolves escorted them to the edge of Wolf Country. "Here there be dragons," Wulfha warned them. "All types. They are not friendly."

"We'll handle them," Astrid said.

"I'm sure you will. But be aware that they aren't all mindless terrors.

Some are cunning terrors. The Dragon King is there, and he is powerful and unscrupulous. My friend Wesla disappeared several months ago, and a little bird reported that the Dragon King got her, raped her, and made her a lowly servant. He has devastating ways to enforce his will. I would not call it a fate worse than death, but she may wish for death at times."

"What is this about rape?" Astrid asked, annoyed. "Does every male want to rape every female?"

"Only the unprincipled males, with respect to the pretty females. You are at extreme risk in that respect."

"So I have gathered," Astrid said dryly.

The bitch hesitated. "Can I hug you safely if I hold my breath?"

"Yes, but keep it brief. My ambiance—"

"I understand." Wulfha opened her arms and took Astrid in, hugging her tightly, then withdrawing. "It has been an education and a pleasure to know you."

"Ditto," Astrid said sincerely.

Then they made their small formation and advanced into Dragon Country.

CHAPTER 9:
DRAGONS

~~~

They had hardly gotten out of sight of the wolf pack when the first dragon struck. It had been lurking behind an innocent-looking acorn tree beside the path. One moment they were walking in a line; the next, Myst was gone from the end of the line. There was the dragon, swallowing the morsel whole.

"Oh!" Astrid cried, appalled. "There was no warning!"

"That's 'cause there's no danger," Firenze said.

"But Myst is gone!"

"Not exactly," Santo said. "Watch."

Astrid had been about to Stare the dragon into oblivion, but paused, watching. What did the children mean?

The dragon's satisfied smirk faded. Its body quivered and expanded. Its snoot wrinkled as if there were a bad smell. It turned greenish around the edges. What was happening? Then it stretched out its neck, gaped its mouth wide open, and let out a resounding belch. Colored mist poured out. That was odd, because it wasn't a steamer. The mist settled slowly to the ground and formed into the figure of a little girl. Myst was back. She had given the dragon one awful pain in the gas.

"That was fun," she said, laughing.

Weak with relief, Astrid picked her, up, kissed her, and set her down. She had for a moment forgotten the child's nature.

"Are there any more cute little surprises coming?" Astrid inquired, trying to keep the edge out of her voice.

"Some," Squid said.

"But nothing really dangerous?"

"Nothing we can't handle," Win said.

"Yet," Myst concluded.

Astrid sighed. "That's nice."

They walked on. Another dragon appeared. This one was a fire breather. It inhaled hugely, ready to incinerate them with a single blast.

Win stepped forward, revving up her wind. As the dragon let go, the wind jumped to hurricane force. It blew the fire right back at the dragon's snoot, singeing it painfully. The dragon retreated, defeated by its own heat.

Farther along a third dragon attacked. This one was a steamer, and they were well within its range. But the children were not concerned.

This time Squid stepped forward. In plain sight of the dragon she shifted into a small basilisk, aiming her Stare directly at it. The dragon fell over itself in the haste of its retreat; it knew better than to bite a basilisk, or even look at it.

Before long there came a fourth dragon. This one was a huge smoker; their entire party would barely make a meal for it. It would suffocate them with smoke, then chomp them at its leisure.

Santo faced it. "Go away, smudge face," he said. "Or I'll hurt you."

The dragon almost fell over laughing. Then it inflated.

Santo focused on its tail. A hole appeared in it.

The dragon whipped about as its smoke dissipated into the sky, thinking it had been speared. But there was only the hole, now bleeding. It whipped back, inhaling again, ready to blast out its hot smoke.

Santo holed it again, this time in a foot. "I warned you," he said as the dragon lost a second lungful of smoke.

The dragon still didn't make the connection. It inhaled a third time.

Santo holed it through the snoot, leaving it no good way to aim its smoke. At last it realized that it was overmatched, and retreated with its wounds.

"Now it gets more difficult," Firenze said. "We'll have to stay close together."

Astrid formed the children into a tight group following Firenze, while she brought up the rear. They moved on.

This time it was not one dragon, or two, or three. It was a battalion of them. They formed a virtual wall before the group, their wings overlapping like a phalanx. "I think I should tackle these," she called to Firenze.

"Not yet," he called back. "I can handle them."

"Are you sure?"

"Yes," Santo said.

So the children had Communed, and knew. Astrid had to trust that, though she was not at all comfortable with it. Any mistake, and they would all be dragon snacks.

They marched up to the wall of dragons. Then Firenze's head heated. Sparks and fireworks radiated from it.

The dragons were not impressed. They had firebreathers of their own. They could handle heat.

Firenze's head became red hot. Then white hot. The air around him flickered as it heated. Wind came in from the sides as the air around his head expanded explosively and rose into the air. Soon a circulation developed, forming a fiery tornado. Coruscating heat whirled into the sky, picking up dust, rising into a turbulent cloud.

The dragons backed off. They were getting some respect. Firenze walked straight ahead, and the children and Astrid followed him as closely as the heat permitted. The dragons tried to come closer, but Firenze turned his head this way and that, and balls of fire formed where he looked, making even fire dragons pause. They were not accustomed to receiving fire, only sending it. He was forging a trail through the center of the dragon mass.

They came to a massive stone wall. That seemed to be the end of Dragon Country. Beyond it could be their escape. The path the children were following indicated that they did have to get by it, at any rate.

But now they were literally up against a wall, with the dragons closing off any possible retreat. The moment they tired or slept, the dragons would charge and swamp them.

"We have to get through this wall," Squid said. "Our way is beyond it."

"But it's hard," Win said.

"And dangerous," Myst said.

It was time for Astrid to organize things. "This wall can't be infinitely thick. We need to find a thin spot. Then Santo can make a hole through it."

"There's something complicated about this wall," Firenze said. "Something we don't understand. But we do need to get past it."

"It will take a lot of energy to make a hole big enough for us to go through," Santo said. "I can't make it both big and long."

"Can you make small test holes?" Astrid asked him.

"Yes, but—"

Astrid was impatient because of the encroaching dragons; they needed to get away from here soon. "When a test hole shows the way, then make a big hole."

"Okay," he agreed, seeing her strategy.

"Myst, you can mist through the holes to tell which one gets through," Astrid said. "Win, you can send air through them. You should be able to spot the right one the moment it appears. So you two help Santo."

"Yes," the two chorused happily.

"Meanwhile I will hold off the dragons," she said. "Firenze and Squid, you can stand on either side of me and warn me of any dragons trying to sneak by my Stare."

The two nodded, and took their places beside her, while the other three children faced the wall.

The dragons, as if catching on that the prey was up to something, became bolder, trying to get into burning, steaming, smoking, or snatching range.

"Stay back, dragons!" Astrid called. "I am a basilisk. I will Stare you if you get too close."

But the dragons continued to nudge closer. "They think you're bluffing," Firenze said.

"Because I bluffed them," Squid said.

"Well, I gave them fair warning," Astrid said, removing her glasses.

A huge dragon charged, breathing fire. Astrid caught its eye, and it plowed into the ground, dead.

"I regret doing that," she called. "But I did warn you. Get away from here."

But another dragon, a steamer, perhaps a stupid one, charged. Astrid caught its eye, and it too dropped to the ground.

"That should be clear enough," Astrid called. "I can do this all day if I have to. But I'd rather not. Go away and stop harassing us, and you'll be safe."

Still they did not stop. A smoker charged. Astrid oriented on its snoot and couldn't find its eyes. Either they were closed, or smoke obscured them. "We're in trouble," she murmured tersely. "I can't kill it from a distance."

"I'll do it," Firenze said. His head heated, quickly turning red. He stepped forward, intercepting the dragon. The dragon's mouth, guided by smell, came down on him. Firenze's head became a ball of fire, and the dragon's mouth was filled with flames. It quickly flinched back, too late; its teeth were charred and its tongue was a mass of sodden ashes. It was painfully out of commission.

Now at last the dragons heeded the warning. No more charged, but neither did they withdraw. They were still watching for an opening.

"Got it!" Santo exclaimed behind them. "Myst found a hole through."

Astrid turned. There was a series of middle-sized holes in the wall. Santo was working on one of them, enlarging it to a hole a person could crawl through. It wasn't instant; it was happening slowly. She realized that he was tiring, having done a lot of work. But there was no other way, so she let him continue.

Finally it was complete. Light showed at the end of a short tunnel. "Get on through, children," she said. "I'll guard the rear."

They scrambled through, until only Astrid was left. She faced the dragons, knowing the moment she turned around they would charge. She had been able to do it before because Santo was there, but now she was alone.

She glared around, then spun about and dived into the hole, changing to basilisk form as she did; that was better for this sort of running. She scrambled for all she was worth, knowing that a dragon would send fire or steam after her. She tumbled out the other end just as a tongue of fire forged though. That had been too close a call!

"Quick, close it up!" she gasped as she changed back to human and recovered her footing.

"I can't," Santo said. "A hole through water I can let expire; it collapses naturally. But stone doesn't."

"Fetch a rock, then. We don't want a slender dragon following us through."

But there were no rocks. They were not out in the open; they were in what appeared to be a stone passage behind the wall. They moved away from the hole, having to leave it open behind them. That made Astrid nervous, but what choice did they have?

Then she realized what it was. "We're in a castle!" she said, amazed. "We just punched through its outer wall!"

"But it's huge," Firenze said. "What's it doing here in Dragon Country?"

"We'd better find out, if we can," Santo said. "We knew there was something about the wall."

"Something wrong," Squid said. "But we were in a hurry."

The children linked hands and Communed. Then separated, their faces mutually grim.

"What is it?" Astrid asked, alarmed.

"We think it's the Dragon King's Castle," Win said.

"Awful," Myst agreed.

"I have not heard of this," Astrid said.

"We know of it historically," Firenze said.

"From when it emerged from Storage and became the capitol of the dragons in all Xanth," Santo said.

"Maybe ten years from now," Squid said. "It's a tourist attraction we visited."

"After the Human/Dragon war," Win said.

"Awful," Myst repeated.

Astrid had almost forgotten that the children were from the future. There would be a war between the humans and the dragons? That did not look promising.

"This way, please, honored guests."

They turned, startled. There was a goblin woman, pert and pretty as they all were. "Who are you?" Astrid asked.

"I am Goldie Goblin, lowliest servant of the Dragon King. I must make you comfortable in your suite."

"Suite?" Astrid asked blankly.

"As his future Queen, you must have the very best. Please follow me."

Astrid's mouth worked, but nothing came out. Future Queen?

"We're in trouble," Firenze murmured.

"But we'd better play along for now," Santo said.

They followed Goldie down the passage, which soon expanded into a hall. It led to a palatial suite, with a living room, family room, dining room, rumpus room, bathroom and several bedrooms. "If there is anything you want, simply snap your fingers," Goldie said. "A servant will appear to do your bidding."

This was so different and unexpected that Astrid clamped tightly down on her reactions. She needed time to think and to consult with the children before even expressing wonder. "Thank you. We will manage."

The goblin curtsied and disappeared down a side hall. They were alone for the moment.

"If we are guests here, we shall have to make ourselves presentable," Astrid told the children. "We are filthy. We'll clean up and change clothing. But first, a little ceremony of appreciation for the courtesy of this residence."

She extended her hands. The children took them, Firenze on her right, Myst on her left, the others in the order of their ages, forming a circle of six. They could touch her hands briefly without suffering much damage from her corrosive skin. And for the first time Astrid participated in their Communion. It was amazing. Suddenly all their minds were linked. It was as if they shared one Communal thought.

We are captives of the Dragon King. There is great danger. We must escape within a day, or all is lost. But we must not give any indication that we have any plan to escape. We are being watched. We must pretend to accede to the

Dragon King's demands.

Astrid released the hands. "Very good, children," she said. "We do appreciate this residence in the spirit it is offered." Which was not what it seemed. "Now the two boys will use the bathroom first. I see there are basins, washcloths, and towels there, and changes of clothing. Use them." She formed a token frown. "And wash behind your ears. Then give the girls our turn."

The boys dutifully obeyed, closing the door behind them. In two moments they were done, garbed in the fresh blue outfits provided. Then Astrid took the girls in, and in four moments (there were more of them) they were clean and in the assorted nice pink dresses provided. Obviously someone had seen them coming, and set things up for them.

Astrid snapped her fingers. A lovely human woman appeared, garbed as a servant. "Wesla at your service."

Astrid recognized the smell. "You're a werewolf!"

"A captive," Wesla agreed. "Now I serve the Dragon King."

Wulfha had mentioned that her friend had been captured, raped, and forced into servitude. Wesla had surely suffered sorely.

"Goldie Goblin said something about my being a future queen. Do you know anything about that?"

"Yes."

"Do you care to tell me?"

"Yes."

There was a pause. It seemed that these servants had been instructed to volunteer little unless directly asked, and they were rigorously true to that directive. That spoke another volume about the discipline the master enforced. "Then tell me about this, please."

"The Dragon King means to make a political marriage with you so he can extend his hegemony beyond the dragons. A beautiful basilisk would seem to be perfect, serving as a threat to other species that might be resistive. If he can tame a basilisk, he can tame anything."

Tame her? Astrid rankled. "I am already married."

Wesla did not respond.

"Doesn't that make a difference?"

"No. Relationships outside Storage are null."

"Not to me!"

Silence.

It seemed that the Dragon King was the law in this realm. Astrid had sympathy for the werewolf, but suspected she was a lost cause. "Please arrange for us to be fed."

"Lunch is ready."

And there in the dining room a competent meal had been laid out. Astrid hadn't thought to check when she emerged from the washing up. "Thank you."

No reply.

They went to the dining room. There was something for everyone, including eye scream and boot rear for the children, and has beans for the adult.

After the meal, Astrid encouraged the children to lie down and rest, perchance to sleep. "You have had a difficult morning," she said. "You are surely overtired." She was thinking especially of the way Firenze and Santo had labored with their talents to deal with dragons and a wall. They needed to restore their resources.

"Can we take the big bed?" Myst asked.

"Welcome to it."

All the children piled onto the big bed, linking hands. With luck, the watching Dragon King would not know the significance of linking hands, and would assume they were merely reassuring each other. Soon they were asleep.

Wesla and Goldie were now in the dining room, cleaning up. On impulse, Astrid joined them. "I don't want to make any trouble for anyone," she said. "But since there is a chance I will be joining you, in one capacity or another, I would like to get to know you a little better. Would that be out of order?"

The two exchanged a wary look. "If knowing us encourages you to join us, it is in order," Goldie said. But she volunteered nothing else.

"Out in Xanth proper I was able to help save three goblin girls from captivity by a troll. I have little use for goblin males, but those girls seemed nice."

"We try to be," Goldie said with a bit of a shudder. Then Astrid realized that she had probably also been raped and brutalized. An accommodation spell could have facilitated the first. She also realized that the spying probably wasn't just visual; their dialogue might be overheard. That would help explain the extreme reticence of these captives.

Astrid glanced at Wesla. "We passed through Wolf Country on our way here. I met Wulfha."

Now the werewolf unbent a little, if only to ask a question. "What did you think of her?"

"She is one smart, tough bitch. I call her my friend."

Wesla did not speak, but her mouth twitched in the suggestion of a smile.

Astrid decided to let them be. At least she had established some basis for acquaintance, just in case.

There was a knock on the outer door. Astrid went to open it. There stood a regally unfamiliar woman. "I am the Dragon Lady," she said. "We should talk."

"Do come in." This promised to be interesting.

They settled in easy chairs in the living room. "As you know, the King has his eye on you," the Lady said.

"Unfortunately I do not have my eye on him. We are only passing through."

"Not so. You will remain here until you have satisfied his desire."

"I'm a basilisk," Astrid said, changing just her head into her natural form for a generous instant so as not to mess up her nice pink dress.

"And I'm a dragon," the Lady agreed, doing the same. "I have come here at the behest of the King to clarify your situation."

"There are few creatures who seriously think they can force a basilisk to do anything she doesn't want to do, and fewer who would ever want to marry one."

"The King is one of the few."

This remained curious. "What is your relationship to the King?"

"I am his mistress. I hope in time to become his wife."

"Then why are you talking with me? I surely am not good for your design."

"I would be happy to see all of you dead," the Lady said candidly. "But that is not my decision to make. I am obliged to persuade you to marry the King and give him an heir to the throne."

Astrid digested this. Not only a political liaison, but summoning the stork, or whatever dragons summoned? That might be a considerable challenge for the King, and anathema to her. "The King has you so much in thrall that you must come to persuade another creature to marry him and oblige him in bed and give him an heir instead of you doing these things? Thus ruining your own aspirations?"

"Exactly."

This spoke volumes about the Dragon King's powers of coercion. "Unlikely. Tell him your mission failed."

"The King thought you might be a bit slow to appreciate the nuances," the Lady said. "Hence my visit."

"The King must be quite persuasive."

"He is. No one says no to the King."

Until now. "Just how does he propose to persuade me?"

"His program is basic. You came here with five children, to whom you are evidently attached. You will have one day and night to make your decision. If it is negative, the smallest child will be taken and caged with the male troll laborers, who are notoriously crude and corrupt. You may imagine the use they will try to make of her through the bars of her cage. They won't be able to ravish or kill her, but they will seriously demean her and forever destroy her innocence. You will then have another day and night to change your mind. If you do not, the cage will open and the trolls will have their loathsome and lethal way with the child. Her screams will be broadcast throughout the castle, so you will know it is happening. Then the second smallest will be similarly caged for a day and night. In this manner all five children will be disposed of in turn. Thereafter you yourself will be hooded and caged, with a day and night to decide whose bride you will be: the King's or the trolls. He hopes you will be reasonable before that point."

Astrid shuddered inwardly. The King evidently had no mercy on his victims. He was after all a dragon.

"And you, Lady—what is your hope?"

"That you will hold out and be raped to death. Then the King may be more inclined to consider my suit, where rape is unnecessary."

"But suppose I accede to the King's wish. Won't that destroy your chance?"

"Not necessarily. The King can be fickle. He may tire of you before too long, as he has with other prospects, and then you and the children will go to the trolls anyway, or be served for dinner. But this would delay my suit yet again. I would rather be rid of you at the outset."

"You might avoid complications by simply enabling us to escape this castle."

"I would be tempted, but for two things: I would not survive the King's rage, and escape is impossible."

"We broke into the castle. Why can't we break out of it?"

"Because you were supposed to come in. The dragons herded you here; didn't you notice? But when you try to get out—the King knows you will try, which is why he grants you that first day for the effort—you will run afoul of the illusion maze. Then you will come to understand the folly of even thinking of escaping the will of the King."

"Illusion maze?"

"Perhaps it has to be experienced to be properly appreciated. But I can give you a hint: if you encounter a wall, it may not actually be there, so you will waste your effort trying to get around or through it. If you set out across a level floor, it may conceal a pit of acid. You will be able to trust nothing you see. If a troll comes at you, it may or may not be real. Even if you could clearly see the whole of it, it's a maze: you would have trouble finding your way through it. So by morning you would be hopelessly lost. And of course the only real gate is guarded by alert dragons; there will be no exit there."

"That is a good hint," Astrid agreed.

"You may prefer not even to make the attempt. Simply submit to the King's will and it will be easier for you, and much easier for the children. If you are really obliging, and actually give him some pleasure, you could have a good life, you and the children, for some time. I will simply have to endure it."

So they would both be in misery, while Astrid suffered what the Lady desired, ironically. "I will consider it."

"Have a pleasant afternoon and evening," the Lady said tersely as she departed.

Astrid pondered. Her prettiness in human form had gotten her into the usual difficulty, and this trap was more sophisticated than that of the fiend. But there had to be a way out. The children's sense of the correct path had not faltered, and she believed it remained valid. But at times like this her faith was sorely beset.

The children woke and came out to join her. "We had a dream," Squid said.

"About a mean old queen dragon who came to threaten you," Win said.

"But you weren't scared," Myst said.

It occurred to Astrid that here in the Dragon King's castle they would be well advised to pretend they didn't know that their dialogue was not private. "Let's play a game," she murmured. "Do you know about crossed fingers?"

"Sometimes we hate you," Firenze said, crossing his fingers.

"That's it," Astrid agreed. She crossed her own fingers. "Of course no dragon queen threatened me. She was perfectly reasonable, in her view. She did have a forceful case to make. I need to consider it quite seriously."

They smiled, understanding.

There was another knock. Astrid went to the door. There was a handsome man in a kingly robe. "I believe you know who I am," he said.

"I believe I do," Astrid agreed. "Come into my boudoir, Dragon King."

The children faded into the background, visible but not intrusive, the very models of docile youth. They knew how to play a role.

"I would like to make you my consort and recognize your children, with their several talents, as heirs to important offices in the Kingdom. It would be a better life than you are likely to find elsewhere."

"I talked with the Dragon Lady," Astrid said. "She was persuasive. But I am as yet uncertain that this is a life I wish to have, or that the children should have. We are only passing through this vicinity on our way back to our home in Xanth proper."

"The only exit to Xanth proper is through the Dungeons and the Mad Birds domain, and thence through the Playground," the King said. "I understand that has been shut off."

"We hope to find another exit."

"We know of none. I fear you will not be able to depart Storage for some time. In the interim I would dearly like to have your favor, lovely basilisk. You have demonstrated qualities to be admired in any creature, and should make an excellent Queen."

"You understand that my direct gaze is lethal, and my ambiance intoxicating and also lethal in fairly short order? I am not a very embraceable creature."

"The embrace I contemplate can be accomplished in seconds. That should suffice. Not even a kiss is required. Thereafter we would sleep apart."

"Assuming I am amenable."

"Assuming," he agreed with another smile. "Please say you will consider it."

"I will consider it," Astrid said. "But I have not made up my mind."

"We shall talk again tomorrow," the King said, smiling as he departed.

Astrid was privately amazed. The Dragon King was so personable and polite! But he had made sure she understood that his offer was not to be denied. There was sharp steel under that velvet.

"I think he wants to kiss you," Squid said. "Even if he says he just wants a hug."

"Something like that," Astrid agreed. "But he also wants us to stay here, and not go home." She crossed her fingers where they could see. "That might not be so bad."

"It's a nice castle," Firenze said, fingers crossed. "And it might be fun having all those servants helping us."

"Instead of struggling through more dangers," Santo agreed, fingers crossed.

"Well, let's think about it, and sleep on it," Astrid said. "Then in the morning we can decide."

"After a good night's sleep," Firenze agreed.

"In any event, there's no point in even thinking about leaving the castle," Astrid said. "It has an illusion maze." She uncrossed her fingers and described it. Then she crossed them again. "So I don't want any of you trying to find any way out. That would only get us all in trouble. We would not want to annoy our gracious hosts."

"We won't," the children agreed, all fingers crossed.

"I'm glad we have that understanding," Astrid concluded. "Sometimes you can be pretty annoying brats." Her fingers were plainly crossed.

"And sometimes you smell bad," Squid said. The others laughed.

Then the children joined hands. They had a serious escape route to figure out. Astrid hoped they would succeed.

The rest of the day was quiet. The children ran around, played, napped, had a sumptuous dinner and finally, after routine fussing, went to bed. But Astrid could not relax. The Dragon King knew the talents of the children, having seen them in action against his dragons, and surely the castle and its denizens would be prepared to foil them. How could they come up with an escape that the minions of the dragon would not balk? She believed in the children, she had confidence in them, and yet she couldn't help doubting. And if they did not succeed in escaping, what could she do except agree to the King's demands? She couldn't stand to see any child tortured.

Well, what would be would be. Tonight would be the test. The King expected them to try to escape, and to fail. If they did fail, he well might achieve his desire. The thought appalled her, but she was a realist.

As darkness closed, the children quietly roused. No words were spoken; Firenze simply took Astrid's hand. He led her to the bathroom, where there was a laundry chute. They would go down that.

Fortunately the chute was narrow enough so that they could push against its sides to let themselves down slowly. It was dark, but Astrid could see reasonably well in the dark, as could Squid and Myst. The boys seemed to be able to manage by feel. Astrid suspected that they had fathomed the route in their Communing, so they knew where they were going regardless of any illusion. Most of the illusion was nullified by the fact that they weren't using their eyes anyway.

They crossed what must be the laundry room, now deserted, and came to what might be a large air-circulating vent. This was a thoroughly modern castle; it seemed the Dragon King wanted only the best. They crawled along the tubing. Then they paused as Firenze made a faint light with his head, so that Santo could see to make two small holes. Then they lifted out a loosened panel and climbed down into a cellar region. Astrid was glad the children knew where they were going, because she would have been thoroughly lost even if she had known the route.

Now they came to a lighted but deserted cave, perhaps below the castle foundation, never filled in. It was crawling with nickelpedes. But the children walked right through it. The nickelpedes were an illusion! No one in his right mind would have gone here. How had the children known?

Then Myst dissolved into fog and floated toward a wall—and through it. That, too, was an illusion. Squid assumed her natural form and followed her, feeling the floor with her tentacles. Between the two of them, they were having no trouble with the illusion. The two moved slowly onward, and the others followed them, silently.

They came to a blank wall. Was it an illusion? No, this one was solid. Myst sifted through a crack in it, then returned to explore another crack. She paused by the third crack: this was the one.

Santo approached the wall and focused. A hole appeared in it. Astrid was glad she had seen to it that he got good rest so that he was able to hole stone without soon tiring. The hole enlarged until it was big enough for them to crawl through. They did.

The other side was simply another section of the foundation. They walked along the rough passage formed by supportive walls until they came to another dead end. Then Myst went to work again, locating the exact place it could be safely holed, and Santo holed it. They crawled through.

This time there was water beyond. The back of the castle was built up from a moat or river, as some were. Was there a moat monster?

There was. A huge greenish snout appeared. Firenze's head started to heat, and Santo oriented to make a deadly hole.

"Don't." It was a voice behind them.

They whirled. There were two figures: Wesla Werewolf and Goldie Goblin. Astrid removed her glasses.

"Don't!" Goldie repeated. "We're not stopping you. We want to escape too. We followed you without telling, or there would have been an army of trolls here now. We can help you. Just let us go home once we're clear of here."

Astrid hesitated. Could they trust these two, or was this merely a tactic to delay them while trolls closed in?

"We'll show you," Goldie said. "We'll tell Moatie you're friends."

Beside her, Win nodded. The children knew.

"Do it," Astrid said tightly.

The two forged out into the shallow water. "Moatie!" Goldie called. "We're friends. You remember us. We gave you treats, dropping them from the turret."

The monster eyed them. It nodded. Then it sank silently back into the deeper water.

"Where do we go from here?" Astrid asked the children.

The children linked hands. "We wait for the Dragon King," Firenze said.

"We what?" she asked, startled.

"Please don't turn us in to him!" Goldie begged, terrified.

"Of course we won't," Astrid said.

"His spies saw where we escaped," Santo said.

"Too late to stop us," Squid said.

"He's mad," Win said.

"He'll try to burn us all up," Myst said.

"That will be better than if he captures us," Wesla said seriously.

"So why are we waiting for him?" Astrid demanded, exasperated.

"You'll see," Firenze said with the type of smile normally seen on the snoot of an attacking dragon.

"They know what they're doing," Astrid told the goblin and werewolf. "We have to trust them."

The two did not look greatly reassured.

"What *are* you doing?" Astrid asked the children.

"We have to fight the dragon," Santo said. "But my talent is tired from making holes through stone."

"I can dive to save myself, but that wouldn't save anyone else," Squid said.

"My mist would just evaporate in the fire," Myst said.

"And my hot head wouldn't stop long-distance strafing," Firenze said.

"So it's up to me," Win said.

Astrid realized that Win had spoken out of turn, letting the others give their reasons. But all of them had known. "Myst will fend off the dragon," she told Goldie and Wesla. She hoped.

There was a light in the night sky. It was a streak of fire emitted by a huge dragon. The Dragon King was coming.

Firenze and Santo took hold of Win's arms and held her up against the castle wall, facing outward. "Get down," Squid said. "Hang on."

Astrid, Myst, Goldie, and Wesla got down in the cold water and grabbed onto outcroppings of the foundation.

A wind started. Astrid realized that it was from Win. But her wind never had any backlash; it really originated from her body. Why were the boys holding her?

The dragon evidently spied them in the gloom. He oriented, coming in for a strafing run. A terrible jet of fire shot toward them. The goblin and werewolf quailed.

The wind leaped into gale force. The fire wavered and bent aside.

Then the wind became hurricane force. It blasted at the dragon, causing him to pause in the air despite flying vigorously forward. But he was determined, and put on more power, resuming his advance.

The wind climbed to tornado force. The shaft of air from Win was a straight column, but the air around it was still, and where the two touched there were tight screws of friction. The surface of the water was whipped into a lather by the surrounding turbulence. Spume splashed into the wall, drenching the children there.

Now Astrid saw why the boys were holding Win. It was to prevent her from being blown away by the whirlwind!

The dragon was literally blown out of the sky. He fell tumbling, his fire trailing in a corkscrew of light. He splashed into the water.

But he wasn't finished. He righted himself, there in the roiling cloud of fog, lifted his snoot, and inhaled.

"Dead ahead," Squid said. "Down."

The boys aimed Win ahead and down. The spear of air shot directly at the dragon, blasting him out of the water. He flew backward, spinning out of control, disappearing into the darkness, leaving only a corkscrewing pattern of dissipating fire.

Now at last the wind diminished. Win had done the job, but now she hung loosely between the boys, unconscious. She had given her all.

Myst scrambled up and across to hug Win. "She's all right," she reported. "Just pooped."

"We have to move on before he recovers," Firenze said.

"We have maybe fifteen minutes," Santo said.

"Let me help," Wesla said. "I can carry her." She got up, went to the girls, and picked Win up, cradling her like a baby.

"We never saw the like," Goldie said, awed. "Such a little girl."

"They are remarkable children, all of them," Astrid said. "I knew I couldn't let the dragon have them."

"This way," Squid said, swimming in her natural form.

"He will come after us," Wesla said.

"My home is not far distant," Goldie said. "We'll be safe there."

"We don't trust male goblins," Astrid protested.

"We have a queen. She'll grant you visitor status."

"Is this feasible?" Astrid asked.

"It's on our escape route," Myst said.

It was feasible. They slogged on through the shallow water. Soon they reached a footpath leading out of the water to a hole in the adjacent mountain.

"Not there!" Goldie said. "That's a wormhole."

Indeed, the blind snout of a giant worm poked from it. They quickly bypassed it and continued on around the mountain.

A light showed behind them. The dragon had recovered and was questing. "We need to get under cover soon," Astrid said.

"There!" Goldie said.

It was another hole, this one guarded by a truculent-looking male goblin. "Fresh meat!" he exclaimed, seeing them.

"Goofus, it's me, Goldie, escaped from the Dragon Castle," Goldie told him. "With friends. The dragon is after us! Tell the Queen!"

Goofus, recognizing her, disappeared into the hole. They followed him into the mountain as the Dragon King spied them and flew down. But almost immediately a squadron of armed goblin males charged out, eager to do battle with the dragon. They had long spears, water bombs, and broad heavily insulated shields.

Astrid and the children collapsed in a warm cave. They were safe. For the moment.

CHAPTER 10:

GOTCHA

They had hardly gotten settled before the Queen arrived, identified by her crown and royal robe. Her hair was a golden yellow mane, unusual for a goblin. She immediately oriented on Astrid. "Are you the basilisk? I have heard good things of you via the grapevine." She held up a grape to illustrate that it was literal.

"I am," Astrid agreed cautiously, hoping this was not more mischief.

"I am Queen Golden Goblin. Welcome to Goblin Annex."

"I am Astrid Basilisk-Cockatrice. Goldie said it would be all right to come here. We do not mean to intrude."

"We seldom recover captives of the Dragon King alive. Goldie has been battered and ill-used, but she is alive and should recover her spirit in time. She escaped because of you. We appreciate that."

Astrid smiled. "We can't claim credit. We did not know she was following us."

"She followed you because you treated her courteously. Not everyone does that, in or out of the Dragon Castle."

"No one deserves the sort of treatment I suspect she got at the castle. A werewolf bitch also escaped with us. I hope we can arrange for her safe passage back to her Pack."

"Goldie has already asked for that. She said Wesla treated her kindly, being a fellow captive of an esthetic aspect. That meant unkind male demands.

We will see that the bitch gets home safely." The reference clearly was not pejorative. "Our association with the Pack has been mixed. Perhaps it will improve hereafter."

"It surely will, Your Majesty," Wesla said.

"Goldie tells me you did not know her identity."

"Her identity?" Wesla said. "She was just another captive, like me. A common girl. We got along because we faced a far greater horror than any differences of species or personality we might have had."

"Ditto," Astrid said.

"She is my daughter. Princess Goldie."

Astrid and Wesla looked at her, mute.

"We made no commotion, because that would have been counterproductive. But I was sore of heart to lose her, and measurelessly gratified to have her back. Now relax. Be assured that you will not be ill treated here." The Queen departed.

"I believe her," Wesla said. "Now I realize that Goldie was too refined to be common. But the Dragon King would have held her for ransom had he known, and tortured her if it was not promptly paid. He tortured her some anyway; it was routine. But it could have been worse. She had reason to conceal it."

"She had reason," Astrid agreed.

Wesla lapsed into wolf form and went to sleep.

Astrid saw to the welfare of the children, then slept herself.

In the morning the goblins had a fine breakfast awaiting them. Then a contingent of armed males supervised by an elite female—Goldie herself—made ready to conduct Wesla safely to Wolf Country.

They both hugged Astrid as they parted. "I knew I could trust you when you spoke well of Wulfha," Wesla said. "She does not bestow her friendship lightly."

"We hope to escape Storage," Astrid said. "But if we do not, and we survive, we hope to return to associate with the Pack."

"Wulfha would surely like that," Wesla said. "So would I."

Then they were gone. "We must move on," Astrid said to the Queen. "We thank you for your hospitality, but will not impose on you longer."

"About that," the Queen said. "Your route, I believe, lies deep within the mountain. We do not go there, though we are underworld creatures. It is complicated and treacherous, buttressed by deadly illusion."

"We have navigated illusion before. It is predatory monsters that concern us more."

"We know of none. But of course we have not penetrated far."

"We hope to find a route to the outside world. This seems to be it."

The queen shook her head. "There may be something hidden in those awful caverns, but we have no certainty that it is an exit from Storage, other than that of death. I know that the children have remarkable abilities, but I fear this is beyond their competence. I understand the Dragon King was able to obtain some of that illusion to mask parts of his castle, but only the simpler parts. I feel you would be better advised to travel back to Wolf Country."

That was interesting, but not as fearsome as the Queen evidently thought. "My friends are in Xanth proper. So is my husband. I must return to them if I possibly can. It is also important that the children return. The welfare of Xanth itself may depend on it. I thank you for your concern, but we must make the effort."

"I understand. Farewell, Astrid Basilisk."

Then they were on their way. The goblins guided them to a tunnel marked ALL HOPE ABANDON in the farthest reach of their domain and watched grimly as they entered it. This time they had torches they could light when they needed them, though the goblins thought they would not be useful. Astrid wondered why, but did not inquire. The tunnel wall emitted a soft glow, so it was easy to follow.

Before long the tunnel opened into a truly impressive subterranean chamber. Its ceiling was marvelously high and grown with stalactites, while its floor was so far below that it was lost in the darkness. Everything was in shades of gray. From the ceiling dangled assorted ropes, supporting swinging platforms. There seemed to be no way across, yet it also seemed that their route required them to cross.

"I could float across," Myst offered. "Maybe see what's there."

"And what if you got caught in a draft?" Astrid asked.

"Trouble," the girl agreed. Because she would not be able to get out of it by solidifying; she would drop into the fathomless gulf.

"We'd better consult."

The children linked hands, Communing. Then they separated. "Across," Firenze said.

"Using the swings," Santo said.

Astrid remembered that this was the Storage section of the Playground. Naturally they had swings in reserve. But she wasn't clear how they applied.

"Swing from one to another," Squid said.

"And let them swing back," Win said.

"For the next person," Myst concluded.

That seemed treacherous to Astrid, just as Queen Golden had warned.

"Over that gulf? Suppose someone falls?"

"It's not as deep as it looks," Firenze said. He squatted down and put his hand into the void. "Feel."

Astrid did the same. Perhaps a foot into it she felt hard rock. "Illusion!" she exclaimed. "How did you know?"

"Squid put a tentacle down. But it could be deep farther in, so we don't trust it."

"So we'll swing," Santo said.

Astrid gazed at the swings. The nearest one hung tantalizingly close, tied to two stout stalactites above, but just out of reach. "We need a hook, which we don't have."

Win smiled. She faced the swing. The wind passing her increased, pushing the swing away. Then the wind stopped, and the swing swung back. Close enough for Firenze to catch its rope.

"That isn't big enough for more than one person at a time," Astrid said dubiously.

"We sense it's part of the magic," Squid said. "One person per swing."

"So one person swings out over the gulf," Astrid said. "What then? The gulf is huge."

"We catch the next swing," Win said.

"And the next," Myst agreed. "A chain."

Astrid remained supremely uncomfortable with this. "And where does this chain lead?"

"Across," Firenze said. "Where we have to go."

Astrid sighed. "I have to trust you, the group of you. But this makes me nervous as bleep."

They were silent, waiting for her decision.

"Oh, I guess we'll have to do it," she said without grace. "I just hope your confidence is justified."

"This part is," Santo said.

That did not reassure her much. "Who swings first?"

"I do," Win said. "Then you."

"Do it," Astrid said tightly.

Firenze held the swing for Win, and she got on it, standing, holding on to the two ropes. He let her go and she swung forward. She arced out over the seeming gulf. Then back again, and forward, the travel diminishing, until she came to rest directly below the supporting stalactites. Astrid opened her mouth, and shut it again; the children surely had something in mind.

Win stood and blew at the next swing. It moved away from her, then back, and she caught it with one hand. Then she stepped across to the new swing, still holding a rope of the old one. She let go of the old, swinging forward on the new, facing back. She let herself swing slowly to a stop, as before.

"Ready?" she called.

"Ready," Astrid answered, suppressing her nervousness.

Win blew. She remained still, but the first swing swung away from her. It came to where Firenze could catch it. He held it in place.

Astrid nerved herself and climbed carefully onto the swing, standing. The board was solid and the ropes firm; that much was reassuring. Then Firenze let it go, and it swung forward. She gazed down into the gulf and quickly away again, as it made her giddy. Maybe it was not deep at all, but it looked almost infinite.

She let herself swing back and forth until she came to a halt. What now?

Win turned around and blew at the third swing. Soon she caught it on the back-swing, and transferred again. Then she blew the second swing back to Astrid. Astrid caught it, and transferred. She let the first one go, and it swung back to the rim of the gulf, where Firenze caught it.

Myst was next. But they did not send her on immediately. First Win and Astrid had to move on respectively to Swings Four and Three. They did, and Astrid let Swing Two go, waiting for it to settle.

Then Myst swung forward to catch Swing Two. Now there were three of them on the swings. They had established a kind of procession.

In this manner they proceeded slowly across the gulf. It seemed precarious, but actually the platforms were firm and the ropes provided firm handholds.

When they were strewn out in a line of six directly over the center of the gulf, there was a flicker of motion to the side. Oh, no! It was a small gray flying dragon! Right when they were unable to avoid it.

"Santo, can you hole it?" Astrid asked.

"Sure," Santo said. He was the fourth in line, after Myst. He focused on the approaching dragon.

The creature continued flying toward them. Now it shot out a thin stream of gray fire.

"Any time now, Santo," Firenze said. He was the last in line, after Squid.

"I'm doing it!" Santo snapped. "But it's not scoring."

"Then I had better do it," Astrid said grimly. She lifted off her glasses and oriented on the reptile. She needed to have it actually look at her face, in order to score. "Hey beastie!" she called. "This way!"

But the dragon ignored her. It flew right toward Santo, who raised an arm to fend it off.

And past him.

No, *through* him.

"Illusion!" he exclaimed. "That's why I couldn't hole it! There's nothing there. Even the fire's not hot."

That was also why it had ignored Astrid's call, and why her Stare would have had no effect anyway. There was no dragon, just the semblance of one.

Weak with relief, Astrid let her pulse slow. She had been more worried for the children than herself, but regardless, it had been an unpleasant incident. The dragon's purpose might have been to scare someone off a swing, to drop into the void. That was surely mischief, regardless how deep it was or wasn't.

"Let's move on," Astrid said briskly to cover her uncertainty.

They swung on. Other creatures came, including silent harpies—the lack of screeching was a dead giveaway—a small roc bird, clouds of biting flies, and of course more dragons. All illusions, all quickly gone.

Win came to a divide in the swings. The main swinging path curved gently to the left, but there was a lesser one curving right. She hesitated.

"The right," Firenze called. "I can feel its relevance."

Win promptly oriented on the closest small swing to the right and blew it into motion. She caught its back-swing and moved on.

Astrid was uncertain. "The left side swings are larger, and continue across the gulf," she said. "The right one veers into a blank wall. Are you sure we should take that one?"

"He's sure," Myst said. "I remember too."

Astrid did not argue the case further. She simply had to trust what the children knew, as usual, odd as their choice might seem at times.

As they progressed, Astrid looked back, gaining a different perspective on the route not taken. Now she saw that the swings went only so far before stopping. That was the true dead end.

Win caught the last swing before the wall. Was there a ledge there? A hole? Astrid strained to see, but saw nothing.

Win got on the swing and swung forward, directly into the wall. Astrid winced as she collided.

And disappeared. Had she dropped into the gulf? No, Astrid had been watching her throughout. She had simply vanished.

Then the swing came back, and Astrid caught it. It had reappeared—without the child.

"Illusion!" she exclaimed, relieved. "The wall is an illusion!"

The remaining children chuckled. They had known it.

Astrid mounted the new swing and sailed on into and through the wall. She caught the next swing, and sent the old one back through the wall. Win was in the swing beyond, waiting. The line of swings continued on to the far wall.

Before long they were all in this chamber, whose walls were reddish, as were the swings. It seemed that each chamber had its décor.

Then there was a sound. Not loud, but there. A kind of swishing. It seemed to come from empty space well to the side of the line of swings.

Squid sniffed. She had the sharpest senses of all of them: eyes, ears, and nose. "Trouble," she said.

"What is it?" Astrid asked.

"It smells like a little dragon. No, a big bat. It's not friendly."

"But there's nothing there!"

"It's invisible."

"Another illusion?" Santo asked.

"Not exactly."

"The illusion of invisibility!" Astrid exclaimed.

"Yes. We have to stop it before it bites us."

"Santo?" Astrid asked.

"I'll try. Point to it, Squid."

Squid changed form and pointed with a moving tentacle, tracing the progress of the bat. It seemed to be headed toward Astrid; she heard the faint sound approaching. Santo squinted, still not seeing it.

"Hole it anyway," Astrid said nervously.

Then there was a little shriek. An injured bat fell out of the air and dropped into the gulf. Astrid caught only a passing glimpse, but its teeth looked vicious. It had come to feed.

"Now we know," Astrid said. "Here in the red chamber the creatures are real, but covered by illusions. I fear that's more dangerous."

They organized for the new threat. Squid kept close ears and nose on anything approaching, and Santo was ready to send holes where she pointed. Meanwhile the group swung on across as rapidly as was feasible. They needed to get out of this chamber.

But Astrid feared there could be something worse beyond it.

There was another sound, as of a steaming kettle. "Steamer dragon," Squid announced, pointing.

Santo loosed a hole where she pointed. There was an angry hiss, and for a moment they saw a small dragon threshing an injured tail. Then a hole appeared in its head and it dropped.

But now there were several sounds, coming from all around them. "They're mobbing us!" Astrid said, alarmed. "We need a better way to identify them, or we're lost."

"Maybe I can do it," Myst said.

"Do it," Astrid agreed.

The child dissolved into a small thick cloud of mist. Then it expanded, becoming a large thin cloud.

And the invisible creatures showed up within the cloud as blobs of nothing. They remained invisible, but since the mist was visible, their invisibility outlined them. They were like clear bubbles in the fog. "Beautiful!" Astrid murmured.

Santo swung around, sending needle-sized holes toward each hole in the cloud. There was a series of squeaks, squawks, and hisses as the creatures were holed. They dropped down. Soon the cloud was clear.

"Coalesce, Myst!" Astrid called. "Get back on your swing!"

The cloud condensed, and soon the child was back on her swing. "I'm glad there's not a wind," she said.

Astrid hadn't thought of that, in the tension of the moment. A wind would have blown Myst away. "If we come to a windy section, stay solid," she said.

They reached the next wall and swung through, one by one. This chamber was pale blue, like washed-out sky, and the swings matched.

What illusion threat would they find here? Astrid was developing a solid respect for illusions. They could be as lethal as completely solid creatures. "Let's get on across," she said. "But watch for anything even slightly unusual."

They swung on across, getting efficient at this mode of travel. Then, at the center, where they could neither advance nor retreat readily, the next siege began. A small dragon flew toward them.

"Back to visible illusions?" Firenze asked. "We can ignore them."

"I don't trust this," Astrid said. "This should be worse than the others, not a repeat."

"There's something funny about that illusion," Santo said. "It's not flying right."

"Not for a dragon," Squid agreed. "That's more like a bat."

"Let me try," Win said. She stood on her swing and sent a blast of air at the odd dragon as it came at her.

And it was swept backward. It struggled to right itself and resume its approach.

"It's real!" Astrid said, surprised.

"It's not real," Squid said. "At least not the way it looks."

"Santo, hole it," Astrid said grimly.

The boy oriented. A hole appeared in the dragon. The creature spun out of control and fluttered down into the gulf—as a bat.

"I knew it!" Squid said. "A bat—masked as a dragon."

"But why?" Myst asked.

Astrid had the answer. "Everything here is an illusion, of one type or another. So this time the illusion covers real creatures, instead of just making them invisible. So we'll think they aren't real, and they can reach us and chomp us."

"Tricky," Win said, letting her wind fade.

They resumed swinging. Another creature appeared, this one a vicious-looking hawk. "Our swinging alerts them," Firenze said. "So they don't waste their energy going after nothing."

Santo holed the hawk. It growled in pain and dropped, becoming a dragon.

They swung again, passing an intersecting line of swings. Win swung back toward Astrid. "Where are you going?" Astrid asked, surprised.

The child didn't answer. She collided with Astrid's swing, put her head down, and bit Astrid on the leg.

Astonished, Astrid put a hand down and caught the child by the scruff of the neck. But it wasn't clothing she caught; it was the scaly neck of a dragon. It was an illusion!

Now she saw the real Win ahead on another swing. Furious, she hauled the mock dragon up to her face and stared into the supposed child's eyes.

In a moment she held a small dead dragon in her hand. She dropped it into the gulf. Then she checked her leg. The dragon had been small, and her basilisk skin was tough; there wasn't much damage. But it was a lesson.

"Did you see that?" she asked the children.

"Win swung back," Santo said. "Only it wasn't her; it was a dragon copying her. I'd have holed it if I'd realized."

"Suppose it was the real Win?" Squid asked.

"That's what we're up against in this section," Astrid said. "Illusion-covered creatures—including ones that look like us. We don't dare attack them carelessly, lest we hurt one of our own."

"I can tell, now that I know to look," Squid said. "That fake Win was a mirror image."

She could tell a mirror image by sight? She really did have superior sight! "Then coordinate with Santo," Astrid said. "Tell him which ones are the fakes so he can hole them."

"And the fakes can't talk," Firenze said. "So when in doubt, talk."

They resumed swinging. Another figure appeared. This one was a copy of Santo himself. "That's not you," Squid said confidently. "Hole it."

"I suspected as much," Santo said with a bit of a smile as he holed the image of himself. It became a hawk and fluttered into the gulf. "Weird."

There were other attacks, but they dealt with them and continued moving. They had gotten on top of another type of illusion.

They made it to the next wall, and swung through.

The fourth chamber was pale green, from stalactites and swings down in the gulf. There were no illusions visible, but those would surely appear once they were committed to the swings. There was a large stone platform or mesa in the center that could serve as a resting point.

"We need to be ready for anything," Astrid said. "I think Myst should travel as a cloud, ready to condense the moment she needs to. Squid should keep alert for anything, real or illusion, and let us all know. Santo needs to be ready to hole anything she tells him to. I will be ready to Stare anything similarly. Firenze can firework as necessary. We all have to trust each other, even if we see more copies of ourselves."

The children nodded. Then they set out, with Win leading the way, blowing and swinging. It was slow, but no longer very slow as they connected efficiently.

When they got well out into the gulf, things exploded into action. Suddenly there was a host of flying dragons, birds, bats, and huge insects. There were also invisible creatures, as Myst's mist showed. And some of the visible creatures, Astrid was sure, would be not illusions but illusion-covered creatures. All were converging on the swings.

"You know what to do!" Astrid called.

"In the cloud," Squid said. "Three blips."

Santo oriented, and the three blips developed holes, became little flying monsters, and fell down into the void.

"The Astrid behind you is not her," Squid said. Santo whirled and holed the figure of Astrid, and it became a dragon and fell.

"The others are straight illusions," Squid said. "Ignore them."

One of those was a giant flying scorpion headed right for Astrid. She nerved herself and let it collide with her—and pass on through without effect. Firenze stood up to a giant rabid bat similarly.

Thus organized, they made it to the central platform, which was not an illusion. They got on it, relieved, ready to rest before moving on. Myst coalesced into her solid form.

A man appeared. "What are you doing here?" he demanded.

"He's real," Squid said, surprised. "Not human, but not a monster or an illusion."

Astrid faced him. "We are a party of one adult and five children seeking to depart from the Storage rooms of the Playground. Is this something you know anything about?"

The man puffed up to a larger size, literally. "Of course I know. This is my private Storage purse, normally closed to intruders. I made it, I maintain it. There is a penalty for intrusion."

So he was a figure of some consequence. This could be very good or very bad. Astrid put on her most fetching smile, one almost guaranteed to soften the heart or head of any male. "Then let's introduce ourselves. I am Astrid Basilisk, effective nanny for these children."

The man took that in, but neither flinched nor warmed. "I am Dwarf Demon Gambol, specializing in games."

A Dwarf Demon! That must be Gambol as in gamboling, skipping or frolicking, playing games. Even the least of Demons had more sheer power than the whole of the mortal creatures of Xanth. Certainly he would be immune to her Stare. She needed to tread carefully here. She smiled again, winsomely. "Then you are the proprietor of the Playground and all its impressive annexes."

"As I said." But he was beginning to melt. Her smile was in some respects the inverse of her Stare, making men become accommodating. She was a bit nervous employing its power, because if she made too much of an impression he would get an idea that seemed never to be far from a male mind. Even Demons could have somewhat mortal tastes, as the marriages between Demons and mortals indicated.

"We were visiting the Playground because of its fine recreational facilities, especially its Stage for Plays, when someone folded it up with us inside. Was that you, without being aware of us?"

"That was not me," Gambol said. "The Playground is for children to use freely. But they should stay out of Storage, which has become overrun with vermin."

Such as goblins, harpies, werewolves and dragons? "We encountered those. Now we seek only to escape, so we can return to our home. But the path has been arduous."

Gambol considered. "You are near the exit. Considering that your presence here is involuntary, I will let you go. But the children must remain here."

"No," Astrid said firmly. She was fully conscious than a mortal did not say No to a Demon, but she had no choice. "We must leave together. These

152

children are my responsibility and I must get them home."

He considered. "So you do have a bit of backbone, basilisk. How do you propose to buy the freedom of the children?"

And there it was. He was interested in something that could not be done in the presence of children, and that she did not want to do at all. She couldn't even be too explicit about discussing it while they listened. "I am a virtually married woman. If there is any service I can render that does not compromise that, I will consider it."

Gambol smiled. "I like your attitude. I was thinking of a game."

"That depends on the game," she said guardedly.

"The kind children can play. I collect and save all kinds of children's games. Give me a new one, and I will let your party go."

Astrid was at a loss. She did not know of any children's game that he would not already be familiar with.

"We can help," Firenze said.

"Oh, thank you!" Astrid said gratefully.

"First we have to invent it," Santo said.

"Invent it," Gambol agreed.

The children linked hands, Communing. Then they separated. "Please stand here, Aunt Astrid," Squid said, leading her to a spot in the center of the platform.

Then the children quickly sketched a network of lines circling around her, like a big puzzle. Soon they had it completed.

"This game is called 'Basilisk,'" Win said.

"It's a maze," Myst said.

"The object is to start at this side," Firenze said, "and find our way through it to the other side."

"But there's a basilisk in the center," Santo said. "Her Stare is lethal and even her closeness is deadly. So she is hard to pass."

"But all paths go past her," Squid said.

"So there's no way to avoid her," Win said.

"But there is a way to get through," Myst concluded.

Gambol contemplated the maze. He tried walking along one path, then another, and another. But all paths led to Astrid. "I could pass, of course, but I see no way for a child," he said.

The children smiled in unison.

"What is the way?" the Demon asked, faintly nettled.

"Love the basilisk," Firenze said.

"Do what?"

"And trust her," Santo said.

"But she's deadly!"

"And she will love you back," Squid said.

"And let you pass," Win added.

"Unharmed," Myst concluded.

Then they demonstrated. Firenze entered the maze and navigated it to the center where Astrid stood. "I love you, basilisk," he said, not looking directly at her.

Astrid kissed him quickly. "And I love you, Firenze."

He walked on, completing the maze.

One by one the other children did the same, each declaring love without looking, each being kissed and passed along. Then all five of them stood at the far side.

"It will work for any sincere child," Firenze said.

"According to the rules of this game," Santo said.

"Which won't have a real basilisk in it," Squid said.

"Just a pretend basilisk," Win said.

"But we do love our real one," Myst said, taking Astrid's hand briefly.

Gambol nodded. "I like your game. I'll take it. Depart in peace." He vanished.

"Oh, thank you, children!" Astrid said. "You came through, again. I even liked the way you did it."

"We do love you," Firenze said.

"And I love you, all of you," Astrid said, tears in her eyes.

They didn't delay. They set out swinging, heading for the far side of the gulf, where Astrid now saw a sign saying EXIT. No illusions attacked. They were truly being allowed to go in peace.

Win blew the last swing, setting it in motion. It swung away—but snagged on an outcropping of rock that Astrid could have sworn had not been there before.

"Blow it again," she called.

Win did, sending another gust. But the swing stayed snagged. She blew up a gale that tugged violently at the ropes.

And a rope broke, dropping the swing's board into the gulf.

They stared, horrified. Had they lost their way out at the last stage? Without that swing they could not complete their crossing.

"GOTCHA!"

Suddenly Demoness Fornax was there. So was Demon Nemesis, caught with his formerly invisible hand on the rope. So it had not been an accident!

"You are guilty of interfering in a Demon Wager," Fornax told him. "As you did when you folded up the Playground and locked the children inside. This time I caught you. You thought to hold them hostage to force me to comply with your desire, or to intervene myself to save them and forfeit my case. But I lurked throughout, watching, and nailed you. Your backside is mine, Demon!"

Demon Nemesis looked at his backside, abashed. "You caught me," he agreed. "You can destroy my reputation among Demons, a humiliation I can't tolerate. Naturally you have some fell motive in mind. What is your price?"

"I will think about it," Fornax said. "But whatever it is, you will pay it without question, or suffer the consequence."

"I will pay it," he agreed.

"Now repair that swing and begone."

The Demon disappeared. The swing hung there, intact. Win blew it, and got it swinging. They resumed their progress.

"Thank you," Astrid said as Fornax floated beside her. "You saved us."

"It is what a friend does. I did not desert you. I merely had to hide and let you proceed alone so that Nemesis would show his hand. I would have intervened had any of you gotten in real trouble."

That was comforting to know in retrospect. By "real trouble" she meant likely death. But it would have cost the Demoness hideously. "I'm glad you didn't have to."

"But it was nevertheless a great satisfaction to nail Nemesis's backside."

Astrid laughed. "I'm sure. Only you could have done it."

"And that was touching, the love you share with the children. I love you too, Astrid, as a friend. I knew it when I saw that happen."

"Wenda Woodwife was right. Children are the key to friendship and love." Astrid sighed. "But I have a problem."

"I will help you with it if I can."

"We are about to escape this prison and return to Xanth proper. The children will be free. But I don't want to give them up."

"Because you love all of them."

"Yes. I liked them before, but this adventure, which really put us all through our paces, brought out their marvelous qualities, and now I love them."

"And we love you, Aunt Astrid," Firenze said. "We don't want to leave you." There was a murmur of agreement along the swing line.

Astrid had for the moment forgotten that her dialogue with the Demoness was not private. Now she had to argue the other side of the case. "But you have to be adopted into five families, and get your family portraits painted, so that

Xanth will be saved."

There was a sigh along the line. "We do," Firenze agreed sadly.

They let the subject drop, and it fell heavily into the gulf, vanishing without even a splash.

One by one they came to the EXIT sign and swung through the wall. They landed on firm rock in a tunnel whose steps spiraled upward. There was even a convenient handrail. There was a landing at the top, with another door. They opened it and stood on a landing overlooking a pleasant wooded vista. There was a path wending politely down the slope. The air was fresh and sweet.

They hugged each other, phenomenally relieved. They were out.

CHAPTER 11:
HOME

Fornax stood by the side, looking a little sad. Squid noticed, and went to her. "You helped us, again, Aunt Fornax," she said. "You saved me before, and also when you caught that mean Demon. Give me a virtual hug."

Fornax assumed her ghostly form, and the child carefully hugged it.

"We do appreciate what you did for us," Santo said.

"Thank you," Fornax said. Astrid could see that she appreciated this recognition.

"Now we need to figure out where we are," Astrid said. "I thought we'd come out the other side of the folded Playground, but that does not seem to be the case."

"I must not do anything to facilitate your progress physically," Fornax said. "Nemesis is watching, hoping to catch me intervening, just as he did, thus nullifying my advantage over him. But considering that we are here because of his interference, I believe I can safely clarify some details. We are in a placid corner of the Region of Earth; the next volcanic eruption here is not due for a while, so it's safe."

"For a while?" Astrid asked, uncertain whether to be alarmed.

"A century."

Astrid laughed, relieved. "That will do. But why is the Playground exit here?"

"Gambol wanted a convenient site at a fixed place. The Playgrounds—there

157

are several of them—may move around, as folk transport them, but when he needs to enter their common Storage to stock another game he doesn't want to have to search. So the back entrance remains in one place, regardless where the front entrances go."

"That makes sense," Squid said.

"But where is the folded Playground?" Win asked.

"Nemesis flipped it into the Gap Chasm."

They stared at her. "Then it's lost!" Myst wailed.

"Not so. It remains where it landed, caught in a partridge pear tree."

"But we can't get it there," Firenze said.

"You can if you choose to," Fornax said. "You can simply travel there and pick it up."

"But what about the Gap Dragon?" Santo asked.

Fornax smiled. "I suspect Astrid could handle him."

Squid laughed. "I guess she could."

"But the Gap Chasm is big," Win said.

"How could we ever find it?" Myst asked.

"That is part of the beauty of Gamble's system," Fornax said. "He wants to know where the Playground are at all times, in case he want to impress a new child with one. So he set up a pointer."

"A pointer?" Firenze asked.

"Here," Fornax said, indicating an alcove in the mountain behind them. There was a small stand there with what looked like a weather vane. "This always points to the one the person associated with, and the size of the arrow indicates how far away it is. A small point means it is far in the distance; a large point means it's close by. So this means that it is moderately far away, in this direction."

"So we can go that way, that far, and find it?" Santo asked.

"Yes."

"Neat," Squid said.

"Unfortunately the direct way is crowded with dragons, harpies, nickelpedes and some less savory creatures."

"We have had enough of those," Astrid said. "Anyway, it is time for us to get on home to our companions, who surely are distraught about our disappearance."

"Not so," Fornax said.

They all looked at her. "They don't miss us?" Win asked.

"They did miss you, the morning you were lost. Kandy contacted me, alarmed. I told her that you were reasonably safe and working your way through the labyrinth, and would return to them in due course. They were reassured, and went on about their business."

"This was an aspect of your compromise," Astrid said, working it out. "You could not do anything to help directly, but you could provide information about what Nemesis had done."

"Exactly. Telling on him did not constitute a violation of the Demon Protocols, though I did not identify him personally."

"Neat," Myst said, giggling.

"Still," Astrid said, "we should not let them worry any longer. We should return there now."

"But we want the Playground," Firenze said.

"Because we can use it to better plan what to do," Santo said.

"And it's fun," Squid said.

Astrid threw up her hands, almost losing them in the sky. "You really want to rescue the Playground, after all the mischief it brought us?"

"Yes," Win said. "Because that mischief was with you."

Astrid fended off her flush of pleasure. "So you want to search it out. Fighting off all the monsters in the way as we go to the Gap?"

That made the children pause. "Commune," Myst said.

They linked hands, Communing.

"That Communing is really an extra talent," Fornax remarked. "Each of them must have a piece of it, and when they get together, it manifests. I don't recall seeing that in Xanth before."

"Maybe in the future people have learned how to get a bit more than one talent apiece," Astrid said, similarly intrigued.

The children separated. "We have it," Firenze said.

"I will make a hole," Santo said.

Astrid exchanged a glance with Fornax. "A hole?" she asked blankly.

"A big one. From here to there."

"But there are mountains between here and there," Astrid protested. "You get tired just making holes through stones."

"My power is growing, and the other children enhance me. I can do it."

"They are special in the way they support each other," Fornax said.

What could she do? "If that's the way you want it, then do it," she said. "But it's still a long haul."

"Maybe not," Squid said.

Santo focused. A huge hole with a circular rim appeared before him, going in the direction of the arrow. It seemed to be a translucent hole in the substance of Xanth itself, for it started at the slope of the mountain and angled down slightly, passing through the air on the way to the ground across the valley. Inside it was shiny and slightly glowing.

"But it's still a long way," Astrid said. "And not big enough for me to walk upright."

"We'll make a cart," Win said.

They got to work on it, fetching fallen branches and tying them together with vines. Firenze heated his head and burned the edges off three sections of wood to form disks, and Santo made holes in the centers. They put poles through the holes. Before long they had a three-wheeled cart with a sail made of a harvested sheet. They set it in the hole and sat on it with Squid in front, her tentacles wrapped around the steering column of the front wheel.

Then Win, standing on the back of it, started her wind. It caught the sail and pushed the cart forward. It accelerated, and soon they were moving rapidly along the tunnel.

Astrid, seated in the center with Firenze, Santo, and Myst, was amazed. The ride was remarkably smooth. She could see through the wall of the tube as they zoomed through hill and dale, now in the air, now underground. The children had made all this, somehow knowing how to do it.

"Really talented kids," Fornax remarked approvingly.

Something about the way she said it aroused Astrid's suspicion. The children were *too* talented. They had developed not only magic talents of remarkable power, but also the ability to coordinate them so as to accomplish more than seemed likely. This seemed to be way beyond the likely abilities of children. They were receiving effective guidance. They called it Communing. But it had to be more than merely pooling their awareness.

In fact it seemed more likely that they were actually channeling advice and support from a phenomenally more potent source. One who was sincerely trying to understand and assist the children. One who could not help openly, because that would constitute Demonly intervention and be banned by the other participants in a Wager. By passing it through the mechanism of Communing, she could mask the real source. A friend who was not seeking credit.

Astrid could not say a word, lest she trigger mischief. But she realized that just as she loved the children, she was coming to love Fornax too.

The Demoness glided along beside her, pretending to be oblivious.

"We're getting there," Squid said.

The wind eased. The cart slowed. They drew up to the end of the hole.

They scrambled out.

They were deep in a U-shaped canyon whose sides rose awesomely high. This was the dreaded Gap Chasm.

"The Playground will be somewhere around here," Firenze said. "We just need to find it."

There was a puffing sound. "That's a steamer," Squid said.

"Stanley Steamer," Astrid said. "The Gap Dragon."

"We can't go until we find the Playground," Santo said.

"You look for the Playground," Astrid said. "I will intercept Stanley."

She walked out toward the approaching sound. Now she heard a whomping, as the dragon undulated toward her. She stood her ground.

The Gap Dragon rose into view. It was full dragon size, long and sinuous. It had six small legs, two vestigial wings, and a horrendous green head. Steam puffed from its mouth and joints. It moved by lifting a section and whomping it forward like a giant inchworm, the raised section traveling back along its body until it expired at the tail. The raised section seemed not to move; it was the rest of the body that moved, sliding through it. Overall, it was an intriguing and impressive effect.

The dragon spied her and paused. He inhaled.

"I wouldn't," Astrid said. "I give you fair warning that I am a basilisk in human form. I can stun you or kill you before either your teeth or your steam can reach me. I suggest you listen to me before proceeding further."

Stanley considered. Then he resumed inhaling.

Astrid removed her glasses without looking directly at him.

Maybe it was her clear disdain for his power that impressed him. Few creatures acted that way without reason. He breathed out, not firing a jet of super-heated steam.

"Good enough," Astrid said, putting her glasses back on. "I am Astrid Basilisk-Cockatrice, on a mission to eradicate the pun-destroying virus. We are a party largely of children who have lost a rather special Playground. Someone folded it up into a matchbox and tossed it into the Gap. We are here to find it, and when we do, we will depart. We mean no harm to you or the Gap Chasm. We know you, Stanley Steamer, and would much prefer to cooperate with you than oppose you. Will you agree to a truce?"

The dragon considered. Then he nodded.

"The children will be glad to meet you," Astrid said. "They know you by reputation." She turned and walked back the way she had come.

The dragon followed.

"Children!" Astrid called. "Allow me to introduce Stanley Steamer, the dread Gap Dragon. We are in a state of truce."

The dragon nodded again.

"And Stanley, here are the children: Firenze, Santo, Squid, Win, and Myst." Each child dutifully faced the dragon and nodded when identified.

"Ooo!" Squid said. "You're so handsome, Stanley. I adore fearsome dragons."

The dragon's snoot turned a darker shade of green: his way of blushing.

"The children would like to meet you up close," Astrid said. "May they?"

Stanley nodded again. Squid, Win, and Myst ran up to him, hugging his scaly neck and kissing his hot nose. He plainly liked the attention. Before long they were riding him, squealing with delight as they rode the traveling hump and slid off the tail. Astrid was glad to see it, knowing how appealing little girls could be, but she did keep a careful eye out. One never could be quite certain with dragons.

Meanwhile the boys continued the search, but there was no sign of the matchbox. "It's got to be here," Firenze said, frustrated.

"Strike a match," Astrid suggested.

He banged his head with the heel of his hand as if knocking the dottle out. "I forgot." He brought out his match and struck it against a rock. And disappeared.

Astrid looked around, searching for him.

"Over here!" he called.

He was in a large bramble bush some distance to the side. He was holding up the matchbox, having found it where it had fallen out of the partridge pear tree. In a moment his head heated; he put it down and burned off the brambles, and stepped out.

Astrid went to him and kissed him, relieved, as he held his breath. Then she called to the other children. "We have the Playground! Firenze found it!"

The three girls left the dragon, to mutual reluctance, and rejoined Astrid. Only Santo remained apart, standing beside Fornax; the two had evidently been talking. "I think we need to consult," the Demoness said.

"There's a problem?" Astrid asked.

"He's catching on."

"Uh-oh," Firenze said.

Astrid did not ask for details. "We need privacy."

"My place will do."

"Your place," Astrid agreed.

"This way." Fornax ducked down and stepped into the open hole they had used to get to the Gap.

Astrid herded the children after her, sitting them on the wagon, facing in. Then she joined them. Win blew it forward. In a moment they were zooming back through the tunnel.

In another moment they came out. Not by the mountain they had started at, but in a stone castle. "Welcome to my residence," Fornax told them.

"In Fornax Galaxy?" Firenze asked.

"With CT matter?" Santo asked.

"The terrene enclave that I maintain in the ContraTerrene galaxy," agreed Fornax.

"You are safe here, as long as you do not stray beyond the castle environs, and our dialogue will not be overheard. Complete candor is possible. But with it must come complete trust."

The three girls looked puzzled. "Why?" Squid asked.

"Because your lives could be in danger if you break the trust," Astrid said.

Now Squid caught on. "Aunt Fornax's been messing in again!"

"I have," Fornax agreed.

"To help us," Win said.

"As before," Myst said.

"Why?" Firenze asked.

"Because we would not have survived or escaped Storage otherwise," Santo said.

"Tell us how," Squid said.

"And who," Win said.

"And when," Myst said.

"When Squid swam across the underground river I enabled her to change her smell as well as her appearance, so the predators did not recognize her."

"My smell!" Squid said. "I forgot about that! I did not have that ability before."

"When Myst floated under the Dungeon exit door, I gave her cloud mobility she did not have before."

"That's right!" Myst said. "That's when I found I could do it! I thought I was just discovering more of my talent."

"And later I enabled her to expand to a much larger size without losing control, so she could identify the invisible monsters in the gulf."

"That too," Myst agreed. "Thank you, Aunt Fornax."

"When Win blew the dragons away, I enhanced her power."

"I could only do a light breeze before," Win said. "Suddenly I could do

Gale and Hurricane. I thought I just hadn't really tried before."

"When Firenze needed to stop the fiend and dragons, I enhanced his fireworks to full hotheadedness."

"That's when it happened," Firenze agreed. "I wondered. I never got beyond fireworks before."

"And me," Santo said. "For this last trip. Suddenly I could do big, long tunnels without tiring. I thought it was just the natural development of my powers. But then I wondered. I tried to ask Aunt Fornax, but she wouldn't answer. Now I think I know why. She's not supposed to mess in."

"I'm not," the Demoness agreed. "I have been cheating. Nemesis will have *my* backside if he finds out."

"And the Communing?" Astrid asked.

"That was my first gift, along with increased intelligence. They needed to believe in each other."

Which explained the uncommon intelligence and judgment the children had showed. They were far beyond their ages.

"So you have been enhancing us all along," Squid said. "Ever since you helped Aunt Astrid rescue us."

"The rescue was a joint effort," Astrid said. "We were exploring friendship, and believed that working together with children would help."

"And did it?" Win asked.

"Yes," Fornax said, her eyes closed.

"What do you want with us?" Myst asked.

Fornax looked at Astrid. "Must I answer that?"

"I think you must."

"I want to love and be loved. To love all of you, and be loved in return. So that my friendship with Astrid can be complete."

"But how would you expect us to be grateful if we never knew what you did?" Firenze asked.

"I did not do it for your gratitude. I did it because—" she broke off.

"You need to finish it," Astrid said.

"Because I already loved you."

The children gazed at her. "Don't you have a Demon Bet against Xanth surviving?" Santo asked.

"I do."

"But if we survive and get adopted out, Xanth will survive," Squid said.

"Yes."

"And you will lose your Bet," Win said.

"Yes."

"You really do love us," Myst said.

"I do." She had been proving it all along.

Firenze considered. "Can we safely touch you, here in your home?"

"Yes, if you want to."

The children pounced. Suddenly Fornax was buried in hugs.

"We do love you," Santo said. "At least I do."

"We all do," Squid said.

"We just didn't know it," Win said.

"Until now," Myst said.

Now there were tears on Fornax's face. "May I kiss you?" she asked. For answer, they started kissing her, all over.

Astrid watched, feeling the tears on her own face.

After a while the children's brief attention span moved on. "What else is here?" Firenze asked.

"Everything," Fornax said. "Gardens, parks, playrooms, kitchens—"

"Eye scream?" Santo asked.

"A mountain of it."

In little more than an instant the children were reveling in that mountain while Astrid and Fornax watched. "The boredom and loneliness are gone," Fornax said. "The children have banished it."

"They have," Astrid agreed.

"But I can't keep them here. All that will remain is my friendship with you."

"I can't keep them either," Astrid said. "How I wish I could! But the friendship will remain."

In due course the children, tired out from their activities, bounced on the playroom beds and sank into sleep, while the adults sat in large easy chairs. Only Santo delayed briefly. "I meant it," he said to Fornax. "I wish I could stay with you."

"Stay with me for a while now."

He joined her on the chair, curling up on her lap. She put her arm around him, and he slept with his head on her shoulder. She looked as happy as he did.

This had worked out almost too well. Astrid had come to distrust anything that was too easy. Where was the catch?

Hours later, when they all woke, Astrid organized the children for the return. "Aunt Fornax has trusted you with information that could severely damage her among Demons," she cautioned them. "You must never speak of it outside. In fact, don't even show the extent of your talents unless you have to."

They nodded in unison. "We won't," Squid agreed.

Then they entered the tunnel, blowing back to the Gap Chasm. The Gap Dragon was gone, having moved on about his rounds. All they had to do was make a new hole to the original campsite.

"Um, should we do that?" Astrid asked.

"Why not?" Firenze asked.

"It should be a longer trip back to our campsite. If we suddenly appear there, thanks to a huge new tunnel you make, that will reveal the extent of your talent. Maybe it won't make a difference to most folk, but a watching Demon could be suspicious."

"I don't want suspicion," Santo said. "It could get someone in trouble." There was no need to say whom he meant.

"Why don't we walk home?" Squid asked. "We've walked plenty in Storage. We can walk some more in Xanth."

"And see the sights," Win agreed.

"Maybe some naughty ones," Myst said, giggling.

They tackled the chasm wall. There was a small path winding up the slope, cut into the wall. It looked dangerously narrow, but they should be able to navigate it if they were careful. This time Astrid sent Squid up first, in her natural form, so that her sensitive tentacles could feel out the way and make sure it was firm. Then Firenze with a staff made from a suitable dead branch, treading carefully. Then Win, Myst, Santo, and Astrid. Fornax was along, but would not trek with them.

It started well. Then Squid encountered a long large snake going the opposite way. It was a serpent trail!

The snake, annoyed by their intrusion on its path, hissed and threatened them with a fang. But Squid imitated another snake and hissed back. Astrid wasn't sure what she said, but the other snake decided to yield the right of way.

"She charmed him," Fornax murmured. "That's one clever girl."

They reached the top. There was southern Xanth spread out before them.

"Ooo!" Win oooed. "A kitty cat!"

"Don't touch it," Astrid warned, recognizing the species. "That's a cat-atonic. It stuns anyone who touches it."

Win withdrew her hand, heeding the voice of experience. They were back in punny Xanth.

Fortunately that was the only danger at the moment. There was even an enchanted path nearby. That meant they could safely and comfortably travel without worrying about monster attacks. The children skipped along, enjoying it. It was quite a contrast to what they had encountered in Storage.

As the day faded they came to a rest stop. There were pie plants, a tsoda pond, assorted bedding and clothing trees, and a nice shelter. They could relax for the night. They feasted and washed and settled down for a story Fornax told about adventures in weird faraway lands like Earth. Astrid had to admit they were amusing. The Demoness was really catching on to getting along with children, and did seem to enjoy their company.

Fornax stayed with them for the night. "May we sleep beside you adults?" Win inquired as darkness closed in.

"Sleep beside whomever you wish," Astrid said. "But not too close to me. You know why."

"We know," Myst said. Then she and Win lay down on either side of her.

Santo and Squid lay down on either side of Fornax. Astrid knew why: the one had had her life directly saved by the Demoness, and the other had taken a shine to her. That left Firenze, who was satisfied to sleep by himself.

Late in the night a voice spoke in Astrid's head. *Something is happening that we need to track.*

It was Fornax, using her telepathy. *Do we need to get up?*

No. We should stay asleep. But I will relay it to you. Someone is sending the children a joint dream.

That's suspicious, Astrid agreed. *Is it a Demon?*

I believe so. We must monitor it without interference, so as to know what is going on. Then we may know what to do.

Then the dream started, oddly, as if waking up. The children thought it was the real beginning of the day, not realizing that they were asleep. That was doubly suspicious.

The supposed morning proceeded normally, but in rapid motion, a kind of summary that went unquestioned by the dreamers. The children got up, leaving the adults asleep. Then they went outside.

There were five pretty horses waiting for them. One of them caught their eyes and made a little speech balloon over her head. Inside the balloon was not printed speech but the head of a young pretty human woman. "We are Day Mares," she said in a musical voice. "I am Doris."

"Hello Doris Day Mare!" the children chorused, delighted.

"We bring nice daydreams to people whose attention wanders," Doris said. "But we have a problem we hope you can help us with. That is why we are appearing to you as we are, instead of delivering our dreams invisibly."

"What can we do?" Firenze asked.

"We have run low on material for the sweetest dreams," Doris said. "A shipment got lost, and we are in danger of running out. We need to get more, quickly, or many folk will suffer stupidly blank minds instead of nice dreams. That would be awful! The dreams are stored in Castle Innocent, but we can't enter it."

"Why not?" Santo asked.

"Only children can enter Castle Innocent. Adults are hopelessly spoiled by things like the Adult Conspiracy. We mares are unfortunately adult. We know about things like signaling the stork and fading out at the end of life, and we have heard all the bad words. So we can't get in. But you children should be able to enter Castle Innocent and fetch out the perfect stuff of dreams. That will rescue us from failing our mission. Will you help?"

"Of course we'll help," Squid said enthusiastically.

"Thank you so much! Then we will carry you to the castle. Do get on." And the five mares lay down so that the children could mount their backs.

"But I don't know how to ride a horse," Win protested belatedly.

"Don't worry," Doris said. "You will be magically secured so you won't fall off no matter how fast we go."

"That's good," Myst said.

The children got on the five mares, and the horses stood up carefully. Sure enough, although there were no saddles, the children had no trouble staying on. Dreams could be wonderful that way, especially daydreams.

"And away we go!" Doris said, making a friendly little neigh.

The mares started walking. Then they trotted. Then they galloped. Then they flew without wings. The children stayed on, loving it. They looked like accomplished riders.

They zoomed with the speed of thought o'er hill and dale, past stream and meadow, leaping across verdant valleys and over high hills. Soon they reached the lovely Castle Innocent. It was girt with candy-colored pennants on rock-candy turrets sparkling in the sunlight. A tsoda-pop moat surrounded it, with many flavors of lollipops growing on its bank.

"How do we get inside?" Firenze asked as the smaller children drooled.

"The front door will open for you," the Doris image said.

They dismounted and approached the castle. As they did, the drawbridge creaked down. Its boards were made of hard chocolate.

"Are there any cautions?" Sancho asked.

"Just one: don't eat anything inside the castle."

"We won't," Squid promised.

But Win wasn't satisfied. "Why not?"

"Because then you will not be able to leave it. It's a rule."

"Awww," Myst said, looking rebellious.

But Astrid, watching, knew that this was the kind of rule that existed in temptingly dangerous places. This was mischief.

They trekked across the moat. Firenze tried the handle of the door, and it turned readily, letting the door swing inward.

They marched on in. There were piled boxes marked DREAMS. They picked them up one by one and moved them to just inside the front door, which remained open. They weren't at all heavy; it seemed that dreams had very little physical substance.

Myst spied a little fragment of a chocolate chip cookie behind where a box had been. It looked wonderfully good. Who would ever miss it? She picked it up and popped it into her mouth, thinking no one would notice.

Don't do it! Astrid thought, too late.

A siren wailed. The lights blinked. The front door slammed shut.

"Oh blip!" Firenze said. "Someone ate something."

"FEE FI FO FUM!" the castle said. "SOMEONE DONE SOMETHING DUMB!"

"Who?" Santo asked, looking around.

"Not me," Squid said.

"Or me," Win said.

They all looked at Myst. There she stood, with a guilty crumb of cookie on her lip. She was obviously the one. "I'm sorry," she wailed, tears streaming down her face. "It just looked so good."

Firenze tried the door. It was tightly closed and locked. He looked at the windows. They were barred. They were caught inside.

"Now it says CASTLE GUILTY," Santo said, reading the words on the inside of the door.

"How do we get out?" Squid asked.

"THERE IS ONLY ONE WAY OUT," the castle voice said. "YOU MUST CONFESS YOUR MOST GUILTY SECRETS."

Oh, bleep! Astrid thought. *It's a trick to unmask your participation, Fornax. So that's why the dream! One of the Demons must be suspicious.*

Astrid considered that. *Not Nemesis?*

He would not dare, knowing that I have his number. We'd both get called up on charges.

Can we stop this?

Not without giving away the secret. It's a cunning trap for more than the children. We shall just have to watch, and hope.

They watched, and hoped.

"Can we Commune?" Win asked.

The children linked hands and Communed. It seemed that they could do this even in a joint dream.

"Wow!" Myst said.

"I don't know," Firenze said.

Santo considered. "Let me just say something that possibly is only a passing thought. If I knew a secret, such as maybe there being an ugly wart on a certain lady's bottom, and I had to choose between saving myself and betraying her, but I really liked her, I think I just wouldn't want to disappoint her. And I think that if anyone wanted me to betray a friend, well, that would not be anyone I wanted for a friend. So I'm not telling anyone anything."

I really like that boy, Fornax thought. *And I don't have a wart on my bottom.*

He was being careful not to give away the real secret while making his point, Astrid thought. *He's a smart boy.*

He is. I'm sorry I can't keep him.

And that of course was the problem. Astrid and Fornax had both come to love the children, but could not keep them. They could not even touch them, really. Others would have to adopt them so that Xanth could be saved. Astrid knew they were doing the right thing, but sometimes it was harder than it looked.

Santo's discussion decided it for the children. "Me neither," Squid agreed.

"Even if we have to stay here forever," Win said.

"But I'm the one who did it," Myst said tearfully. "So—"

"No," Firenze said firmly.

"We're together," Santo said.

"We all make mistakes," Squid said.

"Any of us could have done it," Win said.

Myst just cried tears of gratitude.

"So let's see what we can do," Firenze said.

"I'll make a hole," Santo said.

"No need," Squid said. "When we Communed, we learned what this is."

"A dream," Win said.

"To make us Tell," Myst said.

Firenze nodded. "So all we have to do is wake."

"I'm not quite ready," Santo said. "I'm mad at this fake castle."

"So am I," Squid said.

"Let me have the honor," Win said.

"Sure," Myst said.

They got together again, holding Win in place. Then the wind started. She aimed it up, and it quickly intensified, blasting at the ceiling. It got worse, until the ceiling blew away, crashing up against the roof. The wind swirled, seeking a way out. Then the roof blew off and went sailing across the sky. Then the walls blew out, and the castle collapsed into rubble around them.

Outside, the five day mares were staring. But the wind flew out to blow away their costumes, and they were revealed as night mares. This had not been a nice daydream, but a nasty nightmare. Then they too were blown away.

"Now we can wake," Firenze said, satisfied as he gazed at the wreckage.

The dream lost the last of its cohesion and dissipated into foul mist as they woke.

They were lying as they had been, with Santo and Squid on either side of Fornax, Win and Mist by Astrid, and Firenze alone. Dawn had not yet come.

The two adults lay silently, as if still asleep. Would the children tell them of their dream?

One by one the children dropped back to sleep, perchance to dream of something else. None spoke of the Communal dream.

Everyone had secrets.

Fornax turned over, as if in her sleep. Her ghostly hand fell across Santo's hand and remained there. He did not pull his hand away.

When true dawn came, they all got up and went about the morning routine. Then they resumed the walk toward home.

CHAPTER 12:
FIRENZE

~~~

"They're back!" Kandy cried, rushing to hold her breath and hug Astrid. Then they were all there. Metria hugged Santo, Kandy hugged Squid, Tiara hugged Win, and Merge hugged Myst. No one hugged Firenze. That bothered Astrid, so she hugged him, briefly.

Then came the long narration of their adventure, omitting only the detail of who had folded up the Playground with them inside; the point was that they had found their way out, and recovered the Playground. Fornax would settle privately with Nemesis when it suited her convenience. The others were duly amazed, especially by the phenomenal development of the children's talents, and their joint maturity in the crisis.

That night Astrid got private with Art, who had built up a lot of unrequited passion during her absence. She was glad to oblige it. She loved being with someone who could freely touch her without endangering his health, and who desired her without wanting to rape her.

I envy you that, Fornax remarked. *I too can't be really close to someone without exploding him to smithereens.*

Astrid had come to know the Demoness well enough not to be bothered by her presence; it was part of her friendship. Fornax had after all been with them throughout their trek through Storage, unseen; she knew what was what. Art could not see Fornax, but since this in no way diminished Astrid's passion for him, it didn't matter. *You could indulge Nemesis,* she replied teasingly.

Sometimes I'm actually tempted. He's one who won't annihilate on contact with me; dark matter interacts too little with either terrene or ContraTerrene matter. That may explain his interest.

I doubt it; he just wants to get into your panties, like any male seeing a female like you, and figures he'll get there if he just keeps pressuring you long enough. It's a male-type challenge. Astrid could not have said that aloud in the vicinity of the children, but this was silent among adults.

To be sure. But I want it to be strictly on my terms, not his. I haven't yet figured out how to permanently bind him, so I can tease him unmercifully without any possibility of parole or release. She formed a little image of herself in translucently straining bra and panties, hovering just barely out of reach of a desperately reaching Nemesis.

Well, I hope you figure it out, Astrid thought. She had no desire to tease a man unmercifully, but she wasn't a Demoness.

All too soon Astrid put Art to sleep in the usual manner, then slept herself. It would take her days to fully unwind from the tension of the Playground sequence.

In the morning they held a meeting of all of them, including the children. "Now that we are all together again," Astrid said, "we need to see about getting the five children suitably adopted so that Xanth will be saved. After the mishap of the Playground, we can see that delay can be disastrous. We suspect that there are those who don't want Xanth to be saved, who might try to interfere. So we need to move on with it without further delay."

No one questioned that. "But these are not the most readily adoptable children," Mitch said. "They are good children, but folk are apt to be wary of a girl who can fog out when they want to give her a bath, or a boy who radiates fireworks when annoyed, or a girl who is actually an alien creature."

"I think such a girl would be fun," Merge said, looking at Myst.

"But you're not an outside person," Mitch reminded her. "Neither are you married."

"I know," Merge said regretfully.

"Outsiders simply do not know these fine children as we do," Kandy said, looking at Squid. "So one is alien; is that stranger than becoming a board?" She became the board.

"An outsider might not want to adopt either an alien or a board," Mitch said.

Kandy returned to woman form and sighed. "True."

"So I think we have to look carefully," Astrid said. "Somewhere in Xanth there must be couples suitable for these children. We merely need to find them."

"There's the challenge," Tiara said, looking at Win. "To find couples who will appreciate these children as we do."

"Even if they don't yet know it," Kandy said.

"We can help," Firenze said. "We can put on a Play, in the Playground, and Commune, and get an Answer."

"So you can," Astrid agreed, relieved. "Let's do it. But this time we want to have someone guarding the Playground from outside it, just in case."

"We'll all do that," Kandy said. "No one should enter that Playground without having a guard outside."

"Let's do it," Santo said.

"Do we have a Play?" Squid asked.

They paused briefly. "Maybe we could could dream up one," Win said.

"A Day Mare Dream," Myst said.

The children laughed, sharing a joke the adults didn't get. Astrid looked carefully blank, concealing her knowledge.

"They are clever children," Fornax murmured appreciatively beside Astrid, audible only to her. "They don't waste perfectly good experience."

Astrid nodded, because she couldn't answer aloud without seeming to be talking to herself.

The children trekked to the edge of camp, where Firenze unpacked the Playground. "I'll go in with them," Astrid said. "Some of the rest of you should too, to make an audience for their play."

"We all will," Kandy said.

"But at least one person should stay outside," Astrid said.

"I'll stand guard," Art said, settling down by the edge.

"Thank you." She kissed him on the ear, then followed the others in.

The adults took seats in the audience section. Fornax sat invisibly beside Astrid. "This should be amusing."

Yes, Astrid thought.

"The Bad Act. Scene One," Squid announced. "Day Mares."

The children mounted the stage and went right into their play, setting up four sawhorses in center stage. Astrid hadn't realized that there were sawhorses there, but somehow the children had known about them, in a supply section under the stage. Squid mounted one sawhorse and changed shape and color, making it resemble a real horse. The other children lay down opposite the sawhorses, then made motions of waking, washing, dressing, and going outside.

They paused, seeing the horses. "Who are you?" Firenze asked.

"We are Day Mares," Squid said. "I am Doris."

"What are you doing here?" Santo asked.

"We bring nice daydreams to people. But we have a problem. You can help us."

"How?" Win asked.

Squid, as Doris, explained the problem, concluding, "Only innocent children can enter Castle Innocent."

There was a chuckle in the audience when Doris explained how the Adult Conspiracy ruined people. They had all been there.

"Of course we'll help," Myst said.

The four children mounted the four horses and made galloping motions. It almost did look as if they were going somewhere.

"They're good," Tiara whispered. There was a general murmur of agreement.

"Scene Two," Squid announced. "Castle Innocent."

The sawhorses were rearranged to form a square in the center of the stage, with space for the entrance. "Look at that," Firenze said. "A castle made of candy, with a tsoda-pop moat."

"Don't eat any of it!" Doris called. "Or you won't get out."

"Oh, blip!" Santo swore.

"We're hungry," Win agreed.

They entered and started moving invisible boxes of dreams. Then Myst spied the cookie and made a motion of surreptitiously eating it.

"Fee Fi Fo Fum!" Squid called. "Someone done something dumb!"

The audience laughed.

"The castle's slammed shut!" Firenze said.

"We're trapped!" Santo said.

"Somebody ate something," Win said.

Myst started to cry.

"Scene Three," Squid said. "Castle Guilty."

"How do we get out?" Firenze asked.

"Confess your guilty secrets!" Squid called.

"But we're innocent children," Santo protested.

"Except for one of us," Win said.

"Me," Myst wailed.

"You were hungry," Firenze said.

"We're not leaving you here," Santo said.

175

"Let's Commune," Win said.

The four linked hands. "Wow!" Myst said. "It's a dream!"

"So let's blow it apart," Firenze said.

Win started blowing. The others knocked the sawhorses over, wrecking the castle.

"Look at the horses!" Santo said, staring at Squid on her sawhorse.

"They're night mares!" Win said. "This was all a fake to get us in trouble!"

Squid hunched over, riding guiltily away.

"Wow," Myst said.

"So let's wake up now," Firenze said.

"And that was the end of The Bad Act," Squid concluded.

The audience applauded vigorously as the five children bowed. "That was a surprisingly original play," Kandy said.

Astrid kept her mouth shut.

Then the children Communed for real. "The question is, how do we find good families to adopt us?" Firenze said.

They held hands and focused.

"Oh, blip!" Firenze said, speaking out of turn. "It starts with me. Aunt Astrid has to take me to the Panhandle, where there's a suitable couple."

"I'll do it," Astrid said. "If you know where to go."

"I do," Firenze said. "I know exactly where. That is, I know the direction and range. But not how to get there."

"We'll figure it out," Astrid said.

"The Panhandle?" Mitch asked. "Take the Trollway, so you can get there and back without taking forever."

"The Trollway," Astrid agreed, not entirely pleased. She knew the trollway trolls were different from the marauder she had encountered, but trolls were not her preferred company. But she didn't seem to have much of a choice.

"I'll go with you," Art said.

The children shook their heads. "It's fastest and cleanest if just Aunt Astrid takes him," Santo said.

Astrid sighed. "Then that's the way we'll do it."

"But I can come along," Fornax said. "Since I'm not really part of your group, but do have an interest in the welfare of the children."

"That will help," Astrid said gratefully.

Then suddenly, they were on their way. They took an enchanted path to the nearest trollway station, which wasn't far.

"You will need to figure out a way to pay for your passage," Fornax reminded her. "I can't do it without interfering, unless to counter another Demon's interference. But you—you know what they'll think of first."

Astrid knew. Males took one look at her and thought of it. She wished she could turn it off. "Firenze, I think you will have to do some work," she said.

"Anything you want," he agreed.

"Now that you can control your fireworks, you can make an interesting display for an audience. That should earn our passage."

"Sure."

"I know you have no more use for trolls than I do. But for this we need them."

"I understand."

"You're very amenable. You're not like the surly kid I first encountered."

"Three things about that," he said, smiling. "First, you showed me at the outset that you would not take any guff from me, and you had the means to enforce it. I respect that. Second, I have come to know you as a really nice person, and I want to help you any way I can. Third, our Communion showed that this trip is important, so I have to do what I can to get it done."

"And fourth, you have matured emotionally," Astrid said. "You're no longer that ornery kid."

"I suppose," he agreed.

"You have," she insisted. "You help with the other children in a responsible way."

"I try. I'm the oldest and they expect it. But it's not because of maturity."

"What is it, then?"

"It's that I think you're better than my real mother was, and I wish you were my mother." He held up a hand to halt her protest. "My folks didn't want me; I was a burden. When my magic showed, they called me a freak, and wanted me even less. Our loving family was just a pretense. That's what made me ornery. You're not like that. You just wanted to help me. You accepted me as I am, including my magic. I—I feel comfortable with you. So anything you want me to do, I do. To try to please you. Without you I'd just be that hotheaded kid nobody can stand."

Astrid was taken aback. "But I'm not even human. I'm a deadly animal nobody in his right mind will approach."

He smiled. "Maybe that's why you understand difficult kids. We're like that."

She had to laugh. But it was sad, too. "I can't even hug you without warning you to hold your breath."

"I wish I could hold my breath forever." He swallowed, and she saw that he was on the verge of tears. "But hugs are only part of it. You truly understand me, Aunt Astrid. I wish *you* could adopt me. If you wanted to."

What could she do? "Hold your breath." She paused in their walk and enfolded him, and kissed him on the cheek. Then she let him go, so as not to hurt him by her closeness. "I wish I could too." There; it was out.

"You do?" He seemed almost reluctant to believe.

"I wish I could adopt all of you five orphans. I wasn't fooling when I said I loved you. I don't think you children were fooling either when you said you loved me."

"We weren't," he agreed. "You—you are what we all need, Aunt Astrid. We all saw that in Storage. You led us through. We don't think anyone else could have, or would have."

"Aunt Fornax was watching. She would have."

"We like her too. But she's not part of Xanth, so she can't take care of us."

"I'd like to be your mother. But there seem to be multiple reasons why it can't be."

"Yes," he agreed sadly.

"It is ironic," Fornax said, appearing for Firenze as well as Astrid. "You wish you could be a family, but can't, because you are trying to save Xanth from eventual destruction. I'd like to win my bet, but can't, because that would mean the loss of all of you. We're all doing the right thing, at personal cost."

"I guess that's what it means to be adult," Firenze said.

"It's what it means to have a conscience," Fornax said. "I'm not used to it any more than you are, Firenze."

"A conscience," he agreed thoughtfully. "It makes you do the right thing, even when nobody's watching."

"Demons are not used to that," Fornax said.

"Neither are children."

"So it seems we are learning together."

"There's the Troll stop," Astrid said, relieved to let the subject rest.

"I'll fade," Fornax said, fading.

Sure enough, there was a small troll-house, with a troll in it, and a sign: STOP: PAY TROLL.

They stopped. Astrid put on her most insincere smile. "I need to arrange for passage for two on a vehicle to the Panhandle. I don't have coins."

The troll looked at her. "There may be an alternate way."

"No," Astrid said firmly. "I forgot to mention that I am a basilisk in human form; my look and touch can be lethal. But the boy has a talent that may amuse other passengers."

"You don't look like a basilisk." His eyes were on her front.

Astrid leaned close, giving him a better view. "Sniff my perfume."

The troll did. Little planets circled his head briefly before dissipating into acrid smoke. "That is the smell of death," he agreed.

"I promise to keep to myself and not make any mischief. We just want to get from here to there."

"Let's see the talent," the troll said as his head cleared.

Firenze made a nice little fireworks display. The troll considered. "I'm not sure that's enough."

"Check your schedule," Fornax said in Astrid's voice.

He checked. "As it happens, we do have a bus transporting restive children to that locale," the troll said, surprised. "Such a display might distract them long enough for their keeper to get them settled."

"Done," Astrid said.

"Here are your boarding passes." The troll passed out two tickets.

They entered the compound and stood beside the trollway, waiting for the bus. "Restive children?" Astrid asked Fornax.

"Convenient coincidences happen," the Demoness said innocently. Even Firenze had to smile.

The bus arrived. They showed their tickets and took their seats. The bus was larger inside than out, with a playroom in back where excited young children romped, four and five years old. But they soon got bored, and started running between the seats and climbing over them, annoying the other passengers.

Fornax nudged Firenze. "Your turn."

Firenze got up and walked to the playroom section. "Do you like fireworks?" he asked, getting their immediate attention. In a scant moment they were standing in a circle around him.

He started slow, with a few small rockets arcing up from his head. "Ooo!" the children exclaimed. Then larger rockets appeared, exploding into colorful displays. "Oooo!" they said. Finally he made a phenomenal multirocket barrage. "Ooooo!" they cried.

Then they got tired, and their handler, a plump female troll, got them to lie down and sleep. "Thank you," she said gruffly to Firenze.

"Welcome," he said politely, and rejoined Astrid and invisible Fornax. Then, to them: "That was fun."

"You did well," Astrid said, squeezing his hand.

"I never thought I'd be good with children. Did you know you would be,

Aunt Astrid?"

"I did learn human ways from secretly interacting with a child, so maybe that was a hint. But it was my friendship with Fornax, and the advice of Wenda Woodwife, that got us into children. So really I didn't know."

"Did you know, Aunt Fornax?" he asked.

"I did not. But you are very special children."

"You made us special, by enhancing our—" He broke off, realizing that this should not be spoken aloud.

"Your self-respect," Astrid said.

"Yes."

In due course the children finished their nap and got active again. The matron passed out sandwiches, and that kept them occupied for a while. But they had to use the bathroom, and there was none on the bus.

"We are coming to a rest stop," the driver announced. "There will be a half hour break. Be sure to be back aboard within that time."

"Just in time," the matron said, relieved.

The bus pulled into the stop and the children piled out, followed by the matron. Astrid and Firenze got out too. It was a closed compound with assorted facilities, including pie trees and milkweed plants.

"I must focus on other business; Kandy calls with Demon interaction," Fornax murmured. "But I will return when you resume traveling." She faded out.

"I do like her," Firenze said. "She really helped all of us." He smiled. "By helping you fetch us back from the future, for one thing."

"We started our friendship as an experimental thing," Astrid said. "But I am glad for it."

They used the facilities, and returned to the bus on time. "Different drivers," Firenze remarked.

"They must have shifts," Astrid said. "The former driver will probably drive another bus back the way he came. It's his territory."

"The other passengers aren't returning."

"This must be their stop."

The matron returned with the children and got them settled. The bus started up and pulled back onto the trollway. It was all very routine.

Fornax faded in. "Business accomplished. Now I can relax." Then she looked around. "There is something wrong."

"It's all been routine," Astrid said. "We have a new driver, is all."

"There's the wrongness," the Demoness said. "That's not the right one."

"He seems to know his business."

"Damn!" Fornax could swear, not being part of the local Adult Conspiracy. "They did it while I was distracted. Now I can't intervene without mischief."

"May I inquire, Aunt Fornax?" Firenze asked politely.

"You may, and I will answer. There is a smell of Demon interference here, as there was when the Playground got folded up with you inside. Someone does not want you to complete your adoption, and without it Xanth will not be saved. Not Nemesis, I think; I am tracking him. But someone with a bet against Xanth. I can't intervene without prejudicing the case, which may be their intention. The two of you will have to foil it, and that will be difficult."

"I don't think we can stop a Demon," Firenze said.

"Not directly. But there are constraints. The Demon set up the ploy, but may not openly support it. If it is foiled by the actions of mortals on their own, that will do. That is what you will have to do. I must not tell you more." She faded out.

"I am competent to handle most threats," Astrid said. "But she seemed worried."

"I fear we will just have to see what happens," Firenze said. "Then figure out how to handle it."

"I agree," Astrid said grimly.

The children became restive. Firenze went again to entertain them with his fireworks display. While they were distracted, Astrid went to talk with the matron. "We fear there is trouble ahead," she said. "We will try to stop it, but may not be able."

"Why should I believe a basilisk?" the matron demanded.

Astrid sighed inwardly and returned to her seat. The woman's attitude was reasonable, actually. Why trust any stranger, let alone a deadly animal?

Firenze finished his show, and the matron set about putting the children down for another rest.

There was a fork in the trollway. The driver took the left one.

"That's not the right way," Firenze said. "My Communal direction knows the route."

"Then this must be the mischief," Astrid said. "I'll tell the matron."

She went back. "Do you know the correct route?"

"I do."

"Are we still on it?"

The matron looked. "No," she said, surprised.

"Could the new driver have gotten lost?"

"New driver? We're not supposed to have a new one."

"Then I fear we're in trouble."

The matron marched up to the front. "Who are you?" she demanded. "What happened to our regular driver? Why are you deviating from the proper route?"

"Shut up and sit down, wench," the driver snapped.

"I will not! I am responsible for the children, and their safety. Turn the bus around and return to the correct route."

The driver pulled to the side and stopped the bus. He got up and walked back to where the children were sleeping. He reached down and picked up a little girl. Suddenly there was a huge knife in his free hand. He held it to the child's throat. "You were saying?" he asked the matron menacingly.

Speechless with horror, she fell back. Astrid removed her glasses and advanced on him.

"Stop where you are, basilisk," the troll snapped.

Obviously he knew her nature. She stopped.

"Matron!" he snapped. "Fetch a sleeping mask. Put it on her."

The matron found the kind of mask used to keep light out so that a person could sleep on a bus. She came to Astrid. "I'm sorry I misjudged you," she murmured. "But I can't risk the life of the child."

"I understand," Astrid said. "Do what you have to do."

The matron put the mask on her. Now Astrid's primary weapon had been nullified.

"Tie her hands behind her back," the troll ordered.

The matron found a cord and loosely tied Astrid's hands.

"Tighter."

Well, she had tried. She tightened it, reluctantly.

"Now go sit with the children."

Astrid heard the matron go.

The troll approached Astrid. When he reached her, he cast aside the child and put the flat of the knife to her throat. "Any resistance from you, basilisk, and I slit your throat. Do you understand?"

Astrid nodded. She understood far better than she liked. She knew exactly what was coming next—and she did not dare try to stop it. The troll was obviously an experienced molester. One of the bad ones, as Truculent had been.

Unless she could shame him. "Are you going to do it in front of the children?"

"Yeah. It'll do them good to see it."

"Such a direct violation of the Adult Conspiracy will utterly freak them out."

"Exactly." He was evidently shameless.

The troll hooked his fingers in her shirt and ripped it open. "Nice," he said. Then he caught her skirt and hauled it down. "Nice," he repeated.

Evidently the sight of her panties did not freak him out. Too bad; she had counted on that. Some males were so jaded that they could resist the freak. Those were generally the worst kind.

"What are you going to do with the children?" she asked, playing for time. The longer he stayed close to her, the more likely her ambiance was to get to him.

"Take them to our little group and dump them in the cooking pot for dinner. What else? Freaked out tidbits are the tastiest."

The matron made an exclamation of utter dismay. She had tied Astrid to avoid harm to one child; now all of them were threatened.

Did the troll realize that Astrid could revert to her natural form, escaping her mask and bonds? She would have to act rapidly to avoid that big knife.

He put the edge of the knife to her throat so that it pricked the skin. "Any trouble at all, and you're dead, no matter what your form, bask," he said. "So you'd better stick to this one, at least until I'm through."

He realized. She was out of options. She would have to submit to the rape and await her opportunity. But the necessity galled her mightily. She wished she could rip off the mask and fry him with her Stare.

Suddenly the bus's engine roared into life. "Hey!" the troll shouted.

There was the sound of grinding gears. Then the bus lurched forward. The children screamed as they were shoved to the back by the motion.

"Who the bleep is driving?" the troll demanded as he was jolted away from Astrid.

The bus careened to the side, the wheels running off the edge of the pavement and spinning on dirt. Then it swung back onto the highway. Astrid and the troll wore thrown back and forth, and the children screamed again as the bus veered madly about.

"Get out of there, brat!" the troll shouted.

Brat? Then Astrid put it together. Firenze! Somehow while the troll was occupied with Astrid he had sneaked up to the driver's seat and started working the controls. But how had he figured out how to drive the bus? Astrid herself didn't know how to do that.

"I'll pulverize you!" the troll said, tromping forward.

Astrid struggled with her bonds, but couldn't free her hands or get the mask off; both were on too securely.

Then hands were on her. "Hold still, bask," the matron's voice said. "I'll free you, then you stop him, if there's time during this distraction."

183

Astrid held still. But she could tell by the speed of the tromping that there was not going to be enough time.

The bus accelerated, swinging madly across the highway one way and the other, the tires squealing their magic protest. But the tromping continued. The troll was holding on to the seats as he worked his way forward.

Then the bus abruptly braked, and everything slid forward in the magic of inertia. The matron held on to Astrid, frantically untying her hands. But it was too late. "Gotcha!" the troll exclaimed triumphantly.

There was a hissing noise. Then the troll screamed in pain. "Oww! I'm blinded by fire!"

Astrid had to smile. Firenze had invoked his fireworks. In the troll's face.

Finally Astrid's hands were free. "Thanks, matron!" she said, immediately ripping off the mask. She scrambled up and oriented on the troll.

But it was no longer necessary. The troll was clawing at his blasted face, totally incapacitated by the pain. Firenze was watching as his head cooled, ready to strike again if he had to.

"Firenze!" Astrid cried, running to him as she put her dark glasses back on.

"Aunt Astrid!"

Then they were hugging, awkwardly, because the driver's chair was in the way. "You're all right!" she said, relieved.

"He was going to do something mean to you," Firenze said tearfully. "I heard him threaten to slit your throat."

"He was," she agreed, drawing away. "But you saved me by starting the bus. How did you ever manage to do that?"

"I—learned," he said. "I guess I was lucky to make it work."

"Learned?"

Then Fornax appeared. "Learning to drive a bus has no relevance to normal Xanthly activity," she remarked. "Obviously it does not constitute an intervention. It was purely an exercise in theoretical information."

"Yeah," Firenze agreed. "And also learning about inertia magic that can throw people about. I guess maybe it distracted the troll."

"Intriguing coincidence," Astrid agreed, hugely relieved. So Fornax and Firenze, working together, had foiled the troll's machinations.

Astrid took hold of the suffering troll and hustled him to the door, and then on out. She pushed him away from the bus. "Be thankful we don't abuse you the way you were going to abuse us," she said. Not that he would have noticed, given the state of his face.

Meanwhile the matron was seeing to the children, who were bruised and frightened but essentially all right. "Do you know the proper route?" Astrid asked, not looking at her directly.

"I do," the matron said.

"Then you will guide the new driver."

"New driver?"

Astrid indicated Firenze. "He's just learning, but I believe will be able to handle it."

The matron decided not to inquire further.

Firenze operated the controls, Fornax hovering invisibly beside him. This time the bus did not lurch. It moved smoothly into a U-turn and headed back along the highway. It would go to the intersection and get back on the correct route.

The matron stood beside Astrid, no longer shunning her company. "Your boy certainly earned his passage," she said. "We are lucky the two of you were traveling with us."

"I'm not sure of that," Astrid said. "The attack may have occurred because of us. I am taking him to be adopted by a good family, but we fear there are those who don't want that to happen."

"Why would anyone go to such an ugly extreme to prevent an adoption? That doesn't make sense."

Astrid was glad not to argue the case. "It does seem far-fetched," she agreed.

"He's a good and talented boy."

"He is."

Then a child needed attention, and the matron went to take care of it. Astrid was left to mull the matter. Was a Demon trying to interfere with the adoption, so as to win a bet, or was it an unfortunate coincidence? She could not be sure, but had her suspicions.

"It's not coincidence," Fornax said invisibly beside her. "Kidnapping and eating the children was just a cover for the real target: Firenze. We foiled it, but there may be similar efforts involving the other children. It's annoying."

"It certainly is," Astrid agreed.

The rest of the trip was routine. They reached the destination station, and the matron explained what had happened. "They were going to eat the children!" she said indignantly.

"It happens," the troll administrator said. "Fortunately this young man acted to foil the plot. He has earned free passage on the trollway for any future trip."

"I should hope so," the matron said. Then she hustled the children off to their destination.

"And you, young man," the administrator said to Firenze. "Should you be interested in employment on the Trollway when you grow up, it will be expedited. We appreciate the way you saved the bus."

"I was glad to help," Firenze said modestly. He knew when to keep his mouth shut.

Guided by Firenze's sense of direction, they walked to an unusual site: a sawmill. Boards and planks were neatly stacked, ready for use, but there was no sawdust. In the center was a man addressing a large log. He put his hand to it, and laser beams shot out, cutting the log into six slices. That explained why there was no sawdust: there was no saw.

Astrid approached the man. "May we talk?"

He glanced at her, and his pupils dilated. She had seen that effect before.

"Hello. I'm Laser."

"I'm Astrid, and this is Firenze."

"If you want boards or planks, we can make a deal. What do you have in trade?"

"Not that kind of a deal," Astrid said.

"Just as well," Laser said. "I'm married."

"Yes. Firenze has a talent in some respects similar to yours: he can shoot fireworks from his head, just as you shoot lasers from your fingers. We thought you might be able to provide a good home for him."

"Now that's interesting," Laser said. "How did you know we were looking to adopt a child?"

"Word circulates. So I brought him to meet you."

"Can you cut a log?" Laser asked Firenze.

"No. I could set fire to it."

"That won't do. We don't like fires. We could use a useful talent, but yours won't do for handling lumber." He turned to Astrid. "So no, we don't want to adopt him. He would not be a good match."

Astrid suppressed her disappointment, which felt almost like relief. "You are surely right. Thank you for your consideration." She took Firenze's hand and walked away.

They returned to the trollway station to await the next bus back. "I'm sorry I wasn't good enough," Firenze said.

"You're good enough," she said. "It just wasn't the right fit. I'm sorry I hauled you all the way out here for nothing."

"I'm not."

"But you were put in danger! It was a bad trip."

"It was a good trip."

She looked at him. "Are we on the same page?"

"I love traveling with you like this. If I get adopted I won't see you again."

"I would visit you."

"I'd rather be with you all the time."

"Firenze, that's—"

"Let me make an observation, purely as an intellectual point," Fornax said, appearing. "The children have to be adopted, and get their portraits painted with their new families. When that is accomplished, Xanth will be saved. There's nothing in that prophecy that says they have to be adopted *out*. They could be adopted *in*."

"Adopted in?" Astrid asked blankly.

"You could adopt me," Firenze said.

"But—but then what was the point of this trip across Xanth?"

"Another perhaps irrelevant observation," Fornax said. "A journey together can be a learning experience. Your time together may have satisfied both of you that you are right for each other, when you were unwilling to believe it before, being locked into the notion that adoption out was necessary. So the point of the trip was not to locate a distant family, but to interact long enough to be able to come to that conclusion. You traveled to find the right adoptive family, and maybe you have found it: your own."

"Can that be true?" Astrid asked.

"I hope it's true," Firenze said.

"You know I'm a deadly animal."

"You know I'm a surly kid."

"You both know you want this," Fornax said.

Decision came upon her like a dive into a pool. "Yes, I'll adopt you! Hold your breath; I'm going to kiss you."

He held his breath. She kissed him. It was decided.

CHAPTER 13:

~~~

They made the return trip without complication, because of the trolls' appreciation for Firenze's assistance saving the children. Astrid still did not much like trolls, but had to admit that it depended on what type she encountered. The Trollway trolls were all right.

But who had set up the kidnapping? A hostile Demon surely, but which one? Could it be the same one who had gotten the children in trouble via the joint dream?

"As I see it, there are three prospects," Fornax murmured. "The Demons Neptune, Mars, and Saturn. Mars and Saturn stayed clear, but Neptune bet against the survival of Xanth."

"That's interesting," Astrid said. "What is his association?"

"Mass/Energy. They are really different forms of the same thing. I run afoul of his domain when I touch terrene matter and convert it to energy."

"Could Neptune have an interest in you, as Nemesis does?"

"He's more interested in sea creatures. But he does resent my occasional conversions of mass to energy. Now that I have in effect changed sides in the Xanth Wager, he may be more resentful."

"So he could be trying to nullify your influence."

"He could be."

"Then he could have sent that dream of Daymares to the children."

"He could. And put an idea into the minds of hungry bad trolls."

"But we can't prove it."

"That is the problem," Fornax agreed glumly.

They continued their trek. In another day they were home.

"So I will adopt Firenze," Astrid concluded her report. "The trip we made did find him a home. It just wasn't the one we expected."

"But—" Art started.

She focused on him. "First I'll marry you, of course. Then we'll adopt him. Then you'll paint our family portrait, using a mirror so you can see yourself to paint. We will have done our part to save Xanth from destruction. Do you have a problem with that?"

Art opened his mouth. Astrid leaned toward him and inhaled. "No," he said, his eyes starting to crystallize. He was immune to her poison, but not to her charms.

Men were easy.

"Lovely," Fornax remarked invisibly.

"But what about the others?" Firenze asked. "There need to be five portraits."

"We'll work on them, of course," Astrid said. "The children will all be placed. Who is next?"

"Let's Commune," Firenze said.

The children linked hands and Communed. "Me!" Squid said, surprised. "I'll find my Family on an island. That way. Tomorrow." She pointed across the terrain.

"An island?" Astrid asked. "I'm sure if we go far enough in that direction we'll come to water eventually. But we don't want to send you swimming alone. I'll have to go with you."

"Sure, Aunt Astrid."

"Crossing water," Astrid continued. "I'm not going to swim among the fins. That means a boat."

"There'll be one," Squid said. "The route line I see curves to catch it. It's small. Maybe a canoe."

"I'm not good with small boats," Astrid said. "I'm more of a desert creature. I have little experience with water, and what I have is not great. I'd likely fall in and drown. That wouldn't be much help."

"No," Kandy said. "You're my friend. I won't let you drown. Ease and I will go with you."

"We will?" Ease asked, surprised.

Kandy turned slowly toward him so that he could fully appreciate her remarkable profile. She didn't even need to inhale; she was already his dream girl. "It's your talent to make things easy. Like managing a canoe."

"We will," he agreed.

They rested a day and night. Then Astrid and Squid set off, accompanied by Kandy and Ease.

And Fornax. "Maybe this time we can get by without covert Demon mischief," she murmured.

"I hope so," Astrid said. "Things are complicated enough without that."

"What's 'covert' mean, Aunt Fornax?" Squid asked.

"Secret. Demons are not supposed to mess in, but sometimes they do it sneakily."

"The way you enhanced our—"

"She's just a bystander, dear," Astrid said quickly with a meaningful squeeze of her hand.

"Oh. Sure," the child agreed, remembering. "And I guess there are other bystanders."

"But sometimes what one Demon does needs to be countered by another," Kandy said. "To make it fair."

In due course they reached the water. It seemed to be an inlet on a larger sea. There was the boat, caught in vines by the shore, abandoned. The children's Communion had known. And that ability to Commune was one of the deliberately unrecognized gifts of the Demoness.

Ease hauled the boat clear. It was a dugout canoe carved from a sturdy log. "Looks seaworthy," he said.

"But there're no paddles," Astrid said.

"One will do," Kandy said, and became the board. Her clothing dropped to the ground, and Ease picked it up and put it in the canoe.

"I love it when she does that," Squid said. "She doesn't pretend, the way I do; she really does change."

"She was a board when I first met her," Astrid said. "But I was never bored."

Squid giggled. "She's fun."

"She is," Ease agreed. Astrid suspected that he meant that in a different way.

Astrid found a reasonably flat fallen branch and adapted it into a crude paddle. Then the four of them climbed into the canoe and pushed off.

"That way," Squid said from the prow, pointing.

They paddled that way. Ease had an easy stroke that propelled the craft rapidly forward; he did have the touch. Astrid helped, so as to contribute her share.

"What's that?" Squid asked, pointing into the sky.

"Oh, bleep!" Astrid swore. "That looks like Fracto."

"The wild cloud?" the child asked. "Part of Xanth's legend?"

"The same," Astrid agreed. "We have brushed with him before. Let's hope he doesn't see us."

But the cloud had already spied them. It loomed close, expanding.

"Or recognize us," Astrid said.

A whirling gaseous eye formed, glaring at them. Fracto recognized them.

"He's a two-bit troublemaker," Ease muttered. "A real airhead."

"Or hear us," Astrid said, concerned.

A blast of cold air blew down on them. Fracto had heard. Now they were in for it. Already the water was getting choppy.

When Astrid had encountered the violent cloud on the water before, she had pacified him by using her female wiles. She feared that would not be enough this time.

"Maybe if two lovely women addressed him," Fornax murmured. "Or three, if the third doesn't actually do anything."

It was worth a try. "Face the other way," Kandy told Ease. "So you won't freak out." The man signed and turned around to face to the rear. One might almost have thought he wouldn't have minded freaking out for a good cause.

Astrid removed her clothing, which was bound to get soaked anyway. The board transformed back to Kandy, minus her apparel, as happened when she changed. She took her place in the center of the canoe, next to Astrid. Fornax floated to her other side, similarly bare, and even more voluptuously formed. The three of them gazed up at the angry cloud.

"Wow!" Squid said. "When I grow up, I'm going to make myself look like that." And of course she would be able to do it, with her powers of mimicry. She would make some young man deliriously happy just before he freaked out.

"We apologize most humbly," Astrid called to the glowering Fracto. "Please forgive us." The three of them inhaled.

The cloud considered. Then he sent down another chill blast, making them shiver. But he didn't swamp them.

Then a stiff wind blew from the rear, pushing the canoe forward. It fairly raced across the water.

Astrid was not easy about this. Before, Fracto had blown them straight into mischief. He was one ill wind.

"Land ahoy!" Squid called. "And it's right where we need to go."

Had that niceness been intentional on Fracto's part? Astrid still didn't trust it. But she assumed her most positive stance. "Thank you, Fracto!" she called.

The cloud floated away, evidently pacified.

Then Squid reconsidered. "Or maybe not."

"Not?" Kandy asked.

"It's along the line, but maybe not there yet. It's hard to tell. The direction's right, but maybe not the distance."

"You know, I saw something," Ease said. "I think it was a honeypot. It made me hungry."

"Yet. It's along the line," Squid said.

He shaded his eyes, looking. "Well I'll be!"

"You'll be what, dear?" Kandy asked.

"It *is* a honeypot! A big one."

"Nothing is as it seems, when spoken by an innocent," Fornax said. "I may not say more." She faded out.

"Gimme the paddle."

Kandy became the board, falling into his hands. He paddled vigorously toward the little island.

Except that it wasn't exactly an island. It was a small mountain in the shape of a huge bee, from whose mouth poured a river of golden honey that landed in a pool-sized pot. The honeypot.

Then Astrid got the rest of it as she put her dress back on. Ease had said "I'll be." And it turned out to be "Isle Bee," a bee the size of an island, filling a pot of honey. Fornax had warned her.

But why had Fornax then faded out? That suggested that she was in danger of saying something that would constitute Demon interference, so she had removed the temptation. So maybe there was more to this situation.

Was that honey safe to eat?

Ease paddled up to the pot. He fetched a dipper from the canoe and used it to dip out some honey. Before Astrid could say anything, he tasted it. "Perfect!"

Now she just had to hope it was. In any event, they needed to know more about this.

Kandy reformed. She took the dipper and tasted the honey. "Lovely."

Too late again. Was the honey safe, or was it not what it seemed? She didn't want to alarm anyone unnecessarily. "Squid, let's you and I wait a bit," Astrid said to the child.

Squid considered. She had heard Fornax, and had learned caution. "Okay."

"Good girl." Astrid knew the child was eager for the honey. "Maybe you should swim around the island to see what you can see."

Squid shaped herself into her natural form and plopped into the water.

Meanwhile Ease and Kandy were dipping and eating more honey. "This is the best honey ever," Kandy said. "You should try some."

"I will, soon," Astrid agreed, gazing at the bee-shaped mountain. It was amazingly realistic. It was almost as if a real giant bee had been frozen in place, except for the flowing honey.

Then an unwilling notion pushed into her mind. Almost?

Suppose that was a real bee, that could reanimate at any moment? Suppose the honey contained a sleeping potion. There were no flowers here in the sea to provide nectar for the bee to feed on; what did it eat? That honeypot could be a deadly trap.

Squid reappeared. "There's something funny about that island," she said. "It's tied to a rock below. It has bee legs."

"It's a bee," Astrid said.

"Oh look! Aunt Kandy and Uncle Ease are taking a nap."

As Astrid had feared, the two were slumped in the canoe. "I think there is sleeping potion in the honey. I didn't warn them in time."

"They didn't get caught in Storage the way we did. They're not par—par—"

"Paranoid," Astrid said. "So it's up to us to get us away from here."

"How? There's nowhere else close enough to go to."

"And we don't even have á paddle," Astrid agreed. "We're in trouble."

"We need Aunt Kandy awake so she can be the paddle."

"We do."

"Why did Aunt Fornax fade?"

Observant child! "She must have seen something that she could not warn us about directly, lest she be guilty of intervening. So she faded to stop herself."

"The way she acted to save me?"

"Yes. So in Storage she didn't dare act. Or here."

"I like her."

"So do I."

"She'll act if she has to, to save us. But then she'll be in trouble."

"That's the way I see it," Astrid said. "We have to save ourselves if we possibly can."

"Maybe I can ask the bee."

"It is hard to talk to a stone creature."

"She's not all the way stone, 'cause she's making the honey. Maybe she's got a mind inside. Maybe I can Commune with her."

"I fear that could be risky."

Squid considered. "Maybe if you take off your glasses, Aunt Astrid, and back me up, I can do it. So that if she comes to life—"

"I can Stare her," Astrid finished. "Maybe that would work."

"I need to touch her to Commune."

"We'll try it." Astrid took the rope that had moored the boat before, and tied it around a rocky outcropping so it wouldn't drift. Then she and Squid stepped out onto the island beside the Pot. They made their way to a spot directly in front of the Bee, overlooking the Pot and the stream of honey. Then Squid moved forward, around the Pot, while Astrid focused on the Bee's closed front eye.

Squid assumed the likeness of a much smaller bee. She touched the face of the big Bee. She Communed.

The Bee's eye flickered. Astrid watched it, but did not Stare. She didn't want to do anything she couldn't undo.

Squid broke contact and made her way back to Astrid. "Wow!"

"What is it?"

"She is a Bee. A small *d* demon caught her and tied her here to produce honey for him. He comes once a day to collect it, replacing the Pot. He's mean; we don't want to be here when he comes. Especially grown women."

"We'll try to get away before he comes," Astrid said, not discussing why. "What else did you learn?"

"Her name is Busy Bee. She hates being caught here. But her feet are tied and she can't move. So she just sort of sleeps, and heaves honey."

"Could you dive down and untie her feet?"

"Oh, sure."

"Then go back and offer her this deal: we will untie her feet so she can escape, if in return she will carry us to the island we are going to."

"Okay." Squid went back to the Bee's face.

Astrid remained alert, just in case.

Soon the child was back. "She says okay!"

"Then let's do it. Untie her feet and get back to the canoe quickly. We don't know when the demon is coming."

"Soon," Squid said. She changed form and dived into the water.

Astrid put her glasses back on and made her way to the canoe. She hauled on Kandy and Ease to make sure they were secure within the boat.

The mountain shook. The Bee's eyes opened. Her mouth closed, cutting off the stream of honey. Her wings spread out, extending far over the water.

Squid reappeared and heaved herself into the boat. "Hang on!" she panted.

Kandy stirred, little planets swirling around her head. "What's happening?"

"The honey is drugged," Astrid said. "You've been asleep. We're about to be carried a distance. Hold on to the canoe!"

Kandy grabbed on as the planets cleared. Ease slept on; he had eaten more of the honey.

The Bee's wing-beat revved up. She lifted out of the water, leaving the Honeypot behind. She hovered, then lowered down toward the canoe. Her feet took hold of the sides in four places. Then she paused.

"Oops!" Squid exclaimed. "The demon!"

He came, looming like a dust storm, swelling up to horrendous size. "FEE FI FO FUM!" he roared. "SOMEBODY'S TRYING TO GO OR COME!"

"We have to stop him!" Squid cried. "Before he ties Busy up again."

Astrid thought frantically, but all she could think of was the way they had flashed Fracto Cloud. Well, the demon was male, wasn't he? "Flash him!" she screamed, ripping off her dress.

Kandy joined her in nudity. Then Fornax appeared. "As long as you two are sunning yourselves, I might as well join you," she remarked.

"Feast your ugly eyes on this, smokeface!" Astrid called. Then all three beauties faced the demon and inhaled.

The demon froze, transfixed. He did not completely freak out, but neither did he move. He was wholly distracted by the scene.

Busy Bee unpaused. She lifted into the air, carrying the canoe. She flew rapidly forward, leaving the demon behind. By the time he reacted, it was too late; they were out of his reach.

In hardly more than a moment, the boat dropped back into the water with a splash. The Bee lifted high, freed of its weight, and ascended into the sky.

"There it is!" Squid said. "That's where we're going!"

So the Bee had honored the deal, delivering them to their stop.

"Oh, bleep," Kandy said. "That's the Island of Doctor Moribund."

Astrid recognized it now. They had been here before. Oh, no! That was the worst sort of mischief.

Or maybe not. They had managed to set the evil doctor up with a nice composite mermaid partner, who might have tamed him in the interim. Could this actually be the adoptive couple? Similarly amazing things had been known to happen in Xanth.

"Maybe we should get decent," Fornax said as clothing formed around her. Astrid and Kandy hastily dressed.

Ease finally woke, seeing them complete their dressing. "Bleep! I guess I missed the greatest show in Xanth," he grumbled.

"Of course you did, dear," Kandy said, kissing his ear. "But I'll make it up to you when I can." That seemed to cheer him somewhat.

"Who the bleep are you?" a voice called from the water. It was an ugly mermaid.

Astrid oriented on it, and recognized her. "Maddy! It's me, Astrid, and Kandy, and Ease. You remember us. The basilisk and the board. We helped you get your tail."

"Oh, yes," Maddy agreed. "You freed me to kill myself, only then I changed my mind."

"How's it working out with Frank?" That was Frankenstein, a man assembled from pieces of other men.

"Great! He's my kind of man, and he loves me."

"That's wonderful."

"We're here this time on business," Astrid said. "Is the master of the island still here?"

"Of course. Frank is serving him now. But Mexine really runs the show."

"They get along well?"

"Very well." Then she reconsidered. "Except for one thing."

"Yes?"

"The stork won't answer her signals."

Astrid exchanged a look with Kandy. This was fiercely relevant. She tried to add things up in her head. How long had it been? "They haven't been together all that long."

"It's faster with mermaids. They've been signaling like mad, but the stork hasn't shown its beak around here."

"Then they should be interested in our visit. We have a child in need of adoption."

"Wow! I'll call Frank to lead you in."

"Thank you."

Maddy put her hands to her mouth, forming a megaphone. "Meat for brains! Get your backside over here!"

In hardly more than a moment the composite man appeared. "Vot's up, dear?"

"We have visitors. Remember Kandy, Astrid, and Ease? They want to see Dr. Moron."

"Me love it when you talk dirty!" Then he yanked his eyes off her. "Velcome, visitors! Ve have not forgotten you."

"Nor we you," Astrid said.

"You're the lovely basilisk. Come this way."

They followed him along the winding path to the great old mansion. A shapely young woman in shorts and a halter emerged to meet them. "Kandy! Astrid!" she exclaimed. "I knew you were coming."

"Mexine!" Astrid said. "I didn't recognize you for a moment. You look so—"

"So human," she said, laughing. "You remember me naked, with the damaged tail."

"Yes," Astrid said, modestly embarrassed. She was the former mermaid with a talent for seeing the future. "I gather that your new life has been good for you."

"Yes it has. I love the sheer mobility that good legs give me, and the magic of panties. I have been empowered. And I owe it all to you folk, who set up the deal. Everything's great, except—"

"Maddy mentioned the stork," Kandy said.

"That's it. I feel my transition is not complete until I make a family. So we've been signaling the balky bird several times a day, but there's been no response. I'm afraid that they have a thing against my composite body."

"But they bring babies all the time to crossbreeds," Astrid said. "You're really a human/mermaid crossbreed, just not done the traditional way."

Mexine shrugged. "It's been less than a year. There's hope yet. Meanwhile, what brings you here?"

Astrid plunged in. "We have a child who needs to be adopted into a good family."

Mexine gazed at her, then at Squid. "This one?"

"Yes. But there are a couple of things you need to know about her."

"She's older," Mexine said.

"Six years old."

"If that's the only problem, it's not a problem. She's cute."

"She's alien."

"What, from Mundania? No magic talent?"

"From another planet. Her magic is a different kind."

"I am intrigued. What can she do?"

"Show her, Squid," Astrid said.

Squid changed into her natural form, with eight tentacles.

"A shape changer!" Mexine said.

"Not exactly. She's a moctapus. A creature who can mold her tentacles into arms and legs, and change colors to resemble clothing. She's a very special girl. We got in trouble on the way here, and she enabled us to get out of it."

"Trouble?"

"There was a—a bee the size of an island, with a pot of honey."

"Don't go there!" Mexine said. "That honey's drugged."

"You know of it?"

"Yes, it's a sad story. A demon captured the big bee and tied her to a rock under the water and makes her make honey for him. We'd free her if we could, but we don't know how."

"We freed her."

"You freed her?"

"Squid dived down and untied her feet. Then we adults flashed the demon so that he couldn't catch her again."

Mexine nodded. "He's male, so he freaked out." That covered that aspect. She turned to the child. "You're some girl, Squid."

Squid reformed as a human child, complete with apparent clothing. "Thank you."

"And you want Dr. Moribund and me to adopt you?"

Squid fidgeted. "I guess."

"You're shy," Mexine said. "Well, come meet the doctor."

Mexine led them to another chamber, where a professorish-looking man was studying a manual. "Heh?" he asked, looking up as they entered.

"Dear, we are considering adopting this child," Mexine said briskly. "I thought you should meet her first."

"She looks like a fine child. Heh. Do what you think is best." He returned to his manual.

"Not so fast, dear," Mexine said. "If we adopt her, she'll be our child. You'll have to train her in biology. You need to be sure you're compatible."

Moribund sighed. He had evidently learned not to try to balk his wife. "What can you do, child?"

"I can change my appearance," Squid said. "I'm a moctopus."

"A moctopus! The only ones I've heard of live on another planet, light-years away."

"That's us. We were visiting Xanth as tourists, and, well, I got caught here. My folks are gone. I'm an orphan. So now I need to find a new family."

"I suspect the halflings on this island would like you. Can you imitate a mermaid?"

Squid shifted into a girl with a green fish's tail.

"Marvelous. My wife was a mermaid before she got her land legs. She surely likes you."

"I do," Mexine said.

Astrid was buoyed. It was looking very good.

"But there are chores to do here. Do you work well?"

"I try," Squid said.

"Let's find out. I dropped the Hopeless Diamond down the water well a few months ago, in a simple exercise of clumsiness. I believe it is poisoning the water we drink, making us feel hopeless. If we could get it out, things would be much improved. But the well is deep and we can't reach the gem, and the bucket can't get it from under the water. If we lower you into the well, do you think you could fetch it?"

Squid didn't hesitate. "Sure."

They went to the well. It was indeed deep, with a winch and bucket. The bottom was lost in darkness far below.

"I don't like the look of this," Kandy said. "What if the rope breaks?"

"I'll emulate a snail and crawl back up," Squid said. "I can do it." She got into the bucket.

Frank turned the winch handle, lowering the bucket into the well. Squid was just small enough to fit inside the narrow channel. Soon the bucket disappeared into the gloom, along with the child.

"Oh, I feel claustrophobic!" Kandy said, shuddering. "It's so tight and deep!"

"She can handle it," Astrid reassured her, though she did feel a quease herself.

There was a faint splash from deep below. The bucket had struck the water.

They waited several interminable moments. Squid was diving under the water, searching for what amounted to a single stone amidst whatever other debris was there, in darkness. Suppose she got stuck? She could drown, and they would be completely unable to help her.

"Remember, the girl is competent in the water," Fornax said. "She can glow in the dark, making what light she needs. This is just a routine point of public information."

Or so it was phrased. It was the Demoness's way of letting her know, without violating any protocols. Squid was not in any trouble.

Then there was a jerk on the rope. Squid was signaling that she was ready to come back up.

Frank wound the winch. The rope went taut. It accumulated around the winch column as the load was hauled slowly up. At last the bucket came into sight, carrying Squid in moctopus form. A tentacle reached out, holding a huge bright blue diamond. She had found it!

"Marvelous!" Moribund exclaimed, taking it. "I'll put it safely away now. Heh." He departed with the gem.

"I believe he is taken with you, Squid," Mexine said. "You have really helped. I'm not sure I credit that business of the diamond poisoning the water, but I do feel more hopeful now. So why don't we set up the adoption?"

Kandy was silent. She looked oddly pained, considering the success of their mission.

"There is one thing," Astrid said. "We will need to arrange to paint your family portrait. This has to do with saving Xanth from destruction."

"Well then, we'll arrange it."

There was a fluttering of a large bird coming in for a landing. They all looked. It was a stork! With a bundle hanging from its beak. A tiny foot projected from it.

"Special delivery for Mexine Mermaid," the stork said. "If you will just sign this receipt."

Mexine stood with her mouth open, too astonished to speak.

"That's her," Astrid said, indicating Mexine. "She didn't expect you."

"I almost didn't make it," the bird said. "The island seemed hopelessly lost. I searched for days, and was about to return the baby to the home office as undeliverable. But suddenly the confusion cleared, and I came on in. It's good to get the load off my beak."

"The Hopeless Diamond!" Kandy said. "It *was* poisoning the water!"

"And once Squid got it out, the water cleared," Astrid agreed. "Just in time."

"It must have been spreading from the well into the sea," Kandy said. "Making the whole island seem like a loss. We felt the effect when we arrived."

Then they both paused. "Uh-oh," Ease said. "Now they don't need a child. They've got their own."

They all looked at Squid. She had rescued the diamond and abated its curse—and effectively nulled the prospect for her own adoption.

"I'm so sorry," Mexine said. "But I can't handle two children. I'm a first-time mother."

"That's all right," Squid said bravely.

Kandy reached out and silently enfolded her.

Mexine finally went to sign the receipt and pick up her baby. It was a little girl, with legs rather than a tail. She had indeed made the transition to human mother.

"Heh," the baby said.

They had to smile. It was clear who the father was.

"Well, I didn't see that coming," Fornax said. "Of course I didn't think to look."

"Let's go on home," Astrid said. What else was there to do?

They walked back to the boat. They got in. Kandy became the board, and Ease started paddling back the way they had come. There was no sign of bad weather.

"What happened?" Maddy asked from the water. "Why didn't you leave the child?"

"The stork arrived," Squid told her.

"Oh." The mermaid faded back. What could she say?

"This isn't over," Fornax said, and faded out herself.

"Maybe not," Squid agreed thoughtfully.

After a time, Ease paused to rest. The board became Kandy. "I've been thinking," Kandy said as they drifted. "Splashing through cool water is marvelous for contemplation. You children Communed."

"Yes," Squid agreed.

"And you got a direction for your adoption that led you to the island of Dr. Moron. I mean, Moribund."

"Yes."

"So why wasn't that the right place?"

"I don't know," Squid said. "It was pretty sure, until it changed."

"It was a paradox," Astrid said. "Your presence there changed it. Your Communing isn't sharp on paradox."

"I guess not," Squid agreed.

"When you went down that well," Kandy said, "I feared awfully for you."

"I was safe enough."

"I know. But my feeling didn't. It was almost as if—"

No one else spoke. She had to come to it by herself.

"As if you were my child," Kandy continued. "I just couldn't help being concerned."

"Yes," Squid whispered.

"And when Mexine said to set up the adoption, I thought my heart would break."

"You too?" Ease asked, surprised. "I know men aren't supposed to get all squishy, so I didn't say anything."

"You mean mushy," Astrid said.

"Whatever. It hurt."

"I didn't want to give you up," Kandy said. "But neither did I want to ruin your prospects, so I stifled it."

"Yeah," Ease agreed.

"Mexine and Doc M were perfect, and it's a great island," Squid said. "But I didn't really want to do it. I didn't want to be ungrateful, but I wasn't sorry when the stork came."

"When I took Firenze to be adopted," Astrid said, "it was much the same. The journey made me realize that I wanted him myself."

"Yes!" Kandy said. "I think what you did influenced me, Astrid, and not just because we're friends. I realized that there were other prospects. And I want Squid."

"*We* want Squid," Ease said.

"And I want you," Squid said. "You understand about changing forms, Aunt Kandy. And you're so easygoing, Uncle Ease. You've always been good to me."

Kandy opened her arms. "Come here, dear."

Squid went to them. They tearfully hugged, rocking the boat. It was clear that another adoption had fallen into place.

Fornax reappeared. "Now it's over, at least what counts."

"Let's get on home," Astrid said. "Before anything else happens."

Kandy became the board, and Ease resumed briskly paddling.

"I do so love a happy ending," Fornax remarked to Astrid. "I wish I could have told you about what to expect, but there are very sharp limits on my behavior."

"We appreciate your incidental observations," Astrid said. "Not that they influence us." But she crossed her fingers.

"I wish I could participate more directly. It's quite an experience, placing these wonderful children."

"And it has enhanced our friendship. Just as Wenda Woodwife suggested."

"It has," the Demoness agreed. "In all the time I've been watching you, I have not been bored once. Nervous, angry, relieved, but never bored."

"That's what mortal life is like," Kandy said. "We don't live long enough to have time for real boredom."

"It's more than that."

"Well, we have souls."

"Your souls don't make you unbored. They merely motivate you to care. Now I am coming to care, and becoming unbored."

"You told me how when Jumper Spider associated closely with several humans, some of their souls attached to him," Astrid said. "So he developed a composite soul that served as well as an original one."

"True."

"Now you have associated closely with me and the children. You may be developing a similar soul."

"Why so I may," Fornax agreed, surprised. "That would account for a lot."

Astrid smiled. "It will do."

"It will do, for now," the Demoness agreed. "But of course the job is unfinished. Three children remain to be adopted. Once that is done, the doubt will abate, Xanth will be saved, and the boredom may return. I dread that."

"We'll still like you, Aunt Fornax," Squid said. "We know we owe a lot to you, and you're nice, and so's your castle."

"Thank you, dear." There might have been a tear in the Demoness's eye.

CHAPTER 14:
WIN

~~~

"So that's how it worked out," Astrid concluded. "Squid will be with Ease and Kandy. We are getting there."

"Now that we see how we can keep the children, instead of sending them away, maybe we don't need to make more complicated journeys," Tiara said. "Mitch and I like Win, and she likes us. We are compatible."

Indeed, the child was sitting with them, satisfied. "We can fly," she announced.

Astrid was surprised. "Tiara can float and you can blow, but that's not the same as flying."

"We'll show you," Win said. She went to sit on Tiara's lap. Tiara's hair lengthened and spread below them, forming a kind of chair. They floated gently up.

Then Win turned around to face Tiara. Her wind blew the woman backward. Then she squirmed around to sit behind Tiara, still on the woman's bed of floating hair. Now her wind pushed the woman forward. "See? We're flying!"

The others nodded. "So you are," Astrid agreed. "That's a clever combination of your two talents. You are indeed compatible."

"Bleep!" Fornax muttered, and faded out.

"Uh-oh," Mitch said. "When she does that, it means there's something she can't tell us about." He looked at the flying pair. "Better come down now, dears."

"But this is so much fun!" Win protested, blowing harder so that they sailed up to treetop level.

"All the same," Astrid called. "We've had a warning for caution."

"We'll come down," Tiara agreed.

"Awww," Win groaned.

They began to settle toward the ground. But then an abrupt gust of wind caught them, blowing them higher. It wasn't Win's wind; it was swishing through the branches and stirring up leaves. It quickly increased, carrying them out over the tops of the trees and rapidly away.

"Oh!" Tiara cried. "I can't—" But the rest was lost in the roar of the sudden storm.

She couldn't come down, because they would crash. They were going too fast, and out of control in gale-force winds. Win could blow, but she couldn't stop this from blowing them away.

Astrid looked up. There was a malignant cloud face. "Fracto!"

"Oh, bleep!" Kandy swore. "He must have been waiting to pounce. This is more anonymous interference."

"To stop the adoption," Astrid agreed. "Stopping any one of the five will be enough to doom Xanth."

"I've got to rescue them!" Mitch said.

"Not by yourself," Kandy warned. "There is more here than a mean-spirited cloud. Even if you could catch up to them, they are likely to be forces beyond your resources."

"But I love them!"

What could they say? The case seemed hopeless.

Fornax appeared. "This of course has no relevance to the problem at hand, but I have restored the Sequins of Events dress. It's purely a guess, but I suspect that certain parties are being taken to a site that just happens to be keyed in by one of the sequins. Experimenting with the dress might, purely by chance, put a person there. Not that this is of any present interest." She faded.

"Well, now," Mitch said, understanding perfectly. The empowered dress had some remarkable properties that had given their group quite an adventure on the way to eliminating the anti-pun virus. Knowing its properties made all the difference.

Astrid delved into her belongings and found the dress. Sure enough, the sequins on it were bright with energy. She quickly changed into it. "I think it is you and me," she said to Mitch.

"Yes. We do know how to do this." He squatted before her and took hold of a sequin. He pulled it off.

The dress became translucent, showing the outline of her legs and panties. But Mitch had closed his eyes, avoiding any freakout. Blindly, he replaced the sequin.

"Farewell!" Kandy called.

Then they were at a new location. They looked around. Astrid knew immediately it was another planet. "Alpha Centauri," she said. "Where the centaurs set up their independent society." They had helped rescue the centaurs from Fornax's clutches. How Astrid's perspective had changed on that!

"They won't be here," Mitch said. "Fracto can't blow across worlds."

"I agree. Let's move on before we have to explain things to the centaurs."

He picked off another Sequin, eyes closed, and her dress did its trick. Astrid was glad that at least she had good legs; bad ones would have been even more embarrassing. He replaced it.

Now they were in a bustling office with video screens all around. "I don't remember this," Mitch said.

"Neither do I," Astrid agreed. "Could it be from a sequin we didn't use before?"

"I thought we used them all."

"So did I."

Then a wall charged into them. They passed though it, and found themselves on a windswept plain.

"The Cloud!" Mitch explained. "It's moving. It just moved on past us."

"The Cloud," Astrid agreed. They had been caught in an electronic cloud infected by a virus, and had had a time getting it clear. "Are Tiara and Win likely to be here?"

He considered. "I suppose it's possible. But this isn't the same kind of cloud as Fracto. I doubt they would get along."

"So do I. This is more Com Pewter's kind of cloud."

"So let's move on, and hope we're right."

"Let's move on," she agreed.

He squatted to remove another sequin.

After a moment, Astrid looked down. "Oh, bleep," she muttered. He had forgotten to close his eyes as the sequin came off. He had seen her panties and freaked out. She put one hand down to shield his eyes, then snapped the fingers of her other hand. "Wake."

Mitch revived. "What happened?"

"Close your eyes. You saw too much, and freaked."

"Oh. I would have thought I'd become partway immune by now. I mean, I've been with Tiara."

"My anatomy is new to you."

"That must be it." He closed them, then found her dress and pinned the sequin back on.

The scene changed. Now they were in a forest near a cave. "Com Pewter's cave," Astrid said. "They couldn't be here, for fear Pewter would return."

"Not a very good hiding place," he agreed.

They did another sequin. This time the scene was of an island amidst other islands, all fairly pleasant. "I don't recognize this," Mitch said.

"I do. It's where we found Tiara, locked in her tower, before we encountered you."

"Tiara," he echoed. "So this is where she came from."

"Yes. There's her tower on the other side of the island."

"Her tower." He seemed bemused.

"I don't believe she wants to return here. Not without you."

"I wonder: could she have been put back in her tower? That would prevent her from returning to us."

"Not since she learned how to use her hair to float. But if they barred the windows, maybe so."

"We'd better check."

They walked along the path to the tower. There at the base was a pretty girl. "Tiara!" Mitch cried.

She turned to look at them. It was not Tiara. Her figure was similar, but her hair was way too neat. "Who are you?" the woman asked.

"I'm Mitch. I—I'm looking for Tiara."

"So am I. I'm Cry, her sister. She has disappeared. It's awful." She started to cry.

Astrid put together the likely pun: Cry Sis, who cried in a crisis. The pun virus had not passed by here. Still, there was an issue. "Didn't you lock her in the tower?" Astrid asked sharply.

"It was for her own good. Her hair was too wild."

"That was because it wasn't meant to be restrained," Astrid said. "Now she can fly with it. That's her talent."

"Oh, it worked!"

What? "What worked?"

"We thought if we put her in a place where she could escape only by flying, she would either develop her hair or tame it. Then she would be complete."

"She could have fallen to her death trying!"

"Apopto was afraid that would happen. But Elip managed to avoid the subject. We were afraid she would never get a man unless she dealt with her hair."

Apoptosis and Ellipsis. More puns, meaning programmed cell death and omission. Astrid decided not to comment.

"Well, she got a man," Mitch said tightly. Then, to Astrid: "Let's move on."

Because obviously Tiara was not here. "Let's."

They walked away from Cry. Then when they were alone, Mitch removed and replaced another sequin, this time keeping his eyes closed.

This time they were in a field they recognized: "This is where we insulted Fracto, and he blew up a storm, flooded us out, and we wound up at the island of Doctor Moribund," Mitch said.

"Kandy and I were just there," Astrid said. "If she showed up there, they would help her return."

"So let's try again."

They tried again. And found themselves in the castle in Fornax Galaxy. No one was there, and of course Fracto couldn't have blown anyone from one galaxy to another.

The next site Mitch recognized instantly: "Punic Curse, my home village. Let me check."

He did, and soon verified that they were not here.

The next site was the maze of paths through tall cornstalks next to the alien Zoo, where they had been trapped for a time. The maize maze. "We don't want to stay here long," Astrid said. "The aliens will try to make us another zoo exhibit."

"Right. We'd better move on." Then he paused. "I just picked up a thought. I think it was Tiara's."

His talent was in receiving and sending thoughts. "Is she here?"

"I think so. Let me see if I can establish better mental contact with her. It's not my normal ability, but I love her, and we have been getting closer mentally." He concentrated. "I connected! She is here! So is Win. We almost missed it. They're an exhibit."

Astrid's feelings were mixed. "That means they're safe. But also that it will be difficult to free them. Those aliens are sharp."

"Don't I know it!"

"Can you send the aliens an idea to free the captives?"

He shook his head. "It doesn't work that way. The idea has to originate with someone else. Then I can relay it. And no, I can't work it out in discussion, as we are doing now. That's not an original idea, it's a manufactured one."

That made sense. Most talents had limits. "When we were here before," Astrid said, returning to the subject, "Ease managed to get away. But he would have been caught, and we all would still be there, if we hadn't managed to recover my dress and jump to another Event. If the aliens catch us this time, the first thing they'll do is take away the dress, and maybe burn it."

"Maybe you should remove it and hide it."

"I don't have a change of clothing. Can you handle my nudity?"

He considered briefly. "No. I'd constantly freak out. You are a very fine figure of a woman, Astrid. I love Tiara, but I can't afford to look at you bare."

She knew he was being honest. "Suppose I change to my natural form?"

"That would not freak me out," he agreed. "But I would be in danger from your Stare."

"I may look funny as a basilisk wearing dark glasses, but I can do it."

"Then maybe that's best. We can sneak in and try to rescue them without the aliens knowing we're here."

"I don't trust this. Those aliens are too knowing."

"They are," he agreed morosely.

"Still, we have to try. About my clothing: suppose I give it to you, and you hide it away, and return it to me once we're there? Then I will dress, and be ready to flash any other male I need to."

"That will do," he agreed. "But first we need to find them. They're within my idea exchange range, but they could be anywhere in the zoo compound. I don't have a mental sense of direction. In fact it's not even telepathy; it's just spot ideas."

Astrid considered. "Win's talent is wind. To always have the wind at her back. An anonymous party enhanced it to enable her to control it and make it stronger."

"Yes, of course. What is your point?"

"The air is still, here. A stray breeze would be noticeable, if anyone thought to notice it. At night few if any would be noticing."

"Win could make that breeze!"

"That was my thought."

"Astrid, I could kiss you!" He paused, reassessing. "Not that I would, of course, because—" He broke off, embarrassed, caught between illicit interest and unintended insult. He was a good man, stumbling.

"Three reasons why no kiss," she said. "One: we are friends, not lovers.

Two: my touch is intoxicating and perhaps deadly. Three: we have more important things to accomplish than any stray dalliance, even if we were inclined, which we aren't."

"Those will do," he agreed gratefully.

"You have become a marvel of diplomacy," Fornax murmured in her ear.

"So I am thinking that such a wind would be convenient," Astrid said. "Once darkness falls."

"I will relay that idea," Mitch said. "That much I can do."

"In the interim, we should find a place to hide, before anyone sees us here."

"Oh, yes."

They walked cautiously along a path through the stalks. This was a good place to hide if the invisible giant didn't come looking for them. It was also a good place to get lost, if they weren't careful.

"Let's lie down and cover ourselves with corn husks and dry leaves, so we are hidden. We can sleep until dusk."

"Good enough. But I am getting hungry."

"There's some ripe corn on the plants."

"That will do."

They ate ripe, raw corn, attended to private functions, then lay down and covered themselves.

"Oh," Astrid said. "My clothing. Avert your gaze." She removed her dress, bra, panties, and slippers. Everything except her dark glasses, because it was dangerous for her to go without them. She handed them to Mitch, who bound them into his voluminous hair. It was amazing how effectively they disappeared; it was an excellent hiding place.

She re-covered herself with corn shucks. It was a warm day, and she really had no need of clothing, apart from human propriety.

"Once you locate them, do you have a plan to rescue them?" Fornax asked, seeming to lie beside Astrid.

"I haven't gotten that far yet."

"I have no knowledge, of course, and would not be free to impart it if I did. But I suspect you are conjecturing that the captives are not simply free to walk away with you. You may suspect that they are in a secure cage, or even manacled to a post, or both. And that there will be an alarm set off if anyone tried to approach them from outside the zoo. You may even conjecture that the captives represent a trap, the object being to capture more creatures for the exhibit. So that while location and approach seem feasible, you fear it will not be safe just to walk in."

"I am conjecturing something along those lines," Astrid agreed.

"You may even suspect that there is a larger purpose to the trap. That the real object may not be to develop a human exhibit, but to obtain a transformed basilisk, which would be a far more impressive exhibit. You may wonder why the zookeepers would go to such an extreme for one mere exhibit, which would seem to be beyond their interest. After all, tourists cannot be expected to gaze directly at a basilisk."

"It does seem far-fetched," Astrid agreed.

"So you might wonder what motive beyond that there could be. Unless they plan to exhibit her hooded, rendering her largely harmless. Nullified danger: the stuff of cheap shows. Purely speculative, of course."

"Of course," Astrid agreed, feeling a chill. The Demoness was warning her of real trouble ahead.

"You might even speculate that they could be interested in publicly breeding her. That would be a show like none other."

Breeding her? There were men and trolls who'd like to try. But even if bound, she would change to her basilisk form, stopping that. Still, it was an ugly threat.

"And you might ponder ways to counter such unlikely plots, so as to escape with all parties intact. Just in case something you could not reasonably anticipate were to occur."

"I might," Astrid agreed weakly.

"I do not wish to disturb you," Fornax said. "Merely to encourage you, as a friend, to consider all alternatives."

"Thank you," Astrid said, knowing that the friendship of the Demoness was a phenomenally valuable thing.

"You should sleep now, so as to be fully alert tonight."

"I should," Astrid agreed. "But I'm pretty wound up. I'm not sure I'll be able to sleep."

"Then I'll sleep. I apologize if my ambiance affects you. I can move away if you prefer."

Astrid did not answer, giving a tacit consent. And suddenly she slept, soundly. It was one more unofficial gift.

She woke promptly at dusk. Mitch was stirring. "I thought of something," he said, not looking at her. "What of Timothea?"

"Who?"

"Timothea, small *d* demoness, who was helping the aliens. She's mischief."

Now Astrid remembered. "Mischief indeed. She knows about the sequins, now. Better keep the dress hidden until the moment I actually need it so she can't snatch it."

"I will."

"In fact we had better assume that she's watching us, the moment we head in to locate them. She is immune to my Stare."

"If this is a trap we are walking into, how can we hope to accomplish the rescue?"

"Only by being prepared for the unexpected. It has occurred to me that I may be the real object of the trap. If so, I may be able to give you a chance to rescue them and escape. Take it."

"But what will happen to you?"

"A basilisk can be difficult to hold. You get away with them while I distract the aliens and demoness. Once you are clear, I will see about my own escape."

"Astrid, I don't like this. It feels like betrayal."

"So they may believe that you won't go without me. That can be our surprise. Promise me you will do it."

"I—"

She touched her glasses warningly. "Promise."

He capitulated. "I hate this. It feels like betrayal of a friend, but I promise."

"Good enough. Now we must spring their trap. We should not speak unless we have to, lest they overhear us."

Mitch nodded in agreement.

They followed a cornstalk path to the clearing around the zoo. There was a half moon out, providing enough light for them to see, though Astrid could see pretty well in almost total darkness.

There was the wire fence around the compound, with the main gate. When they had been here before, an invisible giant had herded them through the open gate and into the zoo. Astrid hoped the giant would not be active by night.

Then came a gentle breeze, where there had been none before. Astrid sniffed it. "Win," she said. The child was doing her part.

"It's coming from inside the zoo," Mitch said.

They approached the gate. It was securely locked for the night. No access there.

"I wonder," Mitch murmured.

She looked at him questioningly.

"I picked up a thought from Win. My talent works with living folk. I never thought to try it on other things. She is now aware of that limitation."

Receiving and sending ideas? How could that relate?

Mitch focused on the gate's big padlock. Then after a moment he reached out and took hold of it. The bar slid out, allowing him to remove it from the gate. It hadn't been locked after all!

"I sent it the idea that it wanted to unlock," he whispered, swinging the gate open.

Astrid stared at him, amazed. Could he really do that?

Then suspicion closed in. "It's too easy. Maybe they made it unlockable," she whispered. "Because they want us to come in, as we did before, then get locked in."

He nodded. "That could be. In which case they'll be watching us. We'd better find a more private way in."

He pulled the gate back closed. Then they walked away from the fence.

There was a huge crash in the cornfield.

"Oh, bleep!" Astrid swore under her breath. She had heard that sound before.

So had Mitch. "The tromp of an invisible giant."

"Who will tromp *us* if we don't go the right way."

"Into the zoo," he agreed. "As before."

It also meant the zookeepers were aware of their presence.

Astrid thought fast. If the zookeepers knew of their approach, and knew that they were coming to try to rescue Tiara and Win, why would they try to herd them in? That was a giveaway that they knew. It would make more sense for them to leave the giant out of it, letting the intruders think they were undiscovered.

Unless the giant was acting on his own, herding anything that he smelled. Not knowing about the need for seeming indifference. A glitch in the trap.

"Let's be herded," Astrid whispered.

Mitch shrugged, surprised, but didn't argue.

They reversed course and ran to the gate. It swung open, admitting them. And swung shut again once they passed it.

"Now dodge to the side," Astrid whispered.

They dodged. Soon they were in a garden area, among flowering bushes.

Astrid whispered her conjecture to his ear. "Maybe," he agreed. "But I fear they do know of us."

"They know, but want us to think they don't," she said. "So they'll leave us alone until we're all the way there."

"Sometimes I suspect that your mind is more devious than mine."

"I'm a woman."

"Oh. Of course."

They sniffed the air, picking up Win's faint scent dispersing from her wind. It seemed to be in the direction of the exhibit they had been caught in before. That made sense. So they circled around to enter it from the side.

There was the glass house, as before. There was a light on, showing its interior clearly. Exhibits were supposed to have no secrets from the sightseeing tourists. Animals didn't mind, but humans could be difficult about this, so they were given no choice.

And there inside the house was Tiara, sitting in an easy chair. She was wearing her usual dress, as exhibits were generally shown in their natural habitat. Where was Win?

"I have a nasty feeling about this," Astrid murmured. "Are they holding Win in a separate cell? To make sure Tiara behaves?"

"Maybe. But she is able to blow her breeze."

Which meant she wasn't locked in a dank cell. Still, there was a wrongness.

"I must go to Tiara," Mitch said.

Astrid didn't like this, but couldn't tell him no. After all, the two were in love.

Mitch quietly entered the house, while Astrid stayed outside. "Mitch!" Tiara exclaimed, standing. "I knew you'd come."

"Tiara!" he said, hugging and kissing her.

Then, oddly, he backed away. "Bleep!"

"Mitch, dear, what's the matter?" Tiara asked.

Astrid wondered too.

"You're not my love."

"How can you say that?" Tiara asked, distraught.

"Come off it, Timothea. You can imitate her appearance and voice, but not her kiss."

"Oh, bleep!" she swore, shifting into her sexy demoness form. "And I had such a warm welcome in mind for you." She glanced in the direction of the bedroom. Then she reconsidered. "You can still have that welcome, if you like. Which form would you prefer me to take? Mine, Tiara's, or Astrid's?"

Which was a clear indication that she knew Astrid was near. She was cruelly teasing him, pretending that any of the women were as good for him as Tiara.

"No form," Mitch said angrily. "Just tell me where Tiara and Win are."

She considered. "After we have our little fling."

"No fling!"

"Maybe you did not pick up on the nature of the deal. Fling, then information."

"Damn you!" He was so angry that the bad word came through despite the possible presence of a child nearby. He took hold of her, not affectionately. "Tell me!"

"What are you going to do if I don't? Rape me?" Her breasts enlarged a size. She looked wildly sexy. That was never an accident, with a demoness or a woman.

He cast her aside and stomped out of the house. Men weren't always mesmerized by the sight of a woman's body. Maybe only nine times out of ten.

Timothea laughed as she dissipated into smoke. Had she really intended to seduce him, or merely to tease him? Or maybe to delay their progress? Fornax's continued absence suggested that something devious was afoot that she couldn't afford to reveal. But what?

Mitch rejoined Astrid.

Astrid concluded that it had to have been a ruse to lure them in without giving them a chance to rescue anyone. So much for any element of surprise. If Timothea knew, the aliens knew. Astrid was disgusted as much at herself for being taken in by it as by the malicious demoness.

Still, there was the breeze. It had not actually come from the house, but from close by. Win was near.

They followed the breeze. It led to a high-walled enclosure open in the center, with seats around the rim, rather like an arena. They found the main gate to it unlocked, and quietly entered.

Suddenly it was lit brightly. Assorted alien creatures occupied the seats. Those would be tourist spectators. "Timothea delayed us long enough for them to assemble," Mitch muttered angrily.

That was it, of course. They were expecting a special show.

There was a billboard: THE TAMING OF THE SHREW.

Astrid stared at it, trying to make sense of it. Shrews were tiny creatures; who would want to tame one?

And there in the center was Tiara with Win. The woman's leg was tied to a stake by a stout vine. Astrid recognized the fastening in the vine: a Gourdian Not. One that would take months or years to untie, if it could be done at all. It must have been conjured there.

Tiara saw them. "Go away! It's a trap!" she cried. Indeed, the gate swung closed with a clank behind them.

"Not without you," Mitch said, running to her.

"You can't free me! You can only get yourself caught. You must—"

She was cut off by his kiss.

There was a stir in the audience. It seemed that many of the aliens had not before observed a genuine native smooch. They evidently found it a remarkable and slightly distasteful gesture.

"You're real," Mitch said as he released her.

"Real?"

"There was a fake version of you in the house," he said. "Timothea."

"Oh, that lady wolf. She's a pain in the posterior."

Meanwhile Astrid was gazing around the arena. There had to be more to this than they had seen so far.

"I'll take care of that knot," Mitch said. He squatted beside it, focusing.

Astrid knew his hope was futile.

Then the knot untied.

"I sent it an idea that it was tired of being knotted up," Mitch explained. "Win thought of it. In fact she thought of doors unlocking. She's one savvy girl."

Win smiled, clearly glad to have assisted.

So he did have the power to unlock doors and untie knots, by sending them thoughts, even though they were inanimate. But the audience seemed unalarmed by this step toward escape. Why?

Unless the woman and child were only bait for the real target. Fornax had remarked on the chance that the real target might be a basilisk. To be publicly bred.

Uh-oh.

Fornax appeared, to her alone. "I have a further irrelevant thought I will share. Some time back there was a fight between two ogres. One ogre, for reasons of complication of plot, had only half a soul. When he fought the other, he was at a disadvantage, and the other ogre pounded him into the ground. But then his girlfriend lent him her soul. Buoyed by that, he returned to the fray, and this time pounded the other ogre and won. All because of the imbalance of souls. It was a curious business. Who would have thought that a soul could make such a difference?"

"Ogres have souls," Astrid agreed. "They are variants of human stock. I don't see how that applies to me. I may be the only one of my kind ever to have a soul, and it's a whole soul, not half a soul. And I'm not looking to fight an ogre, not that I'd even need do; I'd simply Stare him into submission."

"Yes, it's obviously irrelevant," Fornax agreed. "I am sorry I bothered you." She faded.

There had to be immediate relevance, but Astrid was at a loss to fathom it. Just as she did not understand the sign about the shrew. The problem with deliberately obscure references was that they were hard to figure out. The

Good Magician's Answers had a similar reputation. They always made sense, but only after it made no difference. It was frustrating.

"Time to get out of here," Mitch said. "Can you haul me on your hair, Tiara?"

"Yes, I have far more floating power than I used to," Tiara said. "That's why they tied me down. Get on my hair and we'll take off."

"Astrid, too," he said.

"Yes, we can take her too, of course." Tiara's hair spread out into a mat.

There was a loud bong. Astrid looked to see the gate open to admit another creature. It seemed to be some kind of big lizard.

Then suddenly it all made awful sense. It was a cockatrice. Naturally his primary interest would be to breed a nubile basilisk. Her. She was the "shrew," to be tamed, not so much an animal as a willful female. And the audience was here to witness the rare act of forceful mating of ferocious native beasts. It would not be pretty.

"Get out of here!" Astrid said tersely to the others.

Mitch hesitated.

"Now!" Astrid snapped. "If you want to survive."

Mitch nodded grimly, understanding the danger. He fished something from his hair and tossed it to her: the ball of her clothing. Then he joined Tiara and Win. They lifted as Win's wind blew. The aliens did not even try to stop them; their part in this play was done.

"Hey!" Timothea exclaimed, appearing. "They're escaping!" She went to intercept them, but Mitch stiff-armed her. They sailed up and over the wall, the demoness still protesting. Maybe she had not gotten the word.

Meanwhile Astrid got efficiently into her clothing, including the Sequins of Events dress. But before she could invoke a sequin, the cockatrice caught up to her. And became a naked human man. "Well, now, pretty bask," he said. "Why get dressed when you'll have to strip again so soon?"

So he could change forms. She hadn't known any other of her kind could. "Not for you, ugly cock," she said through her teeth.

"You are Astrid," he said. "I have known of you for some time. I heard a tale of how you bullied a young cockatrice into submission, making him a virtual plaything of goblin girls. That could have been my son, had I been there to rape his mother. You are clearly my ideal female. I am Cocksure Cockatrice. I anticipate many happy matings in both forms. Two shows a day, in fact, maybe one in each form. That's why I arranged to have you come here. The zoo proprietors were most cooperative. Timothea too, but doing it with a demoness can't compare to doing it with a basilisk. Especially with an appreciative audience."

So the demoness had been entertaining him in the interim, her way. And he wanted to humiliate Astrid before an audience. This stirred her ire. As it was surely supposed to. He wanted her to fight him, as it seemed this was the way of their species.

What choice did she have except to oblige him in that respect? Certainly she was not going to submit to rape without a fight. Astrid lifted her glasses and Stared him, but he met her deadly gaze without concern. He was after all her kind.

Tiara, Mitch, and Win should be safely away by now. It was time for Astrid to depart also. She reached for a sequin.

Cocksure's hand swooped to intercept hers before it touched the sequin. "I know about that dress, too," he said. "We can do without it."

This was real trouble. He was larger than she, and immune to her nature. If he got her dress away from her, she would be captive. So she fought him, pushing back against his hand. He of course pushed harder. He was bound to overcome her. If cockatrices weren't capable of raping basilisks, the species would have died out long ago. That was the ugly reality she was up against. It was why he was so infernally confident.

Astrid couldn't help herself. Blinded by outrage, she played his game, furiously fighting him. The alien audience was rapt; this was what they had come for. Desperate sexual combat.

Then a look of surprise crossed his face. "How can you be so strong?"

Strong? She was tough for a human woman, but not for her own kind. Yet she did seem to be fending him off. She put more effort into it, and pushed his arm away from her.

Cocksure swung his other arm, with a fist, aiming for her head. Obviously when mating wasn't on his mind, violence was. He would happily beat her into submission. She caught the fist in her open hand and pushed it back. He pushed harder, angry. So did she, as angry. He struggled to push her off her feet. She resisted. He tried to hurl her away. She held him close, knowing that if they separated, he would merely pounce on her again. Cat and mouse, part of the fun.

Gradually it came to her: *she was stronger than he was.* She did not look it, but their actual contact was demonstrating it.

Then the significance of Fornax's remark registered: Astrid had a soul. Cocksure did not. Ordinarily she dealt with souled humans, and he dealt with unsouled creatures, so there was no contrast. Now it was soul against unsoul, and her soul lent her strength. Just as it had for the ogre. It made a difference only when they were in direct contact, but of course they had to be for combat or mating, or the combination.

She shook her glasses loose so that they fell down around her chin and Stared him in the face from point-blank range. He fell back, stunned. Her Stare was stronger too! As long as they were in contact so that her soul had play.

She let him drop to the floor, unconscious. Then she plucked a sequin at random, saw her dress go translucent, making some humanoid aliens freak out, and pinned it back on. The setting changed.

She was in a castle courtyard. She recognized it: Caprice Castle! She had forgotten it was zeroed in on a sequin. Then the castle traveled around, but evidently the sequin tracked it.

"Hey, who are you?"

Astrid looked. There stood two three-year-old children. She hastily pulled her glasses back up. "I'm Astrid Basilisk," she replied. "And you are Piton and Data, Princess Dawn's children. We've met."

The children exchanged a juvenile glance, remembering. "Welcome to Caprice Castle," Data said.

"Thank you. It was just chance."

A woman appeared. "Astrid! What brings you here? You're all mussed up." It was Princess Dawn.

"It's a long story," Astrid said.

"May I touch you?"

"Of course." It was Dawn's talent to know everything about any living thing she touched.

Dawn touched her arm. "Oh, my! That monster was going to rape you, but you fought him off!"

"It was an ugly scene," Astrid agreed.

"What was he going to do?" Piton asked.

Oops, the Adult Conspiracy was cutting in. "He wanted to kiss me," Astrid said.

"Yuck!" both children said together.

"It was a horrible threat," Dawn agreed with a third of a smile. "Come, Astrid, you must relax with us, after your bad experience."

"I really should get home," Astrid demurred. "So they won't worry about me."

The princess nodded. "True. We'll have them all in for a pleasant visit while we catch up."

"But they are far away."

"You forget the nature of this castle. This way, please."

Bemused, Astrid accompanied Dawn to the castle's front gate. There outside stood Astrid's friends, and the children, looking faintly surprised.

Now Astrid remembered. It was a traveling castle. "Thank you," she said faintly.

"Come in!" Data called to the children.

"We've got eye scream!" Piton called. That of course decided it.

Soon Kandy was hugging Astrid. Then Tiara and Win. "You made it!" Astrid said. "I feared the demoness would stop you."

"Win had this idea that Timothea didn't really want to stop our escape," Mitch said. "I relayed it to the demoness. She didn't realize it wasn't her own thought. Win really helped me, again. She's such a great kid."

The little girl blushed with pleasure.

That was a pretty savvy child, as Mitch had said. The two of them had worked together as fruitfully as Tiara and Win had, in another way. They would make a great family. And that, of course, was what this was all about.

All suddenly seemed well.

CHAPTER 15:
MYST

~~~

Princess Dawn was of course a fine hostess. They had a fine meal, and caught up on their assorted adventures, while the children got to know Piton and Data, admiring each other's talents. The Caprice Castle children could assume either skeletal or human form, and loved playfully switching back and forth.

"In the course of our travels we have noted areas where the pun virus still rampages," Dawn said.

"Then we must go there," Merge said. "All of it must be eliminated."

"Yes. Then we will seed back stored puns so that Xanth will be normal again."

"That will be a relief," Kandy said.

In due course they departed the castle, well fed and rested, and found that they were in a totally different part of Xanth. Right where they were needed: the signs of dead puns were all around.

They plunged in, as they normally did, each with a jar of anti-virus elixir. The children participated, holding jars of their own. They spread out in a line, efficiently wetting down the foliage and ground so that no virus could remain. Merge split into her five components, distributed along the line so that the others could get refills without losing their places and accidentally leaving any spot undoused. The children had learned to ignore the bare aspects; they had seen it happen when Astrid changed form, and knew despite the Adult

Conspiracy that there was nothing naughty about it. At least not when among sensible friends.

The terrain was uneven, and soon Astrid was separated from the main group by a sloping forest. She ran out of elixir and had to backtrack to find an aspect of Merge. So she shifted to her natural form so she could scurry through brush without wasting time, wearing only her dark glasses and hauling her jar along behind her by a cord. She found Brown, so named from her rich brown hair. Brown tilted her endlessly pouring urn to refill Astrid's jar, and Astrid returned to her place.

She circled a large tree-trunk, and paused. There was a handsome young man snoozing against a boulder, right in the section she needed to douse. Should she wake him? Her clothing was farther back; he would probably freak out. But if she circled around him, that section would not get doused, and the pun virus might spread from it, reinfecting the rest. That would make her effort pointless.

So she fetched a leaf from a nearby fig tree and used it to cover her bareness somewhat. "Sir!" she called.

The man snapped awake. "Why hello, pretty maiden," he said, smiling. "I am Jon. Who, if I may inquire, are you, and what is your business here in my bailiwick?"

"I am Astrid. I am spreading elixir to eliminate any remaining pun virus," she said. "I need to cover the section where you are. Could you move to one I have already doused?"

"Certainly, Astrid," he agreed. "I apologize for being in your way."

"Uh, I am without my clothing at the moment, Jon. I will have to set aside this fig leaf in order to work. You will need to avert your gaze."

"I have no need of that, miss. Perhaps I can help you in your worthy effort. I have missed the puns since they got wiped out here."

No need? He didn't know about freaking out? She lacked time and patience to educate him right now. So she dropped the leaf and picked up her jar.

Jon took a good look at her fully exposed body. "I must say you are a shapely one."

Astrid paused. She wasn't wearing panties, but even so, the sight of her nudity should have freaked him out. "Thank you." Then curiosity got the better of her. "How is it that you are unaffected by the sight of me?"

"It's a long story," Jon said. "But the essence is, I have been rendered immune to freaking out from the sight of female flesh, even such flesh as yours. Now how may I help you?"

Immune? He was a most unusual man. "If you really want to help, we can use you. I can set you up with a jar of anti-pun-virus elixir to spread about."

"I do want to help. This is my home and I want it restored to its former silly comfort."

"Are you a faun?" she asked. Because fauns, like nymphs, tended to be flighty, and thus unreliable.

"By no means. I am a regular mortal man."

"Then come this way." Astrid turned around and started back to where Brown was.

Jon, having been treated to a good view of her bare backside, took it in stride. "If I may ask, why do you wear those dark glasses, and nothing else?"

"I am a basilisk in human form. My direct stare would kill you."

"Ah. I appreciate the courtesy of your caution." Then, after half a moment: "You intrigue me. Are you romantically available?"

"No. I will soon marry my boyfriend, who is immune to poisons."

"Good for him. I am looking for a serviceable woman."

Serviceable? She let that pass. "If you are interested in only one thing, you will not find such a woman in our party."

Jon laughed. "I am interested in that one thing. Every man is. But not only that. I wish to find a woman who can be a good partner in the long haul."

"Good in what way?"

"She should be physically attractive, have an even temper, and be interested in making a family. I objectively assess any available woman I meet, and believe I will know when I encounter such a one."

Was he rational, or hopelessly arrogant? There was one way to find out. "Then maybe you should meet Merge."

"She is a member of your party?"

"Yes. Here is an aspect of her now." For Brown had just come into view.

The sight of this perfectly formed bare girl did not freak him out either. "An aspect?"

"She is one of five young women whose complete form is a mergence of the five. If you like one, you should like them all."

"Certainly the notion is intriguing," Jon agreed.

Brown paused as they approached her. "This is Jon," Astrid said. "He has volunteered to help. We need to provide him with a jar of elixir."

"We have a spare," Brown said, producing a filled jar.

"Jon is looking for an attractive, even-tempered woman who is interested in making a family."

"Well, now," Brown said, eying Jon up and down. "What is your talent, Jon?"

"I can summon things from the dream realm, one at a time."

"Like a walking skeleton or a night mare?"

"Yes, if I tried. But generally I go for simple objects, because the Night Stallion becomes annoyed if any of his animate creatures goes astray."

"That is sensible," Brown agreed. "Do you know my nature?"

"Astrid says that you are one of five women who can merge into one."

"This does not turn you off?"

"Not if the five and the one are sensible. Especially if they are as pretty as you."

"We must talk," Brown said. "After we clear this region of the virus."

"That is sensible," Jon agreed again, smiling.

Brown smiled back. This looked promising.

In another hour, with Jon's help, they cleared the region. Now it could be safely seeded with new puns. They all settled down for a break.

"This is Jon," Astrid said. "He helped us spread the elixir. He is looking for the right woman, and is considering Merge, or will once he meets her."

"No time like the present," the five aspects chorused. They came together, put their heads in close, and let their hair twine. Soon they merged into one.

"Hello," that one said. "I am Merge."

"Hello, Merge. I am Jon."

"I note you do not freak out at the sight of a bare woman," Merge said as she put on her panties and turned around to provide him a panoramic view.

"That is true." There was no freakout, only interest.

"Please tell us about how you came to be immune to panty magic," Merge said as she completed her dressing. She and the children settled down to listen. The children loved stories.

Jon told them. Astrid visualized the sequence as it was narrated.

He was foraging in the woods one day soon after passing the magical age of 18, looking for new kinds of pie to eat, when he heard a faint moan. He went there and found a lovely nymph with her foot caught in a trap. He recognized the type of trap: it was a supernatural snare, designed to catch only magical creatures. That meant she was magical. A fairy, maybe, or a sprite, or a wood nymph caught away from her tree. Certainly she was beautiful; he had never before seen a creature so fair. She had lustrous long golden hair that swirled around her body, forming a kind of cloak, and her features were simply perfect. Her body was—

"Wake," she said, and he snapped out of his trance.

"Sorry," he said. "The sight of such a—well, it does things to me."

"It freaked you out," she said.

"Yes," he agreed, embarrassed. He had very little experience with women, but he knew about freaking out, having seen it happen to his friends.

"Please help me, and I will reward you."

Just so. But was she a good or an evil spirit? If he touched an evil spirit he might be ensorceled and never heard from again. So he hesitated.

She looked up and saw him hesitating. "Please, kind man," she repeated. "Only a mortal can spring this trap."

"What are you?" he asked.

"I am an angel."

"An angel! But they never leave Heaven!"

"I am a young, naughty angel. I sneaked out because I wanted to explore Xanth. Now I am in awful trouble, unless I get back before they do bed-check. I'll never do it again."

"But where are your wings?"

"They are invisible. But I can show them to you if you wish." There was a buzzing, and delicate pink wings showed at her back.

That satisfied him: she was an angel. He knelt and put his hands on the jaws of the trap. In half a moment he had it open, and she drew her foot clear. In the process her hair slid aside and he saw up her bare leg.

"Wake," she said.

Jon snapped out of it. He had evidently freaked out again. "Sorry. I—"

"My fault, Jon. I moved carelessly." Her hair was back in place so that nothing showed above her knees. "But perhaps before I fly back to Heaven I can help you eliminate that awkward freak reflex. It could be dangerous if you were in the wrong company."

"Uh, I guess," he agreed.

"First a little privacy." She waved her hands, and a scintillating globe formed around them. Inside it was a marvelously soft bed of ferns. "Now your reward."

"I really don't need a reward," he protested. "It just wasn't right to have a lovely creature like you trapped like that."

"Oh, but I promised. I am going to cure you of freaking."

"Well, that's sort of a man thing. I admit it would be nice if I could look without freaking, but it's harmless."

"Harmless? Not necessarily. Suppose you encounter an illusion-wielding vampiress who masquerades as a pretty human girl in panties, then sucks your blood during your freakout? You would then become her love slave, when all she wants is your blood. That would be a draining experience."

"Ugh!" Jon said. "I see your point. It would be better not to freak."

"Indeed." She approached him and started removing his clothing.

"What are you doing?" he asked, abashed.

"I am undressing you. You must be naked for this exercise."

"Uh, well—"

She stood on tiptoes and kissed him. That completely shut him up. In fact had she not been holding him down, he would have floated away.

"Now close your eyes," she said. "Because though human women need things like bras and panties to freak out human men, I do not. I need you conscious for this stage."

"Uh, yes." He closed his eyes.

Then she took his hands and moved them to stroke her marvelously soft body. Again he tried to float. Had he seen what he was stroking he was sure to have freaked out so hard he would never have recovered. As it was, he was in nearly terminal rapture as she passed his hands over all of her body from head to toe.

"Now lie down with me," she said.

Numbly, he obeyed, eyes still closed. She hugged him and kissed him. Not only did he feel as if he were floating into the sky, he exploded into total freakout.

"Wake," she said gently.

Jon found himself lying alone on the bed. The angel was standing beside him, fully clothed in her voluminous tresses. "Did I—?" he asked.

"Yes, you freaked out," she said. "But that was your last one. Henceforth neither the sight nor the touch of a woman will cause that to happen."

He sat up, then stood. He put his clothing back on. "Are you sure? I don't feel different, apart from the, the joy of your touch."

"I will demonstrate." She swept her cloak of hair aside and stood nude before him. She was absolutely lovely in every glorious detail, but while he fully appreciated the sight, he did not freak out.

"Wow," he breathed, awed as much by his lack of freak as by the truly evocative body before him.

"Once you have been made love to by an angel, you are forever spoiled by anything less. Not even the most luscious panties will freak you."

"Wow," he repeated. "Thank you."

"Now I will return to Heaven, having done you this return favor. Farewell, mortal." She spread her gossamer wings and flew up into the sky, the globe that had given them privacy dissipating as she passed though it. He stood and gazed up after her as she rose. He saw up her legs, but did not freak. He had definitely been cured.

"And ever since then I have been immune," Jon concluded. "Experience has shown me that love springs don't affect me, or lethe water. My heart is my own, or maybe the angel's. This allows me to be wonderfully objective in my judgment of mortal women. But so far the ones I have encountered have been largely foolish twits, depending on their panties to wipe out my objectivity and cause me to ignore their faults. I want more than that in a wife."

"In Xanth, romance tends to be simplistic," Demoness Fornax remarked, appearing only to Astrid. "Possibly Jon, no longer subject to panty magic, really is more objective."

"That would be nice," Astrid subvocalized.

"I wonder," Metria said as her clothing dissolved leaving only a bright purple bra and panties on the verge of bursting asunder. Mitch, Ease, and Art froze in place, caught by surprise and freaked out. The women wore expressions of thinly masked disgust, though they were used to it.

"She's testing him," Fornax said. "She considers it a challenge."

"No, it's true," Jon said. "I don't freak." He was nevertheless taking a good look. "You're a demoness, aren't you. They tend to have matchless measurements."

"I meant about the spiritual being," Metria said as the stitching on her bra began to give way. "She could have been a demoness, like me, masquerading as an angel, the better to tease you." Now the panties were starting to tear, exposing a generous buttock.

"Nice touch, the seams giving way," Fornax said. "Considering that they're all demon stuff anyway."

"About the what?" Jon asked, his eyes orienting on the buttock.

"The angel," Astrid snapped before the usual exchange could get fairly started.

"Oh." Jon pondered half a moment. "Would a demoness have deliberately rendered any man immune to the weapon of the freakout?"

"Bleep no!" Metria swore. "It's fun to freak men." Her straining bra and panties developed polka dots with no material in the dots, one of her favorite ploys.

"Lovely," Fornax said.

But Jon still did not freak out. "Are you by chance single?" he inquired.

"Ha! She is scoring," Fornax said.

"I'm long since married," Metria said. "However my alter ego Mentia isn't. But she's a little crazy. She'd probably do anything you wanted." She shifted, becoming a different person, but no less endowed.

"Oh yes, she's setting up a possible relationship for her alterego," Fornax said. "Clever."

"But unscrupulous," Astrid murmured. "Considering it is Merge he is supposed to be checking out."

"It's not working. Now cover it up, lady canine," Kandy said tersely. "We want our men functional." She evidently hadn't picked up on the change of personalities.

Mentia glanced at her. "Am I missing something?"

"Metria was trying to tease an immune man," Astrid said. "Put her back in charge."

"As you prefer," Mentia said. She glanced at Jon. "Some other time, perhaps?"

"Perhaps," he agreed, intrigued, as she faded.

"Oh, all right," Metria grumped as her clothing reappeared. It was as if she were unaware of the intervening dialogue with Mentia.

"Show's over," Fornax said, fading out.

Kandy snapped her fingers, and the three men woke. "What do you wonder, Metria?" Mitch inquired. "I fear I suffered a moment of inattention."

Win laughed. "She flashed you, daddy."

"She wondered whether Jon encountered an angel or a demoness, dear," Tiara said. "We concluded that it was indeed an angel."

"But how did she cure you?" Squid asked. "All she did was kiss you and hug you." The children had not freaked out; bodily displays were the stuff of boredom to them.

The adults did not comment. It seemed there had been an ellipsis in the narrative that left the children confused. The Adult Conspiracy was ever-diligent.

"When an angel does it, that's all that's needed," Jon said.

"So you still appreciate the charms of women," Merge said. "You just aren't freaked out by them."

"Exactly." Jon eyed her. "I find your charms quite satisfactory."

"And what of my ability to fragment?"

"I admit that the thought of being hugged and kissed by five young women like you does not dismay me."

"So you in your objectivity see me as a suitable marriage prospect?"

"I do. Are you interested?"

"Is this adult-speak for mushy?" Santo asked.

"Very much so," Metria assured him.

"I am interested," Merge said. "But there is a condition."

"Let's have it."

"We must adopt a child."

Jon frowned. "I was thinking of the conventional signaling of the stork. Repeatedly. Does the stork not respond to your call?"

Merge colored faintly. "I wouldn't know. I've never tried a signal."

"Then why do you think you need to adopt a child?"

"Because the child needs to be adopted. I like her, and she likes me, and we want to make a family. But it would help to have a man in the picture."

"I see. So you are not abruptly smitten with me, so much as needing a man to complete your prospective family."

Astrid winced. Jon's supreme objectivity was showing.

"That's approximately it," Merge agreed. "It's the converse of your interest in signaling the stork, regardless of the woman involved." She shot a brief irritated glance at Metria.

Jon nodded. "That is sensible. Who is the child?"

"I am," Myst said, smiling sweetly.

"Well, you're a cute one," Jon said.

"Thank you."

"How are you for discipline?"

"For what?"

"Power, control, obedience, no back talk, parent's word is law," Metria said.

"Spanking?" Myst asked, bridling.

"Whatever," the demoness said crossly.

"Yes, when necessary," Jon said. "Can't have a child running wild."

"No spanking," Myst said.

"That is not for you to decide."

"Yes it is."

Jon's eyes narrowed. "So you are an undisciplined child?"

"You bet. No one—"

She was interrupted by the swoop of his hand. He caught her about the waist, lifted her, turned her over, and put her across his knee. He spanked her.

And his hand passed through her to bang his own knee. Myst floated free, a cloud of mist.

Jon nodded. "Undisciplined," he concluded.

"I don't like you," Myst said, making a pooping noise.

"The feeling is mutual." Jon turned to Merge. "Adopting a child, maybe. Adopting this one, no. She would be nothing but trouble."

"But this is the one I want," Merge said.

"Then it seems you have a choice: me or the child."

Merge hardly considered. "The child."

"Then that's it." Jon got up and walked away.

Astrid winced again. Could there be such a thing as too much objectivity?

Metria shifted forms again. Her child ego, Woe Betide, appeared. "Well, I guess you showed *him*," she said.

But now Myst was contrite. "I'm sorry, Aunt Merge. If you really want to marry him, I'll—I'll let him spank me."

"Absolutely not," Merge said. "I don't believe in that form of discipline."

"He did seem a bit too oriented on control," Kandy said. "His way or the highway. Maybe it's because panties don't soften him. His immunity makes him unmanageable."

"Like me," Myst said.

"He didn't like you being like him!" Merge said, amazed.

"It would have gotten worse," Metria said seriously. "If he's making demands during the courtship, he'll be a tyrant in the marriage."

"But now I can't make a family," Merge said tearfully.

"There are other men," Astrid said. "You just need to find the right one."

"I suppose," Merge agreed uncertainly. "But I fear they may be all alike in this respect."

"Not me," Mitch said.

"But you're not available."

"It must be time to get back to work," Mitch said, not arguing that case. Tiara's dawning glare might have had something to do with it.

Metria shifted back into Mentia. "I'm just crazy enough to be intrigued," she said. "I have no children." She puffed into smoke and dissipated, evidently going after Jon.

They got back to work, collectively sobered. That continued for several days, as they searched out remnants of the virus and eliminated them.

Meanwhile Astrid pondered: three of the five children had found prospective adoptive parents, and a fourth was in the offing—if only Merge could find a man to marry. But one thing they were not finding any sign of was such a man. It was as though men didn't exist in this region of Xanth.

One afternoon Firenze was working alongside Astrid. "Is it all right if I call you Mom?" he asked hesitantly. "I know you haven't married Uncle Art yet, and you haven't adopted me, but it feels odd to keep calling you Aunt Astrid."

"Cal me that, son," she said. "We know it will happen. We're just holding up until the others can join us for the five portraits."

"Thanks, Mom." He seemed relieved. "I'm worried about Myst. And Santo."

"Metria has expressed an interest in Santo. She admires his talent."

He hesitated. "I don't want to insult anyone."

"What's on your mind?"

"Metria's pretty flighty. She changes her mind all the time. And she already has a half-demon child."

"More than one," Astrid agreed. "You're thinking of Demon Ted. He's nineteen now."

"Yes. She doesn't mention him or bring him around. I don't think she's much interested in children."

"You think she might renege?"

"Yes. And that she wouldn't be a very good mother anyway. Not for a boy like Santo."

Astrid stopped working and faced him. "What are you saying?"

He backed off immediately. "Nothing. Nothing at all."

"There's something."

"Mom, he told me in confidence. I can't tell."

"But it's enough to make him not right for Metria?"

"Yes," he said miserably.

"Well, I think it will be their decision. We should simply hope for the best."

"I guess."

She let it drop. But she wondered.

Fornax appeared. "He has a point. Santo is special."

"He's not a bad boy!"

"No one said that. But Metria may indeed have a problem."

Astrid knew better than to push for more information than the Demoness felt free to provide. "Meanwhile we have not yet placed Myst."

"There is a divide in the way ahead. I regard the right way as more scenic."

"But the left looks like a better prospect for pools of virus."

"So it does," Fornax agreed, and faded.

When they came to the divide, Firenze went right. He had of course overheard the Demoness, and understood. There was a reason for this route.

There was a young man walking the other way. He looked a bit confused. "Are you okay?" Firenze asked him.

"I don't know," the man replied. "There was this car accident, then blankness, then—where am I?"

"You're Mundane!" Firenze said.

"I don't understand."

"From Mundania," Astrid said. "Never mind. This is Xanth."

"Zanth?"

"Xanth. A magic land. You will need some guidance."

"I will help," Fornax said, appearing as an ordinary woman. "This way, Kribbitz."

The man halted in place. "You just appeared out of nowhere. And you know my nickname. I didn't even tell you my name."

"Your name is Chris Kehler," Fornax said. "Here in Xanth we know things. Walk with me and I'll explain."

Plainly bemused, Chris walked with her. Astrid knew she would set him straight about how to get along in Xanth. The Demoness had intervened so that Astrid would not have to be diverted from her course. What was so important about it? It was strictly routine terrain.

They came across a girl about Firenze's age playing in sand. She was making surprisingly intricate figures out of the sand. "Hi," Firenze said. "I'm Firenze, and this is—is—"

"His mother," Astrid said. "Astrid. We're delousing the pun virus."

"I'm Sand," the girl said. "Sand D. I'm good with sand. Mom's a sand witch."

A pun, of course. "So the pun virus is not here," Astrid said.

"Not here," Sand said. "It would have been awful. But it wouldn't have wiped out Mom. She's not a pun. She conjures sand."

Both Astrid and Firenze laughed. "Good thing you explained," Firenze said. "Your dad must have been set straight early on about that."

"I have no dad."

"No dad?" he asked blankly.

"I'm adopted."

Astrid was beginning to see why this route had been suggested. The girl was cute, and Firenze was obviously interested.

"So am I!" he said. "Or about to be. But—"

"Mom adopted me. She conjures sand, and I'm good with sand, and since I was an orphan, well, she took me in."

"She could adopt you without a dad? I thought that was against the rule."

"What rule?" Sand asked challengingly.

Astrid exchanged a look with Firenze. Was there a rule?

Now it was quite clear why Fornax had obliquely recommended this route. Here was a possible answer to Merge's dilemma. Single parent adoption!

"We don't know of any such rule," Astrid said. "But I have a friend whom I think would like to talk to your mother."

Sand frowned. "If your friend is going to criticize—"

"No, not at all! It's that she may be interested in adopting a little girl herself, and would like reassurance."

The girl smiled, relieved. "That's different. I'm sure Mom will talk with her. Mom's very opinionated about the subject."

"I will fetch my friend," Astrid said. "Um, Firenze—"

"I'll wait here," he said, glancing at Sand, who smiled shyly. They were ten years old, but it was not too young to begin appreciating the opposite gender.

Astrid hurried back the way they had come. Fornax appeared beside her. "I took the Mundane to Kandy, who will help him get oriented. I believe Merge will be interested in what the Witch has to say."

"Yes. It's odd that we never thought of single-parent adoption."

"It's not the only oddity in the adoption process."

"Oh? What else is there?"

"I don't think I should comment yet."

So there was more complication coming. Astrid let it be.

Soon she located Merge and Myst working together. "Merge! There may be an answer, if you want it."

Merge did not need to ask what she was talking about. "I want it."

"There's a sand witch, no pun, a witch who conjures sand. She adopted a child."

"That's nice."

"By herself. She's not married. A single-parent adoption."

"Ooo!" Myst exclaimed.

"That's possible?" Merge said in wonder.

"It seems there's no rule against it. Talk to her."

"I will." They hurried in that direction.

Firenze and Sand were playing in the sand, making sand dollars that looked quite realistic. There were both coin-like dollars and paper-like dollars. The coins clinked as they handled them, and the paper bills folded without coming apart.

"That girl really is good with sand," Astrid murmured. Then, to the children:

"This is Merge, to talk to the Sand Witch. And Myst."

"She's like my little sister," Firenze said as Myst smiled shyly.

Sand D jumped up, shedding sand. "This way." Then, to Myst: "What's your talent?"

"I can turn to mist."

"That's great! So a dragon can't chomp you."

The two adults followed the three children. "Firenze seems quite taken with Sand," Merge remarked. "I didn't realize that he was of age to notice girls."

"They're just friends, surely," Astrid said, laughing.

They came to a small sand castle whose walls resembled sandstone. A moderately young woman stepped out to meet them as they approached it. "Mom, someone wants to ask you about adoption," Sand said.

"Well, I'm not giving you up, regardless," the Witch said.

"I'll show you my room," Sand said, and the three children disappeared into the house.

"That's not it!" Astrid said quickly. "It's that my friend Merge, here, was going to marry a man and adopt Myst, the little girl. But it didn't work out, and she feared she wouldn't be able to adopt her. But if you were able to do it with Sand, maybe she can do it with Myst. So we wanted to talk with you."

"I can guess why it didn't work out. That's the trouble with men," the Witch said. "All they want is one thing. If they don't get it, *pffft!* they're gone. If they do get it, then they want it twice a day and they think they own you. They never think of children. That's no good."

"That's no good," Merge agreed. Her case differed in detail, but she had the sense not to argue.

"When I met him, and showed him my house, which my daughter shaped out of the sand I conjured, all he said was 'Does it have a bedroom?' I said it did. He asked, 'Does it have a mattress?' I said it did. Then he said, 'That's fine. Take off your clothes.' He didn't care about the child at all. That's when I dumped him."

"So you adopted her alone, and there was no trouble?" Merge asked.

"None at all. Except from busybodies who think a family is incomplete without a man."

"Obviously that's not the case," Merge agreed. "Thank you, Witch; you have helped me solve my problem."

"It still requires a man to signal the stork," the Witch said. "Which is too bad. But with adoption you don't need the man."

The children emerged. "We'll do it," Merge said as Myst ran to her embrace.

Astrid nodded. Fornax had quietly helped them solve another problem.

Except for one. They still needed to identify and stop the Demon who was still interfering with their adoptions. He hadn't done it in the case of Myst, as far as Astrid knew, though it might simply have been too subtle for her to pick up on. Jon hadn't worked out, but that seemed to have been an honest difference in child-rearing (spanking?) philosophies. But there was still another adoption to go. They needed to stop the interference before it stopped them.

"An evening walk, alone, can refresh the mind," Fornax murmured, and faded.

A walk alone? Astrid didn't see the relevance, but knew better than to argue.

So it was that Astrid found herself walking alone, after the others had returned to the camp. The problem just wouldn't let go of her. She just knew the anonymous Demon would try again, maybe this time successfully. But how could they stop him?

A figure walked toward her. It was a teenage girl. "Are you the basilisk?" she asked shyly.

"I am Astrid Basilisk," Astrid agreed cautiously.

The girl looked nervously around as if afraid of being overheard. "I'm Fray Cloud. Fracto's daughter. I compressed into compact form so I could tell you."

Astrid hadn't realized that Fracto had a daughter, but certainly it was possible. "Tell me what?"

"My father has been messing with you, like with that woman and her daughter."

"Tiara and Win," Astrid agreed. "Fortunately we managed to recover them safely."

"He didn't want to do it. He's not a bad cloud, really he isn't. But the Demon made him do it. He was going to kidnap me and bind me to this form and throw me in among the brutish trolls." Fray shuddered. "I have half a soul, so I can suffer. I'm only seventeen!"

"He threatened you to make your father do his bidding?" Astrid asked.

"Yes. It was awful. Dad hated doing it, but he couldn't let me be—be—"

"I understand. Of course he couldn't."

"But it's wrong. So I just had to come and tell you, secretly, so you would know."

"I appreciate that," Astrid said. "You're a brave girl, Fray. But there is one thing more I need to know. Who is the Demon behind this?"

Fray looked around again. "It is—"

A bolt of energy struck her. It blasted her to swirling vapor. She didn't have time to scream, let along speak the name.

Appalled, Astrid watched the vapor dissipate. So close!

But as the last wisps evaporated, another figure was revealed. "Gotcha!" she exclaimed.

It was Fornax. It had been Fornax all along, pretending to be the cloud girl.

Fornax reached out and grabbed hold of the lightning bolt, which somehow had frozen in place. It was actually more like a long trident. She hauled on it, and a rotund figure with a crown of seaweed was yanked into view before he could let go of the other end. "Neptune, you fat glob of sea sludge!" Fornax said with satisfaction. "I knew it was you."

"Oh for spume's sake!" the Demon said. "You set me up!"

"I did indeed, you barrel of rancid spit. Your corroded barnacled backside is mine. Now you and I will go private and have a little talk all about terms for not speaking your salty name in connection with a certain wager."

The two vanished. Astrid knew that there would be no more interference from that quarter. Fornax had laid her little trap and caught the malefactioned Demon fair and square. Or maybe foul and globular.

Once again the Demoness had come through for the children, and for Xanth.

CHAPTER 16:
SANTO

~~~

Metria was distraught, which was an unusual state for her. "He's water under the bridge!"

"He's what?" Astrid asked.

"Absent, departed, missing, nonexistent, lost—"

"Gone?"

"Whatever," she agreed crossly.

"Who is gone?"

"Santo. I was going to rouse him for his breakfast, but he's not there."

Metria had been taking care of Santo, and was in line to adopt him. What had happened? "Maybe he's out for a walk, practicing making holes," Astrid suggested.

"No. I'm aware of him, and can normally find him. He's nowhere close."

Astrid was suspicious. There had been subtle interference in their project all along. She thought catching Neptune had fixed it. Was there more? "Did someone abduct him?"

"I don't know!"

Fornax appeared. "This one seems to be natural," she said, and faded.

Natural? What did that mean? That no Demon was involved? "Let's assume that he's not abducted, but is lost," Astrid said. "If so, we'll simply need to find him."

They acquainted the others with the problem. "Santo may have gone exploring, and gotten lost," Astrid said.

All the children shook their heads. "If he got lost, he'd simply make a tunnel back home," Firenze said. "He's not lost unless he wants to be."

Astrid remembered Firenze's prior comments about Santo. "Why would he want to be?"

"I can't say."

There it was again. What did Firenze know? She couldn't ask him directly. "Squid, do you know anything about this?"

"A little," the child answered. "He didn't think he belonged."

"Belonged to what?"

She shrugged. "I don't know what."

"Win. What do you know?"

"He—he thinks he's not like us."

"In what way?"

"Some way," she said, at a loss.

"Myst?"

"It bothers him. Maybe he went away."

"Right when we're on the verge of doing the adoptions, painting the portraits, and saving Xanth?"

She spread her hands. "I guess."

"That doesn't seem like Santo. He knows the importance of the adoptions."

Firenze fidgeted, then spoke. "Maybe he didn't think he was adoptable."

"Of course he is! Metria will adopt him."

"So he went away," Squid said.

"So she couldn't adopt him? I thought he liked her."

"He does," Win said.

Astrid looked at them, frustrated. "He likes her, so he's stopping her from adopting him?"

"Yes," Myst said.

"This is ridiculous!"

The children just looked at her.

"*Why* would he stop her?" Astrid demanded.

"So as not to hurt her," Firenze said.

"What, he's got a crush on her? Doesn't he see her as a mother figure?"

"No," Squid said.

Astrid threw up her hands and walked away. What was she missing that the children knew or suspected?

Fornax appeared. "Not that I want to bother you with irrelevant distractions, but it occurs to me that you have not used all the restored sequins. One might take you where you want to go."

"I don't want to go anywhere!"

The Demoness shrugged and faded.

Astrid went and dug out the dress, which she did not wear routinely. It remained pretty, and the sequins sparkled, the new ones brighter than the used ones.

She contemplated it. There actually was one place she wanted to go to: wherever it was that Santo had gone. So she could talk to him and find out what was bothering him. And she realized that a sequin would take her there. That had to be what Fornax had hinted.

She discussed it with the others. "Santo has gone somewhere. I don't know what's on his mind, but I want to bring him back so that we can do the portraits. I think a sequin will take me there."

"Do you want company?" Kandy asked.

"I think I probably need to talk to him alone."

"That may be best," Kandy said.

"Mom, this makes me nervous," Firenze said.

"Me too," Astrid said. She reached down, took a sequin, and pulled it off. The dress went translucent, showing her underwear, and the men freaked out. They never seemed to learn; it was almost as if they didn't want to learn. Well, the women would snap them out of it in a moment. She pinned the sequin back on. Would it be the right one? If not, she would try again.

She stood in what appeared to be a dungeon. Where in Xanth was it?

Then she noticed that her bright sequins had gone dull. They would not work here. That told her where she was: in Hades.

Santo must have made a tunnel to Hades, and let the portions that passed through water or molten rock fill in after him, so as to leave no followable trail. But why? Fornax surely knew, and wasn't free to tell.

"This is not a pleasant excursion," Fornax murmured beside her. "I will help if I can; I think the Demon protocol allows it."

"This is all unpleasantly mysterious."

"The boy does have a case."

"Well, so do the rest of us. I mean to get to the bottom of this."

"Unkind as the revelation may be."

Astrid was fed up with obscurities. "Santo!" she called.

The boy appeared. "Aunt Astrid! What are you doing here?"

"Looking for you. We need you back at the farm for a portrait."

He shook his head. "I can't do that."

"You can't let us all down, after all the work we've done to set up for the adoptions and portraits."

"I'm sorry about that. But maybe they'll work without me."

"Santo, what *is* it with you? Why are you messing things up?"

"I'm really sorry."

Now she saw that he was crying. "Hold your breath," she said as she went to him and put her arm around his shoulders.

He melted into her, comforted. "I wish..."

She let him go before he had to take a breath to replace what he had lost talking. "We love you and want what's best for you, Santo. You will have to trust me. Tell me what's wrong."

He broke down completely. "I can't be adopted."

She knew this was critical. She had to withhold any judgment. "Why?"

"I'm not worthy."

"How can you say that? You're a fine boy who will grow into a fine young man. You have a potent talent that really helped us survive the Storage. You have friends who truly care for you. None of them think you're not worthy. Why do you?"

"I—I—when I grow up and it's time to marry—"

"Yes, that is the normal course."

He visibly nerved himself. "I'll want to marry a man."

Astrid stared at him. "A what?"

"A man."

"You're gay? How can you know? You're a child."

"I know. I've got nothing against girls, especially you and Aunt Fornax, but they won't do for romance."

She opened her mouth, but found nothing to say. This was wholly unexpected.

Fornax stepped in. "Hello, Santo."

"Oh, hi, Aunt Fornax." He did not seem completely surprised by her appearance.

"Let me see if I understand. You believe you are gay, and that this makes you unworthy of adoption into a straight family? Because you're different?"

"Yes," he whispered.

"Let me remind you about difference," Fornax said. "Every person is different in his or her own way, some more than others. Astrid isn't human; she is a basilisk whose very look can kill. Her kind is shunned by all other creatures."

"Not by us," Santo protested. "She's nice."

"She has a soul. That makes a difference. Without it she would not be the person you know and love. But the point is, you know her. You know how kind spirited she is, and how dedicated she is to your welfare, and the welfare of all the children. So she's a basilisk; we who know her don't care."

"We don't care," he agreed. "But—"

"And consider me. I'm the Demon of Antimatter. I will destroy anything I touch here in the terrene realm. I have to appear here in ghostly form so as not to wipe you out. I am also a pariah among Demons, who have constantly balked my effort to participate in this realm. Sensible folk want nothing to do with me."

"Aunt Fornax, that's not true! You enabled us five children to return from the future instead of dying there, and you have been helping us all along. We owe everything to you, and we love you!"

"And I love you. Do you think I care about a little detail like who you want to marry sometime in the future? Do you think Astrid cares? That's your business. So you're different. You're only a little bit different compared to Astrid and me. In no way are you unworthy. We don't think so, the other children don't think so. You're fussing about next to nothing."

"And we need you to be adopted, and have the portrait painted, to save Xanth," Astrid added.

Fornax smiled. "It would be a shame to have Xanth lost because you mistakenly felt unworthy."

Santo gazed at her, assimilating that. Slowly it sank in. "May I hug you?"

"Carefully," Fornax said, opening her arms.

He hugged her ghostly form, carefully, so as not to overlap too much. "Thank you, Aunt Fornax."

"Oh, you're welcome, dear."

"Now we can go home," Astrid said as they finished hugging. "Can you make another tunnel there, Santo?"

"No," he said a bit sheepishly. "I used all my magic energy getting here, and I don't know exactly how I did it. It will take me days to recover, and then I probably won't remember how to do it."

Astrid looked around. "We're in the dungeon of a castle, obviously. We can go upstairs and out, then see about walking back."

"Remember where you are," Fornax murmured.

"In the dungeon of a castle—in Hades," Astrid said, realizing. "But that's—

on another planet. Pluto."

"Yes," Santo said. "That seemed to be the place for me."

"But that means you tunneled through space-time itself!"

"I guess," he agreed.

Astrid exchanged a glance with Fornax. How could he have done such a thing? It would have taken a lifetime of walking to go from Xanth to Pluto, if walking there were even possible. He had done it in what, an hour?

"Point of irrelevant information," Fornax said. "Space is magical in various ways, one of which is the existence of wormholes. That is, holes between one section of the universe and another, short-cutting distance, such that passing through one can enable a person to traverse in a moment what he otherwise might not navigate in his lifetime. The ability to create such a wormhole might be useful on occasion."

Santo had created a wormhole? That made his talent a magnitude greater than it had seemed before. He might well be a Magician in the making.

"I think we won't be walking back," Astrid said.

"I'm sorry," Santo said. "I didn't know you would come after me."

"Again, consider where you are," Fornax said. "There may not be many castles here."

Astrid considered. She knew of only one castle in Hades: the one Princess Eve had had made so she could live apart from the awful spooks of the nether region.

"Princess Eve!" she exclaimed.

"Princess Dawn's twin sister," Fornax agreed.

"She lives in a castle in Hades. This must be her castle. All we have to do is go upstairs and ask for her help. I believe she has a way to go back and forth to Xanth."

"I understand there is an enchanted path connecting the castle to the River Styx," Fornax said. "And that across that river, by additional magic, is Xanth."

"Styx," Santo said. "I've heard of it. The lethe water in it makes you forget."

"There's a ferryman to transport folk across the river," Astrid said. "Because they can't swim in it; they'd forget where they were going."

"Princess Eve can arrange for a pass across the river," Fornax said.

Astrid walked to the stone stairway at one end of the chamber. It led to a closed door. "This must be the way up."

But the door was locked from the outside.

"I guess I figured I didn't want to be disturbed," Santo said.

"Okay, how about the tunnel you came in on? Can we follow it back?"

"I don't think so. Sections will have filled in."

Astrid explored the chamber and found a round tunnel leading out of it. She stepped into it, using her superior night vision. But it quickly terminated in a blank wall. The wormhole must have closed up at that point. Maybe just as well, because otherwise trolls, goblins, nickelpedes and other horrors might have used it to come after Santo.

What now? Astrid returned to the locked door. "Do you have energy enough to make a hole through the lock?" she asked Santo.

"Not yet," he said somewhat sheepishly.

Astrid pondered anew. Then she tried something different. She knocked on the door. Maybe there was a guard.

"Who's there?" a voice called from the other side.

Ha! "Visitors to see Princess Dawn," Astrid called back.

"She's not here."

Oops. Dawn could well be visiting Xanth, or attending a function with her husband, the Dwarf Demon Pluto. What now?

Astrid gambled that the guard on the other side was not very bright. "Then we'll wait for her return. Please unlock this door and let us through."

"Okay." It worked!

In a moment there was a clank as of a plank being lifted clear, and the door swung open on a small landing. There was a frightful spook with horns and a forked tail. A guard demon.

Astrid flashed him a fetching smile. "Thank you, Jeeves." She and Santo stepped through. "That will be all."

The spook stepped back, recognizing the tone of authority.

"You are clever in your off moments," Fornax murmured.

"It's more like desperation and sheer luck," Astrid replied subvocally.

The landing led to another flight of steps. They mounted these to another landing, and thence to more steps. But eventually they reached the regular cellar of the castle.

There was a boy, about five years old, playing with something on the floor. It looked dead, but it was running around. In fact it was a zombie rat, hideous to behold.

"Hello," Astrid said. "I'm Astrid."

"I'm Plato," the boy said, responding in kind, as she had hoped.

"Princess Eve's son," Fornax murmured. "The future second Zombie Master."

So Eve was out, but her son remained. Someone must be here to take care of him. "May I speak to your nanny?" Astrid asked.

"Sure. She's in the kitchen. She's a zombie."

Astrid suppressed her surprise. This was Hades, after all. "Thank you." They walked on up one more flight of steps and into the castle proper.

"Hello!" Astrid called, to alert the nanny.

A gray-haired young woman appeared. "Who are you?" she asked, evidently alarmed by the intrusion.

"I am Astrid, and this is Santo," Astrid said. "We got caught in the dungeon and wish to return to Xanth. We're sorry to bother you, miss—?"

"Zosi," the woman said. "I'm Plato's governess."

Santo laughed. "He said you were a zombie."

"I am."

There was a brief but awkward pause. Astrid tried to patch it up. "You certainly don't look like a zombie."

"It's a long story. I'm fully alive at the moment. How did you get in the dungeon?"

"That's complicated to explain."

"Maybe we should have enough of a discussion to get to know each other better," Zosi said diplomatically.

"I'm hungry," Santo said.

"Do you like peanut butter and jelly sandwiches?"

"Sure."

"That's good. My talent is to conjure them."

The mention of food brought Plato to join the group, along with his rat, and the boys discussed holes and dead things while they ate. Soon the adults were seated in a pleasant living room overlooking a somber scene of Hades outside. "I really am a zombie," the woman said. "Zosi Zombie. I spent some time in the ground defending Castle Roogna from invaders. But since the retirement of the original Zombie Master the zombies have become fewer. We slowly wear out, and have to be replaced, but there are no replacements to be had. So I was selected to return to life so I could try to deal with the problem. In time I encountered Plato, and Princess Eve prevailed on me to become his governess. His talent is to reanimate dead things, you see, and since I'm a zombie, that doesn't bother me the way it does others, and I don't bother him the way prim finicky women do. So I am here taking care of him and helping him develop his talent. He can't reanimate dead human folk yet, but when he's grown he'll do it, and zombies will no longer be threatened with extinction."

"That's remarkable," Astrid said. "It never occurred to me that there could be a shortage of zombies."

"They're an essential part of Xanth, just as puns are."

"Which bring us to us," Astrid said. "I am a basilisk in a manner roughly similar to the way you are a zombie: I am in human form, and mask my gaze so as not to hurt anyone inadvertently. I have a soul, and the basilisk life didn't entirely suit me, so the Good Magician got me transformed, and I served on a mission to repay him, acting as a bodyguard because of my ability to kill monsters. That mission was to eliminate the virus that destroyed Xanth's puns."

"It never occurred to me that there could ever be a shortage of puns," Zosi said with a smile.

"But it seemed that no sooner had we managed to make Xanth safe again for puns, and start restoring them from the capacious depths of Caprice Castle's vaults, when we learned of another threat to Xanth: it will be destroyed in fifty years, unless we can get five orphan children adopted into new families, and their portraits painted. Santo here is one of the children. He felt unworthy, so he fled to what turned out to be your dungeon. Hence my presence there."

Zosi's brow furrowed. "How did he get in there, and how did you locate him? Hades is far away from Xanth."

"His talent is making holes," Astrid explained. "He made a tunnel to your dungeon."

"A tunnel from Xanth? That would require Magician class magic!"

"So it seems. As for how I found him, I had help from my friend Fornax."

"Fornax! She's a notorious mischief-maker. We had to fight her constantly to eliminate the Bomb that changed beauties to crones. In fact, she made the Bomb. Do not trust her."

Astrid smiled. "Times change. She also made the dress I am wearing, that was instrumental in dealing with the virus. She is my friend."

"I don't think she is anybody's friend. Don't trust her."

Astrid was taken aback. "Maybe if you heard her side of it, you would reconsider."

Zosi shook her head. "I'm not sure of that."

Fornax appeared. "Hello, Zosi. I remember you and respect you."

"The Demoness!" Zosi exclaimed, horrified.

"Listen to her," Astrid said. "She's on our side now."

"You almost got Kody killed!"

"Kody?" Astrid asked.

"Her Mundane boyfriend who visits her in his dreams," Fornax explained.

"I'm his dream girl," Zosi agreed.

"I confess I made mischief for you, Zosi," Fornax said. "And for Astrid's party. But then things changed."

"What could change a malicious Demoness?"

"Friendship."

"She needed a friend, and I became that friend," Astrid said. "She has been a friend indeed, helping me throughout, though it will cost her a Demon bet. She saved the life of one of the children, and got in trouble with the Demons for it. She enabled me to find Santo in your dungeon."

"I find that hard to believe." Zosi shook her head as if clearing it. "Which reminds me: why did he go there? It's not a good place."

"He felt unworthy to be adopted," Astrid said.

"Why?"

Astrid hesitated, uncertain whether to speak of the boy's secret.

"Because I'm gay," Santo said.

"Really? That's wonderful!"

Astrid, Santo, and Fornax stared at her. She did not seem to be sarcastic. "Wonderful?" Santo asked.

"My boyfriend in Mundania is gay." Zosi saw their looks of incredulity. "He's reversed in Xanth, and we love each other. But I would never fit in with his real life."

"You know he's gay, but you don't condemn him?" Santo asked.

"Why should I condemn him? He's a fine man. I'm staying alive because of him. Otherwise I'd have little reason not to return to my full zombie state."

"But you're taking care of Plato!" Astrid protested.

"Yes, and that is worthwhile. But that's my job, not my preference. My will to live is because of my dream man."

"I don't think I quite understand," Astrid said. "Which one of you is dreaming?"

"He is. Awake, he's in Mundania. But he can dream of Xanth. That's when he visits me, reversed. That's what I live for. His visits. It's a dream to him, but he's perfectly solid to me."

"He detonated the Bomb and woke in Mundania," Fornax said. "The Night Stallion gave him a dream pass. I'm glad it worked out."

Zosi looked at her. "You're not here to mess that up?"

"Not at all, dear. I'm here to help save Xanth from destruction."

"I hope it's true."

"It's true," Santo said. "Aunt Fornax helped fetch me from the future, where I would have died, along with the other children."

"How did you get involved with children?" Zosi asked Fornax.

"Wenda Woodwife said it would facilitate friendship," Fornax said. "She was right."

"Wenda! I know her. She loves children."

"She does," Astrid agreed.

Zosi shook her head again. "Then I guess I have to believe you, Demoness. I apologize for speaking unkindly of you."

"No need," Fornax said. "We were on opposite sides then."

"But do they allow you to change things in Xanth, now?"

"No. I will be put on Demon Trial if I interfere."

"Then how can you help Astrid or the children?"

"I don't. I merely observe, and sometimes make incidental remarks."

"They can't prove anything more," Santo said.

Zosi nodded, understanding. "I am glad to have had your visit, Astrid, Santo, Fornax, and I'm sure Plato is glad to see another child."

"Yeah, he makes great holes," Plato said enthusiastically. "See, here's one he made me from golf course junk." He held up a big numeral one with a hole through it. "A hole-in-one. They really like those in Mundania, for some reason."

"I'm sure they do," Zosi agreed, looking slightly pained by the pun.

"I think we have to be moving on," Astrid said. "We have marriages and adoptions to perform, and portraits to be painted."

"You said all this is to save Xanth from destruction," Zosi said. "I don't follow that."

"It's a prophecy," Astrid explained. "Xanth will be destroyed in fifty years, but if we can get the five children adopted and painted, then it will be saved."

"That is a worthy cause," Zosi agreed. "I hope you succeed. It would be awkward for us all if Xanth perished."

They all laughed at that. The tension dissipated.

"I will show you to the River Styx," Zosi said. "Charon, who poles the raft across, can be balky, but he'll generally settle for a kiss and feel from a pretty woman."

"I thought he was married," Astrid said.

"He is."

"Then what's he doing imposing on other women? That's not supposed to happen in Xanth."

"This isn't Xanth."

"Oh." Even the children smiled at Astrid's discomfort.

"There's no Adult Conspiracy here, either," Zosi said. "So brace yourself when we walk the path to the river."

"Something's on the path?"

"Off the path. The demons of Hades know the path is enchanted, so they can't reach you no matter how horribly they threaten. So they try to lure you off the path, and they'll use anything they think might work. You have to ignore them."

"It's fun," Plato said, carrying his half-dead rat.

Astrid did not trust that. "As long as it leads back to Xanth."

"The river is the boundary between Hades and everything else. For folk of Xanth, the other side is Xanth."

"Even though Hades is in another planet?"

"Magical realms know few boundaries."

"This should be interesting," Astrid said.

Fornax smiled obscurely without commenting.

They went to the front castle gate. There was a demon guard there, but he let them pass. Zosi clearly had authority in the absence of the proprietors, and of course Plato was the son of Pluto, their ruler.

They followed the path down the mountain and into a dark forest. A handsome man appeared beside the path, beckoning Astrid. "They are silent," Zosi said. "You can hear them only if you cross the line. Don't do that; you'll never manage to get back on it, and the demons will have their nefarious way with you."

"What would a demon want with me?" Astrid asked.

"But they can hear us," Zosi said warningly.

Indeed, the demon pantomimed embracing Astrid, kissing her, and undressing her. Then he became insultingly more specific.

"But the children!" Astrid protested, before remembering that there was no Adult Conspiracy.

"I don't know for sure what he wants to do with you, Aunt Astrid," Santo said. "But it doesn't look as if it's much fun for you."

"I am certainly not crossing the line," Astrid said primly.

"So there, spook!" Plato called, gesturing with a finger. The demon angrily dissipated into smoke.

Astrid almost swallowed her teeth. No child was supposed to know that gesture, especially not a five-year-old.

"You're right, Plato," Santo said. "It's confusing but interesting on the path."

"You have to endure this whenever you're out here?" Astrid asked Zosi, appalled.

"No. They have long since learned that it's a waste of time flashing me. But you're new here, so they're trying. Just ignore them and they'll go away after a while."

Now a sultry demoness addressed Santo. She had a table loaded with cakes, chocolates, and eye scream. *Come here*, she signaled, *and all this will be yours.*

"What would happen if I went?" Santo asked Plato.

"She'd sprout teeth and eat *you*."

"Too bad. That food looks great."

"Watch." Plato set down his zombie rat. It scurried quickly across the line, heading for the food, or maybe just to hide under the table.

In a moment the rat reached the demoness and scurried up her leg. *Eeeek!* she screamed silently, batting at the rodent. The table collapsed and the food slid to the ground, where it reverted to its real nature: garbage.

The demoness, furious, caught the rat in her hands, which had become talons. She opened her mouth, which had grown fangs, and bit the rat's head off. Then she spat it out again, revolted; evidently zombies did not taste good. She glared at Plato, who responded with another finger. She exploded into vile smoke.

"Let's move on," Astrid said, urging Santo forward. She was not amused, but it was evident that the children found the incident hilarious.

"This is Hades," Zosi reminded her.

So it was, obviously. At least the demons stopped trying to tempt them off the path.

In due course they reached the bank of the river. It was a pleasant, peaceful scene. But there was no raft.

"Charon must be on the other side," Zosi said. "He makes regular crossings. He'll be along soon. Then I'll arrange for your passage across."

"I have to go potty," Plato said.

Zosi choked down what might have been a bad word. "Now?"

"Very soon. I can do it in my pants if you want."

"No!" She took a harried breath. "We have to go," she said to Astrid. "He never bluffs about that."

"We'll be all right," Astrid said. "Thank you for your help."

Zosi and Plato hurried back along the path.

"They're fun," Santo said.

"But Hades isn't."

"Actually—" Then he caught her glare, filtered through her dark glasses, and stifled it. He sat down to wait for the ferry.

"But he's right," Fornax said, fading in beside her. "Hades is a challenge for folk who have labored too long under the restrictive Adult Conspiracy. And that child-eating demoness did deserve it."

"I suppose so," Astrid agreed, beginning to glimpse the humor of it. Then she thought of something else. "The way Santo's talent strengthened another magnitude, and he wound up right under Princess Eve's castle in Hades, where Zosi Zombie just happened to be in charge for the moment. That could hardly have been coincidence."

"I have no idea what you mean."

"The way you reassured him, and then Zosi did. You saved his life by enabling his return from the future, and then you saved his sanity. Taking no credit for any of it."

"Anything you may think I did was purely for friendship."

"You have been such a friend throughout! I don't think I can ever repay you."

"Nor do you need to."

"I wish you could somehow get some of the benefit of all you have done for us."

"Friendship doesn't ask for benefit."

"You have certainly learned about it."

"I learned from you."

Arguing was no good, and neither was trying to thank the Demoness for help she couldn't acknowledge giving. So Astrid simply turned and kissed Fornax's ghostly face.

"He's coming!" Santo called.

Sure enough, the raft was heaving into view. The dark ferryman stood on it, wielding his pole. He brought it to the landing, and the motley passengers got off.

Immediately the demons appeared, gesturing to the depressed folk, urging them to cross the line and enjoy marvelous pleasures. But they had evidently already been warned, and trudged along the path, which surely now led to their final abode in Hades. It really didn't make much difference whether they stayed on the path or crossed the line.

"You're on," Fornax said, and faded.

Astrid stepped up to face the ferryman. "Demon Charon, I believe?"

"Believe what you want," he said, eying her curves in a way that irked her.

"Two of us wish to obtain passage across the river, to return to Xanth. We are not dead, and not fated to remain here in Hades."

"A day and night of vigorous stork summoning, for each passage."

The bargaining was on. "The touch of one finger," she said, thinking of Plato's shocking signal.

"An hour of passionate lovemaking."

"One minute of hand holding."

"One fabulous act."

"One kiss."

He saw that she was tough-minded. "One Kiss and a Feel."

Capitalized? "Done," she agreed without enthusiasm.

"Per passenger."

Oh. "One set at the beginning of the crossing, the other at the end of it."

"Done."

She stepped into his embrace. "Oh—one minor detail I may have neglected to mention," she said, removing her glasses. "I'm a basilisk."

He gazed into her eyes without flinching. He was after all a Dwarf Demon. "And a lovely one." She closed her eyes and he kissed her, thrusting his tongue into her mouth, and grabbed her bottom with both hands, avidly kneading it. This was more of a Kiss and Feel than she had anticipated, but nothing new to her; she could handle it. Hereafter she would better pick up on the capitalization.

Charon was a lecher, but he was also a Demon, and had his own powerful ambiance. Had she not been on guard, and on the verge of married, and a basilisk, she might have been swept into his orbit and become his love slave. That was evidently what he was trying for.

She endured his effort for a reasonable while. She had after all not specified a time limit. Then, when he did not quit, she opened her eyes and Stared him at point-blank range. That, coupled with her intoxicating ambiance, set him back, and he released her.

Astrid put her glasses back on and glanced at Santo. "On," she said.

The boy stepped onto the raft. "I think I'll never understand what you gave him." He was being literal.

"You don't need to. Not until you grow up."

Charon, a little unsteady, started poling. So she had made an impression on him.

At the other side she stepped into the ferryman again. She gave him another deep Kiss and copious Feel, but this time did not have to Stare him to make him stop after a reasonable interval. He had evidently learned about her ambiance.

"You are a fascinating challenge," Charon remarked as Astrid and Santo disembarked.

"Indeed."

"Until next time, perhaps."

"Perhaps." Never was more like it, but it would not be expedient to say that. She walked away. He pushed off and floated back on the river.

"You handled him well," Fornax said. "You needed no help there."

"I'm still glad to know you are near," Astrid said sincerely.

"The next chapter becomes complicated," the Demoness said. "I may or may not be able to participate directly."

"I trust your judgment."

"Thank you."

A path wound away from the landing. Astrid knew it led out of the dark region and back to normal Xanth. They had made it out of Hades.

CHAPTER 17:
PORTRAITS

~~~

Astrid watched as a relieved Metria hugged the boy. "Oh, Santo, I'm so glad to see you aft."

"So what?"

"Abaft, astern, rearmost, hindmost, butt—"

"Back?"

"Whatever," she agreed crossly. "When you turned up gone, I feared you had gone to Hades."

"I had."

"Figuratively."

"Literally."

She looked at him. "There must be more to this floor."

"This what?"

"Fiction, creation, level, elevation, narrative—"

"Story?"

"Whatever! Why did you go? Was it something I said? I know I foul up my words on occasion."

"No, Aunt Metria. It was something I thought."

"You thought we didn't want you? Santo, that's not true!"

"I thought I was unworthy."

"How could you ever think that?"

"Because I'm gay."

Metria didn't even hesitate. "That makes a difference?"

"I thought it did."

"Well, it doesn't. If you thought it did, you should have asked me."

"I should have," he agreed penitently.

"Now we can do the Portraits."

Astrid stepped in. "There's a detail to handle first. You are married, Metria, but the rest of us are not. We need to do it before we can adopt. Except for Merge."

"Then let's get on with it. I know I'll look good in a Portrait." That was evidently her prime interest.

They got on with it by holding a three-couple wedding ceremony, done freestyle, with each person saying his or her vow while the children applauded. Ease married Kandy, and kissed her. She became the board briefly, then reverted to lovely woman form. Mitch married Tiara, whose hair floated over her head as she spoke her vow. Art married Astrid, whose sequins lit up while the dress went translucent, much to the children's delight. Then they all shared a huge chocolate-covered wedding cake with candy candles, which the children evidently felt was the most important part of the ceremony. Then the three newly married couples retired for the night, while Merge and Metria saw to the children.

"I'm glad it's finally happening," Astrid murmured as she hugged Art.

"You have worked so hard for it," he agreed. "For all the children, not just ours."

"They all deserve the best. They're fine children."

"And Xanth does need to be saved."

"That, too," she agreed, laughing.

In the morning they set up for the first Portrait. They decided on Kandy and Ease, for no special reason. The two posed beside a mock-up of a wishing well, as they had first met at one. Then Squid emerged from the well in her natural form, shaped her tentacles into human limbs, and became the six-year-old girl.

Kandy embraced her. "We hereby adopt you to be our child," Kandy said.

"Thank you," Squid said, kissing her.

Then the three posed for the Portrait. Art set up his easel and paints, and sketched the scene. It took an hour to get it outlined; then they took a break while he slowly colored the figures in. They returned every so often so that he could get the details right. By the end of the day he finally had it complete, and it looked great; he was an excellent painter. Ease was supremely handsome, Kandy was marvelously lovely, and Squid was the very essence of a sweet little girl.

As he applied the last brush stroke, there was a ripple of color in the surrounding air, like an invisible implosion centering on the painting. Then it cleared, and the portrait seemed to glow. It was done.

"That suggests portentous significance," Fornax said to Astrid.

"Well, it is to save Xanth."

"That might count," the Demoness agreed.

They celebrated with a great evening meal and a romp in the Playground, taking care to guard it from outside. Everyone was thrilled.

The following day Mitch and Tiara formally married, adopted five-year-old Win, and posed for a pleasantly windblown portrait. At the end of the day the painting was complete, looking a shade better than real life, and there was the rippling implosion of color. Another stage in the saving of Xanth had been accomplished.

Then it was Art and Astrid's turn to adopt Firenze. This required special handling to enable Art to both pose and paint. He set up a big mirror so that he could look at the reflection of the three of them, with him at his easel, painting their portrait. Astrid wore the Sequins of Events dress, and there was just a hint of translucency, enough to enhance her appeal without risking any freakouts. The picture showed in the picture, with a smaller one inside that, making an intriguing sequence. The children liked this effect.

At the end of the day there was another color implosion, rendering the portrait complete. Three down.

On the fourth day Merge formally adopted Myst, and the two posed together. Astrid was slightly afraid that there would be a problem manifesting in some manner, as some hidden rule was violated, but there was no trouble. The five aspects hovered faintly in the background, like supportive angels. This portrait, too, received the color implosion. Four down.

The fifth portrait was to be Metria with her husband and Santo. The demoness was eager for it. "How shall I pose?" she asked. "Sexy?" Her dress shrank so as to barely cover her swelling breasts and bottom. "Crazy?" she changed to her alter ego D Mentia, known to be slightly crazy. "Young?" She became her third form, that of the six-year-old child Woe Betide carrying a matchbox.

Oops. "Woe Betide is younger than Santo," Astrid protested.

"Sure. I'm a perpetual child," the child agreed.

"How can a younger child be a mother to an older child?"

The demoness considered. "I hadn't thought about that." She reverted to Metria. "I guess Woe Betide won't have parenting duties."

"But she's still part of you. She'll always be part of you."

Metria shrugged. "She always has been part of me. Ever since that sphinx stepped on me and fragmented me into three aspects."

"I'm just not sure that's right for this," Astrid said. "The Adult Conspiracy might intervene and ruin the adoption."

"She's got a point," Kandy said. "Santo is a very special boy, and he needs a very solid family. Woe Betide may be okay for other purposes, but not for this."

"Conspiracy smiracy," Metria said. "It didn't object to the single parent adoption, or to the basilisk adoption, or to a mother with five aspects. Why should it object to this, with only three aspects?"

"That's a point, too," Kandy agreed. "Maybe we should try it, and if there's no balk, then it's all right."

They tried it. But when Metria said "I hereby adopt you, Santo Claus," and couldn't get it right, they knew there was a problem. The Conspiracy *was* balking.

"Bleep!" Metria swore, making the local vegetation wilt.

"I'm not worthy," Santo said.

"That's not it!" Astrid snapped so fiercely that the wilting vegetation scorched.

"But it leaves us with a problem," Kandy said. "We are left with no fit family to adopt him."

"And the fate of Xanth hangs in the balance," Mitch said.

Astrid felt guilty for even raising the issue of Woe Betide, though she knew it was not actually her fault; she had merely been the one to recognize the question. Now they were stuck without the fifth portrait. Then she got a wild idea. "Let me ponder this," she said.

She walked out into the forest by herself. Soon Fornax joined her. "This baffles me too," the Demoness said.

"I am having wild irrelevant thoughts," Astrid said. "They hardly relate to anything we are presently considering."

"I have encountered thoughts of that nature," the Demoness said with a smile. Astrid was echoing her own manner, when it was not expedient to make a direct suggestion.

"I am thinking that if we searched long enough, we might find a suitable family for a certain eight-year-old boy. But we really need something now.

Today, actually."

"True."

"He is a very special boy, with a ferocious talent. I have to say that he may not be very adoptable. Some folk might object to his—his social orientation. But there is one who has seemed to have a special interest in him, helping him when he most needed it, both with his talent and his personal outlook."

"He deserved the help."

"One who, if a really far-fetched conjecture were to be made, might make a better mother for him than the one we were considering."

"Intriguing," Fornax agreed, seeing where she was going. "But an unmarried foreign Demoness? That would never be accepted."

"I am also remembering how a certain Demon got his hand caught in an interference in a Storage facility that could cost him a Demon Point, if a certain Demoness happened to make an accusation."

"I believe I remember that incident."

"In fact she now owns his backside, one of two she nabbed. She may be waiting for a suitable punishment for his infraction. One that would sufficiently gripe him for more than a day or a week."

"She may."

"It occurs to me that a Demon who bet against the survival of Xanth might be really annoyed if he were required to take some action that had the effect of saving Xanth and costing him his wager."

"He might be," Fornax agreed.

"Such as marrying a certain Demoness and adopting a certain child and performing thereafter as that child's father, with all that implies. That might annoy him even more, since he had figured to get access to her on less strenuous terms, rather than getting locked into an ongoing commitment of decades."

"Oho! You have provided me some interesting thoughts."

"That's what friends are for."

"They are indeed."

"Not that these thoughts relate to any present circumstance."

"Not that they do," Fornax agreed, laughing as she faded out.

Astrid continued her walk. Would the Demoness do it? The fate of Xanth might depend on it. But Demons were Demons, following their own rules, whatever they might be.

She completed her loop and returned to the camp. The others were waiting for her. "I have an idea, but I don't know whether—"

The Demoness Fornax appeared, with Demon Nemesis beside her. He looked as if he had swallowed an overripe stink horn but was constrained to digest it.

"Santo," Fornax called.

"Yes, Aunt Fornax?"

"Would you prefer to call me Mother hereafter?"

His jaw dropped. "You would—would—?"

"The Demon Nemesis has graciously consented to marry me and adopt you, with all that implies. Do you accept us as your family?"

"Oh, yes!" Santo said, tearfully hugging her ghost form.

"Then we shall marry and pose for our Portrait." She turned to Nemesis. "Smile, dear; it's for posterity." She patted his backside, which she now owned.

Nemesis forced a reluctant smile. It was clear that Fornax had found the penalty that most dispirited him.

Art painted their Portrait, and a fine picture it was. At the end of the day the color implosion occurred, confirming the legitimacy of the Fifth Portrait.

A courtroom scene appeared, with three Demon judges, and three others in attendance. "I am Demoness Venus, presiding because I am impartial with respect to the current issue," the lovely female said. "The others are Demon Saturn and Demon Earth, interested spectators. The issue is whether Demon Nemesis and Demoness Fornax are illicitly interfering in Xanth by filling a blank spot and thereby enabling a change in Xanth's future history. Who speaks for Xanth?"

Kandy tried to hide, but could not. The donkey-headed dragon wiggled an ear in her direction. "I speak for Xanth, as before," Kandy said.

"Who speaks for Nemesis and Fornax?"

Fornax caught Astrid's eye. She was it again. But unlike Kandy, she didn't mind doing it. "I speak for Nemesis and Fornax," she said.

Venus glanced at Xanth. "Make your case, Nimby."

"The Land of Xanth should be for its own characters," Kandy said. "If a child needs adoption, there are surely native Xanth folk who can rise to the task. Demons have their own realms, and do not need to interfere in this one. The Demoness Fornax has been interfering for years, as a recent trial demonstrated, and it's time it was stopped."

It was Astrid's turn. "There was no conviction, so the issue is moot. The prior trial was aborted because Demon Xanth withdrew his complaint. Why is he renewing it now?"

"He withdrew it in the hope that outside interference would cease," Kandy said. "Since that interference has renewed, he must act, lest his land be overrun by outsiders."

"That interference, as he puts it, was to save Xanth from eventual destruction."

"The Land of Xanth can survive by using its own resources. If the outsiders had not stepped in, this could have been the case."

Astrid realized that she needed a stronger case, because she couldn't prove that some other family wasn't nearby ready to adopt Santo. It seemed unlikely, but she needed certainty. So she shifted her ground. "What the Demoness Fornax did was not for the sake of interference, but for the sake of friendship. She is my friend, and has been helping me safeguard the welfare of the children throughout. When there was a need for a family to adopt the last child, she stepped in to do it. She needed to be married, to make a complete family, so she persuaded Demon Nemesis to join her in this worthy effort. Now that child will have a good home. This was worth doing in itself."

She paused to martial her thoughts. "This is also important to the welfare of the Land of Xanth. We know that completing these five adoptions, and the related Five Portraits, ensures that Xanth will be saved instead of destroyed. The Demon Xanth is in no position to object to the steps necessary for the salvation of his Land."

"The Land of Xanth might well be saved without the interference of foreign Demons," Kandy said.

"The prophecy indicated otherwise," Astrid retorted.

"A Prophecy you cobbled together for your convenience. Its validity is questionable."

That was true. Astrid knew she was on weak ground again. So she attacked. "Then prove it."

Kandy turned to the Demon panel. "We request the viewing of parallel frames relating to the relevant portion of Xanth history: one without interference, the other with. For the coming fifty years. That should establish the case."

They could do that?

Demoness Venus made a gesture with her hand. Two windows appeared, side by side. One showed the new family of Nemesis, Fornax, and Santo. The other showed Santo alone. They were not still pictures; they were animations.

The Family picture showed a normal family life, with Fornax feeding the boy and teaching him things like reading and manners, while Nemesis showed him how to play sports and deal with bullies who took exception to his nature. He had no trouble with the children he knew, or their families, but in the larger community there could be ridicule and roughness. That abated when the glowing shadow of the Demon Nemesis appeared, radiating invisible menace. Others might not see him directly, but they knew he was there. It was clear that it would be dangerous to cross him. So without actually doing anything, Nemesis was protecting his son.

In the other frame, Santo was on his own. No family adopted him. No Demon protected him. He had to forage largely for himself and sleep in the forest, having no home to retire to. He managed, but it was clearly less comfortable. When he encountered outsiders, at times he had to use his magic to fend them off, making holes they could fall into. That annoyed the neighbors who later had to fill in those holes. Mostly he avoided them.

Watching, Astrid was uneasy. Something was missing here, but what?

Years passed in both frames. Santo grew to manhood. In the home frame he made his living making holes where others needed them, such as in foundation stones and planks so that the walls of houses could be secured. He became successful and respected, and his talent increased in power and versatility. But in the homeless frame others did not want his services. In fact they did not want his presence, and he was tacitly frozen out. In this reduced manner he lived out his obscure life until he was in his fifties.

Again, Astrid was disturbed. Something was not being shown, but she couldn't put her finger on it. Surely the time-line was accurate, because it was Demon-inspired. This really was the future, unsatisfying as it might be.

Then came the invasion. Ogres, trolls, goblins and human people made a tear in the wall of reality that separated one Xanth timeline from another, and poured in to ravage Xanth. Santo went to stop them, wielding holes like lasers, felling a number of invaders. But there were too many. They overwhelmed him and chopped him to pieces. Astrid winced outwardly, but inside she was screaming. How could this horror be happening? Then they went on to ravage the rest of Xanth. The defenders, unable to stop the invaders, resorted to desperate measures: they devised a virus that did not wipe out puns, but living things. That meant that all creatures in Xanth, residents and invaders, perished. Xanth was dead. Only a few children survived, by escaping to different time-lines as orphans.

But in the home frame it was a different story. Santo was a solid member of the community. When the invaders came he helped organize resistance. Men counterattacked, driving the invaders into a channel. Then a huge hole opened up, and the invaders charged into it and disappeared. It was a Hole to Hell that Santo had made, a phenomenal gap that wiped out the invaders. After that, no more came; they had gotten the message that this was no safe place to be. Xanth was saved.

"So the prophecy is valid," Kandy said. "The intercession of the Demons changes the fate of Xanth by facilitating the ability of one person, Santo, to effectively defend it. Not only this Xanth, but all the similar Xanths in the adjacent frames that follow it, one second at a time, because they are similarly defended by the children from the future. This is the reality that changes the future for everything."

Was she conceding the case? Astrid glanced at Santo, who had seen his two future fates and had to be shaken. But if this secured the right one, he would be a hero.

"Therefore the intercession is confirmed, and the charge against the defendant Demons must be upheld," Kandy concluded. "Their marriage, adoption, and Portrait must be nulled."

Astrid felt as if the ground had dropped out from beneath her. In winning her point she had lost her case!

Demoness Venus nodded. "Before the sentence is voted and implemented, does the defendant have any mitigating circumstance to proffer?"

Mitigating circumstance? Whatever could that be? But Astrid knew she had to try.

She thought of her unease when watching the time-lines, her concern that something was missing. Was there more to the situation than showed? Something that might change the larger perspective? She had to produce it now, or lose everything.

Desperation gave her an idea. "The children!" she said. "All of them needed to be adopted and painted, to save Xanth. But all we saw was Santo. We need to know what the others will be doing as the future unfolds." It was no more than a straw, but it was all she had.

"Does the Defendant Petition for such a review?" Venus inquired.

"I do," Fornax said immediately. Astrid was gratified by her trust in Astrid's effort, but feared it was undeserved.

"The Defendant's one petition is invoked," Venus said.

The parallel time-lines played again, this time showing the activities of all five children. They were there, supporting Santo in each frame. He had not been adopted in one, but the children had never cut him out of their lives. That was heartening for Astrid to see. When the invaders came they were blown about by hurricane force winds, befuddled by thick fog, led astray by dangerous-looking creatures that morphed into other creatures, and repelled by ferocious fireworks. But in the end it made no difference; Xanth was saved in one frame, lost in the other. There was no Hole to Hell in the losing frame. Only with a fully functional Santo was the defense sufficient. Her idea had proven to be worthless.

Yet there was still something. What could it be?

"We shall now vote the verdict," Venus said.

"Wait!" Astrid cried. "There's something else!"

"Your Petition has been expended," Venus said.

"But there are two Defendants," Astrid said, feeling as if she were clawing at a mountain of slippery ice with greased hands. "The other has not used his Petition."

Venus looked impatient, but accepted it. "Does Demon Nemesis invoke his Petition?"

"I do," Nemesis said without hesitation.

Astrid was amazed. He could get out of the marriage and adoption simply by accepting the ruling; Fornax couldn't stop that. Yet he was supporting her.

"What is the Petition?" Venus asked Astrid.

"Another expansion," Astrid said. "To include the adoptive parents."

The time-lines played a third time, now showing the five sets of parents, Merge counting as a set. The home frame showed no change. But there was a deviation in the negative frame, and it was a shocker. It showed Astrid herself, following the decision, disconsolately walking alone. She had lost her case, and with it the salvation of both the children and Xanth itself. She had not measured up to the need, and had failed them all. She walked some distance, and came to the Gap Chasm. She stood at the brink, then abruptly hurled herself into it. In her grief she was committing suicide. There was a moan from the other watchers, both children and adults; none of them wanted this. But it was her decision.

No one rescued her this time; Fornax was surely barred from any such further interference. Astrid fell to the bottom and died. Her poisonous body killed the surrounding vegetation and dissolved into the dirt, leaving a barren section that even the Gap Dragon would not touch. But her soul separated from the heap, formed into her human likeness, and made its way to the River Styx circling Hades. Charon the Ferryman poled his raft to the shore, and Astrid duly boarded. What choice did she have?

"Now you are mine, you luscious creature," he said, and swept her into his embrace. She was unable to resist, being no longer alive, and without her deadly Stare. She was in his power, destined to be his mistress as long as he chose. It didn't matter that she had no interest in him; her body, animated by her remaining soul, was all he wanted.

"I worked for this ever since you and the brat crossed out of Hades," Charon said between Kisses and Feels as he worked up to the Main Event. Astrid, dispirited, offered no resistance. "I finally got my chance when I volunteered to do the dull time-lines for the Trial. I fixed it so one failed, knowing that would bring you to me. And it did! Victory is mine."

The pictures faded. "I believe we have enough evidence," Demoness Venus said. "The crucial interference was not where we thought. Do we need to vote?"

The Demons Earth and Saturn shook their heads.

"The Defendants are exonerated," Venus said. "Their marriage, adoption, and Portrait stand. We shall now adjourn to the separate trial of the Dwarf Demon Charon." The three members of the Panel disappeared. So did the Demon Xanth, leaving behind only half a heehaw.

The children and adults sat silent, still absorbing this amazing trial and decision. Then Kandy went to Astrid. "Oh, I'm so glad I lost. Again. That was awful."

"Awful," Firenze agreed. "And you killed yourself. Promise us you'll never do that again, Mother Astrid."

"Never again," Astrid agreed, horrified and bemused as her husband and son hugged her.

Fornax faced Nemesis. "Why did you Petition?" she asked him. "You could have been free simply by doing nothing."

"Santo is my son," the Demon said. "I'm obliged to secure his welfare."

That surprised Astrid. Nemesis might have been brought into this reluctantly, but he did take it seriously once he had made the agreement, not taking an easy way out. That was an excellent sign.

But Fornax wasn't satisfied. "Is that all?"

"And I wanted to please you. A Demoness taken against her will is not the best romantic prospect, and you are special."

Fornax nodded, satisfied. "You have succeeded. I *am* pleased." Then, to the others: "Carry on. We will be busy for some time."

Then she went to embrace Nemesis, her clothing dissipating. The two faded out. Astrid knew that Nemesis was in for a far better experience than he had hoped for. He had gambled and won.

"Let's go to the Playground," Firenze said to the other children. "We need to leave the parents alone for a while. They have some serious kissing to do."

The others giggled knowingly and joined him there.

Astrid realized that she was worn out, emotionally. She had seen herself die, and though that was in the timeline that would not exist, it remained a nasty shock to her world view. "I think I need to rest," she said.

"With or without me?" Art asked.

"Definitely with you. You're the kind of rest I need."

They retired to their tent, where they made passionate love, then slept. Whenever the horror of her death returned to haunt her, she clung to Art, and it faded.

In the morning the children announced a play they were ready to put on. It seemed they had been busy, while leaving the parents alone.

"A play?" Astrid asked. "Why? Is there something you need to figure out?"

"Not exactly," Firenze said.

"It's more like an Unveiling," Santo said.

"Of a statue," Squid said.

"A statue!" Astrid said, surprised. "Of what?"

"Of what we like best," Win said.

"In all Xanth," Myst concluded.

They had made a statue to Eye Scream and Chocolate Cake? Astrid decided not to comment. Children would be children.

Fornax and Nemesis appeared, looking slightly mussed. "We're here to see the Play," Fornax said. "Before we return to savage lovemaking."

The nine Parents followed the five children into the Playground and took their seats as the Audience. Astrid sat between her husband, Art, and Demoness Fornax, touching the hands of each. There on the stage was the statue, a man-sized shape covered by an opaque shroud. It didn't look very promising.

Then a figure emerged from the DO NOT ENTER section. It was the Dwarf Demon Gambol, whom they had met in Storage. Behind him came several others, taking seats in the Audience. Gambol had evidently facilitated their passage here.

Suddenly Astrid recognized one. "Wulfha Werewolf!" she exclaimed, getting up and running to hug her friend. "What brings you here?"

"Oh, I wouldn't miss the Unveiling," the bitch said.

"But it's just a statue the children made," Astrid protested. "Nothing really important."

Wulfha glanced at her, amused. "That depends on your perspective." She took her seat beside Wolfram the warrior wolf, and Astrid returned to her own place.

Then she had to get up again, recognizing another. "Goldie Goblin!"

"It's good to see you again, Astrid," the golden-haired goblin princess said. "I owe so much to you. You saved me from the dragon."

"And you're here just to see a statue uncovered?"

"It's not just any statue," Goldie said.

"I hope you're not disappointed."

"I don't expect to be." Goldie sat down beside her mother the Queen Golden Goblin, whose hair matched that of her lovely daughter.

There was the sound of hooves at the Playground entrance as a horse trotted in. Astrid recognized her: it was Doris Day Mare, of the children's erstwhile dream. What was she doing here?

A speech balloon appeared over her head, with the face of a human woman inside. "I apologize for the role I was required to play before," the face said. "I really do value children, and have come to see their Play and of course the Unveiling. I brought two other visitors." She took her place beside the chairs, not needing one herself.

And there were the two others at the entrance. "Zosi!" Astrid exclaimed. "And Plato!"

"We just had to attend," the zombie woman said. "Princess Eve understands."

Indeed, there now appeared two lovely young women, one with hair as bright as day, the other with hair as dark as night: the twin princesses Dawn and Eve. They stepped forward to greet Wulfha and Golden as equals, then took their seats.

A huge wolf arrived, carrying an elf woman. "Jenny!" Astrid exclaimed, surprised. It was the one she had met at the grave of her lost daughter.

Jenny dismounted as the werewolf changed to manform. She came to talk with her. "Astrid. I finally realized why you were familiar that time we met. It's your soul."

"My soul? It joined me when I was sleeping."

"Yes, out near Jone's grave. That was her soul."

Astrid was chagrined. "Your daughter's soul? I did not know. I never meant to cause you that grief."

"No, no! It found a person worthy of it. One who could complete Jone's mission. I'm glad you were the one." Jenny walked back to rejoin her husband, who was talking with the Princesses Dawn and Eve as if they were old friends.

"I think you do not properly know Jenny Elf," Fornax said.

"I met her once. I'm not clear why she came here."

"She is Princess Jenny, wife of the king of the werewolves, whom she rides."

"Princess?" Astrid repeated blankly. "She never said."

"She is modest," Art said. "She is of course here for the Unveiling. Now we know why your soul was so set on saving Xanth."

Another person arrived, hauling along a grumpy old husband. Astrid jumped up to greet her. "MareAnn! My first friend!"

"We had to come," MareAnn said, glancing back at the Good Magician Humfrey. Then she went back to find seats.

Yet more folk were arriving, filling the seats. Even the donkey-headed dragon Astrid recognized as the Demon Xanth, with his wife, Chlorine.

Well, as long as they were here, Astrid had a question for them. She got up and went to them. "One thing I'd like to know," she said. "The Demoness Fornax and I were struggling to save the children and Xanth. Why did you oppose us?"

It was Chlorine who answered. "My husband can be a bit mule-headed at times." She glanced fondly at the donkey head. "Even asinine. He just didn't want to admit that outside help was needed to save Xanth. Especially not help from a chronic troublemaker like Fornax. Now he knows he was mistaken, and he is sorry." She glanced again. "Say you're sorry, dear."

The donkey head wiggled one ear.

"Thank you," Astrid said gratefully, and returned to her place, carefully suppressing any smile that might have lurked.

She gazed out across the expanding audience. There was Ginger Goblin, whom Astrid had helped save from Truculent Troll's cave. She was sitting beside Truman Troll, the halfway decent one they had made a truce with. Astrid remembered how Ginger had naughtily kissed Truman before the truce ended. Maybe that had led to something more. Kisses could have remarkable effects.

And there was Wenda Woodwife, with her friend Dwarf Demoness Eris and her husband, Jumper Spider. They had recommended that Fornax and Astrid try adopting children, which had resulted in a novel's worth of adventures. It seemed that everyone was here.

Astrid shook her head. This couldn't be for a stupid statue. But in that case, what was it for? It was hard to imagine why so many illustrious people would come to a simple children's presentation. How did they even know about it?

A corpulent Demon Neptune appeared before her. "I notified them. That was part of my assignment." He vanished.

Apparently Fornax had known that something was coming up, and made him handle the details. Maybe the children had asked her to spread the word. But that hardly explained why so many others had chosen to attend. The mystery remained.

It was time for the Play. The children took their places onstage.

What it turned out to be was a summary of the adventures the children had had since coming to Xanth from the future. They showed how Fornax and Astrid had rescued them, and how the other adults had taken them in and made them welcome and done their best to find good adoptive homes for them. But there were none, and in the end those same adults had done it themselves, adopting the children. Even though the last ones had gotten in trouble for it. But working together, they had saved Xanth from later destruction.

That was it. Astrid was sure the children had worked hard to arrange it as a presentation, but it really wasn't much of a play. Yet the audience seemed rapt. What were they picking up on that Astrid couldn't get?

There was polite applause as the play concluded. Then the children lined up onstage, facing the audience.

"And now we approach the Unveiling of the Final Portrait," Firenze said.

"The Statue the artisans in Storage helped us craft," Santo said.

"Of the two we owe the most to," Squid said.

"And love the most," Win said.

"We call it Friendship," Myst said.

A statue honoring the abstract concept of Friendship? That belonged as a relic in the back of some obscure gallery, not as the finale to a children's play, let alone a public presentation for royal guests. But of course Astrid would not say anything like that aloud, lest she hurt a child's feelings. She only hoped that the assembled audience would be kind about their disappointment. To have so many come for so little reason—it was mind-boggling.

"We need to say something about this statue," Firenze said.

"It is a copy of one we saw in our own realm," Santo said.

"Which helped us recognize the people we were dealing with," Squid said.

"So that we knew we could trust them," Win said.

"And honor them," Myst concluded.

Astrid could not make head or tail of this. She glanced at Fornax beside her. The Demoness shrugged. "It is masked, from me as well as the audience," she murmured. "But evidently important to the children."

"And here they are," Firenze said, and swept off the shroud.

Astrid stared. So did Fornax.

It was a statue of the two of them, Astrid standing in her Sequins of Events dress, Fornax beside and just behind her like a protective figure. Both of them seemed to glow as if angelic.

"It's us," Astrid breathed, amazed.

"It is," Fornax agreed, similarly surprised.

"Thank you, Mothers Astrid and Fornax," the children said together. "Thank you for saving us—and Xanth."

Then the applause began. All the rest of the audience joined in, including their husbands and friends, turning to face the two of them. Then they all stood, forming a massive circle, still applauding.

"I don't understand," Astrid said. "What I did was for the children. I never sought any applause."

Fornax's mouth quirked. "And I did it for friendship. Evidently the others also value Xanth's future."

The children ran down from the stage and came to cluster adoringly around them both as the applause continued.

Children. Friendship. Leading to an adventure like no other.

Overwhelmed, Astrid felt tears on her face, and saw them on Fornax's face too. They were finally beginning to understand.

AUTHOR'S NOTE

I wrote this novel in the ogre's months Marsh and Apull, 2013, and edited it in Mayhem. I usually write Xanth novels in the months of SapTimber, OctOgre, and NoRemember, but pressures of originally self-publishing caused me to move up the schedule. There are fewer puns this time because there were six months less for them to accumulate from readers with pundigestion. Apart from the anti-pun virus, of course, which I suspect did not extend to Mundania to stifle pun suggestions. Just so readers can get a notion of the times, this was when the Boston Marathon was bombed. Bad things happen in Mundania just as they do in Xanth.

A decade before, a reader had suggested that I include a gay man as a major character in a Xanth novel. I wasn't sure, so I queried my readers in my www.hipiers.com blog-type column. Their verdict was overwhelmingly negative: no gay protagonist. It wasn't that they were bigoted, but that they felt that Xanth, where funny incidents and silly puns abound, as you may have noticed, was not the proper venue for such a serious matter. Xanth parodies things, such as mundane attitudes toward sex, in the Adult Conspiracy, but a parody of homosexuality would not be funny. Also, I am unalterably hetero myself, loving the look and feel of women, and might well bungle any attempt to sympathetically portray a gay man. So I kept the subject out.

In the intervening decade there has been a sea change in the public attitude toward things like gay marriage, which a majority now favor. A gay reader asked me to check again, so I requeried my Column readers during the writing of this novel. The vote was small, partly because a virus infected the HiPiers site and kept many readers away, but there was a significant change. Now a majority favored it.

But was that enough? The readers I sampled at my website were only a tiny fraction of my full readership, and perhaps not typical of that full readership. The majority vote was far from a landslide. Doing it would be a gamble. I'm a commercial writer, which means I cater to readers rather than critics. I don't much like to gamble with my career. Yet neither do I like to exclude any part of my readership, regardless of its size.

So I compromised. There is a gay character in this novel, but he's only a child, and not the protagonist. It will take him a decade or so to mature. By then maybe the will of the readers will have clarified, and he will be able to be a main character. I suspect this will disappoint both the pro- and the anti-gay readers, and I will lose some, which is sort of the nature of compromises. Sigh.

What about the genesis of the larger novel? I had built up a cast of characters in the prior one, *Board Stiff*, and not all of them were safely situated. The pun virus still needed to be cleaned out, and Merge had not yet found a man. I thought she might be the protagonist (main character). But let's face it, searches for romance are a dime a dozen in literature. Was there anything more original? Well, a reader suggested that there be a wave of orphaned children from the future. I pondered that and concluded it was viable, though I reduced the number to be more manageable. Then I realized that there was one character who really was different: the beautiful but deadly basilisk. Suppose she had to deal with the children, when it was difficult for her even to touch them without hurting them? I also thought about friendship: suppose someone even worse about touching were also involved? Such as the Demoness of Antimatter. From this muddle of notions this novel coalesced.

Once I had the main characters, and their mission, they more or less took over and did the job. The more I saw of Astrid, the better I liked her. She means so well and tries so hard. But why would the most vicious and deadly of creatures ever care for people and children the way she does? Hence I had to give her a soul. There are readers who feel that a novel should spring full-blown from the head of the writer, without any creative effort, as with Athene from the left ear of the Greek god Zeus, but the truth is it takes work and sometimes missteps to craft it. Authors are not necessarily the geniuses they try to appear to be. (I hope this doesn't get me hanged in effigy by other writers for blabbing the secret.)

Here are the reader credits for this novel, roughly in the order of the appearance of their ideas, with duplicate ideas grouped together. I had a computer mixup and lost some of the credits; I hope I found them all again.

Quilting Bees—Karen. N-Trail, Heaven Nickel, Quarter, Dollar, Hell Cent, etc., Blue Music, Pun Dancing, the Gates, Ann Droid, Sun Dial and Pun Dial Soap, Belts: Asteroid, Bible, Rust, Sun, Eye-V, Ear-E, Brain-E, Cheek-E, Hair-E, Vein-E, Sas-C, Sis-C, Tea V drink, Talent of changing homonyms, Beds: Flower, River, Sea. Talent of shooting laser beams from one's fingers. Sand D, Sand Witch.—Tim Bruening. Smarty Pants, Rose Colored Glasses, Troubleshooter, Snow Shoes, Billi Ant, Firenze, Myst, —Mary Rashford. Skepticals—Chris Weaver. Yell-O Jacket—Geri Maisano. Pine Needle that sews curses—Kerry Garrigan. Santo—David Freedman. Orphaned children from the future—Naomi Blose. Talent of always having the wind at one's back—Owen Marrow. Playground—Alex Guelke. Weird birds—Avi Ornstein. Neigh Kid—Joseph McRyan. Boon Docks—Mark Caselman. Medium Coffee—John Hewison. Cecil and Tea Cup story—Rick Lippincott. Catatonic—Steve and Tom Pharrer. Exploring Daymares further—Laurie. Talent of summoning things from the dream realm—Brant Tucker. A mortal made love to by an angel no longer freaks at less—Andrew Jonathan Fine. Chris "Kribbitz" Kehler—Kristyn Cain

This novel was proofread by Scott M. Ryan, who stepped in when I lost my prior proofer, Rudy Reyes. Yes, I proof them myself, but I seem to miss half a slew of errors.

At this writing I am not sure what the next novel, Xanth #40, will be, but I do have a suggestion from a young reader. Probably it will not involve the characters developed in these past two novels, but we'll see.

TALES FROM
THE LAND OF XANTH

FROM OPEN ROAD MEDIA

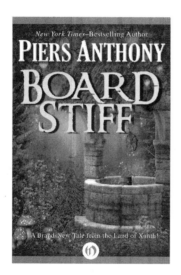 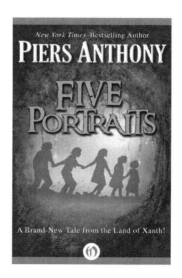

Available wherever ebooks are sold